Book One

Circle for the Earth

A Time Travel Saga to Forge a Sustainable Future

Daphne Singingtree

This is a work of fiction. Names, characters, and incidents are products of the author's imagination. Any resemblance to actual persons, living or dead, is purely coincidental. The setting is based on a real location, and historical figures are referenced. For details, please refer to the *What Is Real* section at the end of the book.

ISBN 978-0-9674431-2-6

Illustrations: Savanna Stamp, Yosama Sun, Carlos Proveda, Robert Gillespie, Van Halen Cunanan, and D.A.Suraj
Editing & Formatting Team: Janet Russell, Nakiska Papenfuss, Michael Pilgrim, Calvary Diggs, Lili Marlene Booth, and Amanda Shellnut
V24.2026

All proceeds from this book will be donated to Zaníyan Center, a nonprofit 501c(3) that promotes health through plants and connection with the earth.

Circle for the Earth

Dedication

To the modern warriors who protect the water
and defend the earth, fight to reclaim stolen lands,
work toward food sovereignty and self-sufficiency,
who teach, learn, and believe in a better future.

Contents

Important Note About Language and Content

The terms *Native American*, *Indigenous*, and *Indian* are used interchangeably within tribal communities. In this book, *Native* refers to those from the twenty-first century who were brought back in time. *Indigenous* refers to the people who lived in these lands in this time period. The term *Indian* may be used by characters from either group and reflects common usage.

Lakota words are written with full diacritics (pronunciation marks) the first time they appear, for those who wish to learn them. A pronunciation guide can be found on page *i*. After the first use, simplified English spellings are used, with occasional accent marks retained for clarity.

In dialogue, there is an occasional racist slur or offensive language reflective of the 1790s. These words are included to portray the brutal reality of that time. If you find them offensive or disturbing—*good*. They're meant to be.

Some readers may be impacted by content that includes profanity, racism, slavery, rape, sexual violence, mild sex scenes, and LGBTQ+ themes.

This book is political, with a strong progressive and anti-colonial stance. It advocates for Indigenous sovereignty, climate justice, and a better world for future generations.

Introduction for Those
Who Hate Introductions

I'm an avid reader who almost never reads introductions. Now I've written my first novel, I realize there are important things for the reader to know before they start the book.

This is a work of fiction, totally make believe. The people are fictional, but the places are real. It takes place on two adjacent Lakota reservations, the Lower Brule and Crow Creek, and the thirty miles around it, containing small towns, all in South Dakota. There's a real loop of the Missouri River where the fictional casino and resort are located. Currently, it is farmland. Almost everything else included in the book really exists within the thirty-mile circle from that loop of the Missouri River that was brought back in time, except for a few fictional places. Please look at the *What is Real* section in the back of the book for more resources. While I attempted to maintain as much accuracy as possible, I took artistic liberties as a fiction writer.

What I wrote about the Lower Brule and Crow Creek reservations isn't specific to those reservations, but an amalgamation of many Lakota reservations. I didn't intend to denigrate anyone or anything in the area. If I have unintentionally offended anyone, please accept my apologies, and let me know so I don't do it again in future editions.

My heritage includes Lakota, of the Standing Rock Tribe, as well as Scottish and Spanish. While I've spent time on reservations, my experience is not the same as a full-blooded Indigenous woman raised on one. I don't presume a full understanding, but hope to capture what I've learned from others. I'm also not African American or gay. Writing from the perspective of those from a different culture means you make a lot of presumptions, which may or may not be accurate.

I'm sure all of us imagine how we'd change the world if we had enough money, power, or magic to do it. That is what fiction is — creating an imaginary world. I've used my hopes, dreams, and life experience to create a world that I'd want for my grandchildren.

Lakota Pronunciation Guide

Consonants

IPA	Examples	English approximation
b	bló	about
tʃ	wašíču	check
tʃʰ	héčhena	choose
tʃ	šič'éši	check, but with a pause afterwards
g	ógle	again
ǧ	ǧí	French parlor
h	wóžuha	hat
x	ȟóta	Spanish jota
k	ská	skin
k'	k'éyaš	skin, but with a pause afterwards
kʰ	wakhéya wakȟáŋ	cab
kˣ		like cab, but sharper
l	hokšíla	life
m	makes	man
n	iná	neighbor
p	tópa	spot
pʰ	ophíye pȟeží	pot
pˣ		like pot, but sharper
p'	p'ó	spot, but with a pause afterwards
s	tiyospaye	sun
ʃ	tóške	shoe
t	witkó	stand
t'	t'élanuwela	stand, but with a pause afterwards
tʰ	mathó	torn
tˣ	tȟáwa	like torn, but sharper
w	tuwá	well
j	wíŋyaŋ	yes
z	wazí	zip
ʒ	maǧážu	measure

Vowels

IPA	Examples	English approximation
a	akézaptaŋ	hat
ɛ	iye	bed
s	iš	bit
ɔ	kȟolá	thought
ʊ	táku	push
ə̃	waŋží	huh
ĩ	siŋtésapela	bit, but nasalized
ũ	uŋkiye	push, but nasalized

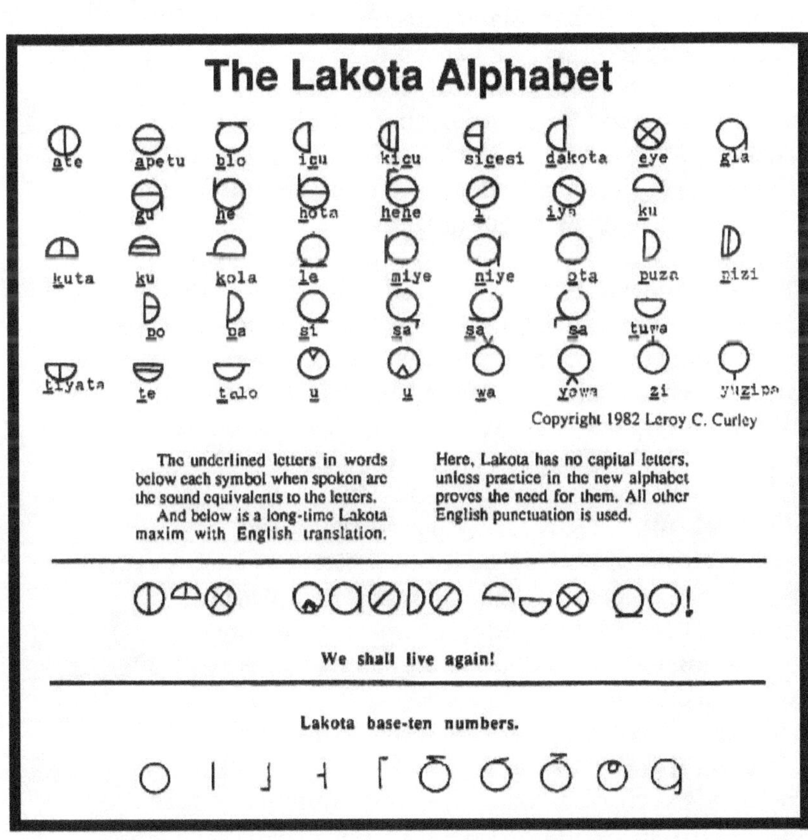

Cast of Characters

Adam Diedrich: Chair, Banking Committee
Anna May Worthington: Displaced former socialite
Anthony Norcross: Member of the First New Orleans Expedition
Billy Fast Dog: Security Chief at Omímeya
Chaton Begay, MD: Head of the new medical school
Clyde Folsom: Former South Dakota State Senator
Darren Iron Cloud: Black Hills/Paha Sapa Expedition
David Cornell: Former State Attorney; Law Committee Chair
David Kim: Information Technology at Omímeya
Doris Stewart: Administrative Assistant at Omímeya
Duane Nelson: Executive Council Member, Communication
Ed Robinson: Brule County Commissioner
Ed Tilson: Native member, Black Hills/Paha Sapa Expedition
Elliot Gray Owl: Secretary, Law Committee
Gift of Thunder: Indigenous to this time and place
Hotah Chasing Hawk: Rose's ex-husband, father of Kimímela
Jack Tilson: Native member, Black Hills/Paha Sapa Expedition
Jamal Alston: Displaced attendee, Permaculture Convergence
Jenny Abrams: Events Manager at Omímeya
Jerome Brown: Executive Council Member, Agriculture
Jonathan Gardner: National Guard Colonel; General, Changleska Guard
Karl Bauer: German tourist, Lewis and Clark Expedition tour bus
Kathy Williams: Driver, Lewis and Clark Expedition tour bus
Kimímela Chasing Hawk: Daughter of Rose and Hotah
Kyle Ward: Emergency Preparedness Director at Omímeya
Larry Tilson: Black Hills/Paha Sapa Expedition
Lois Robinson: Brule County Tax Assessor
Lou White Mountain: Sergeant, Changleska Guard
Martin Worthington: Displaced former executive
Mary Landrau: Executive Council Member, Education
Nels Hansen: Displaced attendee, Permaculture Convergence
Oliver Jackson: Executive Council Member, Defense and Law
Phil Gallo: Casino Manager at Omímeya
Richard Russo: Executive Council Member, Infrastructure
Rose Chasing Hawk: General Manager and CEO of Omímeya
Shawn Caris: Executive Council Member, Human Services
Theresa Martinez: Executive Council Member, Medicine
Travis Hazelhurst: Mary Landrau's assistant
Two Elks: Lakota leader indigenous to this time and place
Wayne Becker: Facilities Manager at Omímeya

Maps

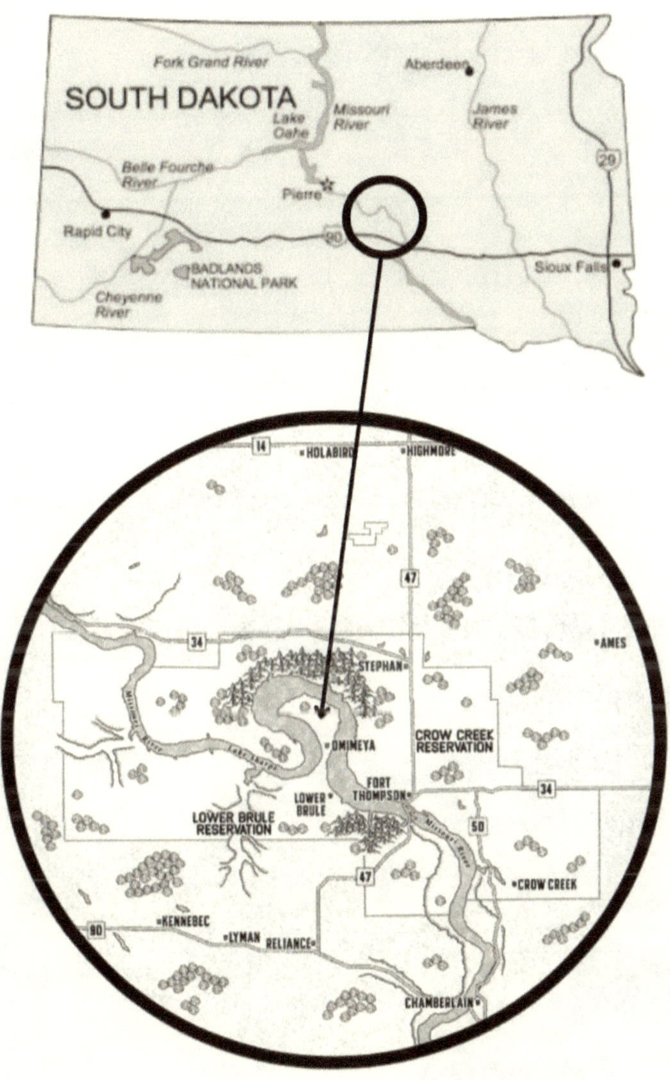

Location of Thirty-mile Circle Brought Back in Time

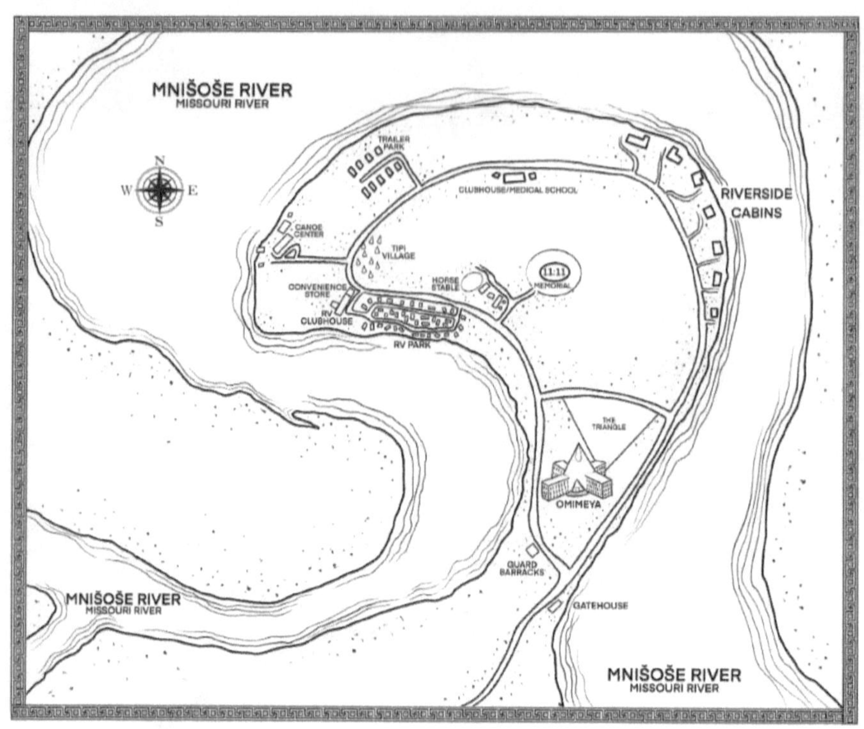

Omímeya Casino and Resort

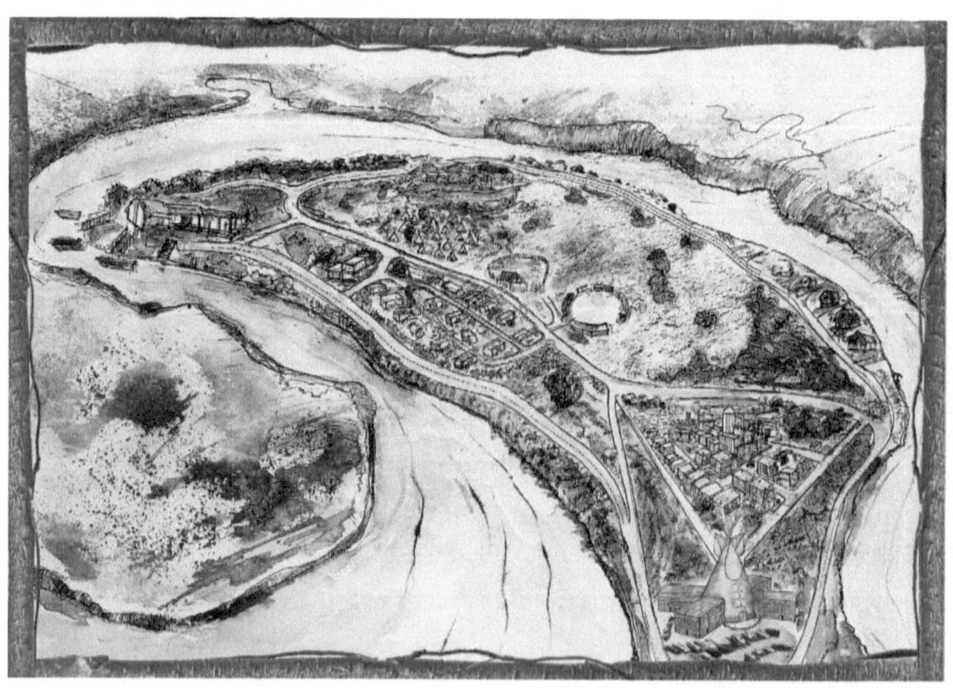

The United States in 1791

Tribal Nations of the Louisiana Purchase 1803

PART I
Day One

Time stays long enough for those who use it.
— Leonardo da Vinci (1452–1519), Italian artist and inventor.

I-90 West, cut off at the edge of the Circle.

Chapter One
Rose

WHEN THE MORNING sun shone on Rose Chasing Hawk on Saturday morning, she was blissfully ignorant she'd wake up in a different world tomorrow. To spend time with her kids, she always worked early on the weekends, trying to arrive home by three or four. Unfortunately, something frequently came up, like last week. As they were about to leave for a school event, she got a work call and had to drop them off and have someone else bring them home. In juggling the priorities of life, the balls that got dropped often included her kids. She thought work-life balance was an oxymoron. Rose loved her children as fiercely as any mother, and wondered how other working mothers managed, especially now she was mainly on her own.

Teenagers were challenging, 'only a phase' her friends told her. She hoped it was true. Rose recalled the argument yesterday with fifteen-year-old Luke, sullen and rebellious as usual.

When Rose said, "Homework before video games."

Luke responded, "I shouldn't have to learn geometry. When am I ever going to use it?"

"You need it to graduate."

"Don't need to graduate. Jake never graduated, and he is doing fine," mentioning a relative who works construction.

"I want you to have opportunities and options. Just do your homework."

Typical argument on a typical day. Her daughter Kimi recently turned thirteen. Since her coming-of-age ceremony a few months ago, she'd become more withdrawn, and Rose was concerned.

Yesterday Rose asked her, "Kimi, do you want me to bring back anything from the store?"

She replied in Lakota, "No, why don't you call me Kimímela, like I asked?" Rose apologized, recalling her repeated request to use her full Lakota name, which means butterfly. Not calling her Kimi was a hard habit to break. She only wished to speak in Lakota, but unfortunately, Rose's Lakota wasn't good. It created distance between them, which Rose was sure was her intent. Kimi's father, Hotah, and his family were traditional and fluent, unusual even on the adjacent Crow Creek and Lower Brule Reservations where they lived, where only a small percentage of the adult population spoke Lakota. Rose believed in preserving language and was grateful for the integration into local schools. She knew she wasn't the only parent whose child spoke Lakota better than she did. It was still annoying.

Luke's Lakota wasn't good either. It didn't help that he wasn't a tribal member. Rose was one-quarter Yankton Sioux, but Luke, as one-eighth, wasn't eligible for tribal membership. He had a different father than Kimi. His father was white and an asshole. Surprisingly, growing up primarily white in a reservation school, Luke never mentioned being bullied or ostracized. Yet, he didn't have many friends. Around here, people considered blood quantum and tribal membership a big deal.

Getting dressed for work felt like putting on a suit of armor. Rose hated the constricting pantsuits she wore. She could afford nice clothes and needed to project a professional image to be taken seriously, but honestly, she felt her body looked terrible in pants. Her big butt didn't help. Rose preferred long, flowing skirts, which hid her problematic features, but emphasizing femininity didn't work when you needed to portray authority, especially when working with men in suits.

After fourteen years in hospitality, Rose ran the Omímeya Casino and Resort, juggling the hotel, RV Park, Tipi Village, Canoe Center, and eight shops and restaurants. The management of the casino was completely separate. Although she was on the same level of the organization chart as the casino manager, Phil Gallo, he treated Rose as a subordinate. And since the casino brought in so much money, it was the tail that wagged the dog and he treated her like his bitch.

The general manager, Tom Durrell, was supposed to oversee both of them, but Rose did most of his work. Tom deferred to Phil on almost everything else. With virtually all the department heads being men, Rose became adept at acting sweet, smiling away her frustration, getting her way by pandering to egos, asking questions she already knew the answers to, or requesting help she didn't need. Someday, she hoped to become general manager, but it didn't seem likely in the foreseeable future.

=..=

Rose headed out the door, surprised by how cool it was in the third week of September. As she was about to get in her car, she saw a flash of color in the field of brown stubble across the driveway. The bold red color stood out from the dry prairie hues of the fields; it was a person standing wrapped in a red blanket. *What the hell?* She thought. Their home was an old farmhouse down a road no one else lived on. Rose could see no other cars or trucks. The silence was palpable, broken only by the rustling of the wind through the grass. She shivered, feeling a sudden chill.

She called out, "Hey!"

They didn't turn around or appear to hear her. Rose walked towards the field, seeing someone with long dark hair blowing in the slight wind. They weren't responding to her shouts. She got closer, noticing the blanket—the red Pendleton from her couch—before recognizing her daughter. A wave of relief washed over her, she let out a long, slow breath. She couldn't believe she had been so worked up, not recognizing her own daughter from a distance. Kimi didn't turn around, because she was gazing to the east with utter concentration as the sun rose. When Rose approached her, she jumped, as if awakened from a trance, and looked at her mother, perplexed.

"What are you doing out here?" Rose asked in a curt tone. Walking out to the field annoyed her with Kimi not answering.

Kimi looked at her intently, holding her gaze as if wondering how to respond. She said quietly, in Lakota, "It is coming."

"What is coming?"

"*Tȟáŋka wakíŋyaŋ.*"

4

Kimi was serious and looked solemn. Rose stopped being annoyed and instead became concerned.

"Speak English. I want to understand you," Rose said.

"Big Thunder is coming. Everything will change after today; we'll lose so much, but what is coming is more important."

"I don't understand."

Kimi gave her mother another intense look and said, "You will soon." first in Lakota, then translated for her, "Big Thunder strengthens the Circle, the Circle protects the Earth."

Rose knew enough Lakota to realize that English missed subtleties in meaning. The word for circle Kimi used wasn't Omímeya the shape, but changleska which means a hoop or a circle encompassing the unity of the people, or the cycle of life. The word for big, thanka, meant not large, it could mean great in any way, or significant. Wakíŋyaŋ is a Lakota word for thunder. It could also mean sacred wings or thunder spirits, which play a significant role in Lakota spirituality, stories, and culture.

Rose took Kimi's arm and led her back to the house, her mind buzzing with questions. "What did you mean, Kimi? What's coming?" she pressed, her voice tinged with concern.

She remained silent, her gaze fixed on the horizon. "I can't explain, Mom," she finally replied, her voice barely above a whisper. "You'll understand soon enough."

Rose sighed and said, "Come inside and stop getting the bottom of my nice Pendleton all dirty. You're not dressed." She was still in her nightgown and slippers.

As she walked back to the house with her, Rose's mind was racing. She prided herself on her rationality, her reliance on logic and reason. But faced with Kimi's cryptic words, she couldn't shake the feeling of unease that had settled in her stomach. The words echoed in Rose's mind, their meaning elusive yet haunting. She'd always respected Hotah's beliefs, but they'd never been her own. Now, standing in the quiet prairie with her daughter, she couldn't help but feel the weight of something ancient and profound in the air.

As she returned to her car, she noticed her ex-husband, Hotah, had backed his truck up by the side of the barn. He only backed it up when unhooking his trailer, which he had parked under an overhang he had built. He was supposed to be gone for a few more months working construction off the Pine Ridge reservation. If he was home early, he had probably quit before he got fired. He didn't communicate well, one cause of their marriage's failure.

Aside from that, he was a good man, a great father, and a good stepfather to Luke, who'd been three when they married. Since Hotah moved out, Luke disrespected him often, like calling him by his first name instead of "Dad." Mostly, they ignored each other. Luke didn't enjoy any of the activities Hotah did. He didn't ride his horse anymore, hated hunting and fishing, and spent his time playing video games. Kimi loved horses, fishing, and hunting. She was a great shot and loved being outside with her dad, uncles, and cousins.

As Kimi returned to the house and Rose walked to her car, she said, "Looks like your dad is home early."

Kimi hesitated and said in Lakota, "He's not alone anymore. He has someone else now."

Although Rose understood more Lakota than she could speak, she didn't comprehend at first. As she took a moment, she realized what Kimi meant, and her heart sank. It'd been almost three years since she and Hotah last slept together, and over a year since he bought the trailer and moved into it. They were legally separated, not divorced. They hadn't resolved how to divide the property or share custody. It was easier to ignore the problem.

A couple of months ago, he'd come into the house and said, "Let's finalize the divorce." She was so taken aback, she didn't respond.

Hotah continued, "You tell me what you think is fair. We can do this without lawyers."

She agreed but never followed through, too busy as usual. Now she knew why he had asked, but the pain persisted.

She told herself he deserved to be happy—they both did. God only knew they hadn't made each other happy after the first few years. He had stuck it out for Kimi. She should be grateful. She took a deep breath and willed herself to let it go. After hugging Kimi, her strange, beautiful daughter, to let her know she was okay with it, she got in her car and headed to work.

As she left the house, Rose glanced back at the field, a sense of foreboding lingering in her chest. She couldn't shake the feeling that something momentous was about to happen, something that would change everything. Kimi always had unusual abilities, which Rose mainly ignored. Rose liked numbers, logical things that fit together in an orderly manner. She didn't consider herself a spiritual person or a believer in the unseen. Everyone from Hotah's family believed Kimi had a special connection to the spirit.

Hotah came from a traditional and spiritual family, which had an *inípi* or sweat lodge on their property and held ceremonies often. His father and aunt were spiritual leaders in the community. Before she passed, his grandmother was a keeper of knowledge of plants, healing, and Medicine Ways. Hotah's grandmother and her parents never lost the Lakota language or the teachings. If Hotah's grandmother spoke English, Rose never heard her.

In the last year of her life, Hotah's grandmother lived with them and significantly influenced Kimi. She started using a wheelchair and couldn't access the bathroom in her old trailer on the family property and moved in with them.

Their house, built in 1920, had undergone several remodels over the last 100 years, needed significant work. Hotah and Rose bought it and the 160 acres it came with for the cost of the land because the bank considered the house a loss. Hotah believed he could restore it. They sold 150 acres of the farmland to the neighbor and, using funds from her father's estate and a construction loan, they started the project. Upstairs, the house had four small bedrooms, while downstairs it had the kitchen and two front rooms: a living room, and a parlor later converted into a recreation room.

The previous owners installed a bathroom between the rec room and the kitchen, but the doorway to the bathroom from the hall was narrow. Hotah tore out the wall between the bathroom and rec room and created a wheelchair-accessible bathroom with a roll-in shower and grab bars. He did a beautiful job, but that was the extent of his care for his ailing grandmother. His mother, aunt, and female relatives did the rest of the work. Rose did what she could while working full time and caring for the children. Toward the end, they had help from home care nurses.

Kimi was nine when her great-grandmother moved in, and she spent a great deal of time with her, even helping her with bathing and getting to the toilet. Rose often listened to them from the other room, singing and laughing. Although Rose understood little Lakota, she knew Kimi was being told stories and was being taught about plants and healing.

The day before she died, Kimi came to her with her eyes full of tears of deep sadness and said, "*Unčí* (grandmother) is going to pass to the stars tomorrow."

Rose knew from the nurses the end was coming soon. There was never a question about her going to a hospital or nursing facility; they knew she would die at home. She was still mentally very much with it, if increasingly frail, so Rose expected her to live for some time yet. Rose tried to reassure Kimi that while unci would pass sooner or later, there was no way to know which day it would happen.

Kimi looked at her and said, "Of course I know. I told Unci, and she agreed."

Not knowing how to react, she said, "I know how much you love her and will be very sad when she passes. It's okay to be sad."

Not long after, a troop of relatives came to say goodbye. After most had gone home, Kimi said Unci wished to speak to Rose.

She seemed so tired but spoke directly to Rose, with Hotah translating. "Kimímela is a shining star who comes to Earth only once every seven generations. She brings sacred medicine. If you listen to her, she will bring healing to the Earth."

Okkaay, Rose thought, not knowing what to think, especially not having much belief in supernatural visions. Every mother thought her child was special, but she knew Kimi was unusual. But to say she'd bring healing to the earth was different. However, she respected Hotah's beliefs, said nothing, and they both went to bed. At four in the morning, Kimi came into their room with tears streaming down her face.

"She's gone."

Hotah's aunt had spent the night and told them later how Kimi came downstairs around three am, sat on her great-grandmother's bed, held her hand while she slept and slipped away. Rose had never been around death. Her own father had died a few years earlier, but she hardly knew him. Her parents divorced when she was four, and he moved from Sioux Falls back to the Yankton reservation. They rarely saw each other.

She never expected someone to die in her own house. They waited until later in the morning to call the nurse and the relatives. Rose stood in the room's corner as the female relatives washed and dressed her for burial before the funeral home came and took her away. It was moving and beautiful in a sad way.

On the drive to work, Rose thought about how she had dismissed Kimi's great-grandmother's words. Now she wondered. There'd been other times when Kimi showed prescience. When she was five or six, she was at her uncle's house. Her dad and cousins were preparing for a hunting trip, and the men gathered around the kitchen table. They were looking at a large map and discussing where to camp. They had chosen and agreed on a spot.

Kimi came into the kitchen and said, "Don't camp there. It will flood tomorrow."

The men looked at each other and laughed nervously, but chose a different site on higher ground. A sudden rainstorm brought a flash flood to the area the next day. Later, they heard reports of other hunters being caught in the flash flood, requiring rescue and losing several horses and vehicles. No one in the family forgot her warning.

Uneasily, Rose was trying to reconcile her analytic mindset with Kimi's inexplicable insights and reached no conclusions as she turned onto the road that led to her job.

=..=

The Omímeya Casino and Resort was a large circular structure, with wings extending on four sides. The center resembled a tipi, built with seventy-foot steel poles painted and textured to look like wood. Just before the opening of the front entrance, the poles met with a large teardrop-shaped skylight. Four-story buildings extended from the lodge in all four directions. With 320 rooms, it won many awards for architecture and sustainable design—100% clean energy, 75% self-sufficient. Solar power, supplemented with hydropower from the nearby dam and wind power, provided electricity.

The nearby wind farm was owned by an out-of-state corporation who sold the power to faraway utilities. There were plans for the tribe to build and own their wind farm, for which Omímeya was underwriting the lengthy and expensive process. A small geothermal plant provided heating, cooling, and hot water. By utilizing hot reservoirs within the Earth which are naturally renewable, geothermal is sustainable indefinitely as it uses no fossil fuels or outside resources like sun or wind power.

Omímeya was on Lower Brule tribal lands, close to Interstate 90, but still far enough away from other casinos. The tribe was too small to fund a sixty-million-dollar casino resort, so a consortium of Indian casinos funded and managed it. They chose the site for its extraordinary natural beauty, with excellent hunting and fishing opportunities. Located in a loop of the Missouri River that encircled the entire five-mile by four-mile site, it was more of an oval with an opening than a circle. A circle sounded better, so it was named Omímeya.

One drawback was the three-hour drive to the big airport; the closest in Pierre was small, with few connecting flights. This kept away many of the larger conferences and high-end gamblers. Only being in operation for eight years, two of which were closed because of the pandemic, it was struggling. There were expansion plans in the works, such as an eighteen-hole golf course set to open next year. There was talk about a private jet runway being built.

The casino revenue decreased post-pandemic, but the resort surpassed expectations. Rose had pushed for a family-friendly vacation spot instead of an adult playground, and it was paying off. Despite the improvement, Rose couldn't shake the feeling of unease as she reviewed the latest financial reports, knowing corporate pressure for profitability could jeopardize her efforts to promote Lakota culture. She spearheaded the Canoe Center, which offered canoe rentals, with displays of Indigenous canoes from the Mississippi River basin and from as far away as the Pacific Northwest. Rose started the annual canoe races, bringing an economic boost to the entire area. She loved watching the families enjoy the Canoe Center, knowing she had played a part in creating a space celebrating Indigenous culture while providing a recreational experience.

Not all her projects were profitable. She kept the horse stables open, calling it a loss leader. Horses and their upkeep were expensive, requiring additional staffing and insurance. Guests' photos of the resort's horses, ponies, and tipis posted on Instagram brought favorable attention. The stable offered riding lessons, which was an excellent activity for children.

Prairie Abundance restaurant was another with red ink. The main restaurant, the Red Oak, was a buffet offering typical made-to-order

American fare, with the addition of fry bread tacos. It was popular with both locals and resort guests and was profitable. Prairie Abundance served high-end Indigenous food featuring game and wild harvested foods. However, because of the distance from major population centers, it didn't attract sufficient guests to justify its high costs. Despite favorable reviews, the restaurant had already limited its operations to weekends and might have to close entirely.

Rose liked the highly rated chef, Jeffery Medicine Bear. He was active in the food sovereignty movement and led groups to identify and gather wild plants. She understood the need for profitability to be sustainable; however, she also believed the horse stables and Prairie Abundance had an intrinsic value that outweighed the bottom line. If only she could persuade corporate.

Rose was excited to have landed a big conference this weekend, with over 150 rooms booked. The Native American Physicians Association. Omímeya had hosted smaller and regional Indian Health Service (IHS) meetings before, but this one was national and more prestigious. Most doctors would bring their spouses, children, and their large discretionary incomes. She expected the gift shops and resort services would do a banner business because she didn't think doctors were big gamblers. It was their first year with this group; she was looking forward to the numbers, possibly showing up Phil, the casino manager. Between the medical conference and other events, they were eighty-five percent booked this weekend, unusual for this time of year. While some doctors worked for the IHS, many didn't. The president of the association, Dr. Chaton Begay, was one of the best neurosurgeons in the country. A graduate of Harvard Medical School, who practiced and taught at Johns Hopkins. He'd come with his wife and two teenage boys. They'd come a week early for a family vacation. As the family explored the resort, Rose noticed the curiosity and wonder in the teenagers' eyes, a testament to the transformative power of the resort's offerings.

One perk of choosing the resort for their conference was it upgraded them to one of the premium Riverside Cabins two miles away from the main building, right on the river. Calling them cabins was misleading. They were two-or three-bedroom 2500-3500 square foot houses, beautifully furnished with vaulted ceilings, stonework, wood interiors, enormous fireplaces, covered decks, a private dock, and modern kitchens with all the amenities. There were four currently, with four more in various stages of construction.

This was the Begays' first time at the resort. Rose included in the welcome gift basket not only the usual specialty foods and products made by various Native companies but extra coupons for the arcade for the teenagers, complimentary spa tickets, canoe and fishing gear rentals, drinks for the casino bar, and a few small denomination poker chips. Rose understood how important guest satisfaction was, especially for VIPs. The richer they were, the more they liked free stuff.

Rose parked and plugged in her car at the staff charging station, under a pitched roof covered in solar panels. She had an excellent electric SUV, a company car with the resort logo on the side. There were empty spaces at the charging station, as the airport shuttles weren't due back for a few hours.

Rose got to her office on the fourth floor on the north wing, pulled her in-house radio from the charger, dropped it into her pocket, put in the earpiece, powered up her military-grade work tablet, ready to start her day. After a couple of hours of routine work, she went downstairs to check out the conference vendors. Rose liked to walk around the vendors at eleven am because the second morning sessions were beginning, and the room was quiet. She couldn't help but smile at the sight of Dr. Begay's sons eagerly grabbing up the branded pens and notepads, penlights, and other swag surprisingly better than the average conference goodies, as many vendors were drug and medical suppliers.

=..=

As the vendors' room lacked outside windows, Rose heard the raised murmur of voices before she saw anything. As she walked to the lobby, she could see through the skylight the sky was strangely dark. Stepping outside with the others, Rose encountered a dense, dark fog swirling around them. The air was thick with an eerie darkness, as if night had suddenly fallen. An ominous rumble filled the air as the fog swallowed the world, muffling all other sounds. The sound grew louder, like an oncoming train, rumbling louder and closer. Suddenly, one large, sharp, roaring explosive clap of thunder, so loud it hurt her ears, like a bomb going off. Then, silence. The fog vanished. The small crowd outside all cried out variations of "What the fuck?!"

All at once, everyone reached for their phone, including Rose. There were no weather alerts. She could see people trying to make calls, but nothing was going through. *Circuits must be busy*, she thought. She tried various websites, but the Internet seemed to be down too. Staff were on the front desk phone. People lined up for the lobby courtesy phone, since the landlines were still up. Guests were milling about, returning to lectures, and others were looking confused while poking at their phones over and over. Rose realized she needed answers, so she hurried back to her office.

She received a radio call from Jim Fredrich, the assistant facilities manager. He said, "Wanted to let you know the generators kicked in automatically as soon as the outside power went out. Perfectly as planned."

"I didn't know the power was out," Rose replied.

The lights were all solar, so there were few noticeable changes when the power went from the major lines to the generator.

"Any idea what happened?" Rose asked. "Sounded like an explosion. Is the plant okay?"

"First thing I checked," Jim answered.

They were talking about the geothermal power plant behind the resort. Geothermal plants could conceivably explode. Chances were remote with the small, newer generation one they had.

"Some kind of weird storm, probably lightning blew transformers. I'll call the LBUC (Lower Brule Electric Company) to find out what they know and see about the timeline for repairs."

"Thanks."

Rose was glad to know Jim was on it, although she didn't remember seeing lightning, but whoever heard of thunder without lightning?

She quickly texted the kids to check if the power was off at her home. They had a generator and a few solar panels. Power outages were common in the Dakotas, so they'd be fine if the power were out. She was glad Hotah was home, as she wasn't sure if Luke remembered how to start the generator. Rose didn't hear back because the text was in a waiting queue, which worried her, as she wanted to know they're okay.

She fielded a few radio calls from various departments, wanting to know what was happening. She let people know there was no cause for alarm. Although the credit card terminals didn't work, guests' transactions had to be cash only. She authorized staff to charge up to $100 to each room. Internal software was working, but not outside lines. The landlines and cell phones operated by Tribal TeleComm, the tribal-owned company, worked, but not other carriers.

On her office landline, she tried placing a call to Kyle Ward, the Emergency Manager for the resort and the regional Federal Emergency Management Agency (FEMA) coordinator. The circuits were still busy; she pulled up the Emergency Response software and texted him. An immediate automated response stated he wasn't currently available but to dial *1 if it was an emergency. She groaned and dialed *1. She hoped he wasn't out of town. Kyle attended many emergency planning meetings all over the state, but usually not on weekends. He lived on the resort grounds in a nice fifth wheel at the RV Park.

Rose pulled up the software to see who was next on the list, Charles Archambault, from security. She clicked on his name to see his work schedule and was glad to see he was working. She switched to the security channel and waited for a break in calls before requesting he come upstairs to coordinate in Kyle's absence. Security had their hands full of hysterical guests, but they were good at that. Always polite and calm, even when faced with unreasonable or intoxicated guests.

She looked through the Emergency Response software when she got to her office. It had a lot of features, links, references, and helpful step-by-step instructions. As per emergency protocol, she sent a notice to department heads to come in. She felt less overwhelmed, but this wasn't her job. They had an emergency manager for this very reason, and she had enough to do with everything else. Rose's mind raced with questions and concerns, but she pushed them aside, focusing on what needed to be done.

She got a radio call from John Murphy, Red Oak's manager. The natural gas stoves stopped working in the middle of lunch service. He tried maintenance but didn't get a reply. Remembering there was a plan for this, she checked and told him they could convert each stove to propane using the part taped on the back. Rose told him to send someone to maintenance in person as they were probably too slammed to answer calls. She texted Jim, who oversaw maintenance, considered it handled, and moved on.

Soon, Charles lumbered in, a big Native man on the heavier rather than fit side. Rose didn't remember whether he was former military, although many of the security guys were. She didn't know him well, but seemed like a nice guy.

He reported, "No word yet from LBUC. The local cell phones are functioning, but the circuits are overloaded. Anyone using Verizon or T-Mobile cannot get service. Landlines work only in the immediate area. The internet is also down. IT was doing a hard reboot as I left, it may be back up shortly."

Charles' voice was steady, his demeanor calm and collected. "I'll get on the radios and give you a better update soon. Phones work if not connecting, so it wasn't an EMP (Electromagnetic Pulse), but that doesn't rule out another kind of attack."

Definitely ex-military, Rose thought, because a terrorist or military strike hadn't even occurred to her. South Dakota no longer had nuclear silos. All the big air force bases were hundreds of miles away. She didn't think they could hear a bomb from that far. Rose was sure the phenomenon was natural. She remembered, with stark suddenness, Kimi's words this morning: "Big Thunder is coming."

Whatever was going on, Rose had over 600 guests and 150 employees for whom she was responsible. She needed to make an announcement, but didn't know what to say. They rarely used the public address system, designed for fires or similar emergencies. She made a bland announcement the storm had created disruptions to some cell services and the internet, and while outside power was down, they had generators. While there may be delays or disruptions of services, she informed guests to continue with their planned activities.

"Any idea where Kyle is?" asked Rose.

"On the river," replied Charles.

Rose remembered Kyle was training for next year's canoe race. Then, Rose received a text from him, saying he'd be there in about forty-five minutes. Better than out of town, thought Rose.

In Kyle's office, Charles requested Rose to get out the satellite phone while he attended to the radios. All kinds of radios stood on the shelves of a long table, set up L-shaped with Kyle's desk so two people could access radios at the same time.

"Where is the sat phone?" asked Rose.

She forgot where they kept it. She performed the quarterly drills, as did all staff, but honestly, she thought if something happened, Kyle would be here.

"In the Faraday cage," Charles replied.

"Where?"

Then she remembered what looked like a closet door at the back of the office. She needed a code and a swipe from her card to open it. Fortunately, she could access all the codes from her tablet with a six-digit pin. The Faraday cage wasn't a cage at all, but a large walk-in closet lined in metal mesh, with wire shelves neatly organized and alphabetized with all kinds of electronics. She grabbed one of the satellite phones. Rose connected the charger, looked up some numbers, and started trying to make calls. She heard a brief sound, then nothing. The screen showed a spinning wait icon and displayed, "Searching for a signal." She thought she was doing something wrong, but not wanting to interrupt Charles, who seemed to be speaking to several people at once on the radios, she pointed at the phone and gestured it was not working. He motioned to leave it, and she returned to her office.

Manuel Torez from the shuttle service radioed and said the front desk had guests who wanted to check out because they were anxious about not reaching their families. He wondered whether they could arrange an early shuttle. Guests didn't know how complicated the shuttle service was. They had two big buses that did the Sioux Falls airport run in the mornings and late afternoons, and smaller electric minivans that went to the Pierre airport on a similar schedule. There were no taxis or Uber. She needed to make it happen, so she gave permission and left it to them to coordinate the logistics.

Jim radioed Rose and said, "LBUC reported many power lines are down. Although the transformers are okay, the entire system shut down as a safety precaution until the lines are repaired. Repairs would take time, days or even weeks."

Jim relayed other bad news. He informed her the fuel reserves were on the low side. The backup generators ran on diesel. They used four large underground tanks for the big shuttles and the construction equipment. Every three months, they'd bring another tank online as one emptied, and then they'd fill the empty tank. This was to keep the diesel fresh, with an ample supply on hand for emergencies. He said the current tank was 3/4 empty and was due to be filled on the first of the month.

"How long do we have?" Rose asked anxiously.

"About a week per tank is normal for the generator. Less with the shuttles," he added. "If we cut power now, it would drastically extend the time."

She wondered when Wayne, Jim's boss, would get in since he didn't live too far away. She wondered if she should wait for him, then realized he trained his people well. If Jim said to cut power, it should be done.

"What do you suggest?" asked Rose.

"Check the power usage on your tablet. It shows the biggest energy draws."

It took Rose a minute to realize the biggest draw was from the casino slot machines. She didn't think she had the authority to make such a decision and told Jim to hold off until she could get word from corporate. Then, she realized she couldn't call anyone from corporate or her boss, Tom Durrell. He lived in Pierre, didn't work weekends, and often flew off on all-expense paid trips to other Indian casinos or corporate meetings. That meant she was in charge. She needed to act like it. She figured she'd allow herself an hour to get through to corporate. Surely the phones couldn't be down for long. In the meantime, she'd shut down the arcade, another big energy draw.

She saw Kyle approach his office. She was so relieved she wanted to hug him, but it wouldn't be professional. While Charles talked on the radio, she filled him in. The sat phone still wouldn't reach anyone or anywhere they tried, and the internet was still down. IT put up a splash page, stating the outside internet was temporarily down. However, the internal servers and Wi-Fi were working, conference schedules and resort activities were still accessible, and internal calls could be made with Wi-Fi.

Rose got an emergency alert from her phone. *It's about time,* she thought, then realized that Kyle had sent it from his FEMA account, part of the wireless emergency notification system. It reached everyone within range of the closest cell tower, regardless of which phone carrier the person used or if the satellites were down. The alert was short and said there'd been a power outage and a disruption to some communication systems. The warning instructed people not to approach downed lines and provided a number to call for reporting. They also gave radio station numbers to tune in to for further instructions.

She listened to the radio in Kyle's office.. Something strange was happening. All communication outside the immediate area had been cut off. The National Guard couldn't reach the military channels anywhere. No one from the state capital of Pierre was responding—no governor to declare a state of emergency, no FEMA. Much of Chamberlain, the Brule County seat, was in contact. The county sheriff's office did most of the reporting.

Kyle and Charles were talking about roads. Rose didn't understand how the streets could be closed, then heard the reports. Roads weren't closed; they ended abruptly. Trees, plants, and even creeks stood in their place. There were houses, cars, and a boat inexplicably cut in half. As reports of strange phenomena continued to come in, Rose felt a growing sense of unease. What started as a simple power outage now felt more sinister, something beyond their understanding.

The county sent rescue services out to two pileup accidents on I-90, one in Chamberlain and one in Presho. It was bad, and they were all scrambling to respond. As Rose listened, she realized with all these people injured; she had a resort full of doctors. Rose radioed Jenny Abrams, the events manager, to make announcements in the meeting rooms and find volunteers to be shuttled to the hospital. She felt good about that, at least.

Kyle said, "We need more bodies for communications. Also, get both Tribal Council members in here for an emergency planning meeting."

Despite the chaos unfolding around them, Kyle remained focused and composed, a testament to his years of training and experience. *Kyle is so calm,* Rose thought. *Houses cut in half. What thunderstorm could do that?* Rose's mind raced with questions and concerns, but she pushed them aside, focusing on what needed to be done. She was determined to use Kyle's example to be calm and lead her team through the crisis, no matter what. She needed to take one step at a time.

Rose knew their troubles were far from over. She remembered what Kimi said this morning. Whatever had caused this bizarre phenomenon was still out there, waiting.

Chapter Two
Jackson

OLIVER JACKSON WAS looking forward to using his taser on white cops. He knew he shouldn't enjoy it since they were his fellow officers, mostly all great guys and one gal. He was a Sioux Falls City cop, currently in Chamberlain to give in-service training on nonviolent arrest protocol and to issue a new state-of-the-art taser. Usually, as part of the training, officers all got tased. Since most got it in basic training, it wasn't required a second time, but as a trainer, he could require it, and he did. He believed if officers used more non-confrontational approaches, there'd be less need for tasing. If they remembered how awful it felt, they'd tase less and talk more.

He enjoyed teaching these nonviolent policing seminars, not so much the tasing. Jackson had witnessed the effects of excessive force firsthand and was determined to make a difference. He'd witnessed the damage it could cause, both physically and emotionally, and was committed to promoting nonviolent policing. He'd been considering quitting the force and doing this full time. During the training, Jackson emphasized the importance of de-escalation techniques and the use of non-lethal force.

He encouraged officers to think critically about their actions and the impact they had on the community. Jackson knew he was funded to attend seminars nationwide and asked to give in-service training because he was Black. That was no problem for him, as he was among only two Black officers in the Sioux Falls Police Department. South Dakota had plenty of Native Americans and Hispanics, but very few Blacks. He preferred the term Black over African American, the same as many Native Americans called themselves Indians, or more recently, Indigenous. Personal choice.

His class comprised fourteen officers, mostly highway patrol, with a couple from the South Dakota State Police office in Pierre. One woman was a trooper and the pilot for the new police plane, a Cessna 206. They flew in five officers from Rapid City, saving themselves a three-hour drive; the others drove in from nearby squads based along I-90.

The cramped but functional classroom had rows of chairs facing a large screen. They were watching the mandatory training video from the taser manufacturer. Jackson thought the video was a waste of time because it was a sales pitch espousing the various features rather than a helpful training tool. Since the state already made the purchase, there was no need for the sales pitch. He had several boxes in his truck he'd issue to each person and others to pass on to departments to do their own training.

As the room was dark and attention was on the screen, no one noticed the dark fog outside and the sounds of approaching thunder. The noise quickly overwhelmed the video. People were getting up to investigate when they heard a loud, explosive clap of thunder. As Jackson and his fellow officers rushed outside, they were greeted by an eerie sight. There was a dark mist, barely noticeable as it faded away, but not a cloud in the sky.

A few minutes later, the dispatcher came out and said, "I could use help. The power is out, radios are going nuts, no one knows what's going on."

As they returned to the squad office, the mood was tense. The officers were on edge, unsure of what was happening and what they should do next. Two troopers in uniform who were on duty during the training immediately went out to their patrol cars. Other than the pilot, the rest were in off-duty clothes. They filed back into the squad office. Someone took charge of activating the emergency protocols, including starting the generator out back, and others helped with the radio.

Jackson tried calling his girlfriend, Denise, although he knew she was working, to leave a voicemail. She worked as a nurse in the emergency department at a Sioux Falls hospital. The call didn't go through or ring. He noticed a few others doing the same thing. The dispatcher reported a pileup on the I-90 east ramp less than a mile away. A couple of guys who drove offered to help. They were all given radios and first aid kits.

He grabbed Doug, one of the Rapid City guys, introducing himself while they got in his truck. "Call me Jackson, everyone does." It had started as an army thing, but now even Denise called him Jackson.

As they headed up the on-ramp to east I-90, he noticed the traffic backed up. The pileup started just past the ramp, so they used the shoulder to bypass traffic. He could see flashing lights ahead from one of the patrol cars and came across several cars that looked like they'd rear-ended each other. The cause was an overturned tractor-trailer in one lane, but when they approached, they saw something so weird, so unfathomable, it was hard to grasp. The freeway abruptly ended, giving way to a vast expanse of prairie. Tall grasses and sagebrush swayed gently in the breeze. Fully grown trees dotted the landscape, their branches reaching toward the sky. The highway was neatly severed, revealing a clear line on the other side where the ground appeared greener.

They stopped as far off the shoulder as possible. Further down the road, the traffic was backing up. People were outside their cars and walking to the cut-off freeway. In the distance, he saw someone in an SUV driving off onto the grassland. In one car, a woman with a head wound was bleeding. The airbags had been deployed, but the door was stuck so she couldn't exit the vehicle. She was conscious and alert but anxious to get out of the car as a toddler was screaming his head off in the back seat. Doug checked the child and reported him unhurt. Then he unhooked him from the car seat and held him up to show the mother he was okay. Unable to open the door, she tried talking to the child to soothe him. Doug reached into his pocket and pulled out his car keys with a little toy plastic animal that squeaked. He unhooked it from his keys and handed it to the child. Sure enough, the child calmed down.

Still holding him, he said, "I'll watch the mom. You check the other cars."

He put the kid on one hip, the first aid kit on the hood, and gave the mom a bandage to put on her head to hold pressure. They soon heard an ambulance driving up the shoulder to the cars ahead, slowly weaving between cars. There were only a few seriously injured. According to the drivers, it could've been worse because a dense, dark fog had come down, forcing everyone to slow down. They noticed no traffic on I-90 east going west, only backed up west coming east.

They returned to the squad office, pretty freaked out. Making small talk to calm himself, Jackson asked Doug if he had kids. He said no, only a lot of nieces and nephews. Doug told him he bought the toys by the dozens at the dollar store and always had one on his key ring. He laughed and said that sometimes they'd squeak if they got knocked about in his pocket, so the guys called him Squeaky. They had a good laugh, which they needed. Just when Jackson thought he knew cops, someone like this surprised him.

A few of the other troopers headed out to a pileup on I-90 west by Presho, about 30 miles away. The freeway abruptly ended there, too. Hoping to improve communication, the Rapid City cops were heading to the plane to return. The commander of the small squad asked for help to bring emergency communication gear up from the armory. Jackson and two other guys followed him to a large warehouse surrounded by a big fence topped with barbed wire. Using a key code, they entered the building. Inside were several Bearcats, the big tank-like vehicles used by SWAT teams, and shelves of various supplies on the back walls.

One trooper pointed to an area and said, "You'd like this, Jackson. We have the largest supply of less-than-lethals in this part of the state."

Stacked up were rows of body armor and helmets, riot shields, crates marked with tear gas, rubber bullets, stun grenades, etc. It looked like enough to quell half the country.

"Many riots in Chamberlain?" asked Jackson wryly.

"Standing Rock Protests," answered the trooper. "Afterwards, they set armories up close to every Indian reservation. A lot of donated military surplus is here, too."

Sioux Falls police had a riot squad. Jackson was required to attend the training, but he didn't think he could fire on peaceful protestors. They might be called less than lethal, but it didn't mean less than dangerous. There were reports of serious injuries, even fatalities. He'd attended workshops with slides showing horrible images of injuries because of these types of weapons. Everyone carried boxes of communications equipment back to the small squad office. As Jackson and his colleagues prepared to investigate what was going on, they knew they were facing something unlike anything they'd ever encountered before. Little did they know this was only the beginning of events that would change their lives forever.

Jackson was asked if he could assist with police coordination at a meeting at the county courthouse. It was tricky to figure out how to get downtown with the off-ramp being nonexistent. He needed to drive onto the prairie for a bit before returning to the road. He was getting low on gas, and the gas stations he passed all displayed closed signs, painting a stark picture of the situation's severity. Evidently, none had generators for the pumps. As he drove, he scanned the radio stations and only found two working. Both saying the same thing, informing listeners power and outside communication were down. They were calling it Big Thunder, and talked about the roads being cut off. So far, they had no new information.

Routinely, Jackson downloaded copies of Google Maps to store on his phone, as some places in South Dakota didn't have cell service. He easily located the county courthouse and made his way upstairs to where the emergency response group was holding their meeting. It was a madhouse with people all talking over each other, milling about, and voices rising in heated discussion. Jackson felt a sense of urgency in the air, like the calm before a storm. He felt a mix of frustration and concern as he navigated the chaotic meeting. He wanted to go home, but a sense of duty compelled him to stay and help in any way he could.

In one corner was a young man in a military uniform standing quietly. Jackson thought it was an excellent place to start. He introduced himself and met Lieutenant Tim Warren with the National Guard unit based in Chamberlain. Jackson asked questions, and they talked quietly. The meeting was people arguing, which wasn't worth their attention. He discovered the unit was the 200th Engineer Company, with sixty-two members based at Chamberlain National Armory, with people from Pierre, Mobridge, and the surrounding areas. The 200th Engineer Company had been deployed in Iraq in 2017 when he was there, but Warren hadn't been in the Guard then. They were doing their monthly weekend training when the shit hit the fan, or whatever this was. Having a military presence reassured Jackson. Warren was calm and amused by the chaos. When someone in the meeting mentioned the National Guard, they fell silent.

Lt. Warren began to speak. "My commanding officer was very clear. We cannot deploy without an order from the governor. I'm here to offer what help we can, such as communication or rescue. As soon as we get the deploy order, we're ready to go, but as you know, we couldn't reach anywhere outside the immediate area. We have four vehicles doing reconnaissance as we speak. Last I heard nothing new. The outside area is all prairie and trees."

Jackson guessed a pompous-acting person wearing a suit was in charge. The lieutenant identified him as Brule County Commissioner, Ed Robinson.

Robinson said, "The FEMA guy at the casino wants to issue a state of emergency within the hour, by two pm."

That brought up a new chorus of people shouting, "He can't do it!" or asking, "What authority does he have?"

Robinson held up his hand for quiet and said, "The emergency group they formed have the legally elected Tribal Councils for both reservations. They have a State Attorney there. Kyle Ward is in charge. Without Janet Spencer, he's the highest-ranking FEMA official. They're asking for us to send a county official up there to coordinate. The state of emergency measures is all reasonable under the circumstances." Then he started reading them off: "a dawn-to-dusk curfew, a price freeze, severe penalties for looting, etc."

"The only thing not standard is a moratorium on gas sales, limited to police, fire, and public utilities." That brought a wave of protests since most had gas generators at home.

Robinson again held up his hand and said, "If we're really cut off from the outside world, and the electricity is off for weeks or even longer, does anyone know how long the generators that power the water and sewage systems will work? I don't know about any of you, but running water and flush toilets are on my priority list. I'm sure we can figure out exemptions for those with special circumstances."

This shut everyone up, probably thinking about how they might get special exemptions.

"Another thing," Robinson continued, "They recommend limiting gun sales to one long gun and one pistol per person."

This brought another howl of protests. This was gun country. No background checks were required to buy guns and open carry was legal. Most people hunted and were National Rifle Association members.

An older woman stood up and said, "These are valid concerns, but this is an emergency order only, not a permanent law. Let's coordinate with them. If someone has a different proposal, bring it before 2:00 pm The more important issue is we don't know how long this power outage will last, or what being cut off from outside means. What'll happen if we can't bring in trucks? How will we ensure a long-term food supply? What about the availability of medicines and other essential supplies?"

Jackson didn't know who the woman was, but he thought she was one of the few grown-ups in the room. Afterwards, the meeting went back to the previous level of chaos.

Jackson asked the lieutenant, "FEMA guy at the casino?"

"Kyle Ward was a former army medic with a lucrative business advising corporations on preparing for natural or manmade disasters. Omímeya Casino hired him around the time of the pandemic to be their emergency manager. He was high up in FEMA as a regional coordinator."

Jackson listened again to the meeting, and the reports coming in via radio. There was rampant speculation—most of it was crazy. If it was a Russian or Chinese attack, how could they plant trees where the freeways were? Or cut cars in half? While aliens seemed plausible, the idea was absurd!

Then a call came for quiet to hear the most recent report. Earlier, a rescue helicopter had been transporting someone injured in the I-90 car pileup to Sioux Falls. I-90 ended at Chamberlain and never reappeared. Where Sioux Falls was supposed to be was prairie. No downed buildings, no bodies, a city of 196,000 people just gone. They flew around as much as possible but had to return because of fuel. Bizarrely, they reported flying over a massive herd of buffalo was more extensive than they'd ever seen or even heard of.

Sioux Falls was gone. Jackson felt like he got punched in the gut. *Denise, what happened to Denise?* Jackson thought. The meeting erupted with questions, opinions, and theories. Someone speculated on time travel. Jackson tuned everyone out. As the meeting progressed, the sense of unease grew.

Jackson could see the fear and confusion in people's eyes, mirroring his own. He needed to get out of there, but he couldn't go home. Home was gone. Then he heard someone at the meeting asking for people to go to the casino and liaise with FEMA. Everyone was reluctant because it was on an Indian reservation. He heard the term tribal sovereignty bandied about. The tension between the county officials and the Tribal Council added a layer of complexity to the situation. Jackson observed the dynamics, trying to understand the underlying tensions.

When the call for volunteers came, Jackson's hand shot up without hesitation. He knew he had to do something. Anything was better than sitting in this meeting with all these crazy white people. No one paid him much mind, but he got directions from the other person who volunteered, a woman named Lois Robinson. She was the one who made helpful comments earlier. She was the county tax assessor, of all things.

Lois said, "Might as well be useful somewhere. I'm a county official. No one is going to want to deal with taxes for a while, I imagine."

As Jackson and Lois prepared to go to the casino to liaise with FEMA, he couldn't shake the feeling things were about to get even more complicated.

=..=

After Jackson got to his truck, he sat in the front seat, stunned and in shock. He couldn't believe Sioux Falls was gone, Denise with it. Jackson had planned to propose to Denise next week. They'd been dating for two years and lived together for six months. The weight of his loss settled heavily on his shoulders. He couldn't imagine a future without Denise, the woman he planned to spend the rest of his life with. Reluctant to commit, he'd been with a lot of women, even in Iraq, where there were few eligible possibilities. He was tall and good-looking. Women threw themselves at him, and he usually caught them. He only had a few long-term relationships. Nothing ever took until Denise. To his shame, he had cheated on previous girlfriends. Although the thought of only having sex with one woman was daunting, he didn't want to marry and be a cheater, so he stayed single. He was thirty-seven years old and thought it was high time he settled down.

Jackson met Denise over a combative drunk. He'd brought the guy into the ER to get sewn up. In the process of trying to restrain him, his partner slammed the guy's head into the sidewalk, and he was bleeding like a stuck pig. These things happened, typical for the job. But the guy wasn't allowing the nurse to clean him up. Even while handcuffed, he was kicking and thrashing about. Jackson was holding the guy down as they were trying to handcuff him to the bed. Another nurse came in, an attractive Black woman, a little younger than him. They looked at each other over the thrashing guy and smiled. They both caught each other checking out the other's hand, looking for a wedding ring, and laughed. After the guy was restrained, he hung around and got her number, they'd been together ever since.

Jackson wondered if Sioux Falls was gone, what about Chicago? What happened to the outside world? A wave of fear hit him thinking about his mother, his sister, and his grandmother. He had an overpowering sense of loss. Despite the distance, they remained a close-knit family, though not as close as before. He'd seen them last Christmas and taken Denise, the first girlfriend he'd brought home since high school, to meet them. They got along like a house on fire—all strong Black women. Were they all gone, dead, or never to be seen again? The question of it all, the not knowing, was frightening.

Jackson lost many good friends in Iraq and learned how to compartmentalize. He took a deep breath, realizing he needed to get going. He could get on I-90 because the bridges were intact. When he exited I-90 at Reliance, he saw an open gas and convenience store with a sign saying "Cash only. No EBT." They weren't selling gas, but luckily, he still had a quarter tank, plenty to go for thirty miles. Jackson had little cash on him, preferring debit or credit cards, but had a couple of hundred stashed in his emergency go bag. He realized he should probably arm himself after seeing the go bag. He had a small gun safe with a biometric lock bolted to the floor frame between the two front seats. A shallow console with a drink holder sat on top to hide the safe. He lifted the console, thumbed the lock, and removed one of the two pistols. He placed his Glock .22 service pistol in the back of his pants, put on a hoodie he had tossed in the back, and wished he had brought his shoulder holster.

The store was a hive of activity, murmurs of worried voices, people with carts more full than usual for a convenience store. Jackson first headed to the restroom, then planned on getting something to eat. As he exited the bathroom, he noticed three guys entering the store and heading to the checkout counter. His "cop radar" went off. They looked like gang bangers, unlike the ones he knew growing up in Chicago's south side wearing gang colors, clearly druggies and thugs. Two Hispanics and one Native, who looked like a meth head, skinny with bad teeth, and all three sported lots of visible ink. One of the Hispanic guys, who wore a thick gold chain and fancy cowboy boots, had the air of being in charge. Jackson tensed, ready to intervene with one hand on his weapon. He surreptitiously moved up next to the aisle that ran up to the counter, while keeping his eye on them. The clerk, a man in his early twenties, reached under the counter and seemed to have pushed a button. He pulled out a shotgun and held it to his side.

"Hang on, dude," said the one in charge. "We got cash. We're not going to rob you."

He produced a big roll of cash from his jacket pocket. The tension in the room went down. Several customers were waiting in line. Everyone breathed a sigh of relief except Jackson. He knew trouble when he saw it. He took out his cell phone and took pictures of the thugs as best he could without being noticed. Just in case, he rechecked his cell. Yep, still no service.

The other Hispanic guy approached the counter and said, "I want cigarettes."

"Sure," the clerk said. "What kind?"

"All of them."

The clerk looked confused when an older man, presumably a manager, came up and said, "Is everything okay here?"

The clerk said, "These guys want to buy all the cigarettes. They have cash."

"That is fine," the manager replied, "except if any of these people in line first want any." A few people in line nodded, and started pulling out wallets and counting their cash.

"No problem," the man replied.

The manager took the shotgun and set it down so he could easily retrieve it. "Teddy, you help the others. I'll help these gentlemen."

The meth head had found a small shopping cart and was filling it with hard alcohol. He looked at the boss and said, "This is adding up quickly. You sure you want all of it?"

"Yes," he answered angrily, obviously not liking being questioned.

The guy waiting for cigarettes walked over and said to the meth head in a low tone, "Ever see *The Walking Dead*, man? This is like the zombie apocalypse. Money ain't going to be worth shit soon, maybe for wiping your ass, speaking of which, see if they have any toilet paper." He pointed to the cart. "This will be the real cash soon."

Jackson thought, *they have a point.* He grabbed a cart and started filling it up with lighters, first aid supplies, and toiletries. The toilet paper was already gone. He added shelf-stable food items, snacks and candy, while monitoring the thugs. As he filled his cart with supplies, Jackson exchanged nods with other customers, a silent acknowledgment of their shared plight. Jackson took his time, got coffee, and passed on sandwiches from the cooler. It had only been a couple of hours, he mused, but why take a chance? Then, he went to the alcohol section and snagged a couple fifths of whisky and a couple of six-packs of beer before all the alcohol was gone. He wasn't a big drinker, but today, he might make an exception.

The boss man nodded at him, not recognizing him as a cop but seeing a big Black man, another dangerous fellow. Jackson dawdled until the thugs filled several carts and boxes, and the manager brought a cash counting machine to the front. He didn't overhear the total, but it had to be in the thousands, maybe tens of thousands. When they left, he followed them outside and took a picture of their vehicle and license plate as they drove away.

Jackson wondered where he was going after this meeting at this casino. If only he had enough gas to drive out and see Sioux Falls with his own eyes! He realized he was now homeless and unemployed. He could sleep in the truck since he had his sleeping gear in the canopy, along with the boxes of tasers and other random stuff he would need to set aside. As Jackson drove to the resort, he heard the radio announce the state of emergency and the restrictions, including the ones about guns. He guessed the county couldn't find an alternative in time. The announcement sounded official, which was oddly comforting. *Zombie apocalypse* indeed, he thought, *not on my watch.*

Chapter Three

Mary

MARY LANDRAU WAS the Chair of the Tribal Council of the Lower Brule Tribe and the Director of the Lower Brule Community College's teacher training program. Today, she was a grandmother trying to figure out what to feed her grandkids for lunch. Her daughter Bridget had dropped the girls, Cecilia, age eleven, and Amanda, age nine, off with practically no notice. Mary was annoyed; this happened regularly. Bridget figured she would always be willing to babysit, which was true, but it'd be considerate for Bridget to give more notice.

Bridget was going shopping in Pierre with her friend Cindy. Mary had planned to go to Pierre herself to shop, her usual Saturday activity. The local grocery stores were small and high-priced. It was worth the thirty-five-mile drive to Walmart in Pierre. She was low on food the girls would eat, like chicken nuggets and tater tots. Mary looked through the cupboards, not finding anything they'd like. She had a box of mac and cheese in the garage pantry. They'd eat that, and she could throw in frozen peas for vegetables.

With the two girls settled in front of the TV, she went to check on her husband Daniel, watching a game in his "cavelet." Not so much a man cave as it was only a corner in the garage. He carved beautiful little animals in wood while watching TV. It was only a hobby, as he worked at a farm equipment supplier during the week. He'd occasionally sell his work at arts and crafts fairs, but with so many cheap Asian wood carvings on the market, he could never make a living from it.

The garage had small windows. With the lights on, neither noticed the falling darkness that came with the fog. Between the two television sets, they didn't hear the approaching thunder until it became deafening.

Mary flung open the front door as a thunderclap roared, so loud she yelped. Black mist swirled, then vanished, leaving a sunny morning that felt all wrong. She saw a few neighbors outside conferring, most seen the fog she missed.

Cecilia came outside whining, "Unci, the TV stopped working."

She returned to the house. Sure enough, the power was out, knocked out by the storm, presumably. She realized she'd need to go to the store to stock up if the power was down for a few days. The tribe owned the local electric company. She knew on the weekend they'd have a hard time getting people to fix anything promptly.

Daniel said, "I can't start the generator. We don't have enough gas." They didn't fill the cans to prepare for winter outages until a bit later. "The freezer will be fine for a few hours. No one open it until I get the generator going."

They talked about the strange thunder, and Daniel made a comment about Wakíŋyaŋ, the Lakota thunder beings of legend, and they smiled at each other. He put a couple of gas cans in the rear of his truck, put a couple of coolers in Mary's trunk saying, "Be sure to pick up ice," and drove off.

Mary got both the girls into the car. Still whining about the TV and not wanting to go to the store, she bribed them with promises of candy. As she drove across the bridge to Fort Thompson, ten minutes away, she heard the notification sounds from many incoming texts. She ignored them all, not wanting to make calls or texts while the girls were in the car. She wished she had a newer car with a hands-free system built in.

Arriving at Dave's ValueMart, she saw the parking lot filling up with people with the same idea. When she parked, she answered a text from Lou White Mountain, another member of the Lower Brule Tribal Council, asking what she knew and proposing they should meet at the tribal office as soon as possible. Mary texted back she'd get there as soon as she could, as she was in Fort Thompson with her grandkids. She didn't know what was happening. Could he please call LBUC?

At the store, the sign on the door said, "Cash only, no credit, debit, or EBT." Shoot, Mary thought. Normally, she used debit cards. With her emergency twenty tucked in her wallet, her cash totaled thirty-four dollars. It'd have to do. Then remembered she had her checkbook in her purse. Hardly ever used checks anymore, but rarely cleaned out her purse.

Long lines snaked through the store. The atmosphere was tense, with people rushing to stock up on supplies, voices being raised. The store got the generator going and was unsuccessfully trying to get the registers to connect with the payment gateway. Many people were talking about the weird thunderstorm. She approached the checkout counter to ask about checks to make sure before she started shopping. She saw a few people arguing with the clerk about not accepting EBT or food stamps.

Mary heard one woman say, "It's the law. You must take them."

It wasn't the law, but Mary didn't want to argue with agitated people.

Mary asked loudly over the crowd, "Excuse me, will you take local checks with ID?"

"Yes," said the clerk, obviously relieved to have said yes to something.

'The crowd murmured, some saying they'd have to go home and look for checks. A few left full carts in the front or started putting stuff back to make smaller purchases.

The line to the cigarette counter was long. As she walked by, Ed, the manager, came out from behind the plexiglass, waved, and called her name. Mary knew him; she knew almost everyone on the reservation. His wife was her son-in-law's cousin, but they weren't close. He only called out to her because she was on the Tribal Council.

Ed asked, "What is the deal, Mary? When is the power coming back on?"

People nearby looked at them, listening. Everyone knew who she was. "I should get word soon," she replied, pulling her phone out of her purse to look more official. She glanced at it but didn't see a text from Lou and ignored the rest.

"It'll probably be awhile, Ed; it always takes longer on the weekend. The linemen all come from Sioux Falls. I expect a couple of days."

Eavesdroppers quickly spread the word. People started moving more swiftly about the store. Shelves emptied here rapidly. Small, like all grocery stores on the reservations, Dave's ValueMart didn't have much back stock.

"The thing is," said Ed, "we only have generator power to run the registers and the security system, not the freezers or refrigerators. After four hours, we're supposed to throw all the food out, according to safety regulations."

"That's ridiculous. We should at least try to get it to the tribal food pantry." She realized she was unsure how much freezer space and generator power they had. They were closed on weekends, and she wasn't sure if she could reach the director.

"Why don't you sell all the food needing refrigeration or in the freezers for half off?" Looking over and seeing another crowd hassling the clerk about not taking EBT, she added, "Let everyone with an EBT card take a grocery bag and fill it for free. That'd be better than throwing it out."

"Gee, Mary, I don't have the authorization for that. I already tried calling headquarters, but the phones don't go through. I can't even leave a voicemail."

She didn't know what company owned Dave's ValueMart, but she knew it wasn't anyone on the Crow Creek or the Lower Brule Reservation. It was another company taking advantage of her people. The prices were super high, which is why she didn't shop there. She also knew it burdened those without reliable vehicles or gas to drive to Pierre or Chamberlain.

"Total it up; if the company insists on charging for food they'd have to throw away, the tribe will pay for it."

"OK, I'll wait to announce until you get your stuff."

"Thank you much," she said, and hustled off before word got out.

As Mary navigated the crowded store, she encountered people arguing over the last of certain items. Obviously, everyone's frustrations were mounting. She lucked out. There was one bag of chicken nuggets, two loaves of bread and plenty of ice cream. Regular milk was out, but there was soy milk, which no one liked, but better than nothing. When Ed made the announcement and put up the sign, there was a mad scramble. She had the girls pick out extra candy to have later.

As she went to her car, the lingering shouts of the angry crowd still echoed in her ears, her shoulders tense with stress. Then she realized she'd forgotten the ice. Seeing the crowds inside, she figured they'd have to make do. Mary and Daniel always kept a couple of gallons of plastic milk jugs filled with water in the freezer to make it run more efficiently. They used the frozen jugs in the coolers for camping, it also kept them from getting gross with melted ice water.

Mary sat in her car and looked at her texts. Lou had contacted LBUC. Evidently, there were lines down all over. Mary knew without power; the tribe would face difficulties in maintaining essential services. She felt the weight of responsibility on her shoulders. More texts arrived from various people asking her for information she didn't have or informing her about someone who needed power for medical equipment or lacked a generator or had various other problems they expected her to solve.

One text from Bridget read: "road gone OMW home." *What?* She thought, *how could the road be gone?* It must be a text-writing error.

After she got home, she unloaded the groceries, and Bridget arrived, visibly upset.

"Mom, you won't believe what happened," Bridget exclaimed, recounting the strange event on the way to Pierre, the fog, the clap of thunder, the road gone.

Mary thought the entire story sounded absurd, but knew Bridget was a solid, practical sort, not given to hysterics. Her phone started dinging with text messages, reminding her to get to the office. She quickly glanced through them, not finding anything she needed to take the time to answer immediately. However, one from Cindy's aunt confirmed Bridget's story and asked her what she planned to do about it. Mary thought, *honestly, how much power did she think a Chair of a small Lakota tribe had anyway?*

She asked Bridget to stay and help her father with dinner. He didn't cook, ever. He'd eat sandwiches and canned soup if she were working, but like most Lakota men of his generation, he assumed the kitchen was the women's place.

When Mary was getting in her car, she was surprised when her phone rang. It was Rose Chasing Hawk from Omímeya who said the full emergency committee was meeting there and Kyle Ward asked to get both Tribal Council members in as soon as possible. Rose told her she'd already contacted Crow Creek members. Mary was unsure if she should say anything about the road ending. The situation was more complex than she'd imagined.

Rose answered her unasked question. "Weird stuff is going on. Come as soon as you can, bring your laptop and plan to stay a while."

Mary had met Rose many times over the years, but didn't like her. They'd had a few conflicts in her role as Tribal Chair. Mary thought Rose was too attached to the Omímeya corporate bottom line. She was better than her boss, Tom Durrell. He was a Lower Brule tribe member, not that he contributed to the tribe, just the opposite. She'd heard disturbing rumors about him. He had an expensive boat and a big house in Pierre, and his family members seemed to get the best-paying jobs and contracts.

She knew Rose's husband's family, ex-husband now, she'd heard. The community held the Chasing Hawk family in high regard. She thought it was too bad that Rose and Hotah gotten divorced, especially with kids. There was a touch of smugness in her thoughts as she considered her thirty-six-year marriage to Daniel. They'd never considered divorce. Raised Catholic, they had attended Mass every Sunday, and actively took part in church activities. Mary knew the Catholic church had a shameful history with colonization, but her church embraced Lakota traditions. She saw no conflict between the two. Mary felt comforted by the rituals of church services, the shared faith, and a sense of community. She felt a spiritual connection at church services.

Both of her parents had attended Catholic boarding schools. In her parents' day, they cut the boys' hair and punished them for speaking Lakota. She knew her father had terrible experiences he never talked about. She grew up speaking only English and learned Lakota as an adult. Her parents lost what they learned as children and spoke English for the rest of their lives.

=..=

Mary couldn't believe despite the millions the casino and resort brought in, they couldn't return more funds to the tribe. Despite her frustrations with the casino, she acknowledged they offered scholarships and invested in state-of-the-art technology at the community college. But some projects, like the wind farm, when operational would benefit tribal members, but would also lower the casino's energy costs. Mary would have liked to see more funding to the tribe's pressing needs, such as housing. She understood the need to repay the building loan, but the building process never ended. Now they're building a golf course. The resort was supposed to be the financial salvation for Lower Brule and Crow Creek tribes. But tourist dollars were all spent at the casino. While they offered preferential hiring to tribal members, most jobs were low-end service types. There were more Hispanics and whites working at Omímeya than Natives.

It didn't solve the unemployment problem on the reservation. The reservation's unemployment statistics still rated among the country's worst, since not everyone could take advantage of the jobs offered. What people didn't realize was the impact that generational trauma, poverty, and cultural genocide had on people. Substance abuse and mental health issues were deeply entrenched problems without simple solutions. Mary believed education was the solution. This was why she moved back to the reservation after college. She could make more money anywhere else, but wanted to see a positive change for her people.

A large Lakota museum project was planned for Fort Thompson on the Crow Creek Reservation. It was a multimillion-dollar project, not run by the casino, but a separate foundation. It was supposed to bring more jobs to the area, but Mary was cynical. St. Joseph, the Catholic boarding school, ran the Akta Lakota Museum in Chamberlain. That museum and the fifty-foot statue of a Lakota woman in a shawl called "Dignity of Earth and Sky" drew many tourists. The hope was the same thing would happen in Fort Thompson. With all the controversy about boarding schools, many wanted a tribal-owned museum. Mary questioned the need for another museum. She thought St. Joseph's did an excellent job of preserving Lakota culture and language at both the boarding school and the museum.

Although the museum completion was years away, the casino was buying artifacts, family heirlooms, old books, and maps as they became available, displaying them at the resort with plans to donate them to the museum when it opened. Mary thought it was self-serving, as people came to the resort to view the displays. The resort expanded their library to create room for the old documents and books. It may or may not end up helping both reservations. Mary didn't have faith in big corporations, even Indian ones.

As she drove up to the resort, she didn't experience the sense of awe many people had when they first saw it. She thought it was a 60-million-dollar gimmick. A seventy-foot tipi? Really? For a fraction of that money, they could provide a nice home for every tribal member on the reservation, since many still lived in poorly insulated old mobile homes. She tried to tamp down her resentment and take the long view that other tribes benefited from casino dollars, with some tribe members getting hefty monthly payments. That didn't happen on the poorest reservations, like the Lakota. But on others, she knew.

Mary hadn't been to Omímeya for a long time. The oak trees were growing fast. Tall berms reaching six feet high, created from the spoils of construction digging, lined both sides of the river, and the resort's entrance road to protect against flooding. It'd have to be a major flood to reach that far, but with climate change, it was possible. Omímeya hired experts who planted native plants and fast-growing oaks, which would prevent erosion, add shade, and beautiful colors in the fall.

She returned her thoughts to the roads being cut off. It was strange, inexplicable, and frightening to not knowing what was happening. With her deeply held faith, she believed God had a master plan and everything would unfold the way intended. She said a brief prayer and went inside.

Chapter Four

Rose

ROSE HATED THE unknown. She didn't even read or watch mysteries. She wanted to study economics in college but got pregnant with Luke in her first year and switched to accounting. When Luke was a year old, his father left. Rose quit school before completing the accounting degree to work full time. The only job that fit her babysitter's schedule was at a hotel. She might have been bored as an accountant, but she loved the simplicity of putting numbers in the right places, in the proper accounts. No mysteries.

Rose struggled with the uncertainty brought by Big Thunder. She wasn't sure how she could cope with anything so outside her experience. One Lakota term for the Great Spirit or Creator is Great Mystery. That's what Big Thunder brought: Great Mystery. The spiritual aspects of her culture made Rose uneasy, possibly because she was raised by a white mother in Sioux Falls, with limited exposure to her father's Lakota culture. Although she was respectful, she found the spiritual aspects unsettling.

Thinking of Kimi made her think about Hotah and the divorce. Rose met Hotah when Luke was almost three years old. Her friend Katy begged Rose to go to her cousin's wedding on the Lower Brule rez with her. Katy's sister babysat while Rose attended the wedding at the small Catholic church. Because the Lower Brule rez was dry and prohibited alcohol sales or consumption, reception guests wandered into the community center parking lot throughout the night to drink. Katy, despite being Rose's ride home, was no exception. Once Katy found relatives and the fun of the parking lot, Rose stood alone, bored, and wanting to go home. It wasn't long into the evening that Rose noticed a guy staring at her. Rose asked Katy who he was.

"Hotah Chasing Hawk," Katy said, explaining that Hotah was Lakota for gray. He'd recently gotten back from Iraq. "Are you interested?"

Rose laughed. "I'm a single working mother with a toddler. I don't have time to date."

Hotah approached her and asked who she was related to. At first, she didn't understand. Then she realized at a wedding this small, about everyone was related to everyone.

She explained about Katy, saying, "You aren't making trips out to the parking lot."

"I don't drink."

She didn't know any young men who didn't drink. Coming from a family of alcoholics, she found it impressive. They talked for a while—or rather, she mostly talked while he stared intently at her.

When it was time to leave, he said, "I want to see you again."

Rose had plenty of interest from guys since having Luke. She knew how to shut it down quickly. "I have a son; he's almost three." That inevitably worked.

"What is his name?" asked Hotah without missing a beat.

She told him and said something vague about seeing him around. Since they lived more than three hours apart, she never expected to see him again. The following week, she came home to see him waiting by the door to her apartment building. Katy had given him her address.

Slightly disconcerted, Rose said, "You could have called."

"I don't have a phone."

Even fourteen years ago, that was unusual, but so was he—like no one she'd ever met. She invited him in. They moved in together three weeks later and were married within six months. He'd never lived in a city before. He'd gone from living on the rez to the army. Although he served in Iraq, he never saw combat; he worked construction in the green zone. With those skills, he found a good job in Sioux Falls. Rose worked fewer hours, went back to school, and got a degree in hospitality management.

The resort was still under construction and needed workers. As a tribal member, Hotah had preferential hiring. He wanted to come home. They moved to a small apartment in Fort Thompson since she didn't want to live with his family. She was hired at Omímeya before it opened eight years ago.

Telling herself to focus, Rose returned to the present. A few employees Rose had texted began to filter in. Doris Stewart, who was indispensable, lived locally, was a Crow Creek member, and knew everyone. Seeing Doris, Rose was so happy she wanted to hug her, but Human Resources (HR) discouraged hugging, emphasizing that subordinates should not be touched. Instead, she had Doris direct people to help as needed.

Rose got a radio call from Manuel. "Both shuttles to Pierre and Sioux Falls returned because the roads are cut off. What do you want me to tell the guests?"

"Inform them the credit card payment gateways aren't working, but we can check them into the rooms they just vacated. We need to let them know the rooms haven't been cleaned yet."

Now Rose wondered how they'd pay. People carried little cash anymore. The system would usually charge their card when they checked out. How long could she let people stay without paying? Hoping the internet would return, Rose authorized the front desk to allow credit card payments in offline mode. A few credit cards might be declined, posing a minor risk. The greater risk was that the internet would never return. In that case, what would she do? Rose figured if that happened, she'd have bigger problems and tried to focus on things in her control.

Rose studied India's hospitality culture in one of her hotel management courses. A common saying in India is "Atithi devo bhava," which means "Guests are forms of God." One assignment was to watch a film about how hotel staff saved guests at the risk of their own lives during the Mumbai terrorist attacks. If the internet doesn't return, this could be a massive disaster, bringing an unprecedented level of chaos. The internet was integral to the functioning of so many systems, its failure could cause a cascade of problems. Rose felt responsible for her guests' safety. She took that seriously.

Kyle asked her to check to see whether doctors had left for Chamberlain yet. He needed them to wait to send some communication gear with them. Communication was fragmented and limited. Police and fire radios reached only ten to fifteen miles. Most of the ham radios were the Baofeng handhelds, which had an even shorter range. The advantage was many people owned them, and Omímeya had quite a few, so they could set up relays. Usually, a ham radio license was required to operate them, but this was waived during disasters. They also had extensive shortwave radios, including transmitters. All the radios together provided better coverage.

While cell phones from Tribal TeleComm worked, it was a single cell tower that only covered about fifteen miles. Normally, the company bought coverage from other carriers' towers, but since those relied on satellites, they were down until reprogrammed.

The resort owned a mesh cell phone system called goTenna for emergencies when cell towers were unavailable. Rose didn't know the emergency planning budget; it was outside her purview, like the casino budget, but she knew it was substantial. The goTenna system worked using hardware in each phone as a peer-to-peer network that spoke to each other over short distances. It was possible to extend it with additional compatible routers. The operating system was called Aspen Grove, which worked like interconnected aspen trees. The National Guard had a similar system, but it was incompatible with the resort's system until reprogrammed. Kyle had tried to convince all the surrounding counties to purchase the goTenna system to avoid this exact problem, but they didn't, even though the system wasn't prohibitively expensive. Emergency preparedness was often at the bottom of budgets. The casino donated the older system to the tribal police and fire department during the recent upgrade. There was a mesh app that worked on a similar principle, but it needed many people to use it for it to be effective.

Since the local cell phones worked, the goTenna phones would only be necessary if they ventured beyond a ten to fifteen-mile radius. However, beyond that required the installation of routers at ten-mile intervals. Fortunately, the chargers and routers required minimal electricity, making them compatible with their solar battery banks.

Kyle wanted to send the portable radios and phones to the hospital, radio stations, police, and county authorities, but he needed to figure out places for the routers. Rose suggested they could send the radios and phones to be dropped off and figure out the router placement later. Then she realized her house was halfway to Chamberlain. They could install a phone and router and be able to stay in touch with Hotah. He could drop off the rest once they found good spots. A side benefit was that she could talk to her kids. She hated being out of touch.

Kyle said in frustration, "I was prepared for emergencies for the resort and the rez, but not emergency services for the entire area."

The emergency manager for Brule County hadn't checked in and could be out of town. She was the other FEMA regional director and would typically be in charge. The Lyman County emergency manager was communicating via ham radio, but coordination was difficult without better communication tools. Kyle let everyone know he had designated the resort the FEMA command-and-control center as they had electricity and phones. There were complaints from Chamberlain, but no one else seemed to care, relieved that someone else was in charge.

Rose seated Mary and the tribal council members in the staff meeting room. She mentioned the need to find places for the routers, knowing that Mary was related to or knew just about everyone on both reservations. Kyle sent a Google map satellite view of South Dakota to the LCD projector, which showed on the large screen. As he zoomed out the image again, it showed drop pins in various places surrounding the resort. He explained the pins marked everywhere the roads ended.

Mary gasped, "It is a circle, with Omímeya at the center."

Rose felt a chill down her spine and said softly in Lakota, "Big Thunder strengthens the Circle, and the Circle protects the Earth." Mary, one of the few who understood her, looked up and everyone else moved on.

Someone came in and motioned to Kyle, prompting him to step out and return shortly with a new report about the helicopter that flew to Sioux Falls. It seemed impossible, but Sioux Falls was gone, like it'd never been there. Several people rushed out of the room to make phone calls to family. They couldn't believe the report about the buffalo herd's size. The tribe owned a small herd, and they knew the huge amount of land that many buffalo required.

Kyle reported a state police airplane was heading to Rapid City, and they dispatched a couple of crop duster planes south, but they hadn't heard from them yet. He also said a freight train derailed near Twin Bridges. There were only minor injuries; one car was cut in half, and corn spilled everywhere. About ninety cars remained; besides grain, it held windmill parts, others steel beams.

Kyle told the group, "I know it's scary; there's much we don't know. This doesn't fit any of the emergencies we've planned for, but we need to look at what we have. There're no reports of fatalities, all the infrastructure is intact, and the electricity can be back on in a few days or weeks at most. While communication with the outside world is cut off, it will improve soon in the immediate area. My job is to plan for worse-case scenarios. We'll have problems if the power and communication outages continue, but we must work one problem at a time."

Mary took over the meeting, listing top priorities and people's suggestions on the whiteboard. Rose left the meeting to answer messages and saw Neal Suttle, the food services manager, who had the office next to hers, come in. There were three restaurants and two snack bars across all the facilities. They needed an immediate plan to conserve food. What if the trucks never returned? She still couldn't grasp that Sioux Falls and Pierre were gone; it made no sense. Neal had heard what was happening, but he was resentful when she asked about his plan.

Neal said, "You know Kyle has addressed supply chain disruptions in the Emergency Plan, right here," patting his work tablet.

"Fine, when I come back in twenty minutes, let's review what you've come up with. Let's aim for zero food waste."

"You don't have the authority to demand changes to my department. I've been attending meetings where we've discussed these plans, and I've never seen you there."

"I have the authority now and will be in those meetings from this point forward. Count on it."

He looked unhappy and left. Realizing she couldn't put it off any longer, she had to face Phil Gallo, the casino manager, about shutting off the slot machines to save power. Rose would need to beard the lion in his den. Management school had taught her to always hold difficult discussions with subordinates in person and in private. She realized she was in charge and likely would remain so.

Years ago, she had attended a meeting in Minnesota with the corporation that managed Omímeya. She was having drinks with one of the corporation's vice presidents, the only woman at that level. Rose asked her how she did it.

The company executive replied, "No one will give you power; you must take it. It is okay to be ambitious, to be ruthless, but make sure you're more competent than anyone else."

Rose realized she could no longer cater to Phil's ego. She had to be decisive and take power. She took the elevator down to the first floor and passed through the lodge lobby on her way to the casino in the west wing. The lobby was filled with people milling about, clearly not in the meeting rooms. The lobby was usually empty this time of day. She could see people sitting on chairs or couches, guests huddled together, a few crying or being held, others whispering anxiously. Rose sensed fear, confusion, and barely contained panic in the air. She hustled to the casino, not wanting to get waylaid by staff or guests asking her questions to which she didn't know the answers.

The casino, usually bustling with people, the lights and sounds of the slot machines, was quiet. The rooms with the big screen for sports betting were closed as there was no cable or internet. Phil Gallo looked up as she knocked and walked into his office without waiting for a reply.

Phil said angrily, "Look who finally showed up! I sent you a text an hour ago wanting to know what's going on. IT is clueless, the phones are down too. I can't reach anywhere."

She nearly apologized but remembered what the company executive had told her and said sharply, "I didn't have time. This is a crisis. Do you realize the reason we can't reach anywhere is Pierre and Sioux Falls aren't there?"

"Bullshit."

"Talk to Kyle and listen to the radio traffic yourself if you don't believe me," Rose said sharply. "The only reason I'm here is to say we must shut down all the slots. There's an issue with the gas for the generators. You can keep the table games and roulette, anything that doesn't take power."

She expected an argument but then noticed his face. He looked stunned.

"Fine, it's on you."

"Yes, it is. Tom isn't likely to come back, which means I'm in charge of both the resort and the casino."

"What do you mean Tom isn't returning?" he said worriedly.

He paled as she explained about the roads and the helicopter. Then she realized Phil lived in Pierre with his wife and three little girls, and they were probably gone.

"I am so sorry, Phil."

Rose had seen him with his wife and girls many times. He had a suite he used when working late; often, his wife and kids would come for the weekends as he worked. His wife would go to the spa and his kids would swim and ride horses. Not every weekend, but often. She'd see them on Sunday mornings, all dressed up, going to mass at St. Agnes's together.

She'd never seen Tom's family. He had one of the riverside cabins and entertained the VIPs or high-end gamblers. She heard gossip about lavish parties, the better-looking cocktail waitresses, and female blackjack dealers getting bonuses for "entertainment." Rose wasn't naïve and assumed Tom would do nothing legally actionable. She didn't think he cared about the company, but he cared about his cushy job. She asked HR to check in with the women to ensure they felt safe. Apparently, the entertainment gigs were highly sought after.

"I have to go, have Mike take over," said Phil before walking swiftly out of the room.

Rose felt both frustration and guilt. She knew she had to make tough decisions, but breaking the news to Phil like that, in a fit of pique, made her feel like shit. Then she had to track down Mike and let him know. She had him shut down the bar, as things were crazy enough. She didn't want security to deal with drunks as well.

Rose heard from Jenny, who said the wedding and reception planned for 4:00 pm was in absolute turmoil. Many of the guests hadn't arrived, including the bride's father, who'd been coming from Pierre. The bride was hysterical. Omímeya was a popular wedding venue. There was a small non-denominational chapel with a beautiful stained-glass cross that could be a four-direction symbol. The Riverside Grove boasted beautiful landscaping, a gazebo, and a wedding arbor for bigger weddings or outdoor ceremonies. Normally, Rose might have handled wedding disasters. They happened—dropped cakes, ruined dresses, family fights, but this she left in Jenny's hands.

Rose headed back and stopped at Neal's office. Most of his proposals were acceptable, but she told him to stop serving made-to-order items at the Red Oak. Changing the self-service buffet to cafeteria style, with staff controlling portion size, would reduce food waste. Rose didn't suggest, ask his opinion, or smile sweetly, as she might have done yesterday; she told him flatly. He sputtered, looking like he wanted to argue, but in the end he kept his mouth shut.

She gave him positive feedback for switching snacks from coffee, tea, and cookies to popcorn and Prairie Tea Blend. A local woman's small herb company made the tea. She grew and wild-crafted many of the herbs herself. The company sold tea bags, but the resort bought bulk tea and served it by the gallon, next to coffee and hot water with standard tea bag selections. They featured the teas prominently at the resort shops. They made the tea from local herbs, the prairie tea plant, bee balm, elderflower, and rose hips. Popcorn was locally grown by the literal ton and cost practically nothing. The Lower Brule Tribe grew commercial popcorn for brands like Jiffy Pop.

The amount of food bought never matched the amount consumed. There were a lot of leftovers. Technically, leftovers were to be donated to the tribal food pantry, but there was often more than the pantry could handle. Even with the staff taking home leftovers, they threw away enough food to feed a small village. The staff who took home leftovers needed it. Many of the kitchen and housekeeping staff were Hispanic and supported their families back in their home countries. Rose knew the resort paid better than similar jobs, but not that much better.

Reviewing the spreadsheets and their discrepancies, she assumed that Neal's family never went grocery shopping. His relatives likely didn't either. This kind of low-key corruption was all too common and bothered her. She tried talking to Tom, her boss. He told her not to make waves and to mind her own business, saying he'd deal with Neal. It probably meant he'd back his truck up at Neal's house. But now things were different. Rose was in charge, and she needed to be ruthless.

Rose said to Neal, "We won't discuss what's happened in the past, but I am going to review all food stores to make sure what's on the inventory is here. No more missing food, not so much as a can of beans, do you understand?"

Neal sputtered at her, "You can't do this. This is my department."

"I can," she reminded him. "Believe me, if I find that missing can of beans, we'll review everything over the last year. I'm pretty sure it will add up to a felony or two."

She returned to the emergency meeting where a guest, a state attorney, was insisting he didn't have the authority to deploy the National Guard. Someone had pulled him into the meeting so the group could claim state authority.

Mary stepped out to take a call but returned shortly after, ashen-faced. "Tribal police received a report so hard to believe you all need to hear it firsthand. Two guys are on their way here with a story and photos to share. It's going to take them a while to get here, so let's take a twenty-minute break. Since it's getting crowded, we'll move to the Otter Room downstairs."

With that, she found Kyle and started making phone calls.

Chapter Five

Jackson

DESPITE HAVING HEARD about Omímeya, Jackson was amazed, upon arriving at the resort, at how its unique design seamlessly blended with the rugged beauty of the prairie and how the calm flow of the river created a striking visual contrast. Denise had mentioned the possibility of visiting for the weekend. Their conflicting work schedules made it difficult for them to spend time together. He would come to regret not dedicating more time to her.

He parked and approached the front entrance, a double-width glass automatic door, with another set of doors farther in. Something that looked like hide or canvas, with folds and slight imperfections, framed the doorway. Above the door, it appeared that tipi lacing pins reached a large, teardrop-shaped skylight. As he felt the "tipi cover" by the door, he noticed a wall painted like a hide. *Very cool*, he thought. As he entered the lobby, he looked up. It felt like a cathedral. Inside were beautiful rugs over a stone-tiled floor, comfortable leather chairs, conversational groupings of loveseats, and a large, circular stone fireplace in the middle. Everything was in shades of earthy colors—browns, greens, with pops of red. Four wide circular staircases with polished wood led to the second floor. Below the mid-height railing was the faux tipi cover. He could see many people walking about. Lining the lobby walls in places were glass cases with Native American artifacts.

Unlike other casinos and hotels in the area, the resort lacked the taxidermied pheasants, cougars, and sometimes larger animals that were ubiquitous elsewhere. This gave the room a more inviting and authentic feeling. He also saw no slot machines, though he noticed a large sign directing him to the casino.

On the right after the entrance was the check-in desk, with a big monitor displaying a list of meeting rooms. Sure enough, at the bottom, it said, "Emergency Planning, Staff Meeting Room 420 North." Helpfully, next to it was a map with a "You are Here" star. He found the elevator and headed up. Passing hotel rooms on either side of the hall, he saw Room 420 at the end. A sign read "Omímeya Administration" in front of a wide door with a stained-glass insert. In a small waiting area, a middle-aged Native woman sat behind a reception desk.

She directed him to the back, to a large open-plan office with a dozen desks and computers, and a few people sitting, typing, or making calls on cell phones. Surprised, Jackson pulled out his phone but still had no service. *Strange*, he thought. Around the perimeter were offices with half-glass walls, some with closed blinds. It looked very corporate. He wasn't sure what he'd expected, maybe dream catchers? Jackson was directed to Kyle, who stood outside his office while a couple of people inside listened to radios.

Kyle Ward was about his age, fit, and tanned. The funny thing was, they both dressed alike. Both wore black cargo khakis, black polo shirts, and black running shoes. Jackson's shirt had the Sioux Falls Police logo on the top left; Kyle's had the Omímeya logo.

Jackson extended his hand. "My name is Oliver Jackson, but call me Jackson," he said. "I've been working as a cop in Sioux Falls and have been asked to liaise with FEMA for Brule County."

Jackson shared his experience at the convenience store on the way here. He had wanted to report it immediately, but he didn't have a working phone or radio.

Kyle said, "I'll set you up to make a report soon, but there are bigger priorities. Join us for the briefing to explain what's going on. I'm warning you, though—it may bring more questions."

"What do you mean?"

"Better you hear it directly. Wait a few minutes."

Kyle leaned forward. "You military?"

"Yeah, Army, Iraq."

They exchanged nods, the silent understanding shared only by combat veterans from the sandbox. After Kyle heard about his military experience and realized he had been displaced from Sioux Falls, he asked Jackson if he wanted a job. Casino security wasn't Jackson's cup of tea, but he couldn't be picky. Then Kyle told him he wouldn't be working for security. The recent information made him realize he needed someone with military experience for outside threats.

Kyle said, "I should run it by the boss lady. Hang on a minute."

When Kyle returned with his boss, Jackson stood up to greet her. She gazed up at him and gave him the "look." It was the same look that almost every woman close to his age, and a few that weren't, had given him since he was fourteen. He sighed, prepared himself for the coy smiles and flirtatious, inevitable, and often uncomfortable comments, especially from a woman who could be his boss.

Rose Chasing Hawk was a head shorter than he was, probably about five feet three inches without heels; she wore a dark-green pantsuit and long, beaded earrings. Around her neck was her staff ID card on a beaded lanyard. Her hair was in a tight bun in the back. When she turned her head, a large, beaded barrette fastened it. She wore lovely turquoise jewelry and a little makeup. She was what was called pleasantly plump, with light brown hair, a fair complexion, and gray-green eyes. If he'd met her out of context without the jewelry and not knowing her name, he wouldn't have guessed she was Native. Jackson thought her severe hairstyle, clothes, and demeanor masked her attractiveness.

Instead of smiling coyly at him as he expected, she took a breath and turned away. Rose asked Kyle, "Are you sure you need him?"

"You decide. Think about what is coming."

She surprised Jackson by asking what his MOS was. Few people knew it meant Military Occupation Specialty. He was an 89D (Explosive Ordnance Disposal Specialist). He'd disarmed improvised explosive devices, or IEDs. She inquired about his law enforcement career. He'd worked for the Chicago police for a year before Sioux Falls.

"Why only a year?"

He surprised himself by being honest and said, "There was too much shooting and too many bad cops."

After that, he'd wanted to be a small-town cop, but Sioux Falls was hiring. As she delved further into his experience and training, he found himself saying "yes, ma'am" and "no, ma'am" to her.

Rose's voice softened. "Do you have any family back in Sioux Falls?"

Jackson's eyes welled up. "My fiancée," he managed to say, the pain still fresh. *She would've been*, he thought.

Rose and Kyle turned away to give him a moment, both saying they were sorry. Kyle looked haunted by sorrow as well. Jackson didn't ask, but knew from his expression Kyle also lost someone.

Rose asked what he'd earned working for the Sioux Falls police, then offered him a salary that was twenty percent more.

She said, "You can get a room here, but even with a staff discount, it's expensive. You should find another place soon. Usually, HR helps with this sort of thing, but the HR manager lived in Pierre, so she's probably not coming in."

Rose got a stricken look on her face, took a breath, and said, "Check in with Doris at the front desk. She'll get you an ID and room key after the meeting. The meeting room is ready downstairs; we should head down."

Jackson was drawn to her because of the authority she exuded. He'd worked with many competent women officers. Jackson liked a chain of command and was comfortable taking orders. He felt this woman knew what she was doing. Decisive. He liked that. He hoped she didn't hit on him. That was uncomfortable coming from a boss.

When Rose turned and walked away, her derriere was prominent in the pants she wore. He'd always been a big booty guy. He had an instant, very male reaction, quickly followed by a terrible pang of guilt and grief. Her butt reminded him of Denise.

=..=

People were waiting for the elevators. Kyle motioned Jackson toward the stairs, and they both took them down, Kyle going fast, Jackson trying to keep pace.

Kyle said, "I mostly have a desk job, so I always try to run the stairs."

Wow, Jackson thought, *running up and down four flights of stairs regularly? No wonder he looks in such good shape.* Downstairs, they crossed the lobby, then went up a wide curved wooden staircase at a more sedate pace. The layout confused Jackson until he realized the second floor was merely a walkway leading to the various wings. They walked to the north wing. The meeting room had a conference-style setup with a slightly raised platform in front and chairs for the twenty-five or so people attending.

Jackson asked, "What's the deal with the video cameras?" seeing the professional setup complete with what looked like audiovisual staff.

"All the meetings are available on closed-circuit TV live and taped. People like to attend workshops online later. The tapes are downloadable for an extra fee and bring in a nice chunk of change. I wanted these guys briefing us to be on video; otherwise, no one would believe it."

Rose led two older men to a small table set up on the platform. The audiovisual staff placed microphones on their collars. They looked freaked out sitting in front of people while being taped. The presentation screen at the front showed a picture of them on their boat that the staff had downloaded, along with videos from their phones. They told their story, and Kyle was right; Jackson had to hear it directly. It was too hard to believe otherwise.

The two men, Jake Hostler and Brent Cagle, were friends from Chamberlain who drove their boat up to Antelope Creek, about twenty-five miles north of Omímeya, to fish, a regular Saturday outing. They had a small bass boat, nothing fancy. The two were on the water when the Big Thunder struck. They decided to travel to Pierre by boat, anticipating a quicker journey than driving home. As they approached Pierre, the unfamiliarity of the landscape struck them. The once-familiar landmarks, Farm Island and La Framboise Island, were nowhere to be seen. The riverbanks appeared vastly different, now covered with grasslands and trees replacing the buildings they remembered. Not believing their eyes, they were going to get out of the boat to investigate when Brent spotted smoke from a fire farther north. When they got there, next to the river, they saw a small tipi, a smoky fire burning in front with what turned out to be meat on drying racks. Next to the tipi was an open-sided wooden structure, about ten by eight feet, and a large canoe tied up on the riverbank. They found a place shallow enough, anchored, and had to wade in high water to get to the riverbank. The river was much deeper and wider than it had been earlier.

They approached the structure cautiously, neither of them carrying weapons; they both wished they were. Curiosity outweighed fear. They called out to the people they saw on the bank, watching them carefully as the man stared intently at the boat. There was a man, one woman, and two dirty naked children, two or three years old, by the tipi, and one young girl who was feeding the fire and placing meat on the drying rack.

The man was white, although so dirty it was hard to tell. The women and children were Indigenous. Neither of them could speak French, so the man communicated with them using a few words of English, gestures, and some kind of sign language. The sign language was very specific. Some signs were obvious, like up and other directions; others they didn't know. Fortunately, between the man's limited English and signs, they could communicate. The man was a fur trader and wanted to trade with them. Although he wanted to see the boat, they refused to allow him on board. He liked the fishing vests they both wore and was thrilled with the hooks and lures. He had them look at the trade goods he had in the hut; it was stacked high with furs on one side, the other with metal pots and knives, a few rifles, and Hudson Bay blankets. They took pictures with their phones of the whole setup. The phones fascinated the trader. They took photos of him, his woman, and the kids. He really wanted to trade for a phone. He kept offering more and more goods, including nice furs for a phone, and they kept saying no.

Then he pulled the young girl forward. She looked about eleven or twelve, and he asked if they wanted to "putain" her. When it was clear they didn't understand, he used crude gestures, so there was no doubt. The men were appalled and angry.

Brent yelled, "How could you do that to your own child?"

"That's not my daughter," the trader explained, "but a slave I recently acquired. She's older than she looks."

Then the trader roughly pulled up her dress to show her pubic hair. When they saw the obvious signs of rape—bruises on her thighs, dried blood stains down her legs, and a torn dress—they were horrified.

"I traded a good rifle and blankets for her. I'm going to take her back up north and sell her to service the men at the bigger trading post. She is worth a lot, surely as much as a phone."

Jake and Brent didn't know what to do. They couldn't leave a child to be sold as a sex slave. She was skinny, dirty, with bruises showing. Not pretty, with pockmark scars and a wide flat face. She looked at them fearfully.

Finally, Jake said, "It's against our religion to buy slaves, but we'd trade for a hide if we could get the girl for free."

The Frenchman didn't get the phone he wanted, but he got the fishing vest, a lighter, a pen, and a multi-tool. They took a video on their phone of the trader, whom they asked to verify they were given the girl as a gift. They were worried about legal trouble.

Then, they spotted a ledger book on the table and asked to see it. He showed it reluctantly, and they saw the dates on the pages, not believing it, verifying it with him as best they could that it was accurate. They took photos, including close-ups of the ledger entries.

The two fishermen left quickly. The girl was thrilled with the boat, overcoming her fear of them. They gave her a jacket and got her something to eat, which she ate like she was starving. They went back to Antelope Creek, hooked up the boat, and drove toward home. The ride in the truck terrified her at first, then she appeared to enjoy it. Their phones still weren't working, so they took her to the tribal police since she only spoke Lakota.

Back at the meeting, the overhead screen showed photos and even played the short video. The last picture Kyle displayed was a close-up of the ledger, with the date clearly marked, "18 septembre 1791"

Chapter Six

Mary

MARY HAD MORE time than the others to adjust to the news they were in 1791. As soon as the ledger from the fur trader appeared on the screen, everyone in the room started freaking out, several shouting time travel was impossible. Even with the proof on the screen in front of them and two eyewitnesses, people were saying it was fake.

Mary came to the front of the room and called for attention in her best teacher's voice. "Everyone calm down."

Someone asked where the girl, freed from slavery, was now.

"I spoke to Janet Duncan at Tribal Police as soon as I heard. She has called the sexual assault team; they are on the way. Janet speaks Lakota. The girl will get the help she needs."

Brent and Jake left the front table. Rose handed them a couple low-denomination chips that worked as cash around the resort.

"Why don't you get something to eat and check in before you go back? We may need you to do the same thing in Chamberlain."

"I thought that's why you taped it, so we wouldn't have to keep repeating it."

"Videos can be faked. Look what happened here. People didn't believe you. Explaining what you saw in person may be the only way." They said they understood and left.

People were still shouting. Mary instructed, "Please raise your hand one at a time and only speak if you have something pertinent to add or a question no one has asked yet and can be answered. I don't know how this happened, if it was a natural phenomenon, God, or space aliens. I have no idea how to return. Spending time discussing the unknowable isn't the best use of our time today. I propose we spend ten minutes on time travel, get it out of our system, and return to the priority list we were working on before we moved downstairs. This is an emergency planning meeting. Our job of caring for our people just got much harder."

Someone raised their hand and asked, "Do we have to worry about contaminating the timeline, or accidentally killing our grandfather and being erased?"

Lois Robinson raised her hand. "I may have an answer. There're scientific theories about the multiverse being more plausible than the time travel you see in the movies. It's more likely we're in an alternative universe. Everything up to this point will be the same as our familiar world, but anything we do from this point forward will change. Since we have never seen people from the future coming back, the multiverse theory makes the most sense. It's also possible we've been transported to a different world altogether. Once we contact the outside, we can find out if the histories match up prior to this point. For example, perhaps we are in a world where there was no Julius Caesar or Jesus Christ." A few Christians glared at her, muttering.

Someone else asked, "Does that mean we can foretell the future, tell people when they will die, or learn how to avoid war or other tragedy?"

Lois replied, "You have heard of the butterfly effect, where something small causes a chain of ripples that changes everything? This started with our arrival. Who knows how things will change, but we know it will. Don't count on knowing the future."

Another person added, "I don't believe it. We need more evidence. This is insane. You're all idiots."

Lou raised his hand, "If we're not in a different world, but in a version of our own, we can change history. We could keep the white man from taking over and protect the Lakota people."

Rose was acknowledged, "Not only the Lakota people, all people, animals, plants, and water, the entire bio-systems of the Earth."

Then she told people what Kimi said to her that morning, "Big Thunder strengthens the Circle, the Circle protects the Earth." She surprised herself by saying, "I don't know how we were brought back, but I think I understand why. Mankind was killing the Earth, climate change was destroying our children's future, soon we would need to leave the planet to save humanity. Then Big Thunder came. It included a circle of people, not only Lakota, but people from all over. We came back with the accumulated knowledge of 233 years."

Rose added, "Do you know who we have meeting here this weekend? 153 doctors! Think how many people that knowledge can save, how many more people do we have with valuable skills and knowledge? Also, fifteen wind engineers are having a meeting here, along with 200 other people who, judging from their income, are highly educated. Who knows what skills they have? I've never been spiritual, but it's clear to even me there's a divine plan. We were chosen to change this world to protect the Earth."

There was silence for a moment, then applause.

Mary said, "Unless someone else has something relevant to add, it looks like we have several areas that we need to discuss, immediate needs and priorities, goals and longer-term strategies. Even if you don't believe in divine intervention, does anyone have an objection to Rose's assertion? We were brought back to create a more sustainable future. Can we make that a goal?"

No one spoke up. "All in favor, say aye, all opposed say nay," a few said nay.

"The ayes have it, so noted."

The secretary typed it into her laptop, although she had a phone recorder out as well. Mary motioned to someone who pulled up the projector screen and wheeled over a large whiteboard, which she started writing on

Kyle raised his hand. "Before we get too far, we need to decide when to inform the public, I've been providing the radio stations with the reports they've been posting, so far, we've not officially mentioned the roads, but I'm sure everyone has seen them or heard the rumors. FEMA has always believed in handling public announcements that may cause further disruption or chaos with caution."

Someone asked, "Why does it matter what FEMA says? We're in 1791. Doesn't it mean we're in Lakota country, not the US of A?"

Folks in the room murmured agreement. There was discussion on the pros and cons of what to say and when. They tabled the idea and suggested coordinating with the counties.

Lois said, "As the Brule County liaison, I'll see if we can agree on an announcement and get back to the meeting."

Jackson stood. "Suppose I'll liaise with the police, perhaps the military." He sounded none too thrilled.

Kyle said, "There are no satellites or ham radio signals anywhere. After it is fully dark, we can check the stars to 100% confirm that we're in 1791. You need to plan accordingly."

The three of them returned upstairs while the others continued the meeting. Mary took command of the room like any classroom full of unruly students. She wrote on one side of the whiteboard: Priorities, and on the other side: Goals. She transferred priorities from the earlier meeting, which dealt with the power outage. Under Goals she wrote: "Sustainable Future."

The group spent time on immediate priorities, primarily dealing with the power outage. Omímeya had electricity between solar, generator, and while the geothermal plant didn't provide electricity, it heated water, as well as cooling and heating. The local area had no electricity or natural gas. Fortunately, it's not cold yet. Most critical infrastructure had generators, but fuel would be an issue soon. They focused on what they could accomplish, simple things like getting solar battery banks to people who need electricity for medical devices. The group decided to make all resources available to all area residents, regardless of tribal affiliation.

After addressing the immediate priorities, Mary said, "We need to dedicate time to discussing these big picture issues. I'm concerned, we're at a crucial point in history. The United States is nine years old and gaining power, and the genocide of all the Indigenous people in North America is gaining ground with settler land grabs. It won't be long before they find out we are living here. If we don't get our act together immediately, we may never get another chance to change the future. We can't wait."

There were murmurs of agreement around the room, as well as people asking what the rush was, and we should take our time. Others still muttering they didn't believe any of this back-in-time nonsense.

Mary continued, "Let's start with a brief history lesson. I'm not an expert but can frame the conversation with broad strokes. George Washington is still president. I don't remember the exact dates, but around now there was a war over lands in the Ohio Valley. The Indigenous won a battle and lose the war a year or two later. Washington was buying up land and pushing tribes to move further west. He was the first president to break a few treaties to set the example. Spain or Mexico claimed the area we are now in, which is Spanish Louisiana. It extends from the Mississippi

River to approximately the Rocky Mountains. In 1801, Spain traded it with France for land they wanted. In 1803, Jefferson bought the region from Napoleon for fifteen million dollars."

Someone raised a question, asking whether we could buy it instead. Mary wrote the question on the board.

Someone quipped, "I bet the casino has that much."

They all laughed. Most in the meeting were Lower Brule and Crow Creek Tribal Council members, and casino wealth was a sore spot.

Someone gasped, "The Black Hills."

There was an eruption of voluble comments at that. Lakota called it Pahá Sápa, it was a sacred place for the Lakota people. In 1868, the US recognized the Black Hills as part of the Great Sioux Nation in the Treaty of Fort Laramie. A few years later, after discovering gold there, the United States illegally seized the land and nullified the treaty. In 1980, after decades of lawsuits, the Supreme Court agreed the United States illegally violated the treaty and owed compensation to the tribe. The Lakota said they didn't want to sell their sacred land. Even though the tribes that lived around the Black Hills were the poorest in the nation, they still refused to sell. Funds had been in an account drawing interest since 1980; at the time of their arrival over a billion dollars. The Black Hills was also the site of the Mt. Rushmore monument, which many Lakota felt was a desecration.

Rose suggested, "The Black Hills have always been sacred Lakota land. However, to protect it, we may need to mine gold ourselves as Lakota, in a sustainable way that protects the earth and the sacred sites. That way, we could have the funds to pay for the Louisiana Purchase. We could support the tribes that live there, even arm them for protection."

Mary said, "Good ideas. Let's table the specifics. We need a committee." She made another column on the board, under committees wrote: <u>Black Hills/Paha Sapa</u>.

She added, "Before we go farther, we need to decide. Should we join with the current United States of America or make the Louisiana Purchase ourselves?"

There was a long discussion, with many people in favor of staying in the US. "Can I see a show of hands of those in favor of slavery?" Mary asked.

No one raised their hand.

"I need to remind you that Washington is a slaveholder, and slavery is the law of the land. I heard someone mention the constitution. There's no reason we could not use our own. Both of our tribes' constitutions are based on the US constitution. They drew theirs from the Iroquois Nations. We could even simplify or improve it. We could create a bill of human rights closer to the one used by the United Nations."

David Cornell, the state's attorney, said, "We need to get a judge and a legal ruling. You can't just decide to create a new country."

Several people asked, "Why not?" He had no answer.

Lou pointed out that all tribal council members for both reservations were present, and they were the legally elected representatives of two sovereign nations. Together, they represented a majority of the population of the Circle, roughly 8,000 people.

Mary asked, "Leaving aside the question of whether we can create a new country, what we need to answer is, should we?"

Still hearing grumbling, Mary said, "This isn't about a country for only the tribes. Remember, outside there are more white people with more guns. Even if all the tribes joined, we'd lose. I believe Washington still has about 60,000 troops. If Mexico or France find out about the Black Hills, we may end up fighting them. Our best chance is to include everyone brought back in the Circle by Big Thunder."

Kyle had returned, said, "I've spent my professional career preparing for system collapses due to natural or manmade disasters. I believe none of us will survive if we don't work together, and quickly. We may barely survive, but lose the twenty-first century things like antibiotics, and flush toilets. We don't have time for political discussions. I just got off the phone with the Brule County Commissioner's office. They want to wait until tomorrow morning to make the announcement. They're going to look over all the evidence, including what the reconnaissance flights brought back. Who knows what chaos the public announcement of being transported to 1791 will bring? One possibility is a rush of gold prospectors with no intention of respecting Lakota lands. They may arrive tomorrow, not whenever Spain and France find out."

Mary said, "The Black Hills committee can look at ways to prevent that."

Kyle continued, "There was a South Dakota State Senator at the emergency meeting in Chamberlain. He was visiting family in Kennebec. He says he is higher in the line of succession than a state attorney. They are going to swear him in as governor."

"Governor of what?" someone shouted. "There's no state of South Dakota in 1791." People muttered agreement.

David Cornell spoke up. "The state senator is correct. I'm only one of several state attorneys, appointed, not elected. Under South Dakota law, he may be next in line for governor."

David asked Kyle who the state senator was. Kyle replied, "Clyde Folsom."

David rolled his eyes, and a few other people groaned. People had heard about the guy. He was a MAGA crazy, pro-lifer, and antivaxxer.

Jackson had also returned and raised his hand. "You should be aware they are rushing to swear him in to deploy the National Guard. He also can order the state police. I've seen their weapons. We don't want a military conflict. We would lose. I've spent time in a war. Believe me, no one wins. Conflicts begin with the concept of 'us' and 'them'. We must include everyone to become 'us'. It's harder to fight yourself. If we create a government, it needs to be a coalition that includes everyone. We need a framework quickly, even if it is temporary and needs work. We can create a new and better country. I, for one, do not intend to be a slave."

People laughed uncomfortably. Jackson was the only Black person in the room.

Jackson stated, "We have a chance to save the planet. Petty politics has no place. We can say to those who disagree with us, 'There is a place set for you at our table if you choose to join us'."

Mary announced, "Sounds like we need to declare independence, work to buy Spanish Louisiana from Spain or France, and create a coalition government of tribal, county or state, and federal members if we are going to meet our stated goal of creating a sustainable future that protects the Earth." Heads nodded, but a few shook their heads no.

Mary asked, "Can someone who opposes please explain why?"

Alan Tilson, a Crow Creek Tribal Council member, said, "I always believed in the United States of America, served my country in Vietnam. Starting a new country sounds unnecessary."

Someone said, "It's only 800 or 900 miles that way, pointing east. You don't have to stay." Mary shot the jokester a dirty look.

Lou spoke up. "Imposing our form of government on other tribes or speaking for them isn't something we can do. We'd be the new colonizers."

That slowed everyone's roll.

Mary proposed, "What about a commonwealth or a confederation, a group of sovereign nations that work towards the common good? Tribes have their own autonomy, make their own laws, and cooperate with us or not as they wish."

"What about slavery?" Lou asked. Everyone was aware many tribes held slaves. They'd seen the horrible result of the young girl being sold.

Jackson answered, much to everyone's relief, "Trade incentives and economic sanctions. Brent and Jake freed a girl in return for a fishing vest and multi-tool. I imagine tribes would give up owning slaves if they had the possibility of owning a better rifle than a flintlock." People laughed. "Slavery in the south will be a bigger issue we can tackle later, although I have to say, Brent and Jake had the right idea. It's never okay to buy a human being. We need to figure out a policy."

Everyone in the room murmured agreement. The issue seemed resolved.

Someone said, "slavery committee." Mary wrote it on the board. Then someone said, "It probably should be antislavery committee," which drew a chuckle.

Mary restated, "The proposal is to create a sovereign nation, declare independence from Spain, create a confederation and find a way to pay for the Louisiana Purchase, all right away."

Many individuals expressed concerns they needed more time, months rather than days, and the necessity for additional input from others. Other people stated a smaller group can accomplish a great deal in a short time. Someone mentioned again that while elections would happen down the road, this group, as the elected representatives, had the responsibility to decide in crisis situations.

Kyle said, "We don't have time to wait, not even a day. This is truly a case where those who hesitate are lost. We need to act fast while we have the legal authority, because believe me, by tomorrow we may lose whatever legitimacy we now hold."

Mary asked, "All in agreement to move forward immediately on the earlier proposal, say aye, all opposed, say nay." After looking around, "The ayes have it."

Mary suggested, "We can call it the Western Commonwealth."

David raised his hand. "Point of clarification confederation would be better for what you want than a commonwealth."

There was some discussion. No one wanted to be called the Confederates, so they settled on coalition instead.

Mary said, "Until we come up with a better name, let's call it the Western Coalition. Oh, what the hell, why stop at the Rockies? Let's declare everything west of the Mississippi, to the Pacific Ocean, to the Canadian and Mexican borders ours."

Alan asked, "What about Hawaii and Alaska?"

"We don't want them. Let's not get greedy." Everyone laughed again.

"Point of clarification: if the coalition is the entire area west of the Mississippi, what are the borders of our new country?"

More discussion followed. Mary asked Kyle to put the Google map with the pins on the overhead screen. Mary proposed that the borders of the new nation be the thirty-mile Circle that was brought here by Big Thunder.

Lou asked, "What about the Black Hills?"

Mary replied, "We need a vote with all the Lakota tribal members inside the Circle. We should seek their permission for the new nation to administer and protect the mining and sacred lands. Then we need to reach out to the Indigenous Lakota for their permission."

Everyone agreed. Discussion followed about the name of the new nation. They tossed a few ideas about, like wakíŋyaŋ, Lakota for thunder. Most people were leaning towards the name Omímeya, from which the Circle radiated. There was talk about how much money and resources the casino had. They tossed the word nationalization out.

"No!" shouted Rose, louder than she realized. Everyone stared at her.

Rose said, "Omímeya is a business that needs to make a profit to be sustainable and give back to the tribes. I'm now the CEO of the corporation and the general manager. We'll file new corporation papers once a new legal system get in to in place. We built this resort using twenty-first century technology. It must be protected. Once the rest of the world finds out about us, they'll sail upriver in a matter of months. People can come to attend lectures by not only the best medical people in the world, but engineers, farmers with new techniques, experts on every technology our old world offered. People will be able to stay at a premium resort with amenities they've never seen before. Tourism can be a tremendous boon to our economy. Omímeya, the business, will pay enough taxes to help support the government. This will be true of all the businesses within the Circle. Nationalization would be a mistake for anything other than critical infrastructure."

There was nodding and agreement.

"I want to share with you something extraordinary. At six-thirty this morning, my daughter, Kimímela, told me Big Thunder was coming, and we would both lose and gain so much. This was over four hours before we heard anything. Then she said, '*Thànka wakíŋyaŋ wašágya kin čhangléška na kin čhangléška awáŋyaŋka makhówančaya.*'" Rose translated, "Big Thunder strengthens the Circle, the Circle protects the Earth."

She explained the connotations in the word changleska, meaning hoop, the unity of people, protection, connection. That should be the name of our new nation, the Changleska Coalition. There were sounds of agreement and "aho," a sort of Indian intertribal amen.

Mary asked, "Are there objections?" There was still muttering.

"Speak up, or let it go for now. We can figure out details later. These are broad strokes."

Mary restated, "The proposal is to create a sovereign nation called the Changleska Coalition whose borders are the thirty-mile Circle from the Omímeya resort, declare independence from Spain, claim the lands from the Mississippi River to the Pacific Ocean, bordered by Mexico and Canada, which will be held in a commonwealth for the Indigenous people within, and to find a way to pay for the Louisiana Purchase."

Mary was about to call for a vote when the AV staff person said, "Hold on."

He asked Mary to move over so everyone who voted would be in the shot. He exclaimed, "This is historic! Imagine if someone had videotaped the Declaration of Independence."

Everyone sat a little straighter and became more serious. All twenty-eight people in the meeting voted yea.

Chapter Seven

Rose

ROSE HUSTLED OUT of the room after Mary called for a break following the vote. It was thrilling to be part of creating a nation. She thought about the meeting being recorded for posterity. She texted the meeting secretary, asking her to email the exact wording of the proposal and the names of those who voted.

Reluctantly, Rose returned to her usual work. She had turned down her radio during the meeting. She also felt her tablet vibrating at her hip in the special pocket she had sewn into her jacket. Rose always kept the sound muted on both her tablet and her phone. On her way to the bathroom, she read and answered texts and responded to a radio query she thought someone else should have handled. Like all working mothers, she found multitasking as natural as breathing, barely noticeable.

The manager of the resort shops wanted permission to close. There had been practically no sales because of the cash-only policy. The staff wanted to go home early because everyone was anxious. Rose granted permission and offered double time to staff members who could stay. Many second-shift workers had not shown up. Rose had to manage staffing shortages alongside everything else.

The more she thought about the implications of living in 1791, the more overwhelmed she felt. With no internet or credit cards, how would guests pay? How long could they support six hundred guests and one hundred fifty staff? Would she have to close the resort? How was she going to manage? Was she completely in charge? What would Phil think? She asked him earlier who was the CEO now, and he replied, "You do it, I don't want it." Countless critical details raced through her mind. *One thing at a time*, she told herself. She took a breath and started making lists.

After washing her hands and leaving the bathroom, she responded to Jenny's urgent request to talk. Unlike other department heads, Jenny used an urgent tag only when she genuinely couldn't handle something.

"Where are you?" Jenny asked.

"In the north wing, taking a break from the emergency meeting."

"The conference organizers want to speak to you, urgently."

Oh no, thought Rose, *this was bound to happen.* Chaton Begay was the one she was eager to impress. If he requested an urgent meeting and brought his organizing committee, they would likely be upset. What was she going to tell them? How would they react? They had paid substantial fees for an upscale, well-managed professional conference.

She realized that, despite the power outage in the surrounding area, the resort's services—meeting rooms, dining, horse stables, and the Canoe Center—were operating normally, except for the slot machines and arcade. Omímeya had no control over their displacement to the eighteenth century. She realized she must stop viewing this as a professional conference in her old world, where she had to appease guests to avoid a bad Yelp review. As far as the guests knew, they had left everyone beyond the Circle behind, never to see them again. It was a devastating realization. She would tell them the truth as gently as possible. She felt guilty about how she had informed Phil Gallo.

"Let's meet with them privately. Find us a room in the north wing, if possible. I need to stop at the Business Center. Let me know what room, and I'll meet you in twenty minutes."

Rose stopped at the Business Center, which was empty, likely due to the lack of internet. She sat and drafted a document based on what had been decided in the meeting, it took her longer than she thought to format it, and she had to text Jenny and have her push the meeting with Dr. Begay. She sent the file to a staff member with instructions for a quick turnaround.

Jenny called to say the Pheasant Room was available. They had set it up for a breakout session. The door sign read, "Use of Indigenous Foods for Heart Care Patients." The room was empty except for Jenny and one of her staff, arranging six chairs in a circle near the front.

Four people entered, and Dr. Begay introduced his wife, Dr. Theresa Martinez. Rose noted that, like many doctors, she had kept her maiden name. They had met briefly before. She had not met the other committee members, Dr. Kathryn Little Eagle and Dr. Roger Caris.

Rose steeled herself for a terrible conversation. It wasn't the first time she and Jenny had met with unhappy conference organizers. They rarely brought a committee. They could almost always resolve problems, though it often cost Omímeya a fortune.

Before she could apologize—her default response—Dr. Begay asked, "Can you tell us what's going on?"

Rose glanced at Jenny, uncertain whether she knew everything. Recalling Kyle's preference to delay informing the public, Rose decided he was mistaken. She shared everything she knew, from Chamberlain's reports to Jake and Brent's experiences and the clear evidence that Big Thunder had transported them to 1791. She was surprised that her audience seemed unshocked.

"We heard the rumors," Dr. Little Eagle said. "We saw the pictures."

"What? Where?" asked Rose.

The shuttle had returned after observing the severed roads, and since everyone had a phone, that made sense, but how did they know the year? It had not been long since she had learned.

Dr. Little Eagle said, "Jake and Brent are at Buffalo Burger, telling everyone, showing pictures, and gathering a crowd. They're drinking beer and enjoying the attention, it seems. People are praising their cleverness in rescuing that poor girl without buying her."

Shit, I need to tell Kyle, Rose thought. "Please excuse me, I need to make a call."

She stepped away, called Kyle, and informed him about Brent and Jake.

Kyle said, "It's probably better if rumors spread first; otherwise, people wouldn't believe it. Once officially announced, it'll be more accepted." He said he would talk to Brent and Jake, send them home, and encourage them to share the photos with people in Chamberlain.

"They should leave before they're too impaired to drive with a boat," Rose said, then added, "Find out where they got the beer. I ordered the bar closed." Kyle laughed.

Upon returning, Rose apologized and explained the debate over when to inform the public. Dr. Caris laughed and said, "It's like being a little bit pregnant. Eventually, everyone will know."

Rose prepared herself for the complaints and demands she assumed were the reason for the meeting. Dr. Martinez said, "We want to know how we can help. There are one hundred fifty-three smart, highly educated people here, all freaking out. They need something to do. We can help."

Rose looked at her, stunned.

Looking into Rose's eyes, Dr. Martinez said, "What do you need, Rose?"

Unable to help herself, Rose burst into tears. Dr. Martinez got up and put a comforting hand on Rose's shoulder. Rose couldn't recall the last time anyone had offered to help her.

Rose sniffled. Jenny, also teary-eyed, returned moments later with a tissue.

Jenny asked, "Is your group still planning to show a film and hold a dance this evening? Since the band was coming from Sioux Falls, we can assume they're not here. Do you still want to show the film? I could arrange a DJ instead."

"We're canceling the conference—no film, no dance. We need a group meeting to inform everyone what's happening and organize people."

Rose replied, "Great idea. We can show the photos, and Kyle—our emergency manager and FEMA director—can debrief. Is it okay to open the meeting to all resort guests and staff?"

"Invite whoever you want."

Jenny asked, "We could use the rooms for committee meetings, but you paid for the rooms."

"No problem."

Rose said, "I'll work out a refund for you. Perhaps those funds could cover stranded guests?"

"Great idea. Should we schedule the group meeting for seven pm?"

"Yes," Jenny confirmed.

Rose stood and said, "Then let's get going. We're starting a new country, creating a new government, and raising money for the Louisiana Purchase."

They all looked at her, dumbfounded.

Dr. Chaton Begay and Dr. Roger Caris wanted to participate. The others had things to do.

Rose stood and walked toward the door. "I'll take you to the meeting. You're welcome to include others if they'll be helpful."

Along the way, Jenny and Rose conferred on the size of the room for the general meeting. With its expandable walls, the Big Bear Ballroom could accommodate a large crowd.

Right down the hall was the Otter Room. The doctors waited outside the closed door, which bore a sign reading, "Emergency Planning Meeting." Rose strode in, motioning for the doctors to follow. The meeting had started. Everyone looked up as they entered.

Rose said, "These are doctors from the conference. They can help. I invited them to participate."

"Wonderful," said Mary. "We can use all the help we can get."

Rose was relieved. She knew some people could be territorial about their roles.

During the break, someone had set up an easel with oversized Post-it notes because they had run out of whiteboard space. Brainstormed ideas on the Post-it notes would soon be posted on the walls.

"We're developing the structure of the new government, the Changleska Coalition," Mary said. "We propose modeling it after tribal governments to some extent. An Executive Council would comprise seven members, each an expert in a specific area, akin to a cabinet or ministerial portfolio in other nations."

An AV staff member typed on a laptop beside the LCD projector, displaying the words *Executive Council* at the top of the screen. Below were seven columns: Infrastructure, Education, Security, Medicine/Science, Agriculture, Human Services, and Communication/Information Technology.

"These are the areas Kyle outlined. We can adjust them as needed. Not everything will fit these categories, but they're broad strokes we'll refine later."

"A suggestion?" Jackson asked, raising his hand. "The term *security* can mean different things, and since law enforcement is included, what if we call it Defense/Law?" Everyone agreed.

David Cornell asked, "Does that include making laws? Are we going to have a legislative and a judicial branch?"

Mary replied, "Let's do things differently, with only two branches. I suggest committees propose laws within each council member's purview, then submit them to the council for a vote. We'll have no dedicated legislators or professional politicians. No political parties."

Lou said, "No red states or blue states." Everyone laughed.

"The Executive Committee members should be experts in their fields, like the Executive Council members. The Medicine/Science Committee would propose laws related to medicine, and the Executive Council would vote on them." After some discussion, everyone agreed.

David asked, "What about the judicial branch?"

Lou suggested, "Keep it simple: three judges for a Court of Justice, elected, not appointed for life. They can supervise lower court judges."

There were comments about elections being corrupt or unfair.

Mary said, "Let's table elections for later discussion," and the topic was noted. She asked, "Does everyone support a supreme court named the Court of Justice, comprising three judges? We can decide later whether to elect or appoint judges. Anyone opposed?"

She called for a vote, and it passed with a few nays. *Some people just like to be contrary*, she thought.

Smiling, Mary said, "David, I nominate you for the judicial committee. You and other lawyers can work it out and present it to the council. There must be more lawyers among the guests. We found you. Sounds like a fun committee."

Lou said, "Before we can discuss elections, we need to discuss franchise, who can vote."

As the discussion began, Rose's tablet kept buzzing at her hip. She stepped out to answer texts and calls. She realized her input at the meeting was less critical than her financial expertise. Rose knew that without economic stability, their fledgling nation was doomed. They needed a funding plan for their new nation, and she was likely the one to develop it. It was a daunting idea. She hoped there was an economist among the guests.

Back inside, she signaled Kyle to join her and asked about available goTenna phones or ham radios. Kyle confirmed they could spare two phones and four radios. Rose requested their delivery to the area's bank managers. Fortunately, Kyle's emergency plan listed all those contacts, including home addresses. Manuel, who had returned from the Chamberlain run after driving since 5:00 am, was done for the day. Rose wondered whether his family was beyond the Circle. Kyle arranged for someone else to make deliveries.

Rose wrote a brief explanation of why the bankers needed to meet as soon as possible. Though most lived just half an hour away, Omímeya would lend them goTenna phones and radios for remote participation if they couldn't attend in person. Rose enticed them to the seven pm meeting by promising evidence of the situation. She debated whether to inform them they were now in 1791, but decided they might not believe it. She planned to prove they were now isolated, without internet or contact with their management. A public announcement was scheduled for tomorrow morning. Chaos would ensue if people didn't know what had happened to their money. Since all stores accepted only cash, it was critical that they devise a shared plan before the public announcement. She dispatched the letters, phones, and radios and moved to her next task.

Rose looked at her list. She wanted to attend the meeting again, but she returned to the Business Center and picked up the documents. The staff had done a nice job. The top of the paper had an understated Omímeya logo; it was bordered with the four directions' colors, on the finest seventeen-by-twenty-two-inch card stock they carried. In a font that was distinct but readable, the document read:

> On September 21, 1791, representatives of the people brought by Big Thunder from another world gathered at the Omímeya Resort in the Nation of Lower Brule in order to declare independence from Spain, and we claim the lands from the Mississippi River to the Pacific Ocean and bordered by what was in our world, Mexico and Canada. We assert that all these lands belong to the Indigenous people who live there. We recognize those tribes as sovereign nations with inherent rights and responsibilities to their own people and to the Earth. From this day forward, we declare these lands to be held in trust for the good of all. On this day, we create a new sovereign nation, the Changleska Coalition. Its purpose is to protect the lands west of the Mississippi River and the people who dwell upon them. Our covenant as a nation is to protect the Earth and interconnected bio-systems such as waters, plants, and animals from pollution, contamination, and exploitation, to be preserved healthy and whole for future generations.

She was hungry, not having had time to eat since that morning. Had it only been a day? It felt like a year. Rose knew she wasn't the only one, so she called catering. She had dinner prepared for forty in the Pronghorn Room next door to Otter at 6:00 pm. She knew preparing food in ninety minutes would be challenging, but leftovers from the wedding reception would help. Rose kept her order simple: soup and sandwiches. The kitchens could produce that on short notice.

Rose returned to the meeting, noticed they were about to call for a break, and announced the group meeting at 7:00 pm She held up the document she created and asked those present for the vote earlier to please sign the four copies. People smiled and high-fived as they signed. The spaces above the names were uniform, preventing any flamboyant "John Hancock"-style signatures. Someone suggested she have a copy framed and permanently placed in the Otter Room.

As additional people arrived, Rose had Jenny open the slider to the next room and set up in rounds for dinner. Rose got everyone's attention and said, "We've little time left and a lot to do, so let's break up into smaller groups, not official committees yet, but working groups. We need to create the government framework immediately, but other issues also require attention. It is essential that we present the Commonwealth and Changleska as a fait accompli. This way, it will be less likely to be undermined." There was a positive response from the group.

Changing the subject, Rose said, "We'll have dinner brought next door at 6:00 pm" There was relief on many faces. "Tomorrow, we've all the meeting rooms donated by the doctors. I suggest we separate the working groups into our seven categories," as she pointed to the screen.

People started breaking into smaller groups. Rose left to go back upstairs to her office. She sent a group text to staff and guests informing them about the meeting tonight. Neither Kimi nor Hotah responded to her text, but she got one from Luke: "out of milk."

=..=

Rose reached only one banker. Most were in contact, but only five of the twelve bankers, representing four banks, planned to attend the meeting. She stressed the need for a prompt response and asked them to select a spokesperson for a public announcement at the group meeting. They would record the meeting and broadcast it on the radio the next morning. *That'll put a fire under their stodgy asses*, Rose thought.

Rose found Kyle and Jackson upstairs discussing Chamberlain with other staff members. She overheard Kyle say, "Folsom insists on making the public announcement as governor tomorrow morning. The radio had reported on the severed roads, but Folsom had imposed a gag order. They could broadcast Kyle's earlier announcement, but nothing unapproved by Folsom."

"Is that even legal? What about freedom of speech?" Rose asked.

"Under the Emergency Powers Act, Folsom can waive all that," Kyle replied. "Folsom believes that as governor he may do whatever he wants, including taking over Omímeya under emergency powers."

Rose felt her anger rise. "We must stop him."

Jackson said, "It sounds like he wants power. Everyone else is just following. I don't think anyone over there has considered the long-term consequences. They didn't seem highly functional to me. Could we offer him a seat on the council?"

"No!" exclaimed both Rose and Kyle.

"Actually," Rose said after a pause, "we could let him stand for election. When I left, they were discussing appointing acting council members, with elections to confirm them within a week or two. They were addressing voter eligibility when I left. We must ensure he doesn't win."

"Elections are a good idea," Jackson said. "If everyone can elect council members, others might accept us as a nation separate from the United States. People need to feel ownership to avoid conflict."

Kyle said, "I don't know how much we can do between now and tomorrow morning."

Rose replied, "Let's delay Folsom's announcement until 2-3:00 pm Tell them the announcement will trigger a run on stores, with everyone buying up twenty-first-century goods. They'll want to join in and agree. Tell them we'll prioritize announcements from the banks and health and safety updates. This will give us time to prepare and act earlier, say, by noon."

"When you make the announcement, read our Declaration of Independence and describe the new coalition government to undermine Folsom's authority. He is a politician. We need to show a broad base of support," Kyle added.

"Can we get all that worked out by tomorrow?" asked Jackson.

"We'll have to," Rose replied firmly.

Kyle said, "I'll go to Chamberlain tomorrow to meet the National Guard commander in person. I haven't had much luck talking to him on the radio. We need his support, or we'll be the shortest-lived nation in history. I hate to take the time away, but I don't see a way around it."

They discussed the potential run on stores and whether to start buying supplies before the announcement. Kyle had already begun. His emergency plan included lists of items to purchase. Doris was already making calls. The fact that everyone around here was related to each other helped. There would be no shortage of volunteers for shopping runs.

=..=

Rose barely had time to eat before it was time for the group meeting. She met with the bankers and outlined, in principle, what was needed. Jenny had organized the meeting, scheduling times for speakers. A group of drummers, originally scheduled to open the doctors' film night, began playing as people arrived.

Mary had changed from the ordinary pants and blouse she had worn all day into a ribbon skirt, an elegant top, and beaded earrings.

Noticing Rose's questioning look, Mary said, "I didn't have time to go home to change, so I asked my husband to bring me some clothes."

"I wish I'd done the same," Rose replied.

"You look fine, authoritative. People need that today."

Tearfully, Mary said, "My daughter Bridgett isn't here. Her husband was left beyond the Circle. He rarely works Saturdays but had to cover for someone. We're still hoping he'll appear."

Rose knew he wasn't the only one and felt deep down that they were gone from this world. She felt guilty that her children were safe. Then she remembered her mother and sister. They weren't close, but they were her only family. She realized with sadness that they, too, were gone. If the rumors were true, this thirty-mile Circle was the only place transported to 1791.

Rose was relieved that Jenny had opened both sides of the Big Bear Ballroom. About one thousand people attended, including guests, staff, and locals. Everyone wanted to know what was going on.

The meeting began with a prayer from the tribal chaplain, appropriate for both Lakota and Christian traditions. Kyle had provided the AV staff with all the Chamberlain photos—depicting the helicopter, buffalo herd, airplane reconnaissance of a tipi village and abandoned earth lodges, and Jake and Brent's images. The twenty-minute video was professional, given its rapid assembly.

As expected, the video elicited stunned shock, even from those who had heard rumors of their transport to 1791. Its concise presentation made denial harder, though many still expressed disbelief.

Mary asked the high school history teacher to give a brief presentation. Lois Robinson talked about the multiverse theory with great authority. Afterward, Rose asked why she knew so much about it.

Lois replied, "I'm a huge science fiction fan. Many sci-fi authors conduct extensive research for their books."

Rose questioned the reliability of fictional knowledge but appreciated that confident delivery often convinces people.

Then, Mary spoke eloquently about the Declaration of Independence and the formation of the Changleska Coalition. She outlined the organizational framework decisions made so far, emphasizing that they would be straightforward and presented soon. She discussed tomorrow's working group agendas: forming groups and nominating Acting Executive Council members.

"People should come prepared to work," she insisted, "not to talk about politics, as there's no time."

She clarified that the working group meetings were open to all, requiring no tribal membership or US citizenship, and encouraged guests to participate. She invited anyone with expertise in the seven areas to consider serving on the council. Mary acknowledged it was a work in progress, a foundation for moving forward and focusing on survival. Elections would be held in two weeks.

Kyle discussed the challenges they faced, emphasizing they could overcome them through unity. He also addressed Clyde Folsom's self-proclamation as governor and shutting down free speech. He warned of the risks of appealing to George Washington and the threat of nationalization. This prompted murmurs of concern. *For someone who claims he's not political, he's doing great,* Rose thought.

David Kim, Omímeya's IT manager, announced they were immediately hiring programmers and anyone with computer experience.

"Wi-Fi across the resort is operational. Cell phones and computers can access Omímeya's intranet, or internal web pages."

He asked everyone, including guests, staff, and locals, to fill out an important skills survey. He noted that even hobbies or courses taken could be crucial for their survival. The intranet offered job applications and information pages, updated hourly.

He explained that Omímeya was uploading software called *Internet in a Box*, designed for developing nations or emergencies. It included a full copy of Wikipedia, regularly updated with new content, alongside numerous technical websites and resources. Omímeya also provided the full content of Khan Academy, an online K–12 school, and other technical databases.

David stated, "We'll never restore the internet as it was, but with everyone's help, we can create a functional version. When someone visits a website, their cache stores files to accelerate page loading. If you don't clear your cache, we can upload those files to restore websites." He explained that, since many people had porn or other objectionable content on their devices, his team was developing a method to anonymize uploads. This ensured no one could trace which cache came from which source. They would archive porn so that future historians could marvel at what got twenty-first-century people off, but none would be available on the New Internet. He acknowledged that this might appear to limit free speech but noted the servers' limited storage capacity.

He added, "The porn on your computer may be the last in this world." The audience laughed, embarrassed. "Please be patient; the internet will run much slower than you're used to."

Instead of rebuilding social media, they were establishing community forums. Modeled on old bulletin board systems, these forums would facilitate discussions and information sharing. Some working group or committee sections, like Defense, might have restricted access. They would also create a Craigslist equivalent.

Old email accounts, such as Gmail, no longer functioned. Omímeya offered everyone one free email address—theirname@omímeya.com— using legal full names only. For duplicate names, emails would be distinguished as name1 or name2. He noted that each email would be linked to a public profile. Users could choose to keep certain details private or visible only to friends. All posts in the community forum would have a link to someone's profile.

The forum rules prohibited anonymous posts. Legal names were required, and all users had to upload identification. Users could not post hate speech, trolling, sexually explicit content or language, or comments they wouldn't say face-to-face. Violators faced temporary bans, with repeat offenders permanently banned. In building the New Internet, the IT team aimed to create a safer, more informative platform for all. David was surprised to receive applause rather than the booing he anticipated.

Next, banker Adam Diedrich spoke. "First, money remains valid. We're not facing imminent economic collapse. Today's emergency proclamation froze prices at current levels. Price gouging will have severe penalties. Until the coalition government issues new currency, US dollar bills remain legal tender at face value. This excludes gold, as its current price is twenty dollars per ounce. Once the new currency is issued, prices will revert to 1791 levels. Keep in mind the average wage in 1791 was sixty-five dollars a year. Not per week, per year. But a pound of butter cost fifteen cents and a loaf of bread was five cents. Goods will cost roughly the same relative to each other; only the monetary denominations will change. The banking committee is developing economic solutions and has underwritten a substantial loan to the new government, secured by Omímeya property."

The crowd sighed with relief. Diedrich continued, "If you bank with Wells Fargo, Interstate, or First Dakota and we have your records, your account is still valid. Once the local internet is restored, we'll resume online banking and debit card services. Please be patient; we're unsure how long it will take. For those with valid accounts, we'll honor checks. However, if checks are overdrawn, we'll consider it fraud and pursue criminal charges instead of overdraft fees. Regrettably, if your funds are at a bank we don't have records for, there's nothing we can do. This is going to hurt. Many people will lose their life savings and pensions. We'll reopen banks on Tuesday but must restrict cash withdrawals due to a dollar bill shortage; however, you can use checks for payments. Soon, local banks will offer credit cards to creditworthy customers."

When her turn came, Rose said, "Please remember that Omímeya is a resort we aim to preserve as long as possible. Guests cannot stay indefinitely. We'll help you find affordable housing as soon as possible. Omímeya is now the only place of its kind in the world." She reiterated her earlier comments about attracting people from beyond the area.

She paused for applause. "The Changleska Coalition plans to hire most doctors and specialists at salaries comparable to their previous earnings, based on their education and experience. Current staff will retain their jobs, though some may need to transfer to different departments. There will be profit sharing for all employees. I understand the grief many of you feel for loved ones left behind. They're not lost, they simply live in a different place—the old world. We face a daunting task, chosen to transform this world and protect our planet's future. As a parent of two teenagers, I've often worried whether my grandchildren could survive humanity's environmental damage. Now, they have a future. May the hope of our children's promising future ease the grief for those left beyond the Circle."

Rose concluded by sharing Kimímela's morning remarks about Big Thunder's arrival and its significance.

Father Murphy of St. Agnes Church spoke last. "It's clear that God brought us to this time. We don't always understand God's reasons but must trust in His infinite mercy and love. I've prayed about what being in 1791 means for me and believe God's purpose may strengthen my beloved church. With foreknowledge, we could have avoided many mistakes in our treatment of Indigenous peoples, including boarding school abuses and cultural genocide. We could have reformed the church's response to the shameful actions of certain priests. I plan to write church leaders, sharing as much as possible to mitigate harm and uphold the glory of God and His church. Those of us living in this time face immense challenges, but through faith in God and mutual support, we can build a better world."

He announced a special Mass tomorrow to honor those left beyond the Circle, adding that shuttles would transport people to local churches, with sign-ups available via Wi-Fi. He concluded with a heartfelt prayer that touched and resonated with everyone, regardless of faith.

Chapter Eight
Gift of Thunder

THE GIRL COULD only faintly recall her name before it was *Broken Pot*. She barely remembered her life before the Lakota came, killed her father and many others, took her and a few others as slaves when she was nine winters old. The running face sickness took most of her family and had left her village weak. The cornfields lay barren. Few hunters escaped the illness. Everyone was always hungry. The Arikara lived in round earth lodges on the banks of what the Lakota called the *Mínšoše* River. Before the sickness that left her face scarred and had affected so many, they lived well, planted crops, traded with other tribes. Their strong warriors had kept everyone secure. Although most of the memories of her previous life had faded, she remembered sleeping next to her grandmother, warm and cozy, well fed, and safe.

She was just called slave at first, since the Lakota thought she didn't deserve a name. She was given to the leader, Two Elks. His second wife, Many Horses had recently given birth. She'd lost a baby the previous winter and didn't want to leave the child in his cradleboard so she could work, wanting to hold him in her arms all the time. Many Horses was young and beautiful, received her name because of the many horses that were offered for her by the young men of the tribe, but Two Elks claimed her with more horses than ever given for a bride. She shared the lodge with Two Elks, his first wife, Black Rabbit, Many Horses, her new baby, and his father, Sings in the Morning. Two Elks' two sons by Black Rabbit lived in the young men's lodge. She would sleep next to Sings in the Morning to keep his bones warm. She didn't mind. He reminded her of her grandmother. It was hard at first; she spoke Arikara, but Sings in the Morning was patiently teaching her Lakota and told her stories. Others, especially Many Horses, yelled at her if she didn't understand. She had to work hard, but she was used to that. She didn't like Many Horses, who hit and pinched her if she wasn't fast enough. Two Elks ignored her and spent his time with the men.

One day, while carrying a pot of water to the fire, she dropped it on a rock, breaking a pot special to Black Rabbit, given by her mother. Black Rabbit was furious. She'd been called Broken Pot ever since.

She quickly learned to speak Lakota and adjusted to life in Two Elks' lodge. They didn't stay in one place but moved the camp often. It was much work for the women each time they moved, but work was everyone's life. Women and girls prepared food, clothing, cared for the lodges, children, and elders. Men and boys spent most of their time riding horses, playing games that were often rough but taught them how to be warriors. Men would hunt, warriors would scout or go on raids. They traded for corn sometimes, and she would grind and make corn cakes on hot rocks, but they never tasted as good as what she remembered her mother made. She enjoyed working with the women. They'd laugh and tell funny stories about the men while they sewed or cooked, or gathered plants. The children would tease her, call her names, throw nasty things at her, hit her, and tell her she was just an ugly slave. One of her jobs was to gather the juniper, moss, and cattail fluff used in the cradleboard to absorb the baby's messes. Many Horses never did that, although it was the usual mother's job.

When the baby was weaned and out of the cradleboard, it was her responsibility to watch over him. She carried him everywhere, even though it made getting work done harder. When he grew too big to carry, she tied him to her with a long rope because he'd get into everything. She loved him despite the mischief he got into, which earned her slaps from Many Horses. When the boy was three winters old, he was gnawing on a buffalo rib. A camp dog came and stole it right out of his hand. He screamed and bit the dog as he beat it. He was called Bites the Dog ever since.

Winters were cold, hard, and hungry. One winter morning she woke up feeling wet because Sings in the Morning couldn't hold his water. That night he left the lodge out in a winter storm to sleep in the snow forever and to leave more food for the young ones. She felt as empty as her sleeping space was without him. Through Sings in the Morning's teaching of the Lakota language and stories, she felt a sense of belonging to the tribe she never would have experienced without him. He always included her when he told stories to the other children, stories about how *Wakȟáŋ Tȟáŋka* created the world, or teachings of the *White Buffalo Calf Woman*. The memory of his kindness would linger, leaving a bittersweet ache. The others mostly ignored her, mistreated by a few, and hated by Many Horses. But she loved Sings in the Morning and missed him deeply.

After Broken Pot had been with the Lakota for five winters, she began showing signs of her moon. She worried about what would happen to her. She hoped Two Elks would take her to his sleeping robes. After Bites the Dog was weaned, Two Elks never slept with Black Rabbit, only with Many Horses. She was sure that was why Many Horses hated her. The women talked and mentioned that Two Elks was too preoccupied with Many Horses, despite her laziness and lack of concern for the sick or elders, which was unbefitting for a leader's woman. People said he'd give Broken Pot to Lame Leg, even though he was young, as he could never offer much for a wife. They believed he could only get an ugly slave. Broken Pot wanted to be someone's woman. Then she would no longer be a slave.

It had only been a few times after starting her moon when the scouts returned with a report that the *wašíču* (white man) they called Big Stink was trading for furs on the Mínšoše River. Another tribe had given him that name, and he was told it translated to Big Nose, which was also true. Two Elks decided to sell her because he wanted rifles. He'd heard wasicu traded well for young girls, especially if they were pretty, but he couldn't offer him a pretty one since she was the only slave he had. The other Arikari slaves had either married within the tribe or were traded off years ago.

=..=

Two Elks' brother, Fast Tracks, who spoke French, accompanied her with his two sons and another man. They left with several horses packed with tanned hides and other trade goods. After many days, they arrived at the trader's camp next to the river. There was a small tipi and a cottonwood hut full of trade goods. As the men talked and examined the hides and goods, they pushed her forward. Big Stink was very dirty, which she didn't understand. The river was right there; he stank. Why didn't he wash? She couldn't understand him well. He spoke Lakota, but a different dialect from what she was used to. Big Stink argued with the men, saying she was too young. He pushed up her skirt to see the hair between her legs; he pinched

81

her small breasts. Two Elks got only one rifle and a few blankets for her. The men smoked, and they drank from the bottle they had traded for. Two Elks had admonished them not to drink before the trade. They'd heard all the stories from others and obeyed. Broken Pot could hear them all whooping and laughing late into the night from their nearby camp.

The trader's woman was Assiniboine from farther north and had two small children, one weaned and one still nursing. She told Broken Pot she was lucky because they'd take her to the wasicu trading post near her people's location, provide her with a log house to live in, give her food to eat, and all she'd have to do is *kiči* (have sex) with the traders and do very little work. Broken Pot didn't know what to think about that. She had seen and heard Two Elks and Many Horses many times at night, even though it was polite to turn your head and pretend not to hear. As a slave, she didn't get a proper coming-of-age ceremony. However, the older women brought her gifts, showed her what to do and included her in women's talk, when before they had shooed her away. She heard it hurt for the first time, but if the man was gentle, used his fingers first, it hurt less and after that it was enjoyable. She'd put her fingers down there sometimes and knew it felt good. But she didn't want to kichi with men if they smelled bad, like the trader.

Told to sleep by the fire, she'd just fallen asleep when Big Stink came from the camp with the other men. He woke her up and pushed her to the hut. He smelled even worse with the whisky. Being close to him made her want to vomit. Big Stink was larger and taller than any man she knew, even Two Elks. He leaned her over a table, pushed her head down with one hand, her dress up with the other, and after a minute of fumbling, she felt a pain so sharp down there she screamed. That made him angry, and he hit her. She tried to get away, but he kept pushing her down. He was too strong. She cried. He hit her again. After what seemed an eternity, he got up and roughly sent her back to the fireside. He entered the tipi to sleep. She hurt and was bleeding. She didn't have her woman things with her; it wasn't time yet to gather moss, or the other plants used.

Broken Pot, cold, sore, bleeding, and frightened, curled up next to the fire in the one thin blanket she had been given. Maybe the other women were right. It wouldn't hurt so much the next time. She missed her sleeping space in Two Elks' lodge, missed Bites the Dog. She wanted to go home.

The men left the next day without a word. The Assiniboine woman didn't talk to her, didn't even share her name. At night, Big Stink did the same thing to her again. It hurt even more; she kept bleeding, which made him even angrier so he would hit her more. A Lakota man would never get near a bleeding woman. They didn't allow her to prepare food, get near weapons, or even sleep in the same lodge when on her moon. Big Stink did it to her every night, and it made the Assiniboine woman so mad that she wouldn't talk to her.

On the fourth day, while she was washing at the river, hopelessness enveloped Broken Pot, painting a bleak picture of a future riddled with suffering and pain. Was this what her life was going to be like? She hated the repugnant Big Stink. The thought of being with many wasicu men horrified her. As she stood by the river's edge, the water rushed by with a powerful current. Its deep, swift flow mesmerized her. A wave of temptation washed over her, whispering how effortless it would be to let the river carry her away. She imagined all her anguish and torment drifting along with the current.

Succumbing to the pull, she took one step, then another, until the cold water reached her waist. And then, inexplicably, she halted, unsure of the reason but resolved to give it one more day.

After she returned from the river, Broken Pot was drying venison on the fire, when a dark fog came quickly up from the river and down from the sky. She heard thunder. Everyone knew how powerful thunder spirits were. She was afraid. The peals of thunder grew louder and closer. Suddenly, there was an enormous crack, louder than any sound she had ever heard. Then the mist was gone, it was quiet, the sun returned, and it was like it had never happened. She was frightened and sat down with her head between her knees. She didn't know what this meant, but she thought the thunder spirits were angry. Big Stink appeared afraid. Soon, he pushed her up and told her to get back to work.

After a while, they heard a strange noise and a canoe like she had never seen came towards them. It had no oars and came very fast, although it was traveling upriver. It was huge and shiny with bright colors and with two men inside. Everyone stared at each other. Broken Pot thought the thunder spirits must have brought these men. Maybe these men would kill them all.

They got out and talked with Big Stink; she understood little. There was a lot of gesturing and words that sounded unlike French. At one point, the two men produced something that looked like a shiny wood box and pointed it at everything: her, the children, the woman, the tipi, even Big Stink. They called it a "phone." It showed pictures of themselves inside itself. This scared her again. Big Stink wanted one of these things, and kept offering more and more, even a rifle. They kept refusing his offers. Then Big Stink pushed Broken Pot to the men. There was more talking. The men got angry, which scared her even more. Big Stink lifted her dress to show between her legs and it humiliated her. She still had blood on her legs. She had not been to the river to wash since early that morning. Now she hated Big Stink even more.

The strange men talked and brought out trade goods. One man wore a bright yellow vest with pockets full of sharp fishing hooks. One man made fire come from something small in his hand, not like steel and flint but faster. Broken Pot realized Big Stink had sold her when he pushed her towards them. She took her small bundle of things, and they walked towards their canoe. *At least the men were clean,* she thought, and they did not smell bad, only different. They waded into the river toward the canoe, but the water was deep. One man had to help. The canoe was so big they had to climb using a ladder on the side.

They spoke to her in soft voices, even though she couldn't understand a word. One man gave her a coat to put over her dress. Big Stink had torn her dress, which made her angry, as she had only one. He didn't give her any cloth to fix it or make a new one, even though he had bolts of cloth with his trade goods. The men gave her food to eat that was so soft and so good it made her smile, which made them smile. They kept giving her more and more food, which she didn't want to turn down, as that wasn't polite.

They went downstream; the canoe made a strange sound. After a while they stopped, and one man got out of the canoe, waded on shore and brought a strange metal wagon right to the water. She had seen wagons before; the Lakota didn't use them, but traded with those that did. The man used a metal rope to pull the canoe onto the wagon, which was pulled by a bigger wagon, which drove away on a wide, shiny black path. At first, she was so frightened she could hardly move, then as she looked outside, the world went by so fast; it was like she was flying.

Having calmed down for a while, she became afraid again. Broken Pot felt overwhelmed by big cabins or lodges, more metal wagons, and so many strange things. This was part of the river she recognized. Every winter, they come past this area for their winter camp. None of this had been here before. Broken Pot heard no one talk of these things. She'd heard plenty of talk about the whites, their trade goods, their wars, and how tribes were being pushed off their lands like the Lakota drove off the Arikara. She felt scared and unsure, not knowing what to think.

The strange men stopped their wagon. One man walked away, and the other waited in the wagon with her. After a bit, he came back with a man and a woman. They dressed alike, which was strange. The woman, named Janet, had a name that sounded strange to her ears. She spoke to her in Lakota. She spoke differently; it was hard to understand, but not unusual. Lots of tribes spoke in different dialects. The woman asked Broken Pot her name, and when she told her, she asked again. Janet said she didn't always understand the right words. When they asked again, she heard her name, and they laughed again, which made her mad. Who were these people? She did not care if thunder beings sent them; they didn't have to laugh at her. They realized they'd upset her, then said soothing words she didn't understand.

All of them went to the biggest wooden lodge she had ever seen. Inside it, Broken Pot sat with Janet on soft shiny chairs while the men entered a different room. Janet held something she now knew was called a "phone" and talked into it like there were people in the room with her. Janet asked her if she wanted something to eat, but the men had fed her so much she had to say no. Broken Pot asked Janet where she could make water and Janet took her to a small room and showed her what a "toilet" was and how it worked. She was thrilled. Janet showed her soap and told her if she didn't wash her hands every time she used the toilet, she'd get sick or make other people sick. Janet said she was sorry there was no hot water, the electricity was out. The word she used was close to lightning, which made little sense to Broken Pot.

After returning to the front room, the two men who'd brought her emerged from the back and exchanged handshakes with the men. Their expressions and tone of voice showed they were pleased with the men. They stood awkwardly by Broken Pot. She stood up, thinking they would take her with them now. After confusion and translation, they said they were leaving her with Janet, said goodbye, being careful not to touch her, and left.

Broken Pot and Janet sat back down. She was told they were waiting for a healer to come to help her. Broken Pot didn't understand. She didn't suffer any injuries, only sore but not hurt. While they waited, Janet told her a word in Lakota, then the word in English. They practiced many words until two women came in. They spoke gently to her in English and Janet provided translations. The two women apologized for not letting her bathe. She'd need to come with them to a place of healing to be looked at. They assured her Janet could stay with her, and they wouldn't hurt her. They were so nice to her. She was more confused than frightened. Broken Pot went with Janet in a different car. She learned the name as they continued to name things. She enjoyed learning the names; it kept her from being so scared of all the strange things she saw.

Broken Pot and Janet went to a place called a clinic, and the two women, named Barbara and Nancy, took her to a small room with a funny table on it.

Nancy said, "They were sorry, but they had to take pictures."

By now she had figured out that pictures were taken with phones, but Nancy had a bag with her and she took out something she was told was a "camera" that also took pictures. Nancy took photographs with what she had on, then had her take off the coat the men had given her, took even more pictures with her turned around.

Janet and the women kept using the words "Rape Kit." Janet translated. She was confused. Broken Pot knew what rape was. Men would sometimes do it to the women of an enemy, but the Lakota punished men who raped women in their own tribe. Occasionally, such a man would even survive the punishment. But she was a slave. Even if she hated Big Stink, she belonged to him, so how could it be rape? And how could they do anything to Big Stink? He was not of their tribe.

Barbara and Nancy left the room and asked her to please take off all her clothes. They left her a thin dress to wear, but the dress was so thin she didn't know how anyone could wear it without it falling apart. She could not figure out how it closed and so held it around herself when they knocked and came in. They asked if it was okay if they both stayed, as they needed Janet to translate. She agreed and decided that she would never understand them, but they were so concerned about her she felt safe.

Barbara held a thin cloth over her bottom half, apologized and took down the top part of her dress, and took more pictures. Janet translated the whole time. They were very slow and careful, explaining what they were doing each time they did something different. She had to put her legs on the sides of the funny metal things on the table and scoot her bottom down, and they even took pictures there. They did things to her down there, it hurt, they apologized, she bled more.

Then she was done. They let her sit up, told her through Janet how brave she had been. Nancy told her she could wash now, sorry, no hot water because no electricity. These people made no sense to her. There was a sink in the room. They gave her a small cloth and soap. Nancy took clothes out of the bag she'd brought. Broken Pot looked confused again. Janet grasped her confusion and stayed by her side as she washed up and was introduced to underwear and menstrual pads. She was so impressed with them; Janet laughed and asked her what she used. Everything seemed to get better. The clothes Barbara gave her were trousers like some men wear but were soft and a top that was a pretty color.

After getting dressed, Nancy and Barbara came back in and handed her a glass of water and what appeared to be a blue seed or pellet. Through Janet, she was told it would make sure she didn't get pregnant. Broken Pot didn't believe one little seed could do that. She knew of herbs that would do the same thing, but you had to make tea from them, and often they didn't work. Believing these people had powerful medicine, possibly sent by the thunder beings, she swallowed the seed. Janet said Broken Pot would come home with her for a short time while they figured out where the best place was for her to go. Nancy and Barbara asked whether Broken Pot wanted a goodbye hug. They hugged her and told her again what a good, brave girl she was.

=..=

Afterwards, they drove to Janet's dwelling, which was many houses put together. They had to walk upstairs, another new experience for Broken Pot. Janet's apartment was large, filled with strange and beautiful items. It had three rooms, and one was just for sleeping. Janet said it was small, and they were saving money for a house. Like most things Janet said, this made no sense.

Janet tried to show Broken Pot how she could send messages far away by poking fingers at her "phone." Janet was talking to a distant person about "electricity" when her husband Raymond entered the room. He was a big man, bigger than Big Stink. Broken Pot thought it would hurt if she were to have kichi with him. She assumed the men had sold her to Janet, and that they had taken her to the clinic to make sure she was not sick, and could bear children. Broken Pot began to cry when she saw Raymond.

When Janet asked why, Broken Pot said, "I'm sorry I cried when I saw how big he is. I'm sure the kichi would stop hurting soon. I promise to work hard."

Janet appeared extremely upset and asked her husband to leave. She sat next to Broken Pot on the couch and told her the English word was "sex", the most common of many ways to refer to kichi. Janet promised that Broken Pot would never be required to have sex with her husband, or with any man ever, if she didn't want to. Janet told her if any man tried to give her whisky, she should say no because that usually meant they wanted sex. Or sometimes men would tell her nice things or give her presents so she would have sex with them. She told Broken Pot that no matter what, even if she liked the man, she could say no to sex. She could say "stop" anytime. Janet said if a man had sex with her and she didn't want it, it was rape, and he could be locked up for a long time.

Janet told Broken Pot she was not a slave, she was free. The two men wanted to get her away from Big Stink, so she'd be safe. She'd never be a slave again. She said among her people that slaves were bad Medicine. No one around here owned slaves. If they did, they would be locked up. Broken Pot felt better, but wasn't sure what would happen to her if she wasn't a slave or a wife.

Janet poked at her phone, then Raymond came back. Janet rushed into his arms and cried, and they both looked at her sadly.

Raymond didn't speak Lakota well, but said, "I'd never hurt you. If any man tries to hurt you, I'll hurt him." He laughed and said, "If I ever had sex with another woman, Janet would kill me."

Janet punched him in the arm and said, "I have the gun to do it with too," but she smiled, and Broken Pot knew it was a joke.

She could feel they loved each other. It made her happy. Janet sent Raymond out to get food, but he brought nothing back so the hunting must have been bad, but he wasn't gone long. He said the stores were closed. They went into the kitchen and ate cereal, milk, and cheese. Janet said they had to use the food in the refrigerator because there was still no electricity. Everyone was so bothered by not having it. Later, the food disagreed with her, and she was so happy about the toilets.

Janet's mother and aunt came over. They didn't speak Lakota, which she thought was strange. Janet told her the white man came and had stolen their land and language. She said some tribes kept their language more than others, but her tribe almost lost theirs. They brought bags of clothes that had belonged to Janet's younger sister. Janet said Broken Pot was too small to wear anything of hers. It was true, everybody she saw so far was so big, even the women. The clothes were wonderful; she had never seen so many pretty clothes and they were all for her. There were even socks and shoes called sneakers. Even though her moccasins were worn and nothing special, the women admired them.

When Janet told her mother and aunt her name translated to Broken Pot, they didn't laugh, but said the Lakota was too long and hard to pronounce. They refused to call her that in English. Janet said the white man stole their names and made them have English names that were easier to say, so they couldn't do that. But then her aunt said they could give her a new Lakota name. All of them had heard the story about how the fishermen had taken her away from Big Stink by refusing to buy her and insisting on him giving her as a gift. Since she came the day of the Big Thunder, they called her *wóyaka wakíŋyaŋ*, Gift of Thunder. But she would be called Gift in English, as it was easy to pronounce.

She was so happy with her name. She jumped up and down, clapping. Everyone laughed. Even being told she was no longer a slave or could turn down sex anytime didn't give her as much pure joy as her new name.

She went to sleep that night curled up on the soft couch, wrapped in a nice warm blanket, cozy and safe like she remembered from her childhood. It was hard to remember the last time she felt so happy. She was Gift of Thunder.

PART II

Week One

*There is no fundamental social change without collective action. You
have to have organizations and institutions
that make a fundamental difference.*
— Cornel West (b. 1953), American philosopher, activist, and author.

Chapter Nine

Rose

AFTER THE MEETING Rose didn't know whether she'd ever been so exhilarated and exhausted at the same time. Despite her desire to go home, there were still things to do. She was glad to see Wayne Becker, the facilities manager, at the meeting. He retired as a Chief Petty Officer after twenty-five years in the Navy as an electrical engineer on destroyers. After the Navy, he received additional training in geothermal engineering and became the lead engineer in the installation of Omímeya's geothermal plant. He was offered a management position and a large enough salary to move his family from San Diego. He was extremely competent and could fix about anything.

Among all the department heads, their relationship had the least friction, though it wasn't exactly cordial. Rose got the impression that he didn't enjoy working with women. She wasn't sure if they even allowed women on Navy destroyers back then. She appreciated that Wayne sent his reports on time and that they were impeccably done. Although his department had a large budget, it was not bloated like others. She always knew there'd be no missing items or over-ordered supplies in his department. He hired veterans when he could and ran his department like he probably ran his ships. She could use four more like him. Rose motioned him aside to talk privately.

"Wayne," she inquired softly, "your family?"

"Most here, a few behind the Circle, luckier than many." His face was stoic.

"What do you think of all this? 1791, a new country, it's all so hard to believe?"

"Don't know what to think, not my job. Too soon to tell much. Did you get my texts?"

"Yes, but I need clarification."

"I couldn't reach anyone by phone at LBUC, so I went there. Their electric linemen come from Sioux Falls. They could find no one locally and had no clue how to get things back up. I helped them bypass the safety so the lines not cut would work. I sent them electricians from both maintenance and construction. Today, all I could do was prioritize the water and sewage treatment plants, and now both plants are running on main power. Good thing too, they were going to run out of diesel. They were supposed to have a seven-day supply, but somehow it disappeared."

He said this with disgust on his face, knowing that disappearing resources were all too common around here.

"I overstepped, pulling electricians from outside my department without asking you first, but you didn't return my text. I didn't think it could wait."

"That was the right thing to do, thank you." Wayne looked relieved, like he was afraid she was going to berate him.

"Jim recommended we shut down the slots and gave me an update on our generator fuel status. He did a good job. You trained him well."

"We have a good crew, lost seven beyond the Circle, including a tech who'll be hard to replace. Priorities for tomorrow?" he asked tentatively.

Rose thought he assumed she'd prioritize the casino. Corporate would have wanted the slots back up, despite the needs of the community.

"Check with Kyle, but probably nursing homes, police, fire. What we can do may depend on diesel."

"I'd add the cell tower and the phone company."

"Of course, didn't think of those. That's why I need you and Kyle."

Rose gave him one of her usual 'I'm such a dumb female' smiles. Except now she really didn't know what to do, and he did. She didn't need to be competent in everything.

"I hear you're in charge now," he said, looking none too pleased.

"Yes, and I'm going to need your help. This place can use some Navy style organization." He nodded, looking appeased.

Rose emphasized, "Everyone needs to be aware: we'll not allow any more misplaced inventory, sloppy timesheets, or situations like the missing diesel at the water plant that could have jeopardized us all." That improved his mood.

"Have you considered serving on the Executive Council for Infrastructure? I can't think of a better candidate."

"No, too much to do here. The tech in Pierre was the other geothermal specialist. I'm not suited for politics, not sure if I agree with what you're doing."

Deciding not to open that conversation, Rose inquired, "Who would you suggest?"

"Tom Russo. He has the skills, temperament, and unless there is a problem, that dam runs itself."

"Great idea, thanks."

Rose didn't know Thomas Russo, other than he was a civilian, despite being the head of the Army Corps of Engineers that operated the Big Bend Dam.

"Do you know whether he lives locally? Was he home?"

"Yes, I talked to him, but don't know if he came to the meeting."

Wayne let her know he'd locked down the triangle, the industrial complex behind the resort. Only vaguely triangle shaped, smaller on the south end, it contained construction equipment, warehouses, recycling, and the geothermal plant—everything needed for operations. The north end had several mobile homes, a contractor office, three ten-person dorms for housing construction workers, and a mobile home used for a dining and recreation hall. It had gates that were usually left open, but Rose assumed Wayne followed security measures and locked it down. The emergency plan covered a lot of scenarios.

"Let me know what you need. Be sure to communicate with Kyle. He's an excellent resource." They parted.

People continued to mill about. She heard Jenny say, "Please exit if you aren't attending the medical working group meeting; other meetings are upstairs—check the door signs."

Rose marveled that people were still working as it was almost 10:00 pm *Oh no, Jenny*, thought Rose. She tried to remember what she knew about her. She'd worked at Omímeya for less than a year. All Rose knew was that Jenny lived in Pierre and was originally from somewhere back east.

"Jenny, I'm sorry I haven't asked how you are doing. Do you have family in Pierre?" The terrible question of the day. She hated to ask it, but felt guilty if she didn't.

"My family all lived in New Jersey. My boyfriend Paul and I moved here, but we broke up a month ago. I thought we might get back together," Jenny said with a sad look. "I've been too busy to process everything. It occurred to me I am homeless with nothing but this." She waved across her body; she was wearing a hotel uniform.

"Let me check. We should have staff rooms."

Between long commutes, working late, winter storms, or over-imbibing, staff members took advantage of the discounted rooms and stayed. She sent a text to the night manager, instructing him to prioritize displaced staff, if the admin rooms were full to add more. Rose added to her list to bring clothes for Jenny. The back of her closet was full of clothes that she planned on losing weight to fit into.

Rose checked in with Jackson. Doris set him up with a staff card and a room. She told him he could draw from his salary at any of the shops. Rose hadn't intentionally avoided him, but he was so gorgeous it made her uncomfortable. She remembered the feeling she got when he first stood up to greet her. It'd been so long since she'd had such a visceral, powerful attraction to a man. She'd not even felt that way towards Hotah when they met. At the meeting, Jackson was articulate and thoughtful. He even quoted Starhawk, which made him more attractive.

HR had stressed the problems with dating subordinates. When co-workers dated, even when they filled out the forms, HR would transfer one of them, usually the woman, often with less pay or to a faraway location. She'd heard the stories of people getting demoted or fired for fooling around with subordinates; not only men, women could act just as bad.

The thought of dating a subordinate was unsettling, almost like incest. Rose tried to shut down her feelings, but damn, they crept up on her. She felt drawn to him, not because he was so good-looking, but because he had a quality that made her want to be closer to him.

Rose hoped to go home before getting roped into anything else. It had been a long, weird day. Concerned about her kids, the day was so unsettling she wanted to see them with her own eyes before she knew they were okay. She got to her office to gather her things and plug in her devices to charge. Years ago, she'd bring work home. Being indispensable was the way up in management. She'd bring her laptop, sit on the couch while the kids watched television and work. She finally figured out unless she unplugged, she'd be no good to anyone.

Rose saw Kyle looking out the window. Curious about what he could be staring at, she got closer and saw the look on his face and knew. *I'm such an idiot; I didn't even ask about his son*, she thought. Kyle looked at her, as if shifting gears to find out what she needed.

"I am heading out. Before I go, is there anything you need? This must be hard."

His face crumpled, but he got control of himself and spoke. "If he could've stayed another two weeks, he'd been here."

Rose had met his seventeen-year-old son, Jason. He spent summers and holidays with Kyle, but normally lived with his mom in Colorado. He and Kyle loved the outdoors, kayaking, hunting, fishing, hiking, even learning to ride. They were close. Rose couldn't imagine anything worse than losing a child, regardless of the circumstances.

She didn't know what to say to comfort him. She settled for, "Please let me know if you need anything, time off, more help, anything at all. You have an incredibly tough job, not sure what we'd do without you."

He looked relieved she wasn't asking him for anything else. "The only good thing about this situation is I've been so busy I haven't had time to think about Jason. I already had my meltdown. I'm allowing myself one a day."

Rose said, "Take care, and goodnight," and gave him a long hug, thinking, fuck HR.

=..=

Although it was only a fifteen-mile drive home, it felt longer than usual. Rose realized if there was no gas, and her electric car broke, it'd take three hours each way to commute by horse. Living in the late eighteenth century was going to be difficult. She didn't know how she would cope. She liked nice things, soft beds, good food. Rose had enough hardship growing up. She didn't want more.

Hotah's truck was gone when she pulled up. That worried her. She'd counted on him being home to keep an eye on the kids. He left a text earlier saying he would turn on the generator, but Rose had been too swamped to text or call back. What if something happened? She was worried. Rose entered through the back, hearing the generator in the garage. In the darkness, she almost tripped on an extension cord. Using her cell phone flashlight, she could see that the generator wasn't connected to the freezer as it was supposed to be. She opened the big chest freezer. Things were still cold but were thawing. She believed they would probably refreeze okay once she plugged in the freezer again. Rose didn't change the cord back to the freezer so she could investigate what was more important than the freezer. Entering the rec room, she saw Luke playing a video game in the dark house.

He jumped up, startled. Rose was so angry she didn't speak. She pulled the cord from the TV.

Luke said, "Mom, I was on the last level," in that wheedling teenage voice she hated.

She went back to the garage and plugged in the freezer. Next, she got down a crate of LED lights that were plugged into a power strip connected to the solar panels they had on the roof. She carried the lights into the kitchen, trying to calm down before talking to Luke.

He came in and said, "Did you bring milk?"

Rose screamed at him. Her furious rant went on for a while, fueled more by the day she'd had than by the freezer. Nothing had spoiled yet, but she was pissed.

"Hotah told me to turn off the generator for three hours, then turn it back on. I figured since it was off anyway might as well play, cuz there's no TV or internet."

She was desperately trying to calm down. Yelling at kids wasn't good parenting.

"Do you know why he asked you to turn it off every three hours?"

"Dunno," was the sullen reply.

"To save fuel. That may be the last of the gas we'll see for a long time, maybe ever."

He perked up. "I've been getting texts. People are saying we're in 1791. Gotta be a joke, too crazy to be real."

"Yes, it's true. Do you realize your selfishness may cost this family an important part of its food supply?"

"You have a good job, and it's mostly venison in the freezer, anyway. We ate the ice cream."

His attitude and sense of entitlement astounded her, and made her angrier. She'd better change the subject.

"Is Kimi already in bed?"

"Everyone went to *kakà* (grandfather's). Unci and Mina went to Pierre to go shopping and didn't come back. Everyone's freaking out. Kimi says they're not dead, just living somewhere else."

All her anger dissipated like water running down a drain. All she could think was that Luke could have been with them. Seventeen-year-old Mina was Hotah's niece, Luke's closest cousin, although not by blood. When younger, the two kids spent a lot of time together. She and Kimi were close.

Rose hugged Luke tightly. It could've been him. She thought of Sharon, Mina's mom. She had to be devastated. Hotah had lost his mother, and his poor father had lost his beloved wife. Rose found herself crying, not over losing her own mother, but because she loved Hotah's mother.

"Why did you not go with them?"

"Someone needed to turn the generator on and off," Luke said defensively.

"But you didn't do that, did you?" Rose was growing angry again.

Before she could blow up at him again, they heard Hotah's truck. As Kimi entered, Rose ran to hug her, then they both were crying.

When Hotah came in, she could hear him talking to someone on the front porch. "Wait here, I'll get the lights."

Rose looked at him sadly. "Hotah, I am so sorry," and hugged him, still snuffling. They stayed like that for a minute. You didn't share fourteen years with a man without a bond. Before he could say anything else, she added, "Might as well invite her in."

With everything that happened, she'd completely forgotten Hotah's new girlfriend had moved into his tiny travel trailer with him. It seemed like such a petty thing to be upset about after today.

A young woman shyly appeared at the door at Hotah's invitation.

"Rose, this is Nicole."

Rose gasped, "How old are you?" realizing as soon as the words left her mouth how rude she sounded.

"She's nineteen," answered Hotah defensively.

She looks sixteen, thought Rose. Since Kimi looked older, Nicole looked the same age as Kimi. *Creepy*, she thought uncharitably about Hotah. She's young, pretty and thin. I suppose that's the appeal.

Rose struggled with her weight for years and was sensitive about being overweight. Rose believed she was unattractive and intertwined it with the belief she was unlovable. She observed men often tied their self-esteem to their income, while women's self-esteem focused on their appearance. Rose was keenly aware of society's differing perceptions of overweight women and men. It wasn't fair, but whoever said life was fair?

"I'm sorry if I was rude. It's been a day. I'm going to make tea. Would you like some? The LED lights are in here. I took the crate down," she told Hotah, pointing.

"Yes please, tea would be nice," answered Nicole politely.

Rose asked Hotah how much he knew about what was going on and filled everyone in with details they hadn't heard. Luckily, the stove was propane. Hooking up natural gas was one of the many remodeling projects not completed yet.

When the tea kettle went off, she said, "I'm having Sleepy Time. Anyone else?"

Kimi said to Nicole, "Better not, it has valerian. How about red raspberry instead?"

Red raspberry tea, thought Rose in horror. *There was only one reason a woman would drink that instead of valerian.*

Be nice, she told herself. "When are you due?"

Hotah looked surprised that she'd guessed, herbs were never his thing.

"February," Nicole answered.

That's why the sudden need to finalize the divorce.

Rose was trying to think of something nice to say when Luke popped up meanly, "That's why he lost his job. Her dad was pissed."

Rose remembered he was working on a ranch in Pine Ridge, a job that ended early.

"How is your family coping?" Rose asked Hotah, desperately trying to change the subject.

"Dad and Chaske are talking about going out looking. They heard about that girl at the fur trader's and were worried about the women wandering around."

Kimi said sadly, in Lakota, "I told them they're in Pierre and alive, but they don't believe me."

Hotah answered in the same language, "They will, sweetheart."

"They need more time," said Nicole, also in Lakota.

I'm beginning to see the appeal, thought Rose. When Hotah and Rose met, she could only speak a few words.

Luke got up from the table where they'd been sitting around the camp light, frustrated as usual when people spoke Lakota around him. "I'm going to bed."

"Hang on," she told him. "Bring me your game controller."

Luke grabbed a light and left the room. Rose told everyone what he'd done. She was still angry. Hotah had given up trying to discipline Luke. When the divorce is final, he really won't be Luke's stepfather, thought Rose unhappily. When Luke came back into the room angrily handing Rose his game controller, Hotah stepped up to him, putting his hands on his shoulders. They were about the same height now, Rose realized.

He said slowly and carefully, "Luke, it is time now for you to become a man. A man takes care of his family."

Then he sat back down at the table. For the first time since she confronted Luke, he seemed genuinely sorry, got tears in his eyes, and ran out of the room.

Kimi said in Lakota, "A bad spirit stalks him."

"Mom," Kimi said, mostly in English, meaning she wanted something. "*Tȟuŋwíŋ* (aunt) Zitkala is staying at *tȟuŋkášila* (uncle) Chaske's because there's no electricity in her apartment and no way to cook. Probably lost her job." She looked at Rose pointedly.

"Of course, she and the kids can stay here, honey," Rose said. She thought, *at least I'll be at work most of the time.*

Zitkala's current job was in a realtor's office in Chamberlain. Years ago, she used to work at Omímeya, but they fired her without disclosing the reasons to Rose, citing privacy rules. Zitkala could be a flake and went through a lot of jobs, but at least she worked, and didn't drink. Her kids were wild but cared for. After losing Mina, Sharon didn't need the stress of Zitkala and her kids. Hotah's sister Zitkala was a single mother of three, two boys, ages twelve and nine, and one girl, six. Luke and Kimi had bunk beds in their rooms. The cousins spent the night many times.

Rose climbed upstairs and before entering her room, she knocked on Luke's door. He was awake, playing games on his phone. She'd forgotten to take it away.

"Be ready to get up at six am tomorrow. You're coming to work with me."

"Do I have to? You have my controller, so I won't be able to play games. I'm sorry about the generator."

Rose was glad for the apology, the first she'd heard.

"We need all the help we can get. Perhaps you could work in IT. They need people to enter data. There are amazing things happening. I signed the new Declaration of Independence today."

"Is the arcade open?"

Her irritation grew again. "No, you are going in to work. Give me your phone."

"That's not fair. The world is ending. I need to know what's going on."

"By playing games?" She held her hand out, took the phone.

"Be nice to your sister; she and Mina were close."

"I feel bad too."

"I know, sweetheart, I love you. I'm so glad you didn't go into Pierre today. Good night."

Rose had a hard time falling asleep, her brain refusing to turn off. Usually, she watched Netflix to wind down, or had Alexa read an audiobook. More technology she'd have to live without. She wished she had something stronger than Sleepy Time tea, but it seemed like she'd just shut her eyes when her phone alarm went off.

Chapter Ten

Elliot

ELLIOT GRAY OWL missed signing the new Declaration of Independence because he forgot to plug in his phone. He'd regret that for the rest of his life. There had been a party at his house on Friday night. His cousin Theo and his best friend Scott had invited people over. They were all drinking and smoking weed. Elliot didn't drink a lot. He had a two-beer rule and stuck to it. When he was sixteen, his dad had been drinking when he drove off a bridge into the Missouri River, drowning himself, Elliot's mother, and his thirteen-year-old sister. Elliot always wondered if he hadn't been at a basketball game that night, if he could've stopped his dad from driving.

He smoked weed instead of drinking. Recreational cannabis wasn't legal in South Dakota, but he had a medical card. As a lawyer and a member of the bar association, he couldn't risk criminal charges. Someone had brought pot brownies to the party, and he ate two, not understanding how strong they were. They knocked him out. He went to bed and forgot to plug in his phone. When he was awakened at 11:11 am by a loud noise, Elliot looked around blearily. His alarm clock was dead. Everything else looked okay, so he went back to sleep and didn't wake up for hours.

By the time he got up, Theo and Scott had left. The place was a wreck. Scott had been crashing on the couch. It was only supposed to be for a few days, but it'd been weeks. Elliot noticed two totes and a backpack in the corner of the living room with all of Scott's belongings. He wasn't awake enough to be annoyed. It wasn't until he tried to make coffee that he realized the power was out. Then he checked his phone, and its battery was dead. He remembered his auntie had given him a camping LED light that would also charge his phone. He dug it out of the closet. It was still in the box. It'd never been plugged in, so it didn't have any charge.

He really needed coffee, and then he remembered he had Red Bull stashed for when he had a work push. After waking up thanks to the Red Bull, he grabbed a garbage bag and started cleaning up, becoming irritated.

He'd rented the two-bedroom house six months ago, planning on making the second bedroom his office. Hadn't gotten all his furniture moved in when Theo showed up with all his stuff.

"Hey Elliot, cool place. My bed is in Dad's truck. Will you give me a hand moving it in?"

That was the way it was with family sometimes, assumptions not requests. After his parents and sister died, Elliot moved in with his aunt and uncle, and took twelve-year-old Theo's top bunk. The two boys were more brothers than cousins. Elliot tried to look out for Theo and keep him out of trouble. It was difficult, because while academics were easy for Elliot, Theo hated school. He barely graduated from high school and had no interest in college or a job.

In 2016, when Elliot was in his second year at Sinte Gleska University, he was taking general courses. He liked history, but wasn't sure what he wanted to do with his life. He was on summer break at his auntie and uncle's place helping with the harvest.

In August they heard about the protest at the Standing Rock Reservation on Facebook. Against the wishes of the tribe, the Dakota Access Pipeline (DAPL) intended to install an oil pipeline under the river that supplied the reservation's drinking water. If it were to leak, as pipelines often did, it would ruin the drinking water and damage the surrounding ecosystem.

Elliot's entire family went to the protest camp. He had such a powerful feeling when they first arrived. Tribal flags from all over were flying on each side of the road leading to the camp, the Lower Brule Sioux Tribe flag included. It was the largest gathering of Native American tribes that had ever been in one place. The number of flags grew as Indigenous people from all over the world arrived. When Elliot arrived, the protest camp was small, mostly comprising Natives. However, it expanded with global support and attention.

Next to the river, the protesters set up camp and started marches and demonstrations against DAPL. The Standing Rock protests changed Elliot's life. He first stayed at the Lower Brule camp with his auntie and uncle, who brought camping gear, including their tipi. The gathering was nothing like he had ever seen, bigger than most pow wows. There were people visiting, cooking, and setting up needed systems such as first aid and herbal stations, donation depots, and workshops on effective direct action using nonviolence. Each day, people would protest on the front lines. They made signs, prayed, and sang. Elliot became a Water Protector. He faced tear gas, pepper spray, bean bags and rubber bullets being shot at him, sound cannons being pointed at him, and being sprayed with water hoses at night in freezing weather. Elliot witnessed the DAPL security siccing dogs on peaceful protesters. He didn't get bitten, but others did.

Eventually, his aunt and uncle returned home. Theo stayed at the camp until school started and then reluctantly went home. They'd come back on the weekends, bringing donations and support. Elliot canceled his fall classes and remained at the camp. Camp life was intense. Big communal kitchens, so many donations of things poured in, it was difficult to manage.

It attracted celebrities, activists of all stripes, hippies, environmentalists, Rainbow Family, even a big Burning Man contingent.

Elliot attended meetings, argued, debated strategy, and shared with others an overwhelming commitment to protect the water. *Mní Wičóni* were the Lakota words everyone knew meant "Water is Life." He made friends and met people he would've never encountered in his rez life. He fell in love with a Pueblo woman named Tara. They moved into a donated yurt when it became too cold for the tipi. Camp life was tough, especially after the porta-potties froze. North Dakota winters were brutal. This was one of the worst winters, with intense blizzards. The protests continued.

The camp was on land owned by the Army Corps of Engineers, who, after political pressure to shut down the camp, demanded they all vacate. By mid-winter, the camp was full of abandoned tents, many truckloads of valuable donations, of food, medical supplies, clothes, diapers, camping gear, and generators. The nearby reservations, the poorest in the country, could've used the donations. Protesters were prohibited from removing donations and cleaning up the site. Not only were the donations wasted, but they also bulldozed over items, which would eventually pollute the river they were trying to protect.

By February, DAPL had won, and the protesters had gone. The pipeline went through. Although the protesters lost that battle, they had planted seeds for a strong Indigenous environmental movement. Whenever a company wanted to put in a pipeline, it would have to consider the possibility of another Standing Rock protest.

Elliot thought with better lawyers, the Standing Rock Tribe could've won the fight against DAPL. The way they treated peaceful protesters offended his sense of justice. He decided he'd protect the land and water through the law. Elliot finished his undergraduate degree at Sinte Gleska University early by taking as many credits as he could, then went to law school at the University of Oregon because of its environmental law program. He and Tara never made the post-camp life transition together. Elliot wondered if he'd ever again experience such an intense and beautiful relationship.

After he graduated and passed the bar, he returned home. Elliot had been awarded multiple scholarships, one of which covered his living expenses. He knew he was better off than his law school friends, who graduated with student loan debt. This gave him time to find his ideal job.

No matter where Elliot looked, he couldn't find any jobs in environmental law. For a summer, he worked in Washington, DC, at a law firm specializing in Tribal Law, but he hated living in DC. The city where he attended law school, Eugene, Oregon, was small, outdoorsy, close to both mountains and the ocean. Although he loved living there, he had to go back to his people.

With no other options, he took a job at the Tribal Law Center in Fort Thompson. It was mostly defense work, a little family law, not anything he'd planned to do. He figured he'd do it until he found something in environmental law. Most of his clients had legal trouble because of alcohol or drugs. Usually, alcohol was involved in the assault and domestic violence cases. He also handled domestic law, simple divorce, child custody, as well as other legal issues common with people who had little money. No challenging legal problems, but it paid the rent, and he worked pro bono on environmental cases on the side. He filed injunctions based on environmental studies, slowed down mining in the southwest, and a pipeline in the Midwest. He'd kept in touch with people from Standing Rock, but he missed the intensity.

On Saturday afternoon, he felt depressed. Keeping drunks out of jail and living with his cousin and his dorky friend wasn't how he imagined his life. After he cleaned up the house, he couldn't gather the energy to go out, so he ate food from the fridge before it went bad, got a little legal work done before the battery in his laptop died.

Towards evening, Scott and Theo came rushing in. "Why aren't you answering your phone? Everyone's looking for you. Auntie Mary called Mom, and I had to get a ride to come get you."

"Why, what's going on? Is this about the power outage?"

"Don't you know what is happening? We got sent back in time; it is 1791."

Elliot knew they both indulged in drugs beside weed, but this time, they didn't act high. They told him the whole unbelievable story, saying there was a meeting at the casino at 7:00 pm and they would prove it. Elliot needed to get there.

He took a quick cold shower, braided his long hair in his customary two braids, put on cleanish jeans, a clean shirt, a sport jacket, his usual attire if he didn't have court, and drove Theo and Scott to the casino. He plugged his phone into the charger in the car, wondering why he hadn't thought of that earlier. Many text messages flooded in, including several from Mary Landrau. She was not really his auntie—her husband was his dad's cousin, but she was an auntie in the rez way. She requested him to bring his laptop and any materials he had about old treaties and to hurry, for he was the only Indian lawyer they had.

=..=

They got to Omímeya right before the meeting. Auntie Mary cornered him. Elliot apologized and said his phone was dead.

She hugged him hard, saying, "At least you are here, many are not," a little teary-eyed.

She seated him in the front area reserved for Council Members with other people whom he didn't know. The meeting was fascinating. He couldn't believe they'd created an entire country while he'd been home cleaning up beer bottles. Afterwards, he told Theo and Scott to find another ride; he was staying there to work. Mary introduced him to David Cornell. They joined a few others in the law working group, which was not an official committee yet. After many hours of discussion, arguments, and doing legal research, they'd made progress. Finally, they established rules for defining a committee, the authority of the Executive Committee, the role of its chair, and the powers of the Court of Justice. They discussed and disputed franchise and elections. They reviewed the Tribal Constitutions, the United States Constitution and Bill of Rights, as well as the United Nations Universal Declaration of Human Rights and wrote the "Four Freedoms and Four Responsibilities." It was to be announced to the public on the radio tomorrow.

They planned a series of meetings all around the area over the next two weeks to recruit citizens and get people interested in voting or being on a committee. They hoped establishing a government right away would dissuade those who wanted to go to George Washington, and allow people to move on to the business of survival without the distraction of politics.

The Changleska Coalition government was more closely based on a Tribal government model, rather than the United States Government. It would consist of seven members of the Executive Council, representing the various areas of expertise. The Chair had no more power than facilitating meetings and sending out the agenda unless it were an emergency, with all seven members unavailable to vote. Once elected, members would serve full time for seven years, and be reasonably but not extravagantly compensated for their time. The council had the authority to remove members from their positions for a range of reasons, including corruption, using the list of violations derived directly from the Lower Brule and Crow Creek Tribal guidelines.

The Executive Council votes would be by majority rule. They would vote on committee proposals, actions, or changes in law or policy. The Council wouldn't create laws, only approve or deny ones proposed by committees. If they denied a proposal, the Council would be required to provide transparent reasons, unless it endangered national security. Committees might resubmit but must wait one year. Committees would comprise up to eighteen members, including a Chair, Secretary, and a Treasurer. It was the Chair's responsibility to direct the committee's agenda and to present proposals to the Council for voting. The Secretary would handle the minutes, including any relevant documentation. The Treasurer would present a resource budget on proposals, including funds, materials, and personnel.

Citizens would have the right to pass a referendum to bring any issue before the Council, bypassing committees, if it passed by over two-thirds of eligible voters.

They wrote the Covenant, the oath citizens would swear to protect the earth. In addition, they wrote an entire constitution which included governance, citizenship, and rights and responsibilities.

To become a citizen, be eligible to vote, serve as a Council, Committee, or Court member, and receive all the protection and services of citizenship, a person must:

1. Be eighteen years of age or older and either brought by Big Thunder within the thirty-mile Circle or be born to someone who was, regardless of their original tribe, country, or county of birth. Dual citizenship is allowed. If not brought by Big Thunder, the person must have lived within the Changleska Coalition borders or a related community for two years.
2. Swear a sacred oath of the Covenant of the Earth before witnesses, of which one must be a citizen, and be duly recorded in the legal record.
3. Agree to support and defend the four freedoms and accept the four responsibilities freely, without reservations or purposes of evasion.

Oath of the Covenant of the Earth

"I solemnly vow, by all that I hold sacred, to safeguard the Earth and its interconnected bio-systems, including its waters, plants, and animals, from pollution, contamination, and exploitation. I pledge to preserve them in a state of health and wholeness for the benefit of future generations."

Four Freedoms *Every citizen has the freedom and right:*

1. To be free from slavery, torture, or rape. This includes the right to be free of discrimination based on race or ethnicity, religion, gender, sexual orientation, or political affiliation. Citizens have the right to justice, not to be subject to incarceration, cruel or unusual punishment, or death without the judgment of a court of law. Every citizen has the right to basic health care.

2. To worship or not worship as they choose. Everyone has freedom of religion or spiritual practice if they do not coerce or compel others to follow their beliefs.
3. To express dissent: This includes freedom of speech, via written or other forms of communication, freedom to gather, to engage in peaceful protest, and freedom to exit or travel. This freedom does not include the right to foment violence, insurrection, or treason.
4. To bear arms to protect themselves, their family, and their property. This right does not apply to those convicted of a violent crime, or who pose a danger to themselves or others as determined by a court of law.

Four Responsibilities *Every citizen has the responsibility:*

1. To protect the Earth for future generations, to use resources sustainably, and to stop those who would damage the ecosystem.
2. To protect their nation. All able-bodied adults from the age of eighteen to twenty-five shall be required to serve two years of military service either in an active or a support role. Those enrolled in either an educational or apprenticeship program may defer service for up to four years.
3. To aid in the care of those who are vulnerable, such as children and elders.
4. To support the financial stability of the nation by tithing ten percent of all gross personal income. Business income is taxed at a higher rate, depending on the yearly income and number of employees.

It was a long night. What they wrote wasn't perfect. Atheists didn't want to swear by what they held sacred, but finally agreed they held their atheist beliefs sacred and accepted the vow. Everyone knew there'd be amendments and changes, but they had a workable framework, which was extraordinary in its simplicity. This had been the best night of Elliot's life.

Chapter Eleven
Jackson

JACKSON WOKE UP hung over and feeling like crap. He'd stopped drinking like this in his twenties, for this very reason. Last night, after attending the meeting and getting his staff ID, which was also his room key, he was exhausted and mentally fried. He couldn't believe the meeting rooms were still full of people working, and the lobby full of people talking. He went to his truck, grabbed a few things, including the alcohol he'd bought at the convenience store on the way. That reminded him he needed to follow up about the thugs. Something about them bothered him, and he was still too much of a cop to let it go. Too wound up to sleep and lacking the day's distractions, Jackson was left with his grief for Denise and his family. Thoughts of his whole lost world would overcome him, hence the heavy drinking, which didn't help.

Thankfully, he had his gym bag in the truck with a clean pair of underwear and socks. He needed to purchase more before they sold out completely. Jackson wondered what kind of underwear men wore in the eighteenth century, probably not his preferred boxer briefs. After he swallowed a couple of aspirins from the small first aid kit in his gym bag, took a shower, and made coffee from the little pot in the room, he expected someone wouldn't refill it after today.

He ate a few granola bars for breakfast. Jackson had received a text late last night from Kyle, "my office 7am," so he'd set his alarm. Because the resort had Wi-Fi, his phone worked, even the internal web pages. They'd assigned him a lower-end room reserved for staff. Out of curiosity, he checked what the room cost; even with the discount, it was a lot. His commute to work was great. He only had to walk seven doors down. He arrived at exactly 6:50 am Jackson and Kyle smiled at each other, recognizing the military mindset. Early was on time, on time was late.

Kyle said, "You are coming with me to Chamberlain. Are you armed?" Jackson left his weapon in the room safe, but he told Kyle he'd get it.

"Do you have your police belt, by any chance?"

"No, at home with my uniform."

"No problem."

They entered what looked like a hotel room a few doors down. He noticed a discreet biometric lock next to the standard swipe lock. They fit the hotel room out as a small armory. Kyle handed him a bulletproof vest and a heavy gun belt like a police-issue.

"Why the gear up?"

"You never know how crazy things may get today. Word is getting out, plus I want you to look intimidating," Kyle answered with a grin.

"Did you bring any long guns with you?"

"No."

Jackson thought South Dakotans were such gun nuts. Did they all drive around with long guns? Sioux Falls was like any small city. With fears of mass shooters, walking around with long guns was likely to bring police attention, although it was perfectly legal.

"Pick something out," Kyle said, pointing to a wall with weapons all neatly arranged, with ammo in drawers underneath, calibers clearly marked with white label tape.

When Jackson commented on how well stocked it was, he was told, "The fourth-floor armory is the biggest. Smaller ones are on the other floors. When we get a chance, I'll give you a full tour. The casino consortium designed Omímeya as one of their luxury bunkers, in case the shit hit the fan. They gave me an enormous budget. That's how they lured me away from my business."

Jackson picked out a Mossberg 500 shotgun. Kyle took a Remington 870 shotgun and an M4 Carbine. He also gave Jackson a Tribal TeleComm SIM card for his phone, a goTenna phone, and a Baofeng radio. Kyle described how complicated communication was. Jackson mentioned the tasers in his truck and they briefly discussed them. Kyle said Omímeya would buy them, but Jackson might consider waiting until after the price freeze ended to sell them for a higher price.

They went out to the parking lot and through the back to the charging station to get into Kyle's car. He drove a new sporty red electric BMW, which barely fit the long guns in the back.

"Love this car," he gushed, "handles ok in the snow, although when it gets bad, I take a resort 4x4."

Their appointment with Lieutenant Colonel Jonathan Gardner was at 8:00 am. It was a good thing they left early as getting around the missing offramp took effort. Thankfully, Kyle's car, paired with the newly worn down road got through it. They managed to arrive just in time, ten minutes early, and were promptly shown into the office at 8:00 am

Both raised themselves to attention. "Good morning, sir," they said in unison. They didn't salute; they were in plain clothes, not active duty, and were indoors.

"Sit," said Gardner. "Would you like coffee?"

"Yes, please." Being offered coffee was a good sign.

Kyle introduced Jackson and his background, retired at E-7 (Sergeant First Class, Explosive Ordnance Disposal) 89D.

Kyle said, "Here is the goTenna phone and routers, a flash drive with the testimony and photos from the two fishermen."

"You could've sent someone with this. Tell me why you're really here."

"Sir, we want you to join the new coalition government we are forming."

"I swore an oath to the Constitution of the United States of America."

"Sir, do you believe in slavery?" asked Jackson.

"Of course not," snapped Gardner.

Jackson said, "George Washington is a slave owner; United States law allows slavery for another seventy-four years. It allows one human being to own another, to rape, torture, and overwork them in horrible conditions and to sell their children. Is that the constitution you swore your oath to?"

Gardner didn't answer and looked uncomfortable.

"The coalition government has a constitution based on the United States which clearly outlaws slavery and other forms of discrimination, protects human rights, and has freedoms of speech, religion, rights to bear arms, like what you swore your oath to."

"Sir, I heard Folsom ordered your deployment," asked Kyle.

Gardner nodded.

"I'm not sure that was legal. There is no South Dakota. Technically, your commander-in-chief is the King of Spain, Charles IV."

Jackson wasn't sure that was true either.

Kyle inquired, "Can I ask whether Folsom requested you to prepare military plans against Omímeya?"

"You know I can't tell you," he replied, meaning "yes."

"Sir, we are not a threat to you," said Jackson. "We want you to join us. We need you. It is the outside world that is a threat."

"Explain."

Kyle articulated all the reasons he had talked to Jackson and the others about.

Kyle added, "My job at Omímeya was to prepare for all kinds of emergencies, even if they were remote, including a Russian or Chinese invasion. Water surrounds the resort on three sides, and it is easy to block the entrance. We were prepared even if bombs were dropped on us."

"You have SAMs (Surface to Air Missiles)?" asked Gardner, surprised.

"You know I can't tell you that," Kyle smirked. "We have plenty of food and water. With the geothermal plant and solar electricity, we wouldn't even skip hot showers if besieged by Washington, Napoleon or Mexico, backed by Spain."

Smooth, Jackson thought. Kyle informed him Omímeya had powerful defenses without being threatening.

Kyle smiled and said, "Thought I'd prepared for any contingency, even considered alien invasion, although I never considered time travel. We need to consider the tribes who live here. Who knows how hostile they'll be after we appear in their territory? They're fierce warriors. Don't underestimate their military skills like Custer did. Our people speak Lakota, and many other languages spoken by local tribes. Our plans include trade missions, health and education programs, and cultural exchanges. We'll protect tribal sovereignty, not break treaties and steal their land. We'll pay a fair price if they sell it and respect it if they don't."

Jackson added, "I was just hired by Omímeya to prepare for outside threats, train soldiers for expeditions or diplomatic missions. I'm not an officer. I have no background in training troops. We need officers, we need the National Guard. There's no reason to reinvent the wheel. We'd like you to serve on our Executive Council. As General Gardner, you could determine the future of our new country's military. I understand you are an engineering brigade. Ask yourself, would you rather help build a country or destroy one?"

At this, Gardner looked thoughtful.

"Sir," said Kyle, "do you believe in God?"

"I do."

"I considered myself an atheist before yesterday. I'm still not entirely convinced that it wasn't aliens, but consider this: no one died during what we call Big Thunder. The thirty miles taken back in time centered on a self-sufficient Lakota resort that was full of doctors and supplies. This occurred right after the harvest, with silos full of grain. Do you realize the boundary was just outside of the hospital and included your unit, an engineering brigade, who were all here during a training weekend? I could go on and on about the unbelievable coincidences of what and who came with us. Many believe a divine force brought us to save the planet from destruction. Can't say I'm not becoming a believer myself."

"And one more thing," said Kyle. "I'm not sure how Folsom intends to pay you and your troops, but our new government got approved by the local banks for a substantial loan backed by Omímeya. They authorized me to pay you in cash by the end of the week. We'll also pay deployment rates to those who can be released from their jobs."

Gardner said, "You give me something to think about," an obvious dismissal. "However, if I accepted, I wouldn't want to be on the Executive Council. I believe in the separation of civilian and military command."

Kyle said as they rose to leave, "Please let us know as soon as possible. There are time-critical issues."

Jackson ended with, "There is room at our table should you care to join us."

=..=

As they drove away, Jackson and Kyle discussed whether Gardner would come aboard. His last comment about separating civilian and military was a good sign. Kyle asked Jackson what he said as they left, the same thing at the meeting yesterday. Jackson explained it was a quote from a book, The *Fifth Sacred Thing* by Starhawk. They briefly discussed the book, which explored how nonviolence can be used in response to a violent threat.

As they drove past a department store, Jackson asked if they could stop to purchase clothing. As they drove up, the parking lot had already filled up, and a line was already forming for the 10:00 am opening.

Seeing Jackson's evident disappointment, Kyle dialed his goTenna phone and said to whoever answered, "We need clothes for someone displaced. Get winter boots and a coat, if possible." Handing Jackson the phone, he said, "Here, tell her your sizes." It surprised Jackson to be asked about his preferences as well as sizes.

After Jackson hung up, he asked, "Who was that?"

"Can't remember her name, one of Doris's relatives. We hired a bunch to do shopping runs yesterday and today. They are working in pairs with at least one of them armed. I had lists prepared in the emergency planning folder."

"I want to see these lists."

"No problem. I'll get you set up as soon as possible."

"What contingency plan did this fall under, alien invasion?" asked Jackson.

"Close," grinned Kyle, "Infrastructure collapse with supply chain disruptions due to unknown cause."

Kyle announced, "This next stop I couldn't delegate," and pulled into an apparently closed RV and trailer dealership. As they drove around, they noticed someone armed sitting in a truck.

"Wait here for a sec, not ready for you to look intimidating. Don't want anyone shot, especially me."

The man got out of his truck with a shotgun at his side at Kyle's approach, eyeing Jackson in the car suspiciously. Kyle raised his hands and started talking. The man's posture relaxed, and he returned to his truck and grabbed a two-way walkie-talkie, the Family Radio Service (FRS) type commonly used. They were inexpensive, short range, but unlike the portable ham radios, didn't require a license or training and used a common frequency.

They headed towards an office in a mobile home nearby. After shaking Kyle's and Jackson's hands, he introduced himself as Reggie Boyd and said his father was on his way. Reggie animatedly told them stories about the road being cut off, with rumors and wild conjecture, including one from someone who swore they saw a spaceship. Winding down his voluble babble, he asked if they'd heard anything new.

Kyle said, "I know exactly what is going on. If we make a deal, I will tell you both everything, even with proof, but I don't want to tell the story twice."

Reggie looked fit to burst with curiosity. Soon his father, Steve Boyd, came in. Kyle explained he was a FEMA official from Omímeya, and he wanted to buy a lot of trailers.

"How many?"

"All that are in good or easily repairable shape. If they can be easily towed, the RVs may have mechanical problems." They both stared at him.

"For God's sake, why?"

"You heard about the roads being cut and people being displaced far from home?"

"Not sure I believe all that crazy talk, end of the world, aliens, the rapture. Things may go back to normal tomorrow."

"If that happens, you will've gotten a hell of a deal."

Reggie piped up, "We're not taking promissory notes from FEMA."

The number of people who didn't trust FEMA surprised Jackson. Right after Katrina, it was understandable, but FEMA had been doing good work since.

"Cash or gold only, no credit, and no banks. I may want to hang on to those RVs. Prices are bound to go up," said Steve.

"I understand, but if things go back tomorrow like you said, you'll miss out. Did you hear about prices being frozen? Not sure how long that will go on for."

Steve nodded and asked, "Do you want the utility and horse trailers as well, or only the ones people can live in?"

"Depends on the deal we work out, but all of them most likely."

"Don't have a full inventory list printed out. It's on my computer, but there's no power at the office."

Kyle considered and asked, "Any of these RVs have a generator we could bring your computer and printer to?"

"Good idea."

Steve directed Reggie to move the desktop computer and printer to a specific fifth wheel while they continued to talk.

"How are you planning to pay? It'll cost a small fortune."

"The problem with cash is there's a shortage of dollar bills. The banks will open on Tuesday. They'll be limiting withdrawals of bills and encouraging people to use checks."

Before Steve could open his mouth to refuse checks, Kyle said, "If you could tell me who you bank with, I could get him on the phone. He can assure you that we have funds that can be electronically transferred tomorrow. We could pay ten percent down cash today to seal the deal."

"You have that much cash with you? Aren't you worried about getting robbed?"

"Have that much cash, but not worried. That's what he's for," he said, pointing at Jackson. "He was a cop. Makes me feel safe."

Steve asked skeptically, "How can you call my banker? Phones are down, and it's Sunday."

Kyle pulled out his goTenna. "Special phone, what bank?" he asked before dialing the home number of the banker.

After Steve talked to his banker, he received an assurance they'd transfer the funds tomorrow.

"What kind of bulk discount will you give me?" asked Kyle.

"You mean what kind of premium am I going to charge for allowing you to buy all my stock, risking my future profits?"

And off they went, settling for something bound to make Steve happy, which was Kyle's intention. There was no need for resentment. Steve would regret the sale soon enough. To sweeten the deal, Kyle offered additional funds for delivery, as well as gasoline from Omímeya's tanks. Radio announcements about gas restrictions had been running hourly.

Reggie returned with the printouts. Steve and Kyle went over the inventory sheets with a calculator, adding up the eye-watering sum. They decided which RVs would be delivered and which Omímeya would pick up. Utility and horse trailers last. With a handshake, a bag of cash, and a handwritten bill of sale, they promised the titles when the bank transferred the funds.

They were about to leave when Reggie said, "You promised to tell us what was going on." Kyle did so with photos.

Steve said with rancor, "Now I know why you wanted them all. Had I known this, I would've hung on to them. These may be the last RVs in the world."

Kyle pointed out that most of the RVs would go to house displaced doctors and their families. Adding, "We need more if you hear of any. We'll pay a good price. The trailers will haul medical supplies." Steve and Reggie nodded with acceptance.

"You did a good thing here. I won't forget it. If you ever need a favor, I will owe you one. You know where to find me."

Then he handed them a handful of low-denomination poker chips and said, "These are good all over the resort, including for meals and hot showers at the gym. I'm not sure if the pool or spa is open, but the shops will open soon."

Reggie looked excited. "I have never been there; heard it was nice."

Having some free time after they drove away, Jackson and Kyle spotted an open diner with a sign on the door, "Cash only, no coffee refills." The place was packed, but they managed to find a seat as someone left. They could see that in the kitchen, stoves were running on propane and they could hear a generator running.

"Don't have everything on the menu," the harried waitress said, cleaning the table from the last people as soon as they sat down. Both men ordered eggs, bacon, and pancakes.

"I usually eat healthier than this," said Kyle. "I'm not sure how long this'll last, so I'm going to indulge while I can."

"I eat like this all the time," Jackson retorted.

They could hear conversations around them, opinions about what was going on, a few fairly accurate, most wild. The spaceship story was still making the rounds.

=..=

They arrived at the radio station with time to spare. Kyle told him to grab the shotgun as soon as the broadcast started, wait by the front door, and look menacing.

"You expect trouble?"

"I suspect as soon as Folsom hears me on the radio, he'll send someone over to shut down the station. We're unlikely to see violence, just intimidation."

"If he can't stop you from broadcasting, will he go to the other station and make his own announcement?"

"That would be pretty difficult," Kyle said with a grin. "That station's generator is going to go out right about now. It'll take them a while to fix it, especially if they don't have the part."

Jackson couldn't help but appreciate this maneuver, although the cop in him frowned upon vandalism. He came in to meet the radio host, William Andrews, then went to the front to wait. Kyle intended to broadcast a prepared statement, then answer William's questions he thought listeners would want to hear. The program couldn't have a call-in segment, since most people's phones didn't work. Jake and Brent were scheduled for an interview afterwards. They were becoming local celebrities. Kyle had brought a flash drive with the tapes from last night's meeting. William would play the different speakers over the next couple of hours, with judicious editing. They hoped, now that the cat was out of the bag, the gag order would be lifted, and Folsom would receive an invitation for an interview on air instead of a scheduled announcement. This station was a National Public Radio (NPR) affiliate with a liberal host. Kyle guessed he wouldn't go easy on Folsom. The other station featured Christian right-wing talk with country music.

They couldn't keep the other station off the air for long. It would be Folsom's platform. Folsom had the right to free speech, the same as anyone, even though Kyle may not agree with his positions. He wanted Folsom to end his charade as governor and refrain from trying to command the military or convince Washington to launch an assault on Omímeya. After Kyle finished speaking, his plan was to take the announcement, interview, and remaining tapes to the other station. Additionally, he wanted to bring a part for their generator, which he heard they needed.

During the taping, Jackson waited out front, unable to hear what was said on the air. It hadn't occurred to either of them to bring a portable radio. Not that it mattered. It was a repeat of last night's meeting. Kyle didn't mention Folsom by name but stated that South Dakota as a state didn't exist, there was currently no state or federal government, and a new coalition government was being formed, which would include state and county officials. Kyle was clear that although the entire Circle was on Lakota land, the coalition government would respect and protect private property and would negotiate a fair price with the Indigenous tribes to prevent conflict.

About ten minutes into Kyle's broadcast, two state troopers pulled up, got out of the car with long guns, and came towards Jackson, guarding the front door with the shotgun at his side. He recognized both troopers from the training the day before. One local, and one from Rapid City, who wore body armor instead of a uniform.

"Hey guys, what's going on?" Jackson said in a cheerful tone, trying to not look intimidating.

The local said antagonistically, "The governor ordered us to stop the broadcast."

"Now that's funny! We don't have a governor. There's no South Dakota, I'm sure you heard."

"Who is in charge is up for debate, but until that's decided, we'll follow the governor. He ordered the broadcast to be shut down, and we're here to enforce that order."

"Do you have a warrant or a court order?" The troopers looked embarrassed.

"No time for that. This is a state of emergency."

"Do you know who declared that emergency? I was there while county officials were looking for their asses with both hands. Kyle Ward stepped in; he's the man you are trying to shut down. He's the highest-ranking FEMA official here. That's the Federal Emergency Management Agency, and federal outranks state in emergency situations. It's his job to inform the public. Folsom wants to keep everyone in the dark so he and his cronies can buy all the supplies before anyone else. Besides, Kyle will be off the air soon. Broadcasts are important for public order and safety. Folsom has no right, legally or otherwise, to shut down the radios. The Constitution guarantees free speech."

Jackson knew guys like these. The Constitution was their bible. He hoped they didn't know that the government could waive constitutional rights under martial law and states of emergency. Like most people, they weren't aware, and everyone relaxed. They asked for confirmation about the rumors they were in 1791. They'd seen the photos from the helicopter and the police plane and had heard rumors about the fishermen. Jackson promised when Kyle was done, he'd show them the photos.

Jackson mentioned that Omímeya had given him a job with a good salary, and he was confident they were still hiring. The cop from Rapid City looked interested.

Soon, Kyle came out and showed the photos. Before the troopers left, Kyle assured them there were good-paying jobs for cops, or anyone with recent military experience, and they left.

=..=

Jackson and Kyle could hear yelling as they approached the meeting in the County Courthouse. Everyone glared at them as they stood in the doorway.

"Problem?" asked Kyle mildly.

Folsom exploded, "Why were you on the radio? It's the governor's job. What's all this crap about a new government? We already have one."

"I didn't get a copy of your announcement before I left. Last night, with rumors flying, there was impending chaos that could risk lives. I was doing my duty as a FEMA official."

"How can you represent yourself as a FEMA official if the government doesn't exist?" said Folsom smugly.

"You are correct. I will no longer represent myself as FEMA, only Omímeya. We're here to invite all of you to take part in the Coalition's forming government, which will include tribal, county and state."

"Nothing wrong with the old government!"

"Except it doesn't exist in the here and now."

"We can make one here just like the old one. I heard what you said on the radio about this new Coalition government. Sounds crazy. We should contact George Washington, as he'd be thrilled to see the weapons and everything we bring from the future. It'd make the USA the greatest country in the world that much sooner."

Jackson spoke up, saying, "Sir, are you in favor of slavery?" He was sure Folsom hesitated.

"No, but what does that have to do with anything?"

Jackson couldn't believe he was that clueless but restated what he said to Colonel Gardner about George Washington and slavery. Afterwards, everyone in the room was uncomfortable. Jackson was enjoying this. He had wondered why Kyle asked him to accompany him, since there were other guys if he needed muscle. Now he got it.

Kyle was showing his irritation. "Contacting Washington would leave us defenseless when everything we brought with us runs out." He reiterated the same risks he'd discussed earlier with Colonel Gardner. "We must create and build something new. We won't survive otherwise. I don't think you understand the risks."

"Don't talk to me like that. I understand more than you think. I understand how government works."

"It's not just the outside world that poses risks. Consider the risks from the Lakota that live here. We invaded their territory. We're on their land."

Folsom responded with a sneer. "The Indians around here don't have guns. We don't even need our military. Just send a bunch of hunters out. A lot of these guys have AK47s; they'd pacify the entire state in weeks."

Jackson felt he had to respond, although he was trying to deescalate. "Sir, I did three tours in Iraq. I know what I'm talking about. We lost the wars in Vietnam, Afghanistan, and Iraq. Americans, despite our billions in military technology and countless lives, don't like to admit that we lost, but we did. We lost because we didn't learn a basic lesson of warfare. Do not fight Indigenous people fighting for their own homes. They know the land, the people, and the culture. Military might is simply not enough."

Kyle added, "Not only could we lose, but chances are we would. Soon, our bullets will be gone. They have patience. We don't have time."

Jackson stepped in with a calm voice. "If you don't want to join us, no problem. The county governments can be sovereign like tribes. Lower Brule and Crow Creek are keeping their tribal identity and government for now. They'll be allies and favored trade partners."

Ed Robinson looked interested. "What'd that involve?"

"Shared defense, resources. Formal rules are being worked on, and you could be a part of that process. There are advantages to being one entity, but we understand if you're not ready. We'll invite the Indigenous tribes to become allies as well. For a formal treaty for shared defense and favored trade, we'll need concessions such as no slavery and not polluting the Earth. The idea is the Coalition is a circle, when others join it becomes stronger like a chain."

Robinson asked, "If the county becomes independent, we could hold elections, and be responsible for our own taxes and services?"

"Yes," said Kyle with a look to Folsom, "You could elect him governor or even president for all we care. We'd need a treaty to make sure he does not endanger us all by selling us out to Washington."

"You're the one who will endanger people. We can make this country great again, with true Christian values. We can ban abortion to start. This constitution you are proposing says you will protect gay people. The Bible says that is a sin. I would never support that."

Kyle asked harshly, "Do you believe we should kill gay people?"

"No, I never said that. I just don't think we should protect them under the constitution."

"Mr. Folsom, in 1791, being a homosexual is a capital offense. Those caught are hung by the neck until dead. Men and women. Not uncommonly either, you can look it up."

Folsom didn't respond, but Jackson wondered whether he thought it was a good idea to execute gays. Jackson gave Kyle a look. He got it. He needed to make nice. Antagonizing Folsom would only make things worse.

Kyle said to Folsom, "William Andrews asked specifically to interview you." Folsom looked mollified.

"We have created a new government called the Changleska Coalition," Jackson added. "We would like you to be a part of it. You have valuable experience. We have nominated an Acting Executive Council. The elections will determine permanent positions in two weeks. You could run for a seat on the Executive Council if you want an active role in the new government."

"Don't know why we would want to join. We have the National Guard and the state police. I'm not sure what an Indian casino can offer."

Kyle replied, "Resources. With the substantial loan we received, we can pay people immediately. We have 153 doctors, we're restarting the internet, prioritizing making medicines, and recreating technology. We need everyone."

Ed Robinson attempted to placate everyone, saying there was much to think about. They wrapped up the meeting. Afterwards, Jackson asked Kenneth Harris, the Brule County Sheriff, for a few minutes of his time. Jackson told him about the thugs he encountered yesterday at the convenience store and showed him the photos.

"Yep, know these three," answered Harris. "The Native is Anthony Maka, called Squirrel. This guy is Gabriel Lopez," pointing to the last photo, "and this one we don't have his legal name, but he's called Caballo. We believe he is the leader."

"Caballo, doesn't that mean horse in Spanish?"

"Yes, supposedly he has a body part built like a horse." They both smiled.

Harris added, "They're cartel, a real problem, holed up in the boonies on tribal land. They deal fentanyl and operate a big meth lab."

Jackson wasn't surprised about the drugs, but he was surprised to learn that Mexican cartels operated in South Dakota.

"Was there a plan to address the issue?"

"The Feds were investigating, but they can't do anything unless there's a murder. Plenty of people disappear, but without bodies," he shrugged. "As for drugs, tribal police say they don't have enough evidence to get a tribal judge to issue a warrant. The whole thing stinks." He made a gesture that cops make which shows a payoff was involved.

Jackson shared with Kyle what Harris had said during the drive home. Kyle admitted that the rez had drug problems, which seemed worse because they were concentrated among a small population. He suggested Jackson speak to Phil Gallo, the casino manager; he knew the rez underbelly. Kyle reminded Jackson they didn't hire him as a cop, and soon drug problems would go away because, without access to chemicals, the drug labs would disappear. Kyle encouraged Jackson to let it go and focus on the big picture. Jackson could see his point, but he knew the destructiveness of meth and was not sure if he could let it go.

Chapter Twelve

Rose

LUKE SURPRISED ROSE by being up when she got downstairs. He was eating dry cereal. She had more compassion for him, this morning. "We can get breakfast at the Red Oak," she suggested.

"Way cool."

"I must warn you," she continued, "I told Neal to cut way back on the buffet. We need to conserve food."

"But it is Sunday," he protested.

"I know, but we are going to have to change our eating habits. We won't starve, but we will eat a lot of corn and buffalo."

"For breakfast?"

"Not today, but be prepared."

"But I love the chocolate chip waffles. Hey, you are the boss now. Can't you order some for me?" Wheedling again.

"No, ask me to make exceptions for you and you'll find out how much trouble you are still in, buddy."

She returned upstairs. Since the hot water tank was electric, and not wanting a cold shower, she decided to shower at the gym at work. As she looked in her closet, she left the hated pants and picked up a corduroy calf-length brown skirt, a turtleneck, and a suit jacket. All her jackets had the custom pockets for her devices, so she was stuck with them for now. Instead of her normal high heels, she wore her worn, but well-loved, mid-calf Frye boots.

She knocked on Kimi's door, and like a mom, came in without waiting for an answer, "Kimi, honey, do you want to come to work with me, use the shower, have breakfast? We can find things for you to do."

She received no response from Kimi. She was sitting on the window seat, looking out the window. Rose repeated herself, was ignored again. Finally, she got it and repeated herself, using Kimímela and speaking Lakota.

Kimi answered in Lakota, "No thank you, we're going to Kaka's and having a ceremony for Unci and Mina."

Rose nodded. She asked in her halting Lakota, "Sure, but I wanted to talk to you about yesterday. You told me about the thunder hours before it happened. How did you know? How could you possibly have known something like that?"

"I'm not sure how I know these things," Kimi said with a desolate look. "I get these feelings, but they're true. I can feel it in my bones."

"This must be frightening; it's scary for me. Mostly because I don't understand. Can you tell me anything more about how you felt and what you experienced?"

"Wakíŋyaŋ shares with me, not words, only feelings. I know there's danger coming, death. At first, the threats are within the Circle, later from without. But Wakíŋyaŋ tells me a gift is coming for me."

"A gift?"

"I'm not sure," she said, her voice filled with uncertainty. "All I know is this gift holds the power to not only help and comfort me but guide me towards finding the teachers I need."

"Well, that is something, at least. I don't understand any of this, but I love you very much, and please talk to me and I'll try to help." Rose gave her a hug, then left.

As she thought about the whole interaction, Rose felt uncomfortable around the unseen. Hotah's family had strong spiritual beliefs that guided their lives. Even after fourteen years, she was still not a believer.

When Rose and Hotah first got together, the depth of his beliefs surprised her, particularly around things she dismissed as superstition. Rose, raised by her white mother and with little exposure to her Lakota father, felt disconnected from her cultural heritage. One example of their cultural differences was Hotah's strong belief in not allowing her to cook food while menstruating. Rose, influenced by her white feminist upbringing, found this restriction demeaning, as it implied she was unclean. However, Hotah's female relatives explained that her ability to give birth symbolized a woman's power, and that honoring this time of month by taking care of herself and reflecting made her more capable of nurturing others.

Separating from men, their food, medicine, and weapons during this time was a sign of respect for this power. Hotah genuinely believed he'd become sick if she cooked for him while on her moon; he also slept on the couch during those times. While Rose respected Hotah's beliefs, she couldn't help but find the entire prohibition somewhat absurd. Now suddenly her daughter was speaking to thunder beings. She had the proof; they'd been hurled back in time. Rose's worldview had shattered. Overwhelmed, she no longer knew what to believe. When faced with difficult emotional or mental problems, she resorted to her lifelong habit of compartmentalizing them in her mind and focusing on practical matters. She got her clothes, shower things, and Luke, and drove to work.

After arriving at Omímeya, Rose was appalled as they walked through the lodge lobby. It was just after 7:00 am and the place was a wreck with overflowing recycling bins, dirt ground in the rugs, and paper cups strewn everywhere. Many people were here last night, but the crowds were bigger for concerts, and still the staff cleaned up everything by morning. Rose wondered how many janitorial crew members were left behind the Circle. The housecleaning crew would need to help, and they wouldn't be happy. Janitorial were mostly men, housecleaning, women, and the two crews were territorial over turf. Rose didn't care if it was the zombie apocalypse; Omímeya had standards to maintain. This was unacceptable. With a high staff to guest ratio, they emphasized excellence and impeccable attention to detail. The night manager, Ron Stayton, was still on duty at the front desk. Rose strode over.

Before Rose said a word, Ron said, "I know, I know. There were three no-shows last night. One texted, asked for bereavement leave, what could I do?"

"Get the front desk to help. Empty trash yourself, if that's what it takes." He gave her a look of disbelief.

"How many guests are checking in and out? You need to step up or find another job. Looks like janitorial has openings," Rose added harshly.

"Wow, Mom, you sure told him," said Luke when they walked away.

As they approached the restaurant buffet, the hostess recognized Rose and tried to wave them through instead of swiping her ID.

"Don't let anyone pass without paying," Rose said. "We need to track all the food carefully. If there is a mismatch between food served and food paid for, someone may lose their job."

The hostess looked alarmed; she probably had waved a few people through.

Rose *thought I was being too mean*, as Luke gave her a funny look.

She had to admit the buffet looked great, although not as lavish as usual. The first was pots of oatmeal and cornmeal mush, not usually served. There was no omelet station. The only eggs had been scrambled with potatoes, onions, and peppers. A good way to stretch eggs, she presumed and had that instead of her usual breakfast burrito. She heard a server tell Luke to take only two pieces of bacon or sausage, please. They had pancakes and waffles, although not the chocolate chip ones Luke favored. Plenty of fruit, she assumed it would go bad otherwise. She texted Neil and complimented his staff on doing a good job. No one did well if criticized all the time.

She wanted to spend time with Luke and sat down with him instead of grabbing something to go. He'd taken an enormous plate of food. She reminded him not to waste it and realized between his eating and monosyllabic answers to her questions, they wouldn't have a conversation. She needed to get to work.

Rose told Luke, "You are going to janitorial to help with recycling."

"No way, Mom, you said I could work IT."

"You don't have a choice; you need to show some responsibility. Find me at noon. I'll give you a chip for lunch and I'll give you another for dinner."

His eyes lit up. "How big of a chip?"

"Ten dollars for every four-hour shift." He glared at her.

"That is less than two dollars an hour. Isn't that a violation of child labor laws?"

"There are no child labor laws. This is the eighteenth century, remember? Besides, it is two fifty an hour," she relented. "Think of it as an apprenticeship. You can try out various departments, find something you like and then get regular pay until school starts."

"I want to work IT."

Rose thought about it and realized she wanted him away from screens.

"We'll see," she said, the response of all parents who may or may not relent.

"How can I find you if I don't have a phone?"

He had a point. She could be anywhere within the resort. She pulled his phone out of her bag, handed it to him and demanded, "Unlock it." He paled.

Rose knew good parents monitored their children's devices. She knew she was negligent and didn't. However, she had no desire to see what a teenage boy had on his devices.

"I won't read any texts, but if you want your phone, unlock it."

He entered his thumbprint and handed it back apprehensively. She swiped on his apps, and uninstalled every game on it, then handed it back.

He looked at her in horror. "There's no more Google Play Store. How can I get games?"

"You won't, at least for a while. Maybe you'll learn something instead of wasting time."

He glared at her and kept eatin. She instructed him to go to the front desk after he finished. She left, asking Ron to find someone to supervise Luke, and went upstairs.

=..=

After getting to her office, she saw a link to the document written last night by Mary, Elliot Gray Owl, and the legal group: *The New Constitution: The Covenant, Four Freedoms, and Four Responsibilities*. Rose was amazed at how much they'd accomplished in one night. The accompanying note stated they wanted her input before finalizing it. She opened her laptop, made minor changes, grammar and clarification edits, nothing substantive, and sent it back with her approval. Rose texted the whole law group congratulations and sent it to the Business Center to be printed up like the Declaration of Independence with signature lines at the end, including the names and titles of the authors. She added her name even though her contribution was mainly commas. For the title, she wrote Chief Executive Officer, Omímeya Resort. She ordered 100 copies on smaller, cheaper paper to distribute.

Rose wanted to check in with the various working groups before her meeting with the bankers, so she went back downstairs. Staff had been working; the lobby looked better, but she noticed something odd. There were a few people in the lobby looking more disheveled and poorly dressed than the usual guests. There were a few children, more people of color than usual in South Dakota, and even one woman wearing a hijab. Most of them were on their phones. She realized they must have been driving on I-90 when Big Thunder occurred, but why had they come here? She had heard Kyle communicate with the counties. They were supposed to send displaced people to tornado shelters, mainly churches in Chamberlain and Presho. Rose approached one family, and heard one child say he was hungry.

The mom said, "You need to wait. We will find something later." She looked stressed.

Rose went over, introduced herself, and asked, "Are you guests here?"

She didn't think so because of the child's request for food. Breakfast was included with rooms. Sunday brunch had an additional small fee, but almost everyone paid for it.

"No," the dad said, "We heard you had electricity, phones, and the internet here. We slept in the car; the church was full."

Rose doubted that. Tornado shelters held many people. She wondered why they preferred to sleep in their car. Rose told them about no outside internet, explained about the phones and job openings on the Omímeya webpage. Rose decided on the spot, and told them all children under twelve could eat free, then realized they couldn't send the kids through the buffet alone.

"I'll spot you brunch for today."

Rose walked them to the restaurant, swiped her card for the parents, and informed the hostess about the new policy. "Write it down if the kids don't have guest cards; we still need to track everything."

She realized the new policy wasn't entirely workable. She must figure out how to send the kids without their parents. Much as she may want to, they could not feed everyone, but she just signed off on a constitution that said she had a responsibility to feed children.

Rose wanted to check in with the working groups, but many people were at church. She returned to her office.

Neil stormed in about an hour later. "I hear you created a policy to feed all children under twelve for free without consulting me?"

"I did."

"You can't do that."

"I can, I am now CEO and General Manager."

Neil looked like he was trying to counter that, perhaps adding up his allies in the various departments and realizing he was falling short.

"What does Phil Gallo say about this? The casino paid for those extra food stores."

"Don't know. Don't care." Phil hadn't responded to any of her calls and texts, but she suspected he was around.

"If you offer free food for kids, you know we are going to get swamped with"—and he hesitated, Rose wondered if he was going to say those kinds of people or rez Indians, or something else offensive, but he said, "way too many people."

"I know there are going to be challenges. This is temporary. We already have free breakfasts at the schools."

"And what about the parents? Who is going to watch the kids? Do you have any idea what a mess kids make in a buffet?"

Rose sighed. "Yes, we'll need to assign staff."

"I am already understaffed. Those not lost behind the Circle are asking for bereavement leave."

"We need to hire more; hell, hire the parents as meal monitors, pay them in food."

Neil calmed down, but then Rose added fuel to the fire. "I am adding free meals for elders, anyone over sixty-five."

"We can't afford that, even with the reserves."

"I'm working on a plan."

Neil added spitefully, "When something is free, people take advantage, assume they are entitled, and only want more."

Rose had to admit he had a point. She'd seen it not only on the rez but growing up poor in Sioux Falls.

"We'll do our part in feeding elders and children, but it is the responsibility of everyone. It's five miles into town, gas is restricted, and the community centers and schools are closer."

She handed him a copy of the Constitution. "Says right here, all citizens have a responsibility to care for children and elders. We will do our part."

They wound down with other business, and he left. She wasn't sure how on board he was, but what could he do?

=..=

Rose met with the bankers at 10:00 am. Jenny had set it up in one of the nicer rooms used for corporate meetings, with drinks and snacks. Most of the bankers came. She got the impression they didn't grasp the situation and thought things would return to the way they had been. She distributed copies of the Constitution and Declaration of Independence, asking them to share, as paper and printer ink were scarce. One banker said he wasn't sure any of this was relevant since he'd heard the banks would be under county jurisdiction.

Rose explained they were now on Lakota land. They could try to hang on to the old world and be part of the county, but those who became citizens of Changleska and joined would gain the rewards. She pointed out instead of becoming nationalized as likely under control, in Changleska, the four different banks could register as new corporations, with each manager as CEO. The banks could decide whether they wanted to merge. If a bank consisted of multiple branches, the top manager would be CEO. Banks in this new world would be extremely profitable, creating wealth not only for themselves but for the new country via taxes.

Rose let them know that along with the Internet in a Box, Kyle had downloaded the entire patent office database. The banks could make loans to start businesses that would invent products made with eighteenth century tools and materials that were decades, even centuries ahead of their time. Not computers—they'd be too advanced—but better farming tools, medicines, steam engines, radio. The possibilities were endless.

Someone asked who was going to provide collateral for these loans. The new government was already in debt. Rose suggested the banks could consider a percentage of the loan applicants' business or stock if they did not have land or acceptable collateral. There was a plan to set up a stock market. It'd be up to the banks to review business plans and decide based on applicants' prior history. And yes, a few businesses would go bust, but enough would be successful.

Rose reminded the bankers that the United States had become such a force in the old world because of its wealth. It was up to them to create the

131

same in this new world. She mentioned how Europe would beat a path to their door for access to their knowledge and technology. They briefly discussed trade missions and diplomatic overtures to the outside world.

Rose deliberately didn't tell them she now believed the Creator had sent Big Thunder to protect the Earth, or how they could create a better world. She told them they'd get rich, build generational wealth, and have power beyond what they'd ever imagined. She sold them all. Rose thought, *now Changleska may have a chance. Poor countries never win.*

Chapter Thirteen
Martin

MARTIN WORTHINGTON WAS worried about his wife, Anna May. Worrying about his wife was normal for him. Martin worried about how much she spent, what she expected from him, where she was, who she was flirting with, and whether she was cheating on him. He suspected she was but was afraid of finding out—because he also worried she'd divorce him. His upbringing had instilled in him the belief that oaths were sacred. He believed 'until death do us part' meant exactly that.

In twenty-three years of marriage, he had never seen Anna May so despondent, so depressed that she wouldn't clean herself up. Normally, she took extraordinary pride in her appearance. She was always at the spa or the gym, spending money on designer clothes, expensive hairdressers, and cosmetic work she didn't need. She always looked perfect. When she gave birth, she refused to let Martin in the room until she'd fixed herself up. She insisted on C-sections as she thought childbirth was too disgusting. She wouldn't even consider breastfeeding.

He had initially thought she was depressed because both of their sons had been left outside the Circle on the day of the Big Thunder a week ago. Martin grieved for his sons deeply. Peter was nineteen, and Michael was twenty-two, both in college. He was the active parent. Anna May left it to him and the nannies. She'd serve on an organizing fundraising committee for the exclusive private schools the boys attended. Anna May didn't abuse or neglect the children. She loved them in her own way, although he wasn't sure whether the boys ever knew it.

It worried Martin that Anna May wasn't depressed because she would never see the boys, but because they were in 1791. He questioned if she mourned their sons or losing her social status, the house, cars, vacations, and the luxurious lifestyle funded by his money.

Losing all that didn't bother him; he thought living in 1791 might prove interesting. He was sixty-two years old and ready for something different.

Martin wanted to believe Anna May stayed with him for the boys, but he knew she stayed because of the ironclad prenup his dad insisted she sign, which the lawyers updated regularly.

Martin had met Anna May after her father drove down a cliff and died. He'd been the insurance investigator. There were things that didn't add up. Her father's family had been old Georgia money, but through poor investments, gambling, and expensive mistresses, wasted it all. The many financial records that Martin pored over during his investigation clearly showed that. A red flag was the big life insurance policies he took exactly one year before he died. He never carried much insurance before. There'd been no skid marks in the road before he went down the cliff, no evidence he tried to stop. He had a small amount of alcohol in his system, way below the legal limit, more like a shot for courage. Interestingly, he had a medication in his system that was used in the early stages of some types of cancer.

Martin figured out Anna May's father had killed himself to take care of his family. He felt bad for the wife and daughter, but he hated fraud. He was about to close the case and tell the family his findings when Anna May and her mother showed up at his office. Martin rarely saw the families involved in person. The investigation had been going on for months, which wasn't unusual, especially with a large payout. It took time. There could be lawyers and appeals, but this was a clear-cut case. Anna May's mother was attractive and closer to Martin's age, but Anna May was luminescent. He had never seen such a beautiful woman. Both women had a good sense of fashion but chose to keep it subtle. They wanted to discuss the case. Why was it taking so long? What was the problem? Martin was so nonplussed by Anna May that instead of telling them he was closing the case for fraud, he told them the investigation was ongoing. He'd dragged the case out as long as he reasonably could, finding reasons to have them come to the office, even visiting them at home. Did they know about the medication? Could he get permission for medical records? Why was he driving at night? Had he had his vision checked?

At the follow-up visits, Anna May would cry, and her tears made Martin feel helpless as she related her problems. Anna May and her mother had to sell the house, but it was so heavily mortgaged they'd get almost nothing.

She'd started her first year of college studying art history, but could no longer afford to continue.

Martin knew he could rule it was an accident so they would get the insurance settlement. He was well regarded at the company; they'd ask no questions. Martin struggled with the decision, but knew he had to decide against Anna May. He wouldn't compromise his strong set of ethics, not even for her.

He decided to tell her in person and visit them at home. They'd spent a lot of time together by then, discussing a wide variety of topics. The house looked empty, the furniture and family heirlooms all sold. Anna May's mother wasn't home. Although he'd called in advance, he always tried to meet the two women together. Anna May dressed provocatively and made a distinct pass at him, letting him know how important his favorable report would be. Angrily, Martin let her know the result, left the paperwork, and stormed out. Martin didn't see her for six months, but never forgot her. Like a virus, he couldn't get thoughts of Anna May out of his system.

One day, he was in a different neighborhood than usual and as he walked past a tax office, he saw Anna May in the window. He went in and talked to her. She was a receptionist, hired for tax season. Her mom had moved to Florida to live with her sister but had no room for Anna May. She had dropped out of college. She was wearing one of the same outfits she wore when he was investigating the case. It was obvious she was struggling.

Anna May was clearly not happy to see him and was done making polite conversation. Surprising himself, he asked her out. She was about to turn him down when Martin mentioned an upscale restaurant, which he remembered she said she liked. She said yes. He was happier than he could remember in a long time.

They dated for months. He always paid for nice restaurants, the theater, concerts. He didn't lavish her with expensive gifts, but now and then, he would surprise her with a gift card for a high-end boutique, and she began dressing well again. Martin knew he wasn't the only one she dated. They hadn't discussed exclusivity. Anna May was often busy on a Friday or Saturday night. Martin always acted like a gentleman; other than a kiss good night, they weren't intimate. He was raised a Methodist. Not the liberal Methodists they have now with women pastors and gay marriage, but old school: no smoking, no drinking, and no premarital sex.

He wasn't a virgin, but his few experiences had left him so unfulfilled, both emotionally and physically, that he thought he would always be a bachelor. Martin wanted to marry Anna May, but he didn't think she'd have him. He was twenty years older, and she was so gorgeous she could have any man she wanted.

When they went out, they usually went wherever she wanted. His parents were having their annual Christmas party, and she finally agreed to accompany him. When they pulled up to his parents' big Atlanta mansion, the valet parked his car, and the butler greeted them, causing her attitude to change immediately. She wanted to know why he'd not told her he came from a wealthy family. He told her the issue never came up. Martin's grandfather had invented a few medical devices in the 1940s. The family had run the small company, which made them since. His brother was supposed to have taken over the family business, but he passed away at a young age without children. His parents despaired of ever having grandchildren. At forty, it didn't seem likely he'd marry.

Martin had loved detective stories growing up, knew he wasn't cut out to be a cop, and became an insurance investigator instead. He had no interest in the family business. After his brother died, his father planned to sell it when he was ready to retire.

Anna May's availability to see Martin increased after the party. Instead of going to the opera she loved, and he hated, she took an interest in his hobbies, going with him to historical museums. She'd cook dinner for him. She even went to church with him. When it became obvious she was trying to seduce him, he explained in no uncertain terms there would be no premarital sex. They did some heavy petting, but he always stopped before it went too far. He wanted to marry her, and if so, he wanted to do it right. It took a while, but she finally agreed to marry him.

Martin would have preferred to live modestly on his salary, but she wanted more. He loved her helplessly, so to make her happy, he'd give in bit by bit. Anna May thought he could do better at his job, he could be lead investigator, head of the department, vice president. Her ambition drove his career. She'd invite company executives to their home for dinner, flirt, and charm with that thousand-watt smile, and he'd get promoted. Anna May would have lunch with the wives of company executives, gathering all the gossip. Afterwards, a scandal would lead to a colleague quitting or being fired, and suddenly, a promotion would become available.

Upon his promotion to vice president of the Midwest region, they relocated to St. Louis, where the company had its headquarters. His parents had passed by then. He inherited everything, and they lived a life that had all the affluence and social position Anna May wanted.

Martin didn't give in to all of Anna May's wishes; she had a generous allowance but couldn't exceed it. He paid and checked all the credit cards and managed all the household funds himself. For birthdays and anniversaries, he would gift her with small diamonds, a string of pearls, or antique jewelry, but drew the line at extravagance.

Over the years, they compromised, particularly regarding vacations. He took her to Paris or Fiji and she would take a riverboat cruise on the Mississippi River, or visit a historical site he wanted. She wasn't happy about the ten-day bus tour of the Lewis and Clark Expedition. The compromise was his promise to spend fourteen days in Italy at a villa she found online.

=..=

There were twenty-six people in their tour group, mostly retired Americans, a Danish couple, two Japanese couples, and four Germans. Evidently, the old west and especially Native Americans commanded an enormous interest in Germany. In addition, there was Kathy Williams, the driver and tour operator who handled the itinerary, hotels, and meals, and Michael Debray, a history professor at the University of Missouri, who guided these tours twice a year. He had written his thesis on the Lewis and Clark Expedition and had an encyclopedic knowledge of it. Martin enjoyed sitting next to him on the bus. He would pull up his laptop to show maps or journal entries to support a point he was making. Anna May stayed in her seat on her phone, playing games or on social media. She had a big Instagram following.

On day three of the tour, they stopped at Chamberlain, at the rest stop next to the Dignity of Earth and Sky statue. The tour bus had a toilet, but everyone avoided it if possible. People from the bus were exiting the restrooms when they saw the black fog, heard the incoming rumbling thunder and the intense, loud explosive noise now called Big Thunder.

No one knew what was going on. Their phones didn't work. They returned to the bus. Kathy assured the passengers everything was fine. The next stop would be the Akta Lakota Museum. As they drove to the offramp, they noticed a line of cars backed up, and soon a highway patrol officer set up flares and closed the offramp. Kathy got out of the bus, spoke to people in the cars ahead, and walked up to check it out. She came back saying the road was closed, something strange was going on, and it'd be best if they continued to Bismarck, North Dakota, the next stop. Martin was disappointed as he was looking forward to the museum. Anna May complained, not that she cared what they saw. She just didn't like it when things didn't go as planned.

Some people walked up themselves and reported back there were trees and prairie where the I-90 used to be. They'd no problems getting back on I-90 westbound, and drove until they saw a long line of stopped cars. There'd been an accident ahead. They kept seeing cars cross the median line, heading back the other way, and wondered what was going on. Kathy took another walk and came back with an implausible story about the roads being gone.

They turned back to the nearest town, Presho. The power there was out, phones down, and no one had a clue. Hotels and restaurants would only take cash. Kathy had no luck getting anyone to accept the tour company credit card. There was a mini-fridge on the bus for snacks or water, but no food. The passengers were tired, scared, and hungry. Most had little cash, as their tour fees were supposed to have covered meals and hotels, but Martin always carried a couple of hundred in cash. After the group stopped at a small grocery store, Martin noticed people returned to the bus with hardly anything, so he went back inside and returned with sandwiches and drinks, which he offered to everyone. Anna May glared at him.

The radio was making vague announcements, directing those who were displaced to shelters in churches and schools, and listed them by town. Kathy found a designated shelter, and they had been staying there ever since.

=..=

The church basement storm shelter had cots, blankets, and boxes of old canned food stocked, but they were fortunate enough not to have to use them yet. It seemed to be a holy roller or Pentecostal church of some sort, not Martin's kind of church. About another fifty displaced people joined them, and no one had any idea what was going on. Rumors were flying. The rapture and aliens were popular theories. Someone's cousin saw a spaceship in Chamberlain. Or maybe it was an uncle, but it was a relative, and they had seen it with their own eyes. Church members and other locals brought food, clothes, toiletries, and toys for the children. The next day, after services, church members hosted a big BBQ. Church members without generators brought thawed food that was still cold. Everyone ate a lot of game and beef. The church members treated the displaced people well, creating a party-like atmosphere. They brought generators, those who didn't have one brought dehydrators, pressure cookers, and canning jars. The big kitchen was full of women preserving food. The prevailing attitude was: "We are all in this together." After a few days, that changed, with people focusing more on taking care of their own families and leaving the displaced on their own with only the pastor's wife to look in on them.

They didn't hear the initial radio broadcast that announced they were now in 1791. The church radio only played the Christian station. Once they heard the situation from enough people, Anna May hysterically demanded that Martin take her home. She complained these people were all lying. Once she realized they'd lost their boys beyond the Circle, and her life as she had known it was gone, she fell into a deep depression and lay in the cot all day, not brushing her hair, barely eating, and not changing her clothes. Martin worried.

Kathy got one local to go out with his pickup and liberate solar panels from highway traffic signs. She put one on top of the bus to run the radio and the lights. She hung up a sheet across the back and made herself a sleeping space with more privacy than the cots in the basement. Those from the tour stuck together more than other displaced people. They hung out on the bus, played cards, or had endless discussions about what it all meant and what they would do.

Kathy listened to the NPR station on the radio on the bus to hear more about what was going on with Omímeya, the resort, and Changleska, the new country. Martin finally convinced Anna May to get cleaned up by complaining about how badly she smelled. She boarded the bus to get her bag from the overhead and started listening to the radio.

=..=

The NPR station had news and announcements, mostly from Changleska, occasionally from the counties. The IT team discussed restoring the internet; they called it NewNet and encouraged people to upload their caches. The Omímeya staff announced an online media library for books, music, and video. They mentioned there'd be a monthly subscription fee, but they'd waive it if people uploaded original content. They recommended people act soon before the original content ran out. For original technical materials of any kind, including print, they'd pay top dollar in cash.

A doctor discussed smallpox; other than older people, no one was vaccinated against it. It was a virus, and antibiotics wouldn't work. Warnings were issued about contact with the local Indigenous population, people should wear a mask and avoid physical contact if approached. The doctor said the twenty-first century people could decimate the local population with modern colds and flu. There were other discussions about working groups, committees, teams, expeditions, Changleska, sovereignty, allies, citizenship, and the election scheduled for next week.

The Banking Committee announced how people could make more money by starting companies to sell inventions decades or centuries ahead of time than by mining gold from the Black Hills. Gold sold for twenty dollars an ounce. Mining was cold, hard, backbreaking work in hostile territory. Instead, they could start businesses from the comforts of home. The banks offered low-interest loans, as well as schematics and plans of inventions like farming equipment or radios that would sell well.

After hearing all this, Anna May perked up for the first time in a week, cleaned herself up, and started talking to people and gathering information. The next day, there was going to be a Town Hall meeting at the high school about the upcoming election for the Executive Council. Nominations were still being accepted. Some positions were unopposed, others had multiple candidates. To be on the Executive Council, you need to be a citizen of Changleska and have professional experience in one of the seven areas. They defined professional expertise as having made a living in that field, even if retired.

The Christian radio station's daily speaker was Clyde Folsom, who stated he was the legal governor. Folsom declared God brought them back to make America great again as a Christian nation that outlawed abortion, would keep women in their place homeschooling all the children they would need to repopulate the area. He argued to nationalize Omímeya, implying an Indian casino shouldn't have control of the internet, and had resources all should share. He didn't say whether he would run as a Council member but decried the requirement of swearing an oath of covenant to protect the earth and the new constitution. Being a part of a county as an independent allied nation didn't seem to appeal to him, either. Like any politician, he talked a lot and said little.

Anna May convinced Kathy to drive the bus to the meeting, although it was a little more than a mile away, saying it was too far for the retirees to walk. Martin didn't think Anna May had walked a mile in her life except on a treadmill. She wore a nice dress, heels, fixed her hair and make-up, and looked like her old self.

=..=

The radio had announced Omímeya's IT team would be there. They came early and set up the high school with a generator and Wi-Fi, and started uploading materials from people's devices, caches, and media. People had been told to bring Kindles as well as phones and laptops. They could charge their devices, create new emails, peruse, fill out the skills survey, apply for jobs, and post on the Community Forum, even post on a version of Craigslist. The NewNet Craigslist was exactly like the old one, except it had no discussion forums. Craigslist was the only place where posts could be anonymous, because of safety issues with people selling things. Unlike the original Craigslist, it allowed the sale of firearms, which drew a lot of interest.

In one classroom, they created a Citizen Center where people would stand before a video camera and witnesses, swear their oaths, and have their details recorded in the database. Then, someone congratulated them, shook their hand, took a picture, then printed their citizenship card. Before the meeting, a few people became citizens, but after the meeting there was a long line.

Martin found the Town Hall fascinating. The first edition of a new newspaper, the Chamberlain Free Press, was passed around. It'd been the weekly Penny Saver, which was all that remained after the old town newspaper had died off. Now resurrected, it looked like any small-town paper. There were articles and photos about Big Thunder, which was old news by now. The back pages featured memorial pieces for those left outside the Circle. There were even ads from the stores that turned trading posts, with lists of what they were buying and selling.

The main part of the paper contained a copy of the new *Declaration of Independence, Covenant, Four Freedoms, and Four Responsibilities*. There was an explanation of the difference between the Changleska and Omímeya. The explanation provided a detailed account of the workings of the new government, including elections and citizenship. Biographical blurbs of the nominees for both Acting and Executive Council, allowing for the possibility of additional nominees. The newspaper had opinion pieces by locals on the pros and cons of joining Changleska or becoming an ally as an independent county. People received a reminder that county membership would be put to a vote in the future. The radio announced all this before, but people either had missed it or listened to the other station. Having everything written out made things clearer.

The meeting organizers allowed time for everyone to arrive and read the paper, then opened with a prayer from a local pastor and began. They gave public service announcements such as health warnings, but they kept them short. Although Clyde Folsom was not a declared candidate, they allowed him five minutes of opening remarks, which were slightly toned down from his radio broadcasts. Unless unopposed, the candidates could speak for ten minutes, explaining why they should be on the Executive Council.

A young Native man who was a tribal lawyer spoke eloquently about the need to protect the Earth and the water, and the privilege to be sent back with instructions on exactly how to do it.

Last, two girls came forward dressed in traditional Native style. The smallest one had a pockmarked face. With two boys with drums, also dressed similarly, who stood to their side. They sang in Lakota, then in English, 'Big thunder strengthens the Circle, and the Circle protects the Earth,' four times each. People started joining in, mostly the English part.

When the song ended, there was a moment of silence with palpable spiritual power.

The meeting ended with a reminder to sign up for citizenship so they could vote next week, and a prayer from a pastor from another local church.

=..=

Afterwards, people circled around various speakers. Anna May made a beeline for Clyde Folsom, Martin trailing in her wake.

"Governor Folsom, I'm so glad to meet you," with the dazzling smile no one could resist. "And this must be your lovely wife, Ellen? You must be so proud of Governor Folsom doing God's work during such difficult times."

Folsom looked surprised. Even though it had only been a week, you didn't see women anymore wearing nice dresses, make-up, and heels. At forty-two, she was still very attractive.

"I'm Anna May Worthington, and this is my husband, Martin. He was the Vice President of the Midwest region of National Insurance, but his family made medical supplies. We understand you were a Republican?"

"Yes, I was in the State Senate and was here visiting Ellen's family."

"Martin and I were big Republican donors, Martin was active in the local party, they even asked him to run for office, but he is too modest and wouldn't hear of it."

Martin tried not to snort; Anna May was the only one who'd asked him to run for office. She chatted charmingly, careful to include his wife in the conversation. Anna May could immediately spot the male level of interest and could turn on or off the sex appeal accordingly.

She asked Folsom, "I was wondering if you could answer some questions for me? I'm afraid we both have been too upset about the loss of our two sons to pay much attention to what's going on." She quickly wiped away slight tears without smearing her make-up.

"Yes, what can I answer for you, dear?"

"It seems to me you have much more government experience than anyone else on this Council of theirs." This got affirmative nods from both Folsom and his wife. "I am so worried about what could become of us, hostile tribes, smallpox for Heaven's sake? We need strong leadership."

Folsom replied, "I don't agree with all of their policies, rewriting the constitution, swearing an oath to protect the earth."

"There is more I don't understand. Martin usually explains these things to me, so tell me, Governor Folsom, what do you disagree with so strongly it would keep you from running for the Executive Council and keeping us all safe?" She gave him one of the looks Martin knew few men could resist. "If you were on the Council, couldn't you change any policy or law? They said it was just a start."

"Well, putting it like that, Mrs. Worthington—"

"Anna May, please."

Folsom said, glancing at his wife, "Looks like we should give it more thought, right, Mother?"

"If there is anything you need, please let us know," Anna May said, "Martin and I organized fundraisers for a number of Republican candidates. As a matter of fact, he played golf regularly with Senator Baker."

Senator Baker was a well-known conservative whom Martin played a foursome with once because he'd donated to his campaign. He barely spoke to the man.

Martin was once active in the Republican party but hated Trump. He despised men who cheated on their wives and had little patience for the rest of the circus the party had turned into. He was still a conservative and didn't vote in the last election because he didn't like the other guy either.

Anna May took Ellen Folsom's arm and walked away. Martin could hear her saying, "We must get together soon. Guess we can't go to lunch like we used to, but please convince your husband to run. We need him."

Martin walked away quickly before he had to speak to Folsom. He had heard him all week on the radio and found him loathsome.

=..=

When alone after they returned to their two cots in the church basement, Martin asked her, "What was that? How could you support that man?"

"Oh honey, don't you understand? He is dangerous. As a failed candidate, he'll have less power. If he signs the oath and stirs up too much trouble, it'll be considered treason. Didn't you read the constitution?"

Martin reached out. Anna May surprised him by laying her head on his chest. "I'm not sure if I have ever loved you more than this moment," he said.

And he stopped worrying about his wife.

Chapter Fourteen

Mary

A WEEK AFTER Big Thunder, Mary's life had changed so dramatically it was hard to imagine. She made a point of having breakfast with her family to maintain a semblance of normal life. After Bridget's husband had been left behind the Circle, Bridget moved into her childhood bedroom. Mary moved her sewing to the garage. They had converted the boys' old bedroom for the girls' occasional overnight visits years ago. Losing their father was hard enough, but moving to an unfamiliar place would've made things worse.

At least the electricity was back on. They'd never gotten rid of their DVDs after streaming started, and watching movies helped the girls. The girls were starting school in a few days, and Bridget was seeking a new job closer to home. Commuting from Chamberlain had become problematic. She was an occupational therapist at Chamberlain Hospital. Soon there'd be less need as older people and stroke victims died off.

Breakfast, with the girls occasionally squabbling, Daniel looking mournfully at his single small cup of coffee, and Bridget rushing around, provided comforting normalcy. Her family grounded her.

Mary tried not to think of her two grown sons, who had moved out-of-state years ago. She saw them and her grandkids once or twice a year, weddings and funerals mostly, not usually Thanksgiving or Christmas anymore. Being distant eased the pain. Occasionally, it would hit her. *She'd never see or hear from them again.* Not on Facebook, where she could see them on vacation or the kids in their Halloween costumes. They couldn't call or text. Her boys used to call Daniel for advice sometimes. They never wanted her advice.

The shuttle was due to arrive at 8:40 AM. Despite living seven miles away from Omímeya, she took the electric shuttle because of a shortage of gas. Not long before Big Thunder, the Lower Brule tribe bought an electric school bus, which now operated on regular runs. It was too bad there was only one. Electric car technology was beyond their ability to reproduce, in her lifetime at least. Manuel, the leader of the shuttle team, worked out every trip to maximum efficiency and tried to be judicious in their use. Omímeya had two big buses that ran on biodiesel, but they had a limited supply. The Fuel Committee was developing ethanol, which could only serve as an additive, not a standalone fuel. At least there was plenty of corn. They were looking into corn oil as fuel, as converting diesel to veggie oil was simple. Producing large quantities of corn oil was more complex than anyone realized. Fuel from hemp had the most potential, especially for gas cars, but learning how to produce it would be a challenge. Hydrogen cars were too great of a technological leap, for now, but possibly in the not-so-distant future.

What sustained, drove, and humbled Mary was what they were accomplishing—creating a new world, discarding what didn't work from the old, figuring out what might work to protect the earth for future generations.

Mary loved the passion of the people she worked with, especially the doctors. She'd never liked doctors before, not even her own or her kids' doctors, especially when her parents had serious health problems.

The doctors from the IHS, although badly overworked, weren't any better or worse than others. She'd read enough medical horror stories online to know that. Most shared an inability to listen to patients and had a superior and judgmental attitude. She was tired of hearing she needed to lose weight. Did they think she never tried? Or they told her that her blood pressure or cholesterol was creeping up. They would recommend she take this new drug, only to find out a year or two later that the drug caused some problem or another. Mary avoided doctors because of the dominance of the medical insurance industrial complex, which prioritized unnecessary tests to prevent lawsuits.

These physicians who came with them were all early risers. When she got to Omímeya, dropped off her stuff, and went to their meeting room, they'd accomplished more than any other group had by lunchtime. Many of them left family beyond the Circle. Maybe that's why they worked so hard, or more likely, they didn't graduate medical school without being driven, focused workaholics. They were smart, didn't waste time with endless debates, made plans, and carried them out. More than anything, she saw how much they cared. The doctors were upset they would soon lose people from the lack of insulin. They were worried about smallpox, typhus, and cholera. It distressed them losing all the equipment and medicines they needed to save lives, and they worked incredibly hard to figure out solutions.

While she served as Chair of the entire Council, her ministry seat was Education. One project was starting a medical school. Doctors were reviewing the curriculum, thinking of how to teach in the eighteenth century. They wouldn't see students until next year, but wanted to be ready. They had doctors and others who were experts in their field; however, knowing how to do something and knowing how to teach it were two different things. Another project involved expanding the teacher education program at the Lower Brule Community College. Running the program was Mary's job before last week, what her master's degree was in. It was hard not to spend time on this project; it was close to her heart.

Teaching the teachers was the most efficient way to spread knowledge. Each doctor could only treat so many patients, but each teacher could train many more students. They could send teachers all over, not only in medicine, but science, engineering, better farming, all the modern knowledge needed to change the world. Underlying everything would be the values of social and environmental justice.

They planned medical education to start in high schools. They discussed how they would teach health to the Indigenous population while still respecting their traditional belief system. Overhearing a conversation, Mary was amused by the discussion of how to explain to a traditional healer they shouldn't use buffalo dung on wounds. The doctors knew they needed to learn about herbs, although most didn't believe they worked. Smart, compassionate, dedicated, not an arrogant one in the bunch. Or maybe they needed to see patients to put their arrogant hat on. Being sent to 1791 with one hundred and fifty-three doctors strengthened Mary's faith in God. The week before Big Thunder, the resort hosted a conference of tax accountants.

Some physicians were moving to Chamberlain, where the hospital was. The hospital was owned by an out-of-state corporation. The chief hospital administrator, using Omímeya's example, created a new corporation, gave shares to employees based on wages, physicians and administrators getting more than the janitors. Previously, the hospital derived its income primarily from Medicare, Medicaid, and private insurance; only a small percentage was private pay. All the medical insurance companies were out-of-state, including those for the county employees. With no insurance money coming in, it was unclear at first how they'd pay employees and address the upcoming drug and supply shortages.

When the hospital realized Changleska would pay all medical bills for every citizen, they set up a Citizen Center in the waiting room. People took their oaths, presented their cards to pay. For those not wanting to be Changleska citizens, the hospital set up its own insurance; people would pay monthly, and it would cover everything except catastrophic. The monthly amount was about the same as what private insurance cost. This was all theoretical. No one was sure who would make cash money, or if the new system would be sustainable.

The doctors brought a proposal for an immediate Council vote for an Ethics Board, different from a committee, with autonomous authority. The board would comprise twelve members from different medical fields, including nurses and aides, as well as spiritual or religious leaders. No officers other than a rotating secretary responsible for documentation. Six-month terms, with every practitioner required to serve at least one term. It would take a terrible toll; the burden would be shared.

The Ethics Board would decide on who lived or who died. With such limited medical resources, an unknown timeline for replacements, all patients had to be triaged. Triage normally treated critical patients first unless they had a zero chance of survival. The Board would create new guidelines based on age, other medical conditions, and other factors instead of immediate survival. Few decisions were easier than others. With a limited supply of insulin, not giving it to an eighty-year-old with a heart condition was clear-cut, but what about a forty-year-old mentally ill alcoholic? Besides drugs, medical supplies like IVs, chemicals used for tests, gloves, needles, all finite resources for the foreseeable future. Machines like X-rays would be difficult to repair, so conserving their use was necessary.

It was difficult for any doctor to let any patient die, even knowing that decision would allow another to live. They were trained to treat the one in front of them. This was especially hard if they could easily save the patient.

The Board would issue clear guidelines everyone agreed to, which would relieve the burden of choice.

There was debate on calling it an Ethics Board, as they weren't addressing professional ethical violations. No one wanted to call it a death panel. The name Ethics Board stuck. Mary thought the Council vote would be easy. Councilors raised concerns about the proposed autonomy, saying working without Council approval was a slippery slope. The measure passed five to two. Mary saw how a little power affected the Council, who were quickly becoming politicians concerned about their own power base rather than the merits of the proposal.

Although Mary's purview was Education, as Chair, she tried to keep up with other areas. The Council only voted on issues considered immediate, not able to wait until the election, now a week away. The doctors had brought the Council the most immediate proposals that needed voting on. Now it was mostly setting up committees and confirming officers. The committees themselves were supposed to choose a Chair, Secretary, and Treasurer, and if they hadn't done so, the officer choices became a Council responsibility.

If a Committee Chair worked full-time in that capacity, they could be paid. Other officers received a small stipend, while everyone else volunteered. Lunch was provided for working groups, teams, and committees. Although people would soon tire of buffalo stew and cornbread.

At least they'd have buffalo. The Lower Brule tribe had its own buffalo herd. Before Big Thunder, the Crow Creek tribe had opened its own meat packing plant that could process one steer or a buffalo a day. Air reconnaissance showed vast buffalo herds in the area, but they hadn't yet organized a hunt, not having large enough processing abilities. This was hunting country, so there were many small shops specializing in game, but nothing on an industrial scale.

She had sat in on most of the meetings of the other groups, realizing that in nominating Council members, there were bound to be hits and misses. It was so hectic those first few days. Mary, Rose, and Kyle nominated Council members, since there were no official committees in those first few days. Since Mary had been Tribal Chair of the Lower Brule, Rose and Kyle thought it was a logical choice to nominate her Chair of the

Executive Committee. She'd facilitated the early meetings and had co-authored the Constitution and related documents.

Mary felt inadequate for the job now that she knew the extent of it. The Lower Brule tribe had about 3,500 members, of which half lived on the reservation. They had accessed federal funds and used guidelines from the Bureau of Indian Affairs (BIA) and other tribes as a roadmap. Her previous part-time job as Tribal Chair had been comparatively easy, not too different from serving on one of her church committees.

This job was so big. Theoretically, the Chair did not have more power than the other six members, but she had been in enough groups to know that was misleading. The level of responsibility was staggering. Despite her trepidation, she knew she'd feel worse if she lost the election. A new nominee stepped forward who'd run against her. Pamela Norstrom was a recently retired teacher who qualified by having professional work in education but had no other related experience. She attended the same church as Clyde Folsom, who encouraged her and several others to run.

She wouldn't mind losing if the candidate was remotely qualified, but Norstrom, while a sweet woman, honestly didn't have the intelligence for this position. At last night's town forum debate, she couldn't believe how little the woman understood the issues. The truly scary thing was there was a possibility she could win.

As much as they tried to avoid it, a red state and blue state mentality was beginning to take hold, fueled in part by racism. Big Thunder had brought around 8,000 people into the thirty-mile Circle. About 4,500 were enrolled members or residents of the Crow Creek and Lower Brule Reservations, referred to as Natives. Another 1,000 were guests or staff at Omímeya, or people just passing through when it happened. The remaining 2,500 came from nearby towns in Brule and Lyman counties, which had the largest non-Native populations.

Some people couldn't handle no longer being part of the United States. Others bristled at the idea of joining forces with the reservation Natives. That unease had always been there, simmering under the surface. Now it was out in the open. Mary had hoped the shared experience of Big Thunder might bring people together. Instead, the cracks were widening.

A merger between Brule and Lyman counties might have made sense. Creating a single nation that included everyone brought back made even more. Call it Changleska. She could see it so clearly. But she had learned not to expect logic to win out. People didn't like change, especially the kind that made them question who they really were.

Mary had lived in other parts of the country during her college years. When people asked if she was Native American, and asked what tribe, the typical response had been "That's so cool," or "I'm part Cherokee."

She could feel their sincerity. They had respect for Native people. It was different in the Dakotas. Whenever she was off the reservation, people looked down on her and treated her badly. For example, she could sit in a cafe and watch them serve everyone else before her. Some assumed all Natives were alcoholics, poor, or uneducated. It had gotten better over the years, but racist attitudes remained, especially in the rural areas.

Now both Omímeya and the reservation had electricity, phones, NewNet, doctors, jobs, and smart, educated people. Because of the gas shortage, people from outlying areas were moving closer if possible. Omímeya was becoming a capital even in such a short time. Now that things had changed, there was resentment.

Almost immediately, the Omímeya leaders saw the implications of being transported to 1791 and created a system to be better than the old one, to preserve the earth as well as protect the Indigenous people. They responded to an unfathomable situation with a flexible mindset. Not everyone could make the leap. When faced with the unknown, people tend to stick with what they know. In a crisis, they follow those who tell them what to do, since following is easier than leading.

Mary remembered what Jackson said in that first meeting: "Don't create an 'us' and 'them', have them join us." Now everyone in the northern part of the Circle, whether or not part of the reservation, had become, in common parlance, "the rez". The south was being called "the county". It wasn't exactly a red state/blue state situation because plenty of conservatives and liberals lived in both areas, but "rez versus county" was quickly becoming "us versus them."

The leaders could've said, "You all are in Lakota country now. Love it or leave it." Instead, they offered the choice to become an independent ally. They thought eventually allied groups would decide to join them, and in the meantime, no one would lose. Instead, a few people decided on taking up the offer of Changleska Citizenship and were running for Council in a simple power grab.

Mary was afraid the leaders had made a huge mistake. If people like Clyde Folsom, Pamela Norstrom, and others like them won enough seats, they could cause untold damage. Rose and her friends told her not to worry, no one would vote for them. She wasn't sure, because after all, the country elected Trump.

Those who nominated the initial slate of Council seats hoped it would become permanent. They specifically didn't nominate people Mary worked with in the tribal governments, because they wanted a coalition, not only politically, but a group diverse in philosophy, backgrounds, and ethnicity.

They nominated David Kim not only because he was the head of IT at Omímeya, but because he was Korean American. That was a blunder, not because diversity wasn't important, but they had to look at the bigger picture. They should've waited a few days and found a better candidate. Being knowledgeable wasn't enough; communication skills and working in a group were critical, and not in David's skill set. He realized it and wanted to go back to IT. Finding someone qualified in communication or IT was proving difficult. There were two choices: Duane Nelson, a retired employee from Interstate Communication and a ham radio operator, or Joseph Rivera, a web designer recently hired by Omímeya in IT, displaced when driving on I-90. Mary was unsure which of them would be a better candidate. She was determined to get to know both. Folsom promoted someone else entirely.

Mary loved working with Dr. Theresa Martinez, Minister for Medical/Science. Fortunately, no other candidates were running against her. She had been chosen because she was a professor of epidemiology at Johns Hopkins University. Mary had to have it explained. Epidemiology examines the factors that cause diseases to exist, how and why diseases occur in different groups of people. As a scientist and educator, she didn't see patients. Working in academia, she had excellent communication skills and political acumen. She would be a good Chair if Mary lost the election. Council members elected the position of Chair. If Folsom's cronies got a majority, who knew what would happen?

Folsom was teasing a run for the Defense/Law seat held by Oliver Jackson. He qualified because he worked as a state senator. His recent radio broadcasts were toning down the anti-oath rhetoric, the supposed reason he didn't run. Mary nominated Carl Plenty Crow as Minister for Agriculture. Now she knew that choice was a mistake. He was a successful local rancher growing grain, hay, and a small herd of livestock. Mary knew him socially, but had never worked with him. He was a terrible communicator, talking over others, assuming he knew everything. At an early meeting, Carl was talking about the need to recreate pesticides. He asserted it was impossible to grow food on a large scale without pesticides. Elliot Gray Owl, who had stopped by the meeting, pointed out pesticide runoff was a major source of pollution in the Missouri River. That prompted an argument. Elliot, a member of the Law Committee, asked Carl if he had already forgotten his oath to protect the water. Everyone knew Elliot returned from Standing Rock obsessed with protecting the environment. Carl ignored him and continued to talk about pesticides.

The next day, Elliot showed up to the meeting with Jerome Brown, whom everyone called Jerome the hippy. Jerome, a Rosebud tribal member, leased thousands of acres of Rosebud trust lands over on the White River. The tribe leased him the land for practically nothing because they were interested in what he was doing. He was farming using organic and regenerative methods and had a few cattle and horses. Collaborating with South Dakota State University, College of Agriculture, where he had earned a master's degree, he experimented with different crops, including industrial hemp, which drew interest nationally. Carl Plenty Crow thought degrees in agriculture weren't worth much and loved to say how much more he grew than any of the organic farms around here.

There was a farm cooperative called Dakota Lakes that taught sustainable land practices, but Carl never got along with the organizers. They worked closely with Jerome, and the people in the area highly respected them. Elliot couldn't understand Carl's antipathy.

Jerome had started a small nonprofit, funded largely by the Rosebud tribe, teaching Native youth sustainable farming practices. He was active in the Tribal Food Sovereignty movement. Mary had attended seminars in the past with him. She found him highly intelligent, well-spoken, knowledgeable in his field. She'd heard great things about the summer internships he held, wishing more of her tribe's youth would attend.

Jerome was called the hippy, in part, because he was into permaculture, which aims to develop self-sustaining ecosystems by integrating human activity with natural surroundings. Besides the youth program, he held periodic workshops on his land. Once a year, he held a big gathering called a Permaculture Convergence, a conference with speakers and people who helped with various projects like building a new greenhouse or a cob oven. He made a smart move by charging people to attend the event, which allowed him to receive payment and to benefit from a lot of free labor. Jerome minimized expenses by having everyone camp out and built composting toilets instead of renting porta-potties. He managed all this with no paid staff, only a few people who lived on the farm full-time with him and his girlfriend.

Mary had never been to White River Farm, but she'd seen slides at a seminar. They'd dug the greenhouse four feet in the ground and lined the bottom and sides with old tires, which helped conserve heat. The farm had several greenhouses and supplied greens that Omímeya bought. Some slides showed a tiny house they'd built using Hempcrete, a building material from hemp. The little round dome house inside was beautiful, fully self-contained, and highly energy efficient.

There was trash talk about Jerome on the reservation because most of his visitors were white, and a few were so-called "pretendians" who took Indian names, had dubious heritage claims, wore feathers, or engaged in other forms of cultural appropriation. What Mary found interesting was that Big Thunder occurred during the farm's annual Fall Equinox Permaculture Convergence. Eighty-five people were attending from all over the world, all committed to growing food free from chemicals and to living sustainably. Mary thought if God had wanted them to grow food with pesticides, a conference of agricultural chemists would have been meeting at Omímeya alongside the doctors. They needed more chemists, but Mary agreed with Jerome they needed to learn to grow food differently and quickly.

Jerome's people were slowly filtering into meetings, an interesting addition. They often asked people to stand up and take a deep breath if arguments were starting. They used the consensus model at their own meetings. One of them tried to convince Mary to use it instead of Robert's Rules of Order. Voting by majority rule, the woman argued, would create unhappy minorities who would leave the group. Opposing viewpoints were often useful. Mary heard from Elliot that they'd used the consensus model at Standing Rock. He liked it. He admitted it took more time, but Mary felt she was too old a dog to change her stripes. Was that how the analogy went?

Rachel Night Pipe, Mary's nominee for the Human Services seat, was another mistake. Everything had been so rushed. Mary chose someone she knew, figuring her term might only last two weeks. Mary knew Rachel well; she ran the tribal services office, helping with housing, food stamps, utility assistance, all the myriad of services needed by the reservation population. She disregarded the fact that the BIA or the federal government funded those human services. Very little funding came from the tribe. Rachel's lack of willingness to admit being lost and her inability to find solutions, coupled with her reluctance to step aside, even if they could find someone, frustrated everyone.

She stubbornly refused to grasp the new realities of their situation. A guest, obvious from his clothes, made recommendations, which she shot down. He pointed out they couldn't feed everyone; it would be hard enough to feed children and elders. Able-bodied adults should work. If they didn't, they would get hungry and find jobs. The labor shortage was becoming one of their biggest challenges—there was no shortage of work at all skill levels.

Rachel countered, some people couldn't work because of substance or mental health issues. He replied medical had enough to do, Human Services should take on treatment and counseling. She shot that down, and so it went on. Mary knew they needed a new candidate.

Rose had stopped by, listening to one of these exchanges. Mary gestured, and they stepped out of the room.

"Who's that man, the one in the red shirt?"

Rose wasn't sure, but pulled up her tablet. All guests had filled out a skills survey by this time. She could match the photo with the doctor's name she remembered.

"Shawn Caris, married to one of the doctors. It says here he was the Director of Human Services in Spokane, Washington."

"Tribal member?" Mary asked.

He didn't look it, but it wasn't always obvious. It shouldn't matter. Mary wouldn't admit it, but in her heart of hearts, she distrusted white people.

"No, his husband is Nez Perce."

"His husband?"

Rose smiled at Mary. "Yes, Spokane is not South Dakota."

People liked to say that in many tribes, gay people had once been honored as Two Spirits and welcomed. Maybe that had been true a long time ago. But not where Mary grew up. Her experience on the reservation was people discriminated against gay people. When she was growing up, a man was beaten to death for making a drunken pass at another man.

Today, people in rural South Dakota might move to a nearby city if they came out as gay, even though it was more accepted now. Other than Julian Bradley, the Guest Services Manager, Mary didn't know anyone who was openly gay. The woman who ran the herb farm was supposed to be a lesbian, but Mary had never met her.

Rose agreed with Mary they should approach Shawn Caris to see if he would run against Rachel in the election next week. They only had five days until the nominations were closed. Since no one knew him, it was a long shot.

While they were sitting on the bench in the hall, one of the cleaning staff walked by with a cart, emptying recycling bins. The woman stopped by Rose, touched her cheek, and said, "Pobrecita." Rose knew it meant "poor baby" in Spanish. "We're here for you if you need anything."

Rose was confused. This wasn't the first time this had happened. Women staffers were all making sympathetic comments to her. She knew almost everyone had lost someone. She'd lost her mother, sister, Hotah's mom, and niece, but not a spouse or child. Others had lost their whole families.

Rose asked Mary, "Do you know what that's about?"

"You don't know?"

"No, that's why I asked."

Mary laughed. "Oh honey, they may have lost their families and the world they knew, but you had your husband move his nineteen-year-old pregnant girlfriend into your house. That is a genuine tragedy."

Rose protested, "Hotah and I are getting a divorce. He didn't move her into the house but into his trailer," but Mary just laughed again.

They returned to discuss Rachel Night Pipe. Mary said, "This is going to be awkward." She'd nominated Rachel and considered her a friend.

Rose said she'd handle it. Mary smiled at her; Rose smiled back. Mary thought, *not sure why I wasted so much time disliking Rose. She's wonderful.*

PART III
Week Two & Three

Action is the foundational key to all success.
— Pablo Picasso (1881–1973), Spanish painter and sculptor.

A butterfly chasing a hawk

Chapter Fifteen

Rose

BEFORE BIG THUNDER eight days ago, Rose enjoyed driving home from work. It took less than twenty minutes, giving her a chance to unwind mentally, sometimes by listening to podcasts or Lakota language tapes. But for the last few days, she'd dreaded coming home, knowing what she'd face, not wanting to take the steps she knew she must.

Whenever she arrived, she knew the house would be a disaster. Zitkala, Hotah's sister, whose household contribution instead of rent was supposed to be cooking and cleaning, was too busy doing who knows what to clean. Her three kids were holy terrors. At least school was starting soon. She was glad she ate at work because there was never any food left for her. Luke would ask whether she brought leftovers home, complaining the other kids ate everything Zitkala made. She knew teenage boys ate a lot and brought him food home sometimes, feeling guilty whether she did or didn't. She told him he needed to work to eat but didn't enforce it.

Rose's decision to have Luke work at Omímeya was a disaster. The first day he did such a terrible job in Recycling, his supervisor had to let him go before the shift ended. That same afternoon, he used her name to cadge a free meal despite Rose's strict policy on giving away food. The days following were no better. Luke had endangered another worker when she put him in Facilities, forcing her to relent and get him in at IT, another failure. Everything seemed fine for a few days until David Kim, very embarrassed, came to her and informed her that Luke had been caught downloading porn to flash drives. They'd caught him when someone had overheard him trying to sell it.

Rose was at her wits' end. Unfortunately, Luke was not a tribal member, so she couldn't send him to a reservation boarding school. Perhaps if they had room, they would change the rules. Current boarding schools weren't the same as the historic ones. She'd heard good things about the two that arrived with them. Sometimes kids went who had troubled parents or who lived too far away to attend regular school. She knew parents who thought the structure and discipline were good for teens.

Rose wished she could get him into the cooking program that Jeffery from the Prairie Abundance Restaurant started, but they were only taking those with kitchen experience. They were training kitchen workers to become chefs. The training program was a good use of the restaurant's resources. They planned to open once a week with all student help, which would lower labor costs. No one was sure there were many job opportunities for high-end chefs, but learning was always good.

Rose felt guilty about the time she spent working, wondering if her lack of attention caused Luke's behavioral problems. She still held the game controller. With that leverage, she hoped for improvement in his behavior. She wondered why she could deal with troublesome employees but was at such a loss with her own son.

Her house was another source of anxiety. Rose used to love the old farmhouse. When Rose and Hotah first bought it, she pored over magazines, online articles, even started a Pinterest account, finding a modern farmhouse style she liked. She wanted it to be upscale and sleek while still preserving a few of its historical features. Hotah preferred something more basic. Since he was the contractor, it was a cause of friction. The marriage started its downhill slide with the remodel.

Originally, there'd been four small bedrooms upstairs and one bathroom with a tub at the end of the hall, which everyone shared. She wanted an ensuite bath, which Hotah didn't care about. He'd grown up sharing a bathroom with seven people. She won that round. He opened a wall between two bedrooms and put a bathroom with a big shower in the back of one, with two large closets on either side.

Six years later, he still hadn't finished the ensuite. The beautiful stone floor tiles she'd picked out were still in the box in the bathroom corner, sitting on top of the cheap vinyl stapled on plywood that was supposed to be temporary. On Hotah's side of the closet, the nice organizer shelf system she bought was still in the crate, under a few boxes of his stuff. After a fight, she finally got her side of the closet system installed, but not the wooden sliding closet doors. They were sitting out in the barn with all the other building materials for unfinished house projects.

Whenever Hotah got paying outside jobs, he stopped working on their house. This she had understood. He had to make money. What frustrated Rose was the house got put off because Hotah went hunting, or had to help his brother build a barn, or his nephew's roof, or another relative's something. Hotah's usual response to her complaints was to leave and not come back for a day or a week. Eventually, it became obvious that the marriage was over. They had no yelling and screaming matches, no counseling, and no actual plan, until he moved his nineteen-year-old pregnant girlfriend in.

A few days after Big Thunder, Janet asked Kimi to spend time with Gift because they were close in age, and she spoke Lakota.

The next day, Kimi informed Rose—informed—not asked, but in English, "This is Gift of Thunder. She's moving in with us."

Rose didn't want to be insensitive, but taking on a traumatized child with everything going on seemed like a bad idea. The girl would need a lot of care and attention. Rose was having enough trouble with Luke.

In that strange way she had, Kimi said to her, "Gift needs to be here. The thunder told me it would send me a gift to help me. She is it."

Okay, thought Rose, *I guess Gift needs to be here.*

Kimi and Gift spent their days on horseback, gathering plants, exploring the area. Hotah made sure they were armed and taught Gift how to shoot. Gift loved it. She said only rarely were women allowed weapons or became warriors. Kimi excitedly told Rose about all the new plants and their properties that she'd learned. Gift was helpful around the house, entertaining the young cousins, learning English at a remarkable pace. She loved the remnants of the modern world. Her delight in what everyone else took as mundane was a genuine pleasure, especially when the electricity came back on.

Rose wanted to take Gift to a therapist, but Kimi said, "Gift doesn't need therapy."

There were quite a few therapists already here, and some arrived with Big Thunder. None spoke Lakota fluently, so Rose didn't push. They could always do it later.

When Rose entered the house, things were as chaotic as usual. Nicole and Hotah were inside, Nicole doing the dishes. Rose asked Hotah if she could speak to him privately, went into the living room, and handed him a folder of papers.

"What's this?"

"Divorce papers, Elliot Gray Owl wrote them. You can sign and file at the county courthouse as soon as you want."

He said nothing, didn't open the folder, just looked at her.

"I'm giving you the house, all of it. You'll have financial responsibility for Kimi." He looked at her quizzically.

"I'm moving to Omímeya, going to take Tom Durrell's Riverside Cabin. It is a three bedroom, so there will be room for Luke, Kimi, and even Gift."

"Kimímela won't want to go."

"I'm aware, but that option will remain available."

Hotah opened the folder and looked over the papers. "Thank you, this is generous, more than I expected or probably deserve."

Rose paid the down payment for the house, made most of the payments, paid for almost everything related to the remodel. They were lucky. The bank that financed the house and remodel loan was a Sioux Falls bank without a local branch. According to the new law, they now owned it free and clear.

She wanted to start fresh. Big Thunder had changed her. She knew in the winter, Kimi's sibling would be born. Nicole and Hotah couldn't be living in a travel trailer with a baby.

"Give me a few weeks to get my stuff out from upstairs, but Hotah."

"What?"

"Finish that damn bathroom before Nicole moves in." He smiled, and they hugged.

Later that evening, Kimi hugged her and said, "I told Nicole you'd do the right thing." *Of course you did*, thought Rose fondly.

Luke was excited about moving into the Riverside cabin. He'd never been inside, but the pictures featured prominently on the website. He could catch the school bus with the children of guests living at Omímeya. The bus used to shuttle workers would need to be a school bus again. Luke said he didn't want to go to school and didn't need a high school diploma. He planned on joining the Guard when he turned seventeen. Rose told him she would have considered that if he had gotten a job at Omímeya, but he had burned all his bridges. To live with her, he'd need to be in school.

Returning to work the next day, Rose felt lighter. She didn't know how the burden of the house, the unfinished projects, and the mess weighed on her until she let it go. Rose was ready to start a new chapter. She was heartbroken to see less of Kimi, but knew her daughter was no longer fully hers. Hotah would be there for her, as well as for Gift.

=..=

Rose was almost happy to face the collection of crises that was now her life. She hated to admit it, but Neil was right. Free food for children created problems. She hadn't expected people would drive five miles with limited gas just for free food, especially since the tribal food pantry still had plenty. Some people just dropped their kids off, letting them run around unsupervised all day. Omímeya had a small children's play area, offered reservation-only babysitting, but no day care. Paying staff to watch other people's kids wasn't working, so they had to change the policy and put signs out specifying that free food for children only applied to guests. The schools were taking over children's feeding centers. Still, a few children showed up and were fed. She was wrong and had to admit it. She needed to remember what Omímeya was and what it wasn't and to stop trying to be all things for all people.

Rose texted Billy Fast Dog, the head of Security, to arrange a meeting. The sheer numbers of people coming through the doors, combined with a smaller number of staff, had increased cleaning needs, but also increased theft, which Rose suspected would get worse. Guests could use their key cards as debit cards. If stolen, charges could quickly rack up before the theft was reported. The banks would reverse fees if stolen, but didn't pay for Omímeya losses such as food or shop merchandise. One person bought a lot of valuable jewelry with a stolen guest card.

Rose and Billy came up with a solution to put photos on guest key cards. There was a machine that made staff ID cards with photos, but Omímeya had a limited stock of blanks. Almost everyone had a driver's license and a citizen's card. They could place the two back-to-back and laminate them together. Each citizen's card contained a barcode that could link to bank accounts as a debit card. It was simple to add guest room keys to the same card.

After the big meeting on the first day, there wasn't a roll of toilet paper left in any of the public bathrooms. After COVID, the casino consortium had installed quick-install bidets in every bathroom on every property they owned. A sign in each bathroom encouraged the use of "European" bidets to save trees, but the bathrooms also provided toilet paper, which was used more often if the amount of TP they went through was any indication.

The Medical Committee, as part of the health announcements, suggested people fill recycled squirt bottles, like old dish soap bottles, with water as portable bidets. There was much relief at that suggestion.

All kinds of other things were going missing, not only because of visitors. Rose texted all the staff a stern warning: zero tolerance for anyone caught going home with unauthorized items, no matter how small. She suspected everyone knew it was an empty threat; they were too shorthanded to fire people for pilfering, which had long existed. Previously, no one paid attention if the items were small.

Rose worried it would get worse. Kyle made dire predictions based on his models. Guests didn't feel safe, which bothered her. It didn't help that many locals walked around armed. South Dakota was an open carry state, but until now most people hadn't gone everywhere packing heat. She was worried that someone would get shot. Many guests had come from out of state and were perturbed seeing all the guns.

Rose recalled the Monday after Big Thunder; Kyle told her he'd upgraded her security clearance. She'd little knowledge about the various security clearances. Kyle said he needed to give her a tour of the secure facilities to input her biometrics. She told him she had about twenty minutes until her next meeting; he laughed and said she'd need at least two hours.

They didn't get to it until the next day. When they reached the basement, Kyle explained he'd been hired long after it was built. The casino consortium, who had billions, constructed Omímeya as a luxury bunker complex. He didn't know how much it cost to build, but much more than the sixty million reported, with all the supplies, much more. Kyle had a ten million dollar a year budget, but it included other properties, nothing as involved as Omímeya.

Kyle said, "Good thing they were planning on building another one. Their entire operation just disappeared."

Under the south wing, close to the main restaurant, were bulk food supplies from the many farms and food distributors the casinos owned. One person's job was to maintain the complex system of rotation. He was left behind the Circle, Kyle informed her sadly. They stored and rotated ninety percent of the food used at the resort, excluding perishables. Kyle explained that buying what they used in enormous quantities and rotating saved in overall food costs. Big freezers filled with flour and other grains surprised Rose, but Kyle explained that they'd gotten the flour for almost nothing, and with minimal cost for the extra electricity, the freezers would extend storage time for an extra two years. Kyle said they could feed six hundred people for a year, and even longer now, with all the grain silos and buffalo.

Rose had to submit a retinal scan and a full handprint to access the restricted areas. Now she understood the need for security clearances, realizing what a target they'd be. Rose asked about Neil, the Food Services Manager. His clearance level was three out of the four levels. The other level fours besides Kyle were Phil, who had a higher clearance than Tom, his boss, a three. The other level fours were Wayne Becker, the Facilities Manager, and Billy Fast Dog, the head of Security.

Kyle mentioned the need to read more people in, and repeated his common phrase, "Always have a backup. If it's important, your backup needs a backup."

Rose asked who his backup was. He said, "Peter Jorgenson."

"From receiving?"

"Guess he does more than direct packages," they smiled.

Kyle commented, "You were Tom's backup; you need to train yours." Rose looked at him questioningly.

"Any of us could drop dead tomorrow. If all five of us died, everyone else might too."

"Got it, backups for backups, including people."

To properly vet someone would take years, which is why those with prior military clearance would get through quicker.

"But I'm not military. Why the high clearance for me?"

"No choice. Being in 1791 was not on anyone's radar."

"What was?"

"Asteroid strike, EMP, nuclear war, bioterrorism, your usual run of natural disasters, pandemics, and civil disturbances."

Rose asked, thinking she was being funny, "What about aliens?"

"Big plan," answered Kyle.

"Really?"

"An entire government department gamed all kinds of scenarios out. Someone sold us a copy. It'd cost him his security clearance, even jail time, if they found out. The plans took three hard drives, much bigger than all their natural disaster plans put together. They've been working on them for years."

Rose gasped. "Are aliens real?"

"No idea, but the government sure put a lot of money toward preparing for an alien invasion, so maybe."

Kyle showed Rose the medical supplies under the east wing, heavily loaded with PPE (personal protective equipment) they bought a literal ton after COVID.

"Most of these will go to the hospital or local clinics, slowly and carefully, as needed. A few drugs, they don't store well, the data is unclear how long they'll last. We can't rotate drugs like food. No insulin, mostly antibiotics that store well."

After adding her biometrics, they entered the weapons area under the north wing. Kyle told her there was more military equipment in the triangle. As in the medical wing, each door had a barcode, which listed inventory.

Rose asked, "What if the power went out completely?"

"We'd be screwed." At the look on her face, he cracked up.

"Look beside each door." Under each barcode was a long list written in some kind of code. It didn't look English. It was barely visible, painted only a slightly different shade of gray than the walls.

"Who can decode this?"

Kyle took a picture with his phone, adjusted the brightness, then flipped the image. It'd been upside down and backwards.

"This is why so few people have high clearance. Everything has a simple low-tech fix."

Rose pointed at his phone. "Not totally low tech."

"We could do it manually. It would just take a while. There're even physical keys hidden."

"I can't believe the extent of all of this."

"Don't underestimate the power of a bunch of rich people who want to save their own asses."

They went to the west wing to input Rose's biometrics. Rose asked what was there.

"Bank vaults, including personal vaults by various members of the consortium, but we may never get in them. We don't have the codes. They built the vaults to be impenetrable."

Rose asked excitedly, "How much gold is there? Enough for the Louisiana Purchase?"

"No idea, but fifteen million in gold the day before Big Thunder, in 1791, it would only be worth 3,000 dollars at twenty dollars an ounce."

"That is something, at least. We can use that money, correct?"

"Yes, there is a protocol for this as well as everything. Three quarters of all level fours must agree."

Rose already knew what was under the east wing as a level two. She had seen it during the yearly drills. There were normal emergency shelter supplies, such as cots, blankets, bottled water, dehydrated food, MREs (Meals Ready to Eat), and PPE, and other medical supplies. The consortium had overbuilt all the basements to withstand tornados, earthquakes, floods, even planned egress routes in case the building collapsed on top.

Rose said, "I thought only the east wing had the emergency supplies."

"That's what you were supposed to think. A principle of prepping is to conceal items for others to find and keep your main stash well-hidden."

=..=

Rose had to deal with the day's issues. Some were chicken and egg problems. They needed to hire more people. The HR manager had been left behind the Circle, and none were conveniently staying at the resort. Despite being listed all week, nobody applied for the position. Rose would either need to find someone in a different field, or perhaps she could poach someone from the county. One problem begat another problem. A few days ago, a guest approached her and asked her if she planned to run for a seat on the Council. Rose said a Council seat would be relaxing compared to running this place. The poor guy looked abashed.

Rose met again with Billy. She hated the Security Chief's suggestions, but knew they're probably necessary, like checking employee bags as they leave. They could close off the road coming into Omímeya, it was already in the Emergency Plan. They could quickly build an enclosed gatehouse using materials set aside for that purpose, which would only allow those authorized entry. Rose called this proposal unworkable because people were coming for working groups and committees all the time, and most weren't guests.

Billy asked, "Do they need to meet here?"

"I guess not. With electricity now on, we can hold meetings in the library, college, or high school."

Rose considered it a better option, within walking distance, and it would keep the resort cleaner. She didn't like the idea of closed gates. They compromised by putting up the fence and the gatehouse, but leaving it open, with the possibility of shutting it later. Billy said the construction would take four or five days.

Meetings at the high school would be problematic when school started. There were school security issues because of school shootings. NewNet access in community centers and church meeting rooms would solve the problem, but like everything, it was in process.

They now had a plan and said goodbye. Billy's levelheadedness impressed Rose. She thought about how different her work relationships had become after Big Thunder, less adversarial, even with the men she'd had previous problems with. Not always smooth, but she felt she was gaining respect. That they were all overwhelmed made them depend on each other.

She met with Jackson and Billy several times to discuss security, even though Jackson's focus was on external threats. Jackson impressed Rose, and she enjoyed their conversations. They often found themselves walking together to or from meetings, sharing laughs over silly things people said. She steadfastly ignored her feelings towards him.

=..=

Rose remembered her meeting with Phil a few days after Big Thunder. He wasn't responding to texts or calls. They were understaffed; she shut down the casino and reassigned everyone. Casino employees resented that. She knew Phil was in his suite grieving and she heard he was drinking a lot, which concerned her. She had never seen him drunk, although drinking while socializing with gamblers was part of his job.

Rose brought her concerns to Kyle, who told her Phil needed some time. Just in case, he had frozen Phil's security clearance.

"Did you lock him out of the weapons locker?"

"Protocol, but if he wants to kill himself, he has plenty of weapons in his suite."

"He is Catholic. He won't kill himself. Could you speak to him, please?"

"He is your employee, boss, your job."

"Tomorrow."

"Chicken."

The next day, Rose went to his suite, pounded on the door, and yelled, "I know you're in there. Open up or I'll use the master key."

He opened the door, looking disheveled, unlike him, previously impeccably dressed and groomed.

"What do you want?"

"To talk. Can I come in?"

He let her in. She looked around. Obviously, he hadn't let housekeeping in either.

"I am so sorry Phil; I really need your help."

"Why? You shut down the casino." She noted he was more resigned than angry about it.

"We'll open back up, to a limited degree, once we get a handle on the crisis."

Instead of looking interested in a reopening, he looked tired and sad.

Rose asked him, "How much do you know about what is going on?"

"Enough. Spent years planning, didn't expect to survive without my girls."

Rose wanted to tell him the platitudes she'd been telling everyone the last couple of days: They're not dead, just living a good life with Thirty-One Flavors and Netflix.

Then she remembered, "Didn't Amy have a medical condition she needed medication for?" She hoped it would help Phil realize she was better off with twenty-first century medicine.

Phil looked at her harshly. "Do you think I wouldn't have two lifetimes of medicines stored here for her?"

"I don't know what to say. Other than it sucks balls, nothing that I can say will make it hurt less, so I'll stop trying. But I still need your help."

With an enormous sigh, "With what?"

She thought she might as well be honest. "I'm out of my depth here. I didn't know about what was in the basement, the long-term plans, none of it."

"Tom didn't tell you. I thought you were a level three."

"No, a two, a clueless two, but that's not the problem. Having weapons and supplies is an immense relief. We still have serious problems."

She discussed with him all the various issues that Kyle, Jackson, Mary, and others had been sharing.

Rose said, "I know we haven't always gotten along." He rolled his eyes.

"But I respect you. We have different areas of knowledge. I need all the help I can get." She did not, not want to cry, so she took a breath. "Please."

"Since you asked so nicely."

Rose asked Phil what he knew about Clyde Folsom. He got out his work tablet and rattled off a few biographical details. Rose knew the casino kept files on all the state politicians, including potential scandals. They rarely used that dirt, since usually campaign contributions worked just fine. They gave money to all the candidates, regardless of the party affiliations.

Phil said, "Other than being a religious nut, I see no extramarital affairs, no debts out of the ordinary. He comes from a well-to-do ranch family, and he aspired to higher office, but don't they all? Sorry, not much help."

Rose asked him what he knew about the Mexican cartels on the reservation. He knew more than he wanted to admit.

"You know what I need?"

"What?"

"A consigliere, like in *The Godfather* movies." They laughed.

It was an ongoing joke that he was mobbed up, being partially Italian from the East Coast. He had tribal membership; she didn't remember which tribe. Tribal membership was required for his level in casino management.

Phil looked like he was thinking, then said, "OK, give me the rest of the day. I will come to work tomorrow, but you better give me some staff back."

"You got it."

After he returned to work, Phil was more like his old self. While Rose and Phil's relationship wasn't exactly cordial, it was better. He accepted her new authority, and they worked out the casino reopening. The casino would keep its separate accounting and staffing. They repurposed the three sports bars with large high-end TVs to play movies from the media library, as they no longer had cable or the bandwidth for on-demand movies in the rooms. Available for free for guests, while a small fee for everyone else, the popcorn was free. This revenue would go to the casino. Rose suspected it would add up. Few people were gambling, although she wondered about next year when guests would come up the river.

Slot machines took up a lot of space. Now the electricity was back, Phil wanted them kept. Rose pointed out guests hardly used the slot machines and they couldn't replace them if broken. IT was short of space, and their equipment was currently scattered all over the resort, while the casino's slot area had electric plugs every few feet. Phil wasn't happy, but agreed to store most of the slot machines. Rose agreed to leave the ones currently on each floor and a few in the game area. Construction quickly built IT two large, insulated rooms, with secure doors. The casino lost a third of its floor space. Buffalo Burger, which had previously opened onto the casino, lost a few tables. The casino kept its bar and Rose closed the other one. The casino offered table games, roulette, and bingo with small prizes that were in high demand, like candy bars or shampoo. A meal at the Prairie Abundance Restaurant was the big prize. Bingo was popular and even turned a profit, since most the prizes came from the basement storage.

Yesterday, Rose had Tom's Riverside Cabin opened. Kyle added her and overrode Tom's security codes, including the safe. She wondered if Tom knew it could be opened with the right security clearance. There was over a million in cash in the safe, a lot of gold, and a box of identical diamond tennis bracelets. Rose wondered how many mistresses Tom had. When she told Phil and Kyle what she'd found, they said that was why Tom never got a higher security clearance. They suspected him of skimming, but they never proved anything. All the Riverside Cabins were smart houses with features disguised to give a rustic feel. She set the wake word for the house to "Alexa". She missed Alexa. The basement had a safe room behind a hidden door disguised as a shelf of cleaning supplies. Tom had hidden crates of top-shelf liquor, cases of the gourmet goodies used for gift baskets, and several boxes she hadn't opened.

Rose had housecleaning pack up everything and take it to storage. Tom's closet was full of expensive suits. He was a tall man; she wondered whether they'd fit Jackson. She thought about Jackson more than she felt she should. One room's closet was full of expensive women's high heels, dresses, and lingerie, new with tags, none in her sizes, of course. Rose deliberately did not look in nightstand drawers or in the large leather chest in one bedroom. She believed more than a casual sage smudge was necessary.

She asked Hotah's aunt to come before moving any of her stuff in. Her skepticism toward spiritual matters was shifting after Big Thunder. She knew disbelieving what she had witnessed firsthand was illogical. This led her to ponder: if the Earth possessed such immense power as to transport them back in time for protection, what other aspects of the unseen world could be true? While she was aware of sage's antimicrobial properties and understood how it worked to prevent sickness, she now also believed in its spiritual properties, specifically in its ability to disperse negative energy. She now believed that smudging would replace darkness with light. It would purify and protect her home. Once smudged, she could move in, knowing it was a clean and safe space.

Chapter Sixteen
Jackson

IN THE TEN days since Big Thunder, Jackson saw more shooting and murder victims than the entire eight years he'd worked as a cop. He hadn't worked homicide. If he did, it was usually peripheral, such as securing a crime scene. What he saw today disturbed him much more than the previous homicides, and not because of the mutilated corpses. In Iraq, he had seen plenty of gore. It disturbed him to think about the implications for everyone who lived within the Circle.

The first murder occurred on the second day he arrived. He had gotten back from Chamberlain with Kyle and had gone straight to the room marked Defense and Law working group. Most were Native men, many of them older. A call had gone out for veterans. More Native Americans served in the US military than any other ethnicity, including whites.

The meeting was chaotic, with various conversations going on, like, "When I was in Vietnam." Jackson had spent a lot of time in meetings during all his nonviolence training and knew how to facilitate. He called the room to attention.

"My name is Oliver Jackson. People call me Jackson. I was hired by Omímeya to organize a Defense force. Recently I was a Sioux Falls cop, but I served in Iraq three tours as an E-7. MOS was 89D." All the veterans looked at him with respect. They all knew 89D worked with explosives, which required extreme discipline, focus, and a steady nerve.

Jackson didn't feel the undertones of racism he felt in most places. He was the only Black man in a room of about three-quarters Natives to whites. It was because they were military. You depended on your team for your life; you didn't care what color they were. Friendships, especially in combat zones, were powerful and frequently lifelong, often with those you wouldn't normally be friends with. People would talk about the color-blind world we live in today. He knew it was bullshit, as he faced racism every day, some from those who'd be appalled if they were aware of their unconscious racism. He knew Natives experienced the same, but he wasn't sure of the extent. In the military, he knew racism still existed, but he felt more at ease with vets than anywhere outside of the Black community.

Jackson addressed the group. "I have suggestions for this meeting."

People were all ears; he got the impression nothing had been accomplished all morning.

"Today we don't need to figure out how to accomplish tasks, but what those tasks are, then we'll organize the groups and committees to accomplish them. We also need nominations for Acting Executive Councilor for Defense and Law."

Someone quickly said, "I nominate Oliver Jackson."

Someone else added, "I second."

"I'm new here. Anyone else?"

No one else stepped up, and everyone said aye. Jackson reminded everyone his term was temporary, lasting until elections in two weeks. He got started.

"Everyone interested in the legal aspects, political structure, the constitution, and judges, all that should be in the law group, please move over there," he said, pointing to a corner. A few stood and went over.

"All of you with experience or interest in law enforcement gather over here." No one stood up.

"They must be all out keeping us safe; they can meet another time. For the veterans, any commissioned officers, please raise your hands." No one did, which was surprising considering how many were in the room.

"I guess we'll have to work for a living." There was a chuckle at the old joke.

They subdivided the veterans into groups: training, weapons, patrols, logistics, and other areas; after they divided up, each group was small. Jackson encouraged them to recruit others. He told them he'd contacted the National Guard and hoped it would join them, but stressed they needed to proceed as if they were on their own.

Things were coming together when Jackson got a disturbing call from Mary. She relayed a conversation from church that morning which led to her concerns. Someone had mentioned how wonderful it was that Elizabeth White Eagle's daughter, Susan, was working. Everyone knew she was on drugs and had hooked up with Squirrel who was a meth head. The caller saw Susan in the Family Dollar yesterday, working the register. It surprised her to see Squirrel was working there, too. After church, Mary called Elizabeth, who cried about the extent of her daughter's drug habit and claimed she couldn't have been working, especially with Squirrel. Who'd hire him?

Mary remembered Jackson talking about running into thugs at the convenience store with lots of cash going around buying cigarettes and alcohol. Mary had a horrible suspicion. She dialed Phillip Gray Grass at the tribal police. There were only three officers in total for both reservations. Janet was off handling the case of the poor girl who'd been raped. Phillip and the other officer were overwhelmed, now handling a robbery at a convenience store. When she relayed that information to Jackson, he said he'd take care of it. He called Phillip and requested to waive tribal jurisdiction. Jackson knew Big Thunder had caught extra state cops, and they were available with the National Guard deployed. Phillip gave permission and said that with everything going on, tribal jurisdiction would no longer mean much.

Jackson called Kenneth Harris, the County Sheriff, and Nathan Bennett of the state police. Harris stated the cartels were heavily armed, and recommended deploying the SWAT team, but they had to go right away because no one knew how long they would remain at the Family Dollar.

As police raids went, it was a shit show. It was no one's fault. There'd been no time for planning. Communications were poor as radios didn't reach, only a few goTenna phones were available, and the police were concerned about using the open ham radio channel. Another problem was the state police didn't realize there were civilians shopping at the store. They only received information that cartel druggies were holed up at the Family Dollar after robbing it and were heavily armed. Had they known about the shoppers, possible hostages, the entire approach would have been different. It didn't help that everyone didn't show up at the same time. County was scoping out the back when someone noticed a smell and an inordinate number of flies in the dumpster and found two bodies. They were trying their radios when SWAT showed up, one in the back and five of them rushing in the front door. Squirrel reached under the counter, pulled out a shotgun and was quickly mowed down for his trouble, but not before the blast caught one officer in the vest, with a few pellets hitting him. Susan White Eagle shot at the cops, missing, and hitting a fourteen-year-old boy standing nearby. Then, a SWAT officer shot her. She was alive, but it was unclear whether she would make it. Jackson and Phillip, who had finally freed himself up from the robbery, arrived after it was all over.

None of the other shoppers suffered any harm, and the police escorted them out, which left a group of cops in the aisles of Family Dollar. They stared mournfully at the innocent boy on the floor and hatefully at Squirrel's body. Someone was giving Susan first aid, and paramedics were on the way. They informed everyone about the bodies in the back. Phillip confirmed it was the store manager and salesclerk. It looked like they had been there at least twenty-four hours.

Obviously, after Big Thunder, instead of merely robbing the store, the scum had murdered the staff and spent two days working the registers, cash only, raking it in. The store was probably mobbed with shoppers like the other Family Dollar stores in the area. Jackson suspected that Caballo, the cartel boss, still held most of the cash. It was too smart a move for two meth heads. The cartel wouldn't have trusted them with too much money. There may have been runners and shifts involved. Jackson didn't know how sophisticated Caballo's operation was. He had no dealings with the cartel in Sioux Falls.

No one could find the coroner. Instead of wasting more time looking, Jackson realized the resort was full of doctors. He called Kyle, who called Rose, who called Jenny, who agreed to find a doctor and send one over. Jackson realized he needed Rose's number on his phone. And who was Jenny? Did he need her number?

Other cops showed up. By this time, Jackson figured every cop inside the Circle was there, freed from looter patrol by the National Guard. Cartel drug murders were interesting. They were cops, after all.

Knowing he might not get another chance, Jackson gave a loud whistle, a useful skill as a sergeant, and said, "Listen up, everyone."

Everyone knew how badly it had turned out; a dead child still lay on the floor. He introduced himself, although most knew him, and announced he'd been nominated as Acting Executive Councilor for Defense and Law and wanted to say a few things.

"Although things didn't turn out as we hoped, an innocent death is always terrible, everyone was working under horrible conditions. It's a miracle this situation didn't turn out worse, much worse. What I saw was excellent cooperation among all of you. No one worried about jurisdiction or who was in charge. Innocents were in danger, and all of you," he waved his hand across to those listening, "rushed toward danger, when others may have fled." Everyone nodded. "This is why I am proud to be a cop, well, a politician now, at least for the next two weeks." Everyone laughed.

"Because our old world is gone doesn't mean we can leave our dedication and professionalism behind. Some may think we don't need to treat this like a usual crime scene. Who knows what'll happen with the legal system? It's clear what happened here. I want to remind people someone organized this, not meth heads. My guess is there'll be a lot less money here than should be. We need to dot every 'i' and cross every 't', crime scene photos, the works. Even though I know how much everyone loves paperwork." Obliging laughter followed.

"Even if we kill the son of a bitch who organized this tomorrow, and I hope we do, we need to remember we're the example of modern policing. I'm not sure when, probably years down the road, there'll be eighteenth-century police who'll come here wondering how we did things. We need clear documentation, step by step, because long after we are dead and gone, cops will look back and say, 'This is what good policing looks like.' Our role won't change. We're still here to protect and serve."

He looked around and felt the same sense of camaraderie between cops as the military. Jackson, knowing that Caballo was out there, a thorn in his side, had hoped for his swift arrest. There were so many things to do, so many competing priorities. Even with the extra cops Omímeya had hired, there was no time for an investigation.

The next murder took place two days later. Two chuckleheads figured with the power out, security systems would be down, and it was a good idea to rob a gun store. Since the ones in town were regularly patrolled, they targeted a gun store in an outlying area. They didn't realize that good security systems have Uninterruptible Power Supply (UPS), a built-in battery to be used in case the power goes out. Here it was also hooked up to a small solar panel. The owner saw them approach, weapons drawn. When they entered, the owner shot one thug, but the other had time to shoot the owner's adult son, who died before they could get medical help.

There had been five other shooting incidents since Big Thunder. Jackson got reports but didn't visit the scenes. The National Guard shot one looter who was coming out of a store. His arms were full of goods, and when told to stop, he dropped the goods and went for a weapon. Another occurred when an armed robber was shot dead attempting to drag off a gun safe from a basement. The homeowner heard noises. He came downstairs in the dark, realized he was being robbed, and shot the man dead. Afterward, he realized it was his nephew. His nephew had been a meth user, but he was still family. The man would have never shot him if he knew. Another incident was an accidental shooting involving one of the displaced people who had just bought a gun and was trying to clean it. Two other cases involved separate convenience store robberies, where both robbers were shot. The salesclerk shot one robber, while the other was shot by someone shopping while armed.

=..=

The murder scene Jackson had just arrived at disturbed him more than the others because both murder victims had been scalped. Glen and Lisa Ryobi lived on the outskirts of Presho, close to the Circle's edge. They'd lost five hundred acres of prime farmland. Ray, a friend who stopped by to return canning supplies his wife had borrowed, found them. Ray told Jackson the whole sad story.

When Ray pulled into the driveway, he saw a body lying on the front porch in a pool of blood. Not far away were four horses. An Indigenous boy and another man were tying things to one of the horses. He immediately reached for the .30-06 Springfield rifle from the gun rack behind his seat, saw the man notch an arrow in a bow, and Ray shot him without fully getting out of the truck. It was such a bad angle he missed a kill shot. The man fell, wounded. The Native boy helped the wounded one get up on the horse, taking off with all the horses leaving fast.

Ray considered chasing them but wasn't sure if the body on the porch was Glen, or whether he was alive. Turned out that Glen wasn't only dead but scalped and mutilated. After vomiting, he called out to the house, braced himself, and found Lisa inside, in front of the still locked gun case, with her throat cut, scalped as well.

As he looked around, he noticed that someone had trashed the house and there was a pile of random things, mostly clothes, lying in the front yard. He noticed the body of an Indigenous man, dead with a face full of shotgun pellets.

Ray hated to leave, but without the right SIM card for his phone, and the landline in the house did not work, he couldn't report the incident. He drove to the Lyman County Sheriff's office, told them what happened, and returned. He wasn't sure what he could do, but didn't want to leave poor Glen and Lisa alone.

By the time Jackson got there, it'd been well over an hour. Like the Family Dollar incident, about every cop in the area was arriving or there already. Jackson had called Colonel Gardner earlier to see whether the National Guard wanted to send someone, as this situation obviously had security implications for everyone. Colonel Gardner had put off deciding which side of the Changleska County debate to align himself with. He told Jackson privately he would obey nothing from Folsom he'd have considered an illegal order in the old world. Gardner agreed to send someone and emphasized the need for intelligence, and requested an unlikely observer that Jackson wouldn't have considered, but nothing was usual anymore.

After a while, an Omímeya electric work truck pulled up, and Kimímela, Rose's daughter, and Gift of Thunder, called Gift for short, piled out with another man whom Jackson didn't know. The two girls were inseparable. Gift had moved into Rose's house right after she arrived. Jackson couldn't understand how Rose could take on the responsibility of a traumatized teenager with as much time as she spent at work, but it wasn't his business. Gift was learning English fast, but still needed Kimi to translate.

Jackson would've preferred to shield them from this, but knew they needed the intel. Jackson first showed them the dead man lying where the horses had been. Gift walked right up to the body and examined it closely, not disturbed at all, even though his face looked like hamburger. Kimi, standing back, obviously more squeamish, appeared nauseated.

Kimi translated. Gift confirmed it was a Lakota warrior, named Yellow Cloud, one of the Two Elks band. Gift knew him well and recognized the porcupine quill work on his shirt. She said he was a good warrior who had a small son. Before anyone could stop her, Gift went right up to the porch where Glen still lay uncovered as someone took photos, then went into the house and looked at Lisa before she came out. Kimi remained outside. They spoke for a while.

Kimi motioned to Jackson, "You better get a few people to hear this. Maybe tape it too."

Everyone gathered around. Someone holding a police issue video camera started to tape Gift. Jackson got his phone out. He'd seen too many police tapes go missing.

Gift said, looking right at the camera, in English, "My name is Gift of Thunder. I'm fifteen years old, and I live at twenty-four Old Crow Road." She looked pleased to know the address. "I am still learning English, and Kimi has explained how important it is to be accurate." She pronounced that word carefully. "I will say the rest in Lakota, and Kimi will translate."

People looked surprised at her stated age, for she looked eleven or twelve. "Yellow Cloud and two others came to trade. Not wearing medicine paint for raiding or war. Horse trails here are heavy." She walked over and pointed. "Pack horses. Sturdy, not fast. Looks like Yellow Cloud got off his horse here," she said, pointing to a spot near the front porch, "with this pile of furs," pointing again, "trying to trade. He didn't have his weapons out."

A cop interrupted. "How do you know that?"

Gift looked annoyed at being interrupted. "He'd need his weapons when going to the stars. They'd been kept by his side." The cop nodded.

"Don't know what was said, but Yellow Cloud got shot. Another man shot that white man," she said, pointing to Glen. "Probably took his rifle unless anyone moved it?"

They assured her no one had touched it. Some cops wondered why they weren't the ones to notice it was missing.

Through Kimi, Gift continued, "I can't tell who shot him, need to see the arrow. I could pull it from his throat?"

The cops looked appalled. Kimi told Gift she couldn't take out the arrow; the special doctor for the dead had to do it. Gift understood. Different tribes had different rituals for the dead. These people had doctors for everything.

Kimi continued translating. "After the white man, someone killed the white woman. He must have been angry that Yellow Cloud was killed without holding a weapon while trying to trade. The woman he was less angry with, because he slit her throat, that way she dies quick. Man on the porch was alive for a while. The arrow didn't kill him. He was cut while he was alive. Too much blood. Other than scalps, Two Elks' warriors don't cut the dead, only those alive so they can feel it."

The cops all looked horrified, even Jackson, who'd seen terrible things in the war.

"After that he was wounded, not sure by who, the woman did not have a gun."

The cops exchanged a look. No one had told Gift or Kimi anything deliberately to prevent influencing the girls' observations. Someone asked how she knew, and she rolled her eyes.

"No blood coming out of the house. He was wounded here." She pointed to the exact spot. "Not too wounded. Not enough blood, he may live." Gift added, "they had a boy with them about my age to hold horses and learn."

She showed how marks of a smaller horse showed it carried a light rider. Gift pointed to drag marks and a blood trail missed so far by everyone.

"They tried to carry Yellow Cloud home, not loading him on the horse yet. Did not pack the goods on the horse yet either." She pointed to the piles of random stuff by the door. "Maybe someone stopped him, which is why he got wounded and couldn't take the goods."

All the cops stared at Gift.

Then one of the few female officers said to her, "Damn, girl, you would make a mighty fine detective." Everyone laughed.

Kimi quickly translated. She knew Gift hated people to laugh at her. Told her it was a compliment and explained what a detective was.

Gift beamed. "I can't imagine having a job like that, but how interesting it would be."

Chapter Seventeen
Martin

MARTIN KNEW ANNA MAY was anxious to get out of the church basement they'd been staying in, and so was he. It had been ten days, about nine days too long. He appreciated the generosity offered by strangers to those displaced by Big Thunder. All prices were frozen until the election, in five days, so they couldn't find rental properties anywhere. Prices would go up then, and people hung on to their rentals until they could get more money. Because of gas shortages, everyone wanted to live close in, either on the rez or in the county, depending on their politics. That political divide was changing after the Ryobi murders. The radio reported the incident as either a horrible, tragic mistake or a deliberate heinous murder, depending on the station. The paper hadn't put out an edition yet. Martin hoped that the newspaper coverage would present a more balanced perspective.

NewNet posted the video testimony of the young Lakota girl describing what happened online that same day. They provided graphic content warnings, although the bodies were blurred out. Not everyone watched the video because access to NewNet was still limited. They believed that spreading the word quickly, clarifying it wasn't a deliberate raid but a trade mission gone wrong, might discourage people from seeking payback by running out in their 4x4s and guns looking for "wild injuns." They were wrong. A few went out, and none came back.

The realization finally hit many people that they're really in 1791, occupying Lakota land. More people became Changleska citizens. Housing grew tighter as many people didn't feel safe living in rural areas; some moved in with rural relatives.

Martin was concerned even if they could find a place, they had no money. They'd spent the cash they brought with them. Their bank and credit cards were not part of the local systems. They were broke. He heard the banks wouldn't give credit to older people, only to those with marketable job skills. Anna May had almost no work experience. She'd worked occasionally at a friend's art gallery, mostly so she could tell people she worked. Over the years, Martin offered to pay for any schooling or training she wanted. She attempted a class now and then, but nothing she stuck with. It was surprising she had such ambition for him, but never had an interest in a career for herself. He thought she would be successful in any number of fields. Martin felt hopeless and depressed. He had always been the provider. Although he decried Anna May's extravagant lifestyle, he loved he could make her happy with his money. His self-worth was determined by his bank account. Now it was gone, he didn't know what to do.

Good thing Anna May had a plan. Following the Town Hall meeting, she persuaded Kathy to approach Lyman County to request an exemption for purchasing diesel for a bus service. The county was happy to do so. There were few buses, and the nearby truck stop had a good diesel supply and a working pump, although electricity hadn't made it out that far yet. Anna May went with Kathy and convinced the truck stop owner to give her a full tank on credit. Kathy charged people a small fee and made daily runs to Omímeya and stops in the nearby towns.

They planned a trip to Omímeya. Anna May dressed fashionably and convinced Martin to wear a sport coat. Omímeya was impressive, not as big or luxurious as resorts they stayed at in the past, but unique in its beauty. After they arrived, Anna May tried to find the location of the Patent Office, only to find that it hadn't been set up yet. However, someone directed them to a staffer sitting at a desk in an open area on the fourth floor of the administration offices. After being introduced, the young man told Anna May they wouldn't be issuing licenses for several weeks at least. Because so few people held patents, the issue hadn't come up yet.

Anna May beamed at the man. "We don't want a license. My husband Martin here already owns a patent."

"Then I'm happy to help you, Mrs. Worthington."

"Anna May, please. According to the posted guidelines I read, if you or a direct family member have renewed a patent in the last twenty years, there'll be no licensing fee, right?"

The man agreed and checked the records. Martin showed his ID, and they printed copies of the six medical device patents his family had renewed.

The young man said to Anna May, "I'm supposed to charge for copies, but since you are my first customers, they're free today."

With effusive thanks, they left. With a few hours before the next bus, they checked out the resort.

Anna May looked longingly at the now closed spa. "They'll open it sooner or later, don't you think?"

Anna May spent the time talking to people, finding out who the movers and shakers were. They had created an email address earlier; she made an appointment with a banker in Chamberlain for the next day.

It surprised Martin how much better he felt having the patent papers in his hands, but he didn't know how to turn the patent papers into cash. He'd never paid much attention to the family business and didn't know how the devices were made.

However, he was beginning to have faith in Anna May, who said, "Don't worry, dear."

While Anna May was schmoozing, Martin listened in on meetings, synced his devices, and read about expeditions in the NewNet forums. He thought it would be exciting to go on one, but couldn't imagine Anna May roughing it. A cot in a church basement with flush toilets was driving her mad. Martin found river boats fascinating and had some plans for old steam paddlers on his laptop. He posted in the expedition forum to see who else might be interested. The job boards had no openings for insurance executives. There was nothing he could transfer his skills to.

The next day, Anna May insisted he wear a suit and a tie. They met with a banker named Adam Diedrich, who Anna May found out was not only the Chair of the Banking Committee but was running for the Executive Council, the Infrastructure seat. Because the economy was critical to everything else, they placed that seat under Infrastructure instead of Human Services, the other choice. He was running against Thomas Russo, the Army Corps engineer who operated the dam. Martin thought he'd rather have an engineer who knew about infrastructure than a banker in that seat and hoped others would feel the same.

Anna May was her usual charming self, but Diedrich surprised Martin by not falling for it. Diedrich spoke directly to him, inquiring about his plans for the patents.

"Do you want to start a business?"

Anna May rescued him with, "Martin was so busy as the Vice President of National Insurance, manufacturing didn't hold his interests."

She asked Diedrich for his advice. "We were hoping, since you know all the local businesses here, you might suggest someone who'd want to build these important medical devices."

Martin took out the folder and Diedrich perused the paperwork. "You own these free and clear."

Anna May added, "Who knows how long it is going to take the Patent office to issue licenses? It's so complicated. Everyone is so busy."

Diedrich asked Martin, "If you don't want to manufacture these yourself, are you looking to sell the patent?"

Before Martin had a chance to say yes, Anna May interjected, "If we can get the right price; we'd also need a small royalty."

"This may take time to find the right buyer."

Anna May, with that smile, said, "Of course, we were thinking of opening our bank account with your bank. Would it be possible to open an account with a credit line using these as collateral?"

Martin was getting his feet under him. "We don't know the value of these yet, so it'd either have to be a large credit line, or only one device."

They tossed around numbers, and Martin remembered financial details from his family business. They left the bank with a new checkbook, a $15,000 credit line, and three fewer patents, the banker holding on to the others for collateral.

=..=

Anna May posted a housing wanted message on Craigslist, offering to pay the proposed rent increase now in cash instead of waiting until after the election. Anna May claimed she wanted to live as close as possible to Omímeya, because that was where the new capital would be, but Martin wondered how much being near the spa, gym, and pool played a factor in her choice.

The rentals close to Omímeya on the reservation were dismal. They found a big farmhouse nearby for a reasonable amount. The older couple who owned it wanted to move to Chamberlain to be closer to family. It was in good shape, recently modernized, twelve miles from Omímeya, but right on the bus route. As it was too big for the two of them, Anna May surprised

Martin by suggesting a couple of people from the tour bus could move in, as the farmhouse had four bedrooms. People could contribute to the rent when they found work. They offered Kathy the option of using the barn for her bus business and fixing up the loft to live in, using a bedroom until then.

Michael Debray, the tour guide/professor, was one of the new roommates, and the Danish couple, Ella and Soren. Anna May said they could work off the rent by helping around the house until they found jobs. Martin knew Anna May had always had household help, and never cooked or cleaned if it could be helped. Ella and Soren were in their sixties, didn't have transferable job skills, and were unlikely to find other work.

One of the German men found a job on Craigslist after the first Town Hall as a programmer at Omímeya and moved out. He'd been traveling with another German man, both younger than most of the tourists. Everyone assumed they were a couple. Turned out they were cousins, and didn't get along well, which wasn't surprising. The other German man was a disagreeable fellow. He found his own place to live before Martin and Anna May did. He didn't say goodbye to anyone. No one had any idea where he went.

The two Japanese couples stayed at the church in Presho. They started a soy business making tofu, soymilk, and other soy foods in the commercial church kitchen. Silos stood full of soybeans, more than could be used locally. The couples' dream was to sell their business eventually and return to Japan; they desired to experience Japan in 1791, considered a golden age. A few people found places among the members of the church.

Kathy tried to find housing or jobs for those on the tour bus. Anna May helped by continuing to network, gossip, and charm people around them. Anna May went often to either Omímeya or the library, which was becoming another important gathering place. Using NewNet, she joined various online community forums. She started a forum called Displaced Farm Wife, which was filled with pictures of her trying to do unlikely farm chores, which were usually staged, or recipes made by Ella. She was careful not to lie, only imply she did these things. It generated useful tips from locals. It wasn't Instagram; but Anna May was gathering followers.

Anna May met a man on the Human Services Committee who'd told her about a new elder housing program, and she found places for the remaining people. Residents in nursing homes were dying quickly without medicine, freeing up rooms in all the assisted living centers. They had doubled up residents with formerly private rooms to create more space. These centers provided free room and board to couples or individuals over sixty-five for a few hours of daily help. Nursing care wasn't required, but helping with recreational activities, playing cards, or giving attention to residents was. Everyone was expected to take turns helping in the kitchen. Special skills or interests were welcomed. It was a wonderful solution, especially for displaced older folks with no families. When more rooms opened, couples would be eligible for two rooms. Two adjoining rooms could be turned into a suite, using the second bathroom plumbing to create a small kitchenette. There was talk that if more rooms opened, the centers would include day care, with elders helping with the children. They called them Living Wisdom Centers and held classes in the community rooms for tips from people who lived in the Depression or had other forgotten skills.

Michael pointed out the property needed security; the Ryobi murders still fresh in everyone's minds. None of the other household members had ever held a gun in their lives, but Anna May said her father had taught her, and she was an excellent shot. Then asked if Martin would please buy her a rifle and a pistol. *At least it's not dresses or jewelry*, he thought.

Chapter Eighteen
Jackson

JACKSON THOUGHT THE two weeks since Big Thunder were both the longest and the shortest of his life. The old world seemed far away, and everything now moved at super-speed.

The election will be held tomorrow. Jackson was glad it was going to be over. Yesterday, two hours before the deadline, Clyde Folsom declared his candidacy for Executive Council for the Defense/Law seat. The man had a following, especially among conservative Christians. Jackson wouldn't care whether he lost the election. He'd plenty to do without being a Councilor. Jackson worried about the future of his new country, even the fate of his new world, if Folsom were to be elected. The same evening that Folsom announced his candidacy, NewNet and the Chamberlain Free Press posted a photo of Folsom taking his citizens' oath a week prior. This was an issue because for the last two weeks on his now daily radio show, he'd railed against Changleska, the covenant, the new constitution, and the oath in particular. He had told his followers the only way to preserve their way of Christian life would be for the county to remain independent.

Politicians being hypocrites weren't unusual. People assured Jackson that enough voters would back him. Folsom said he changed his mind because of the Ryobi murders. He asserted Officer Jackson didn't have the leadership experience needed to keep everyone safe. Both NewNet news and the newspaper pointed out that Folsom signed his oath two days before the Ryobi murders. Jackson wondered who'd leaked that photo.

He wished he could be in two places today. Yesterday, the county sheriff's office had finally gotten a lead on the whereabouts of Caballo, the Mexican cartel leader they believed responsible for the Family Dollar murders. He operated meth labs, sold fentanyl and other drugs, and committed who knows how many murders and robberies. An informer stated Caballo and his head guys were meeting with another drug dealer to discuss a possible merger. The sheriff knew the man who lived there had an extensive criminal record. It was out in the boonies at the edge of the Circle by the White River. This time, the sheriff wasn't taking chances; they had time to plan. No civilians were present, as the man lived alone. They coordinated with all the police agencies, even Tribal Police. The National Guard would help with communications. Jackson thought Colonel Gardner's participation was a good sign, as police raids weren't the National Guard's normal purview.

Caballo's meeting scheduled at 4:00 pm posed a problem, as it clashed with the last debate before the election. This meant Jackson, who needed to be at Omímeya, would miss the raid. He checked his phone, hoping for an update from the police. He found none, but he noticed the time was 11:08 and he realized things around him had quieted. Last Saturday, there was a moment of silence at exactly 11:11 am, the week anniversary of Big Thunder. At 11:09, a gentle tune from a Native American flute echoed through the resort's loudspeakers. Jackson noticed everyone around him setting down their phones. Most stood up, taking off their hats, waiting respectfully.

At 11:10 am he heard Rose Chasing Hawk, "Thank you for honoring the change by Big Thunder. During our minute of silence, let us do more than remember the lost. Consider what we gained, and how we can move forward in a good way to protect this Earth."

After the minute of silence, she softly sang in Lakota, then in English: "Big Thunder strengthens the Circle, the Circle protects the Earth." Many people sang with her. The ceremony differed from last week's, which had been more of a memorial. Jackson wondered whether this would be every week at 11:11 am. He hoped so. Jackson was feeling a greater connection to what he thought of as God. He had been churched as a child, but he raged at God during his teen years, seeing innocents die in the harsh streets of Chicago where he was raised.

Jackson received a text from Billy Fast Dog requesting a meeting as soon as possible. Billy invited him into his small, private office outside of the main security area, on the ground floor next to the casino. Seeing Kyle there surprised Jackson.

Billy said, "We need to show you something of a sensitive nature. Kyle tells me we won't grant you a security clearance until after the election. Do

I have your word that if you lose the election, you'll not reveal the way we got the information I'm going to show you?"

More curious than offended, Jackson agreed.

"The Riverside Cabins are all smart houses, featuring state-of-the-art security, updated every year." Jackson nodded, not surprised, wondering where this was leading. "Rose and her son Luke moved into the cabin of Tom Durrell a few days ago. When assigning each cabin, the house database includes everyone who will stay there and requires all their visitors to announce themselves at the door, so the facial recognition system can identify them as friendly. Evidently, either Rose or her son didn't read the house manual or get a welcome orientation as a normal guest would. Yesterday afternoon, Luke had two visitors, one of whom is on our watch list, because you put him there."

"What the fuck?"

Billy pulled up a photo, not very clear. It was the Hispanic man he'd seen on his first day, Gabriel Lopez, whom he'd called thug number two in his head.

"Yes, that's him alright. What was he doing at Luke Chasing Hawk's house? Her kid is only fifteen or sixteen, right?"

"He is fifteen and his last name is Trenton; he has a different father than Rose's daughter."

Billy started a video on the screen in his office. They watched as Luke greeted the two men at the door. One was Lopez, the other unknown. The men entered the kitchen off the great room. Luke brought out a bottle of booze, and they poured drinks. Luke grabbed a couple of things from the fridge, then they all sat outside on the deck. Even though there was no sound recording, the quality of the video amazed Jackson. Now he could understand why he needed security clearance. Paying guests would throw a fit if they saw how their privacy could be invaded. Luke and the visitors passed a joint or a pipe, drank, ate, laughed, and talked. The men were attentive to Luke. When they got up, they patted him on the back and high-fived, then went back into the house. After getting more drinks, the three of them entered a bedroom, presumably Luke's. Jackson raised his eyebrows at Kyle and Billy.

Billy said, "We don't have video in the bedrooms, only infrared, in case of a hostage situation. Check it out."

Billy switched to another screen. Jackson could see images of three people, like the infrared images he'd used in Iraq, but clearer, the technology improved. Three guys were sitting in front of a screen, two in chairs, one on the floor, obviously playing video games.

Billy shut down the screen. "That's it. They play for an hour and leave, and Luke cleans up."

"I know you wanted me to confirm it was Lopez, but what's the other reason I'm here?"

"You may have heard that Rose is having trouble with Luke."

Everyone in the resort, which was like a tiny town, knew that Luke got caught trying to sell stolen porn from IT.

"You've more experience than either of us in juvenile law enforcement."

Jackson thought for a minute. "Not sure smoking weed and underage drinking are illegal now."

"That's not it. We think these guys are grooming Luke."

At Jackson's look, Billy quickly said, "Not sexually, although that sometimes happens. We think they're trying to get Luke to divulge security weaknesses, getting him using, so they can pump him for information. We're not sure if they were smoking weed or meth."

Jackson nodded thoughtfully. "I can see that. Still not sure what I can do."

"We're trying to figure out the best way to tell Rose and want your help."

"Oh, hell no!"

Kyle answered, "We've worked with her for years, know her well, and in the last two weeks, we've gotten closer. We need someone objective."

"What about the tribal cops, the sheriff, or state cops?"

Billy said, "Unfortunately, they're all busy planning the raid to catch Caballo. We don't want to wait to tell Rose. The alert came in yesterday. It took a day for human eyes to process it. We want to make sure Luke stays away from these assholes. Rose needs to ensure that. We can heighten security, or eighty-six them from the property."

Kyle added, "If these guys are close to Caballo and get busted, who cares? But if it was your kid, wouldn't you want to know right away?"

Jackson agreed.

Billy said, "This may be a tempest in a teapot, a dumb kid bragging about his mom's important job, showing off his fancy new place, and partying a little. But if it turns out to be more, we must ask ourselves, have we done enough?"

Jackson sighed, knowing he couldn't get out of telling Rose. "I'll tell you from my experience working with juveniles in trouble, they all lie. Every one of them, always. We can tell Rose right away, but I don't think any of us should interview Luke. Tomorrow we can find another cop with juvenile experience to interview him." Billy and Kyle agreed.

Billy added, "We must impress upon Rose not to reveal to Luke about the house security cameras. Rose can tell him we saw the men on the cameras outside the casino. It'd be best if all three of us told her. Jackson, you could fill her in on the plan for the police to interview Luke, and what it may look like from a law enforcement standpoint."

They discussed when to tell her, before or after the debate, and decided to do it sooner rather than later, texted Rose and found a time. Once decided, they all wanted to get this onerous job over with.

The three of them met upstairs in Rose's office. The conversation and viewing of the video went about as well as expected. Billy saw her horrified expression when she saw two grown men entering her fifteen-year-old son's bedroom. He quickly switched to infrared and explained. Rose was obviously upset, angry with Luke, but the mama bear came out,

"Why would you have the county sheriff or another cop interview Luke?"

"For one thing," answered Jackson, "you're our boss."

Rose said, "If you win the election tomorrow, I'll no longer be your boss. Changleska will pay your salary."

Jackson hadn't thought about that. The more he thought about it, the happier it made him. He liked Rose more and more, despite the teenagers. Jackson made it a rule not to date single mothers. It was bad enough breaking women's hearts, but he hated hurting kids. But there was something about Rose. He might break his rule for her.

"Objectivity is important. Driving him to Chamberlain, putting him in an interrogation room, may help him realize the seriousness of who he associates with."

Rose asked in alarm, "He's going to be interrogated? Do we need a lawyer?"

"No, interviewed only," assured Jackson. "He's not being accused of a crime. We just want to know what these guys asked him. We need an honest answer." Rose calmed down.

"Rose," Kyle said gently, "do you think Luke would tell us the truth if we asked nicely?"

Rose had to admit he probably wouldn't. She agreed not to tell Luke about the house security cameras and was pleased she could pull up views on her devices and check on him.

Jackson returned to his hotel room, where he now lived. He appreciated how close his room was to everything. He could afford to keep the room, as he had few expenses. For the upcoming debate, Jackson wore one of the expensive suits that Rose had passed on to him. Her previous boss had been the same height but thicker. However, the hotel laundry service made alterations. After he showered, he put on the now cleaned and well-fitting suit; he had to admit he looked good. Evidently, so did many of the women who admired him as he walked across the lobby to the Big Bear room where the debate was scheduled. Jackson caught their looks and thought that's one way to get votes.

In the last couple of days, a few people had dropped out of the race. Two of the candidates promoted by Clyde Folsom dropped out for unspecified personal reasons. Jackson was curious because he'd heard rumors of scandals, but nothing concrete. Another moved further away because of the Ryobi murders and didn't want to spend two hours a day commuting. The bus service made many stops. It was slow and inconvenient.

The AV staff set up everything for the debate to be broadcast live on the radio and on closed-circuit TV. People could watch in their rooms, or in the movie rooms in the casino. There, they could eat popcorn and talk more freely. Signs all over the Big Bear room asked people to remain silent for the taping. It would be on both radio stations, shown on NewNet but not live; they did not have the bandwidth for live programming yet.

People were filtering in. It looked like it was going to be a sizeable crowd, about 400 people. The first rows of seating had been reserved for family members of candidates and Committee Chairs. He allowed himself the thought that Denise would've been sitting in the front row, proud of him.

On the stage were several long narrow tables for the candidates. In the front was the podium, where each would get ten minutes to speak. At the end, they would give those running unopposed a couple of minutes to make announcements about their seat or deliver a rah-rah speech. *We're all becoming politicians*, Jackson thought with disgust.

A chime sounded, everyone settled, the tribal chaplain said a brief prayer, and Rose came up to the podium for a quick introduction. Since most everyone was sitting down, Jackson noticed five men walking quickly down the aisle, all carrying long guns. That wouldn't be unusual if the men had just come from a security shift, but his cop alarm went off as he realized they were carrying AK-47s. He stood quickly. He rarely walked around armed at the resort and regretted it today.

Yesterday, Jackson had given Billy one of the tasers he'd brought from Sioux Falls to check out. He'd decided at the last minute to bring it. Jackson wanted to see whether it would show in his new suit in his shoulder holster and didn't want to bother getting his service weapon out of the room safe. He was reaching for the taser when he noticed a man hurrying up the stairs to the stage and recognized him as Caballo. The man was approaching the stairs and had at his side a Desert Eagle .44 Magnum pistol.

Jackson shouted, "Gun," and shot him with the taser. It hit the bulletproof vest Caballo was wearing. It startled him, and he stumbled as he came up the steps. Then Caballo raised the pistol, aiming directly at Rose. Jackson leaped at Caballo, tasing him again, this time hitting him in the leg. Caballo fell to the ground twitching, his gun going off.

Unfortunately, shouting "Gun" didn't get the same reaction as it would in a police situation. It took a few seconds for people to grasp what was going on. Pamela Nordstrom was sitting next to Mary Landrau, shouting, "Active shooter," and pushing Mary under the table.

The men with the AK-47s hadn't planned to be noticed so soon. They lifted their AKs and started shooting random people towards the front of the room. Charles from Security ran to the fire alarm and pushed a button marked "AS" which was under the Fire button. Immediately, a loud alarm went off, then a prerecorded voice said, "Active shooter in the building, this is not a drill. Active shooter, shelter in place and find cover. This is a lockdown; police are on the way." The message repeated over and over. Doors to each wing began to shut automatically, isolating the lobby from the wings. Jackson didn't know those doors even existed. They were metal pocket doors on both sides. They shut quickly and locked with a clang.

The room filled with shooting, screaming, and crying. Jackson was on top of the still twitching Caballo, who was reaching for his gun on the floor a few feet away. Although Rose had blood streaming down the side of her face, she steadily picked up Caballo's huge gun, bent down, and held it towards Caballo's head. He was thrashing about, swearing up a storm in Spanish. Someone came and helped restrain Caballo. Jackson was tempted to tase him again, but knew that could be lethal. He wasn't sure if the first shot had gotten through the vest. Jackson threatened to tase him again, anyway. He was sitting on top of Caballo, still on the ground, struggling to get free.

Rose said calmly, "Jackson, if you would please move, I'll shoot him in the knee. If he doesn't stop, I'll shoot both knees. They don't do knee replacements anymore; another thing left in the old world."

Caballo stopped. Jackson looked at Rose. She was looking at all the wounded and dying people, her people. Jackson knew she meant it. He was still too much of a cop. He didn't get up. Caballo was glaring at Rose.

Someone shouted for rope; someone else yelled, "Don't hang him here."

The shooting stopped, the screaming didn't. About half the crowd were locals, many wearing side arms. Every one of the shooters sustained multiple gunshots. Doctors aiding the victims quickly exhausted the meeting room's first aid kit. People started tearing clothes for bandages, pulling off belts for tourniquets. The active shooter announcement was still repeating, but less frequently. Someone asked if it could be turned off, as the shooters were contained, but no one knew yet about the rest of the building. Because they were going to be speaking, neither Jackson nor Rose had their in-house radios with them, so they were left in the dark.

Charles heard on his radio there were still gunshots, and Security was checking floor by floor. There were armories on each floor for this very reason. Usually, the casino didn't arm its security. They locked everything down. That meant the shooters couldn't escape, but that also meant they could keep shooting people. It was rare for guests to be armed; the hope was they'd be locked in their rooms. Rose thought about the movie theaters and the restaurants. The doors to those wings had now been locked, but if there were shooters inside, it would turn into a bloodbath.

Jackson realized the drug deal was a well-planned feint. This was the actual attack; Caballo was attempting a coup. While every Councilor and every candidate were here, every cop within the circle was thirty miles away, probably searching an empty house. Jackson was still sitting on Caballo, and people were trying to find something to tie him up with. Rose was still holding the gun, seemingly unaware of the blood dripping down her face.

Finally, Jackson could get off Caballo, hog-tied with several people's belts, including his own. Several men had weapons trained on him, casually discussing whether they should shoot his balls off. Jackson took the gun from Rose and led her to the table. Rose's family came running to her. They all looked unhurt. He got a good look around for the first time. There were dozens of bodies, most moving, some not.

He heard later that at the same time as he shouted "Gun," Kimi shouted "Get down" but in Lakota, as she had been speaking it to Gift, so few understood. Her family did, and everyone immediately got to the floor.

Jackson walked over to a man, obviously a shooter, judged by the number of men and one woman holding guns on him. He was wounded, slowly bleeding out. A doctor approached, bent down with bandages torn from someone's shirt.

Another doctor put her hand on his shoulder. "Stop, Eddie, remember your oath."

They stood there a few minutes and watched the man expire from blood loss, the doctor with a stack of bandages in his hands, tears running down his face.

Jackson recalled that the Acting Executive Council had passed one of its first measures, which was the creation of an Ethics Board to make tough choices when medical resources were limited. But he had seen the bandages in the doctor's hand. It wasn't a matter of resources to stop the bleeding. Then he remembered Susan White Eagle, who had killed that boy at the Family Dollar. She'd been in the ICU for a few days, may have recovered, with the help of surgeries, IVs, drugs, and a lot of resources. The Ethics Board determined that if a criminal would likely get a life sentence or the death penalty, they were ineligible for medical support. They could be given pain relief if there were adequate supplies for the population, otherwise nothing. When Susan started screaming in pain the next day, Jackson heard one nurse had injected a full syringe of air into each of Susan's carotid arteries. She quickly died of an embolism.

The Ethics Board had stated in its initial meetings that it wouldn't address euthanasia or death with dignity, leaving those decisions to doctors and their families. Everyone who passed on the story about the nurse was careful not to mention her name.

After the Ethics Board published its guidelines, doctors who practiced medicine were required to swear this oath like the Covenant, in front of witnesses, with one hand over the heart:

I swear by everything I hold sacred to use my knowledge and skills to heal those I can, harm none, and recognize the limitations on whom I can serve, for the greater good of all.

Two more people died that night because no one could access the infirmary, located mere feet away on the other side of the steel door. Jackson knew this event would be studied for a long time to learn from mistakes and to find better solutions.

In the Big Bear room, there were twenty-nine wounded, eleven dead, not counting four of the shooters. In the rest of the building, the lockdown worked. Only six were wounded, and the twelve dead were all shooters. If Jackson were thinking like a cop, he'd have thought it suspicious that every suspected shooter received a fatal gunshot, sometimes to the back of the head. Jackson decided he thought too much like a cop. He needed to think like an executive councilor.

Clyde Folsom pushed Rachel Night Pipe in front of himself while trying to get under the table, resulting in her being seriously wounded. Folsom swore it happened accidentally, no matter what the video had been running the whole time showed, or the photo that appeared on NewNet or in the next day's paper.

After the lockdown was lifted, the other police arrived. Jackson heard that upon reaching the location of the raid, they'd discovered two dead bodies—the dealer who lived there and the informer who had told the cops about the meet. They'd been dead at least a day.

After this incident, the Council created a policy that mandated all police officers to be stationed to cover all areas of the Circle instead of congregating in one location. Even if more police had been close by, it wouldn't have changed the outcome, as it was over in minutes. Not much could've been done. Still. Jackson waited until Ken Harris, the Brule County Sheriff, arrived, and he explained about Luke. He asked if someone would take Luke to the Juvenile Detention Center. Harris agreed to find someone because he'd personally take Caballo, now cuffed, to the county jail.

Jackson said, "Make sure the asshole stays alive. All these people," he waved to the room, "deserve justice. Let's not rob them of that." Harris nodded, understanding.

Jackson went up to Rose, still surrounded by family. He told her the police were going to take Luke now. She could visit him soon, not sure when.

Rose looked at him, a horrible understanding coming over her, and said dully, "I suppose he needs a lawyer."

"Yes, it is likely there will be charges, possibly serious ones."

She nodded and went to where Luke was standing next to Hotah. She didn't say a word to Luke, just to Hotah. Then a cop came and escorted Luke out.

After that, Jackson had to leave the room. He found himself in the lobby and was suddenly swarmed by, of all things, reporters. William Andrews, the radio host, as well as a journalist for the newspaper and others he didn't know had their phones out and in his face asking questions about what happened.

Realizing this would be part of his job if elected, he cleared his throat and stated, "This wasn't a mass shooting, so please refrain from using that term. This was the act of an evil drug lord who tried to organize a coup to take over our government. At this time, it seems the plan was simply to block all exits and kill those serving on the Council. The cartels rule with violence and fear. We're lucky Omímeya had prepared for active shooters. This was an attempt to destroy our new country, but they failed. Thank whatever you believe in for that."

After that, Jackson left, craving solitude yet loathing his isolation. Even with her ex-husband's girlfriend comforting her, he couldn't shake his envy of Rose. Violence and trauma had been Jackson's constant companions since childhood, and he wondered about the extent of the accumulated PTSD. Aware that he needed help, but unsure of what kind or how to seek it, he found himself in his room and, despite the early hour, drowned his sorrows in alcohol. As he succumbed to unconsciousness, he realized that this was probably not the help he needed.

The election proceeded as planned the next day. People said if not, the cartel would have won. The election committee had been working hard to devise a system that would make it extremely difficult for anyone to claim that an election was stolen. There were no secret ballots, as the system prioritized transparency. You could become a citizen, get your card, and vote the same day. Citizen Centers were set up at the polling places. Each site was open Sunday, nine am until 4:00 pm all over the Circle—high schools, community centers, and previous poll sites. The committee picked places to be within walking distance, and arranged rides for rural people. A person would take their printed paper ballots in Spanish and English, with photos of the candidates next to their names. After marking their choices, voters would print and sign their names, hold their ballots and their citizenship ID card up, and be photographed by a volunteer who'd have them watch while their votes were tallied in the computer. The paper ballots were put in a lockbox, watched by two other volunteers. Both radio stations announced the results by 6:00 pm.

Clyde Folsom lost the election by so many votes, a joke circulated that the only votes for him had come from his own family. While hypocrisy in politicians had become commonplace, cowardice—hiding behind a woman—was unforgivable.

Adam Diedrich withdrew from the race without giving a reason. Obviously, it was safer to be a banker. Thomas Russo won the seat for Infrastructure. Prior to the election, people joked that anyone supporting flush toilets should vote for Russo. Rachel Night Pipe withdrew. She'd have a long recovery. Shawn Caris ran unopposed. People hailed Pamela Nordstrom as a hero for both saving Mary Landrau and shouting "Active shooter" so quickly, which resulted in her receiving a surprising number of votes.

She said modestly, "I was a teacher. Active shooter drills were a regular part of my life before retiring."

Mary won by a comfortable margin. Duane Nelson, the retired telephone worker, won the Communication/IT seat vacated by David Kim. The big surprise of the night was Jerome "The Hippie" Brown, who beat out the well-known Carl Plenty Crow for the Agriculture seat by a large margin. Evidently, the people who still lived on Jerome's land since attending his permaculture event the day of Big Thunder had campaigned for him.

Chapter Nineteen
Karl

KARL WAS MISERABLE. He disliked this country, the crowds, the food, and what they called beer. It was bad enough to be on a tour bus visiting the sites of the Lewis and Clark expedition, but two weeks ago, Big Thunder had transported him to 1791. Now he was stuck in a church basement, with no money, no electricity, no internet, with a bunch of people he didn't like. All he wanted to do was go back to his beloved Germany.

Karl had no interest in visiting America, but he met this girl, Hannah, who he was very much interested in. She'd always dreamed of coming to America, attending a powwow, and seeing all the Indians in their regalia. Karl had few serious girlfriends, even though he was twenty-eight. After they'd been dating for a few months, they discussed taking a holiday together and planned a tentative trip to southern France. They asked for the same time off from their jobs. Karl was excited. He'd never gone on holiday with a girl before.

One day Karl and Hannah were attending an outdoor festival when an Arab family walked past, with two older children and a woman wearing a hijab pushing a stroller. Karl made a disparaging comment after she passed about how too many Arabs were ruining Germany, going off on an anti-immigration rant. Hannah said little, but went home afterwards instead of going to his place as planned. Later, she said she couldn't date a racist and didn't want to see him again.

Devastated, Karl believed he needed to make a grand gesture to win her back. He searched online, and found this late in the season, the Native American bus tours were all booked. He found one that followed the trail of Lewis and Clark, that included Native American museums. The tour fit in the vacation times they had scheduled for the holiday to France. The American tour was much more than he could afford, but he thought Hannah was worth it.

Hannah refused to answer his calls and texts. Finally, he showed up at her house, showing her the tickets, thinking it would win her back. It didn't. With his broken heart, wounded ego, and diminished bank account, he returned home and got drunk. Three days later, he went online to cancel the tickets and found to his horror that he'd missed the deadline for a refund by two days. He emailed and pleaded, but no luck, no refund.

He'd been looking forward to the tour, thinking he'd go with Hannah. Because Karl didn't want to waste the money, he talked his cousin Leon into coming with him, although Leon couldn't pay for his full share. Without Hannah, this entire trip was a mistake. His cousin was a poor substitute. Karl and Leon were the youngest people on the tour bus.

=..=

The church members requested a volunteer to assist hunters who brought venison. Karl offered, as he was bored. In the church parking lot, there were four guys, two trucks, and two dead deer. The church put out a call for hunters to bring fresh meat. It thrilled the guys they didn't need hunting tags, and the game was so plentiful. The entire process fascinated Karl. Out of the back of a truck they pulled out a portable table designed for processing game, hooked up a hose to the outside water spigot, and quickly broke down both carcasses into manageable chunks.

They shared their beer with him, although it was the terrible American stuff, and asked him questions about Germany. One guy said, "I don't believe Hitler killed all those Jews." Karl said that he thought Hitler made a mistake in putting his energy into killing Jews, that he could've won the war otherwise. They seemed to have similar politics as he did, but the American version. It surprised his new redneck friends he'd never shot a gun. They were planning more hunting trips and invited him along to teach him how to shoot.

Karl found he liked guns and didn't mind the blood and guts of hunting, although he didn't like, but he didn't particularly despise his new companions. They're talking about going to the Black Hills to pan for gold. Karl was considering going with them. He knew nothing about panning for gold, but it sounded like a lot of work for twenty dollars an ounce. Karl thought he could do better, although he didn't think he had transferable job skills, he had worked as a civil servant processing permits.

One guy worked at a beer distributor in Chamberlain. The company was looking to brew beer on a commercial scale. There was no shortage of wheat. They assumed being German, he knew how to brew beer. He didn't, but offered to do research. Karl thought working at a brewery in town would be better than panning for gold in hostile Indian territory.

Karl heard about the town hall meeting at the high school. There would be internet, so he went to the meeting, figuring he'd look for a job if the beer thing didn't work out. He briefly listened at the meeting, but the politics of creating a new country sounded like a Green Party wet dream to him and he wasn't interested. He spent his time online downloading discussion forums to read offline later.

None of the expeditions were scheduled for Europe until next year. This disappointed him as he wanted to go back to Germany, even if it was 233 years too early. Then he saw a post asking for a French speaker to go on an expedition to New Orleans that would depart within the week.

The small expedition would canoe down the Missouri River, connect to the Mississippi River at St. Louis, and then proceed to New Orleans. Although the route was downstream, they would paddle to speed up the journey. The requirements were for someone very fit, prepared to put in twelve-hour days, and able to withstand extreme outdoor conditions. Someone experienced in camping, hunting, and fishing. The only qualification he met was he could speak French. Karl was thrilled. If he could get to New Orleans, he could catch a ship from there to Europe. He filled out and sent the application while he had internet access.

Karl found a forum discussing a science fiction book series called *1632* by Eric Flint, about modern Americans being transported to seventeenth-century Germany. The weird thing was that the books closely resembled their situation. The series emphasized how knowledge of the future could be a source of fortune and influence. How the encyclopedia could foretell the outcome of battles, dates, and the deaths of important people. Karl had never even seen a paper encyclopedia, having grown up with the internet. He immediately realized the value of having information about the future and formed a plan. Karl knew that the French Revolution had started a couple of years earlier and that Europe was in turmoil. In 1791, Germany was not a unified country, consisting primarily of Prussia under the rule of the Holy Roman Emperor. It wasn't until after the Napoleonic Wars that

Germany became united. It was a critical point in history. Karl wondered how he could use foreknowledge of events as a source of power. To do anything, he'd need more information.

To check his email, he got a ride from one of his new friends into Chamberlain. He was pleased to find out he had an interview for the New Orleans expedition the next day at Chamberlain Hospital. The next morning, he packed up all his belongings and left the tour bus without saying goodbye, doubting anyone would even notice. Once at the hospital, he met with the organizers of the expedition along with two other travelers and a doctor named Katherine Moray. Dr. Moray, quizzing him in French, asked about his family and background. She said he was lucky to have a cousin here, as many lost their entire families.

He'd never considered that. He wasn't close to his family and wasn't particularly upset about never seeing them again. She informed the rest of the group that his French was sufficient, but he spoke with a noticeable German accent.

Kyle Ward, one of the organizers, asked directly, "Why do you want to come?" Asked about his experience in canoes. He had none. Asked about his general health and fitness. He lied. He never worked out. Asked about outdoor skills, first aid, and other skills. Karl had none. Karl was getting discouraged and wanted to turn the interview around, so he talked about how interested in expeditions of exploration he was. After all, he was in America on a bus tour for the Lewis and Clark expedition. Karl then asked his own questions, which made him seem more knowledgeable than he was. He asked about what type of canoe, and its cargo capacity, and rattled off several details about the Lewis and Clark expedition he was surprised he remembered. That impressed them.

He met the two men who were going: Raul Muñoz and Anthony Norcross. He was told that Muñoz would be the leader. Although this first expedition wasn't military, future ones would be. Muñoz would expect him to adhere to military discipline and follow commands. Could he agree to that? They asked him questions that suggested they might invite him to join, such as inquiring about his availability to start, whether any health conditions would hinder his participation, and whether he owned a laptop and phone. They asked him whether he understood the risks of being away from modern medicine into an area rife with malaria and yellow fever.

Preoccupied with changing history for personal gain, Karl had thought little about the risks of the journey or life in the late-eighteenth-century. He considered staying and getting a labor job, perhaps making beer, living in a country he hated, with people he despised, and figured going on this expedition was worth the risk. It was the fastest way he could return to Germany.

Kyle Ward asked directly, "Why do you want to come?"

Karl thought about lying and saying the thrill of adventure, but he thought this man would see through it. He told the truth, not all of it, but enough. "I want to go back to Germany; I'm hoping to find passage on a ship leaving New Orleans."

"How are you planning on paying for your passage?"

"Not sure yet, was thinking I might find work. I don't have ship experience, but perhaps they need a clerk." Karl hadn't thought that far ahead and was making it up as he went along.

Ward looked thoughtful and asked a few more questions, mostly about his education and past employment. He asked Karl to wait in the hall. Karl was hopeful. He figured if they're going to turn him down, they'd have sent him home. Since he didn't have a home or job, he needed this. They requested him to come back to the room and informed him they accepted him on the condition he successfully passed a physical examination. The pay was generous. He'd get some funds right away, which he could use to purchase items he'd need for the journey. They provided a list.

This was the first expedition. They planned another expedition to leave for New Orleans in a month with a flotilla that included a barge and modern boats. They expected that journey to take three to six weeks. The canoe journey would be faster. Their job was to provide intelligence about what to expect when the larger expedition arrived.

To maintain a low profile, the canoe crew would dress up as 1791 fur traders and blend in as much as they could. The first expedition would need to keep anything modern, like phones or laptops, hidden. When the bigger expedition arrived, they'd bring out modern marvels and make a big splash. Beforehand, they needed to get the lay of the land, understand the politics, find out the prices of grain and find buyers.

They asked Karl if he was interested in becoming their agent in Europe. If so, they would send him enough for the ship's passage and a small ongoing payment. They explained it would entail sending letters and reports, conducting reconnaissance similar to their plans for New Orleans, establishing contacts, and laying the groundwork for future efforts. Karl expressed keen interest and asked if they had any historical information they could provide him with. When Karl was doing research earlier, any history of this time, or information of anyone born after 1700, wasn't available on NewNet. Whenever he tried to access a particular event or person, a message popped up saying they were still uploading data, but he could email his request. Karl was told as an agent he could access information not available to the public.

There was a hiccup when they wanted to add his pay to his citizen's card. He wasn't a Changleska citizen. Karl had no desire to join their silly new country, and didn't want to swear any oaths. He was a German citizen; he still had his passport. They explained while dual citizenship was possible, Germany as a country didn't exist yet. After discussing it among themselves, they let him know he didn't need to be a citizen to join the expedition, but if he wanted to become their agent in Europe, he'd need citizenship.

Karl thought it would be disloyal to Germany to become a Changleska citizen. Then he realized he needed access to the information on NewNet. Lying and taking their oath would be a small price to pay. He took the oath and became a citizen. Everyone looked pleased, but Karl still felt disloyal. Ward appeared suspicious and wouldn't have accepted Karl if there had been other viable candidates. Karl would depart for New Orleans in a few days. They'd withhold his last payment until the larger expedition arrived. Karl was sure that had been Ward's recommendation. The group didn't fully trust him. After he became a citizen, he received an email with a link and a password, and suddenly he felt he had a chance. With information came power. Now he had a tool he could use to further his aims.

They told him of a motel he could stay in and when and where to meet. He had two days to get ready. After buying whatever items on the list he could find, he visited the library. In the back, he found the encyclopedias. Thinking ahead, he'd brought a sharp knife and a folder. He cut as many pages out as possible on anything that could be useful. He also got articles on Napoleon and all the various battles. When he got online, the credentials to the history websites worked. His computer was then loaded with information to change the course of history in Europe.

Karl had never been a good student, not smart like his cousin Leon, but he was meticulous and focused. He knew those traits would get him far with thorough research and detailed planning. He also knew he had a trait that would serve him best. Karl was ruthless.

=..=

The expedition would travel in an eighteen-foot birch bark canoe. It was a replica of what fur traders used that was on display at the Canoe Center at Omímeya. The canoe size had a limited cargo capacity, but it was lightweight. They didn't expect to portage as the Missouri and Mississippi were big rivers. Just in case, they packed everything in sixty-pound bundles, a more manageable size for the less muscular crew than the usual fur trade voyageurs. They carried food, camping gear, furs, and items to trade either along the way or in St. Louis. Hidden among their belongings were a few modern pistols as they carried flintlocks. They'd obtained most of the goods they carried from a fur trader named Big Stink, whose name everyone found funny.

They instructed Karl to leave a lot of his modern clothing, but provided him clothing they hoped would fit in with the locals. Because of a lack of historical information, a lot of guesswork was involved. Before meeting people, they'd hide the modern rain gear they'd brought.

In the historical briefing, they learned in 1791, St. Louis stood as a pivotal trading post on the rise, boasting a population of approximately 2,500 residents. Among the largest cities in the western region, it thrived as a colony of Spain, governed by a Spanish official. Originally established as a French settlement in 1764, control of the territory had since passed to the Spanish. Despite this, French remained the dominant language, reflecting its origins as a bustling French fur trading hub. In his history, St. Louis would transition to American ownership through the 1803 Louisiana Purchase.

The expedition carried a letter to post in St. Louis to the Hudson Bay Company. They dispatched another letter through another route, hoping one would reach its destination. They also carried letters from Father Murphy of St. Agnes to the Catholic churches in both St. Louis and New

Orleans. While the expedition brought copies of their new Declaration of Independence and Constitution, as well as supporting explanatory documents, these weren't to be disclosed until more proof of their otherworldly origin would arrive with the second expedition.

Muñoz received instructions to have a private meeting with the priest of the biggest church. He was to bring his laptop and show a film Father Murphy produced using the footage from Big Thunder, featuring shots of cars, airplanes, and the resort. Father Murphy asserted no witchcraft or evil was involved, just craftsmanship. The St. Louis priest was asked to recommend others who he thought should view it. They instructed the travelers to visit any other Catholic churches they encountered and gather letters from those priests verifying they'd seen the video.

Eventually, they intended these letters for the Pope in Rome. Father Murphy requested priests be sent to Changleska to convert the Indigenous tribes, as Changleska had planned extensive outreach expeditions for many tribes. Emphasizing the 233 years of advances in science and medicine, he asked the pope to send scholars and priests in those fields. Father Murphy emphasized the importance of speed, as the rest of the world would soon arrive. Although Karl had been told to never use the words time travel, to substitute "from a different world," Father Murphy used the term time travel frequently. Karl later discovered what was in the letters. None of them made it to Rome.

Karl was worried about how he'd manage the rigors of the journey, being stuck with two guys he didn't know in a small canoe, paddling every day. The journey was only expected to take a month. He could put up with anything for a month. To console himself, he reflected on what his life could be like in Europe. He could meet a nice German girl. A farm girl who would love to please him. Then it occurred to him, not a farm girl, he needed to marry into the Prussian nobility, with a politically powerful father-in-law to help him get started. He needed to be patient. He now had the tools, and believed he had the will.

PART IV
Week Four to Six

Chapter Twenty

Two Elks

TWO ELKS DIDN'T think it was a good day to die; as a matter of fact, he would rather not. Since the last moon, he'd felt deep in his bones danger was coming. Now he knew the source, and he was riding toward it. He was not afraid for his life, but for his people. Last moon, during a fair morning, the sky suddenly darkened. Thunder without lightning rolled in, a boom sounded louder than anything he'd ever heard, then the sky cleared, like nothing had happened.

In his tribe, there were people with strong medicine for healing or who had deep connections to the spirits. One *wičháša wakȟáŋ* (holy man) said the thunder beings brought a warning, or it brought a great blessing. He believed a special ceremony was needed. Everyone had a different suggestion. Two Elks respected their words, mostly. He learned he had to find his own way. There was too much mystery to understand what the spirits wanted from him. For twenty-five winters he'd led his people, starting when he was twenty winters old. He'd left his starving camp in a snowstorm and returned with two elks, gaining his name. Back then, his camp was small, his people weak, for the running face sickness had killed many. Little by little, his camp gained strength. He led warriors against the enemy; some strong, some weak. The Arikara who lived in this area were dying from the sicknesses which came from the wasicu. He killed their warriors, enslaved their women and children, and burned their camps so the sicknesses wouldn't spread. His band of Sicangu became a small tribe, growing until it became the largest for many weeks' ride in any direction.

Since the powerful thunder came, his scouts had returned with curious stories from neighboring bands. One was about a large iron wagon seen down a ravine, with many strange items inside—shiny things, clothes, objects like other wasicu had, but different. The day after they saw the wagon, a day's ride south, the scouts saw a white man walking alone. He shouted at them in his language, not French, so no one understood. The man screamed and cried piteously. It was obvious the man had the bad-head sickness, which meant spirit touched him. Best to treat him kindly and leave him alone. They left him food and water, gave him a blanket found in the iron wagon, and left. The man cried and tried to follow them, but they rode away.

Five or six days after the thunder, they were camped by the river when they saw the French trader, Big Stink, and his woman pulling his canoe upstream, their children strapped to their backs. They came ashore and told an interesting story. Big Stink, who no longer stunk, had his formerly long hair cut short, and wore a bright yellow vest with pockets all over it. Big Stink said on the day of the Thunder, a canoe came upriver without paddling—louder, bigger, and shinier than he'd ever seen. Two white men came with objects like he'd never imagined. Their small box called a phone could do astonishing things, such as capturing the exact likeness of a person or object. Big Stink wanted one, and offered many fine trade goods, including his best beaver pelts, but they said no.

When Big Stink offered to trade a turn with Broken Pot, whom he had gotten days before, they grew angry. He offered to sell her for a phone, but they said owning slaves was bad, yelled at him, talked among themselves, then pointed to a deer hide, which was nothing special, and said they'd trade many of their fine things for that hide, but Big Stink must give them Broken Pot as a gift. When doing trades, sometimes you gave a small gift at the end, especially if someone might regret the trade later.

Big Stink excitedly showed what things he got in trade for Broken Pot. Soon he realized Two Elks was getting angry, as he only got an old rifle and two blankets for her. Days later, Big Stink got many wonderful goods. Two Elks realized it wasn't Big Stink's fault. Things happened that were inexplicable. Big Stink continued his story. Four days later, another loud canoe came upriver without paddles. He could see five people on board.

The people in the canoe shouted, "Is anyone here sick?"

When Big Stink said no, two men and one woman came ashore. Two men stayed in the canoe. All the men carried rifles like he had never seen before.

The two men looked and dressed differently from the Lakota he was used to. They were larger and spoke a different dialect, which was understandable with effort. The woman was white, spoke accented but fluent French. Her name was Katherine Moray.

They stood back the length of a person and spoke loudly, saying, "Sometimes when two different peoples meet, a sickness that doesn't affect one, affects the other," so they didn't get close.

Katherine asked Big Stink many questions. He didn't understand why she wanted the answers, but he obliged her, as she was pretty. She wanted to know whether he was a Catholic. Did he work for the Hudson Bay Company? What did he know about the French Revolution? Who was king before the revolution? Who was the King of England? She asked him to name key figures in history. He'd never been good in school, but she seemed satisfied with his answers.

Katherine told a story he found hard to believe until he saw enough to know she spoke the truth. She said her people came from another world, brought by Big Thunder to protect the Lakota and all the tribes from the white man stealing all the land and poisoning the earth and water. She said her people brought many fine goods to trade but wouldn't trade phones as they came from their old world. They couldn't make more for many generations. One man brought out something like the phone, but bigger, called a laptop. It showed moving pictures with sound from their old world. He could see people flying in machines in the sky, cities with buildings so tall he didn't know how they got to the top. Wonders and wonders. Katherine told the truth; they came from another world. Big Stink was born in France. He came to this country as a young man. He knew there was nothing in Europe like what he saw on that laptop.

Katherine said they had powerful medicine and healers. In their world, almost no women died in childbirth, and very few babies. They had wiped out the running face sickness they call smallpox by putting a tiny drop of smallpox under the skin, which would protect people from getting it for the rest of their lives. Called "vaccination," it worked for other diseases too. They didn't bring any, but they could produce them locally. Katherine was uncertain about the time frame, perhaps within a year. They'd vaccinate everyone, as that would be good for everyone.

Katherine had offered to look at him and his family to make sure they were healthy. She said dirt brought illness. If they wanted to be healthy, they needed to be clean.

Two Elks knew it was true, as the wasicu didn't bathe often. Most thought that was why they brought sickness.

Katherine spoke to the men in English. Big Stink only knew a few words but heard his name.

One man asked in Lakota, "Do you like your name, Big Stink?"

Because of his understanding of the word for stink and its connection to the nose, he believed his Lakota name was Big Nose. He didn't like being called Big Stink. He told them the soap here made his skin peel and fall off. In France, the soap was better. He didn't stink as much in France. They said they had soap with them, and later they could trade for more. He said his real name was Claude.

Katherine said, "If we give you soap and you promise to wash every day, we'll call you Claude."

He wasn't sure if he would wash every day, but agreed. Before Katherine would get close to his family, she put a mask over her face, an apron over her clothes, and wore thin blue gloves on her hands. She took tools out of a bag and listened to their chests. She examined their eyes and ears, poked their bellies. Katherine said they were healthy now but could get sick if they didn't keep clean. She told them to wash their hands, especially after moving their bowels. She told Claude to shave his head and be careful to never get lice because that would bring disease. The papers she gave him contained instructions on how to prevent disease, written in both French and English.

She told him if he met any of her people, they wouldn't trade with him because he smelled so bad, they'd be afraid he'd get them sick. They brought many trade goods with them, better than anything he had ever seen or even heard of. They traded for almost everything he had, although they had better goods. Katherine told him that white men's greed for beaver for their hats would mean soon there'd be too few beavers. They said beaver dams helped the earth be healthy. In the future, they'd not trade beaver pelts. At first, Two Elks thought that was ridiculous. Beavers were like stars in the sky, they could never trap too many. Then he remembered his grandfather saying how many more there used to be in one stream or another as they passed by.

Claude learned how a "radio" worked. They showed him by speaking softly into a small box, asking the man on the canoe to raise his right hand in the air, then his left. They told him the radios they had now didn't go far, but someday soon they'd have ones they hear days and days away. He asked to see their rifles. After removing the ball differently than he would with his flintlock, they showed him. They stepped away from camp and shot at targets to show how powerful and fast their weapons were.

Two Elks thought the story sounded like the elders' tales of star people and animals that talked like people, told on winter nights. He listened not only because it was polite, but because it was interesting. Katherine asked him to tell others what he saw on the laptop and to display the trade goods. They promised him gifts if he'd spread their messages. They gave him silver to deliver a letter to the Hudson Bay Company. Along with the letter, they had messages for anyone along the way. He was to spread the word about the Changleska Coalition and the *Declaration of Independence* from Spain, which claimed the lands west of the Mississippi, not to conquer but to hold in trust for the Indigenous people. He was to talk about Changleska, its Covenant, and the Constitution. These thunder people were looking for allies and trade partners. They could teach many things from their old world like medicine, science, better ways to grow food, and machines to make life easier. They'd only trade with those who didn't have slaves. By next summer or fall, they'd have rifles better than flintlocks, but they'd only sell them to favored allies who agreed to the Covenant to protect the Earth.

Claude first came to Canada during the American Revolution; he saw how new countries were born. He was excited to be one of the first to pass on messages and show the wonders these people offered. Claude had his woman bring a bundle from the canoe. Two Elks examined the strange and wonderful objects he traded. He took out papers from a "plastic folder," was one of the many gifts they gave for bearing messages and delivering the letter. He was proud of how the folder protected paper better than oil cloth. Displaying a piece of fine paper, he showed Two Elks words written in English and French. He said that it was a copy of their *Declaration* and Constitution and gave him a copy. Two Elks couldn't read in any language, nor did he know anyone who could, but he saw the colors of the four directions on the sides, and the small picture of a tipi in a Circle at the top. He recognized it as important and carefully set it aside.

Big Stink and his woman presented Two Elks with a bundle of small gifts, not as fine as the trade goods, but unique and special. Claude gave him a small bag of corn and said the thunder people had more they wanted to trade. He couldn't carry much in his canoe. It was full of the new trade goods, without room for furs, because he wanted to go fast and light. He would earn more from these goods than from ten canoes of fur.

Two Elks learned from Big Stink the thunder people inhabited an area one or two days downstream from where he'd been camped. That concerned Two Elks, for he knew the entire area well. If there were strange people living in his territory, why hadn't he known about it? Maybe the thunder really brought them.

After Big Stink left, Two Elks talked to his advisors about what they should do. Some warriors said if the thunder people invaded their land, all their trade goods belonged to Two Elks. Others said thunder beings could be tricky, and it'd be best not to anger them. Two Elks heard about the fearsome weapons and thought he should approach slowly and carefully instead of sending in a bunch of warriors who might do something stupid.

=..=

His camp moved the next day. They were slowly making their way to their winter camp, only about nine or ten days past where Big Stink had his camp. Two Elks sent a trade mission to get more information about these thunder people. He sent his brother Long Tracks, an experienced trader who spoke French, Yellow Cloud, and his younger brother Spotted Calf. They didn't take many trade goods. If things went well, Two Elks would meet with the thunder people himself, surrounded by warriors. Then the trades would be more in his favor.

Two Elks sent out other scouting parties to learn about these new people. A few days later, three scouts returned with four dead bodies on horses. Two Elks was told they heard a noise long before they saw anything. Faster than any horse could run, an iron wagon raced towards them, with no horses pulling. They had heard the story of the iron wagon and the white man sick in the head. They slowed when they were close and the wagon stopped. Two wasicu men got out and shot them one by one, so fast even though they had weapons ready, four were dead before they could finally kill the wasicu men, but it was a near thing. Two Elks' scouts took many things from the wagon, including the weapons. They left the wagon because they didn't understand how it could run without horses.

Two Elks was furious. Big Stink had lied about these people. They were not looking for peaceful allies and trade. This was a trick to make him let his guard down. They had invaded his land and killed his people. Two Elks knew how to go to war. He tightened up camp and sent warriors to high ridges, looking as far as they could. Others closed in for protection, or ready to pass messages. He prepared to attack. He now possessed two of the strange weapons and was trying to figure them out.

Two days later Spotted Calf returned with Long Tracks slumped over his horse, badly injured. He told Two Elks they came to a place where the grass was browner, trees were gone, and the river had moved. They kept going until they saw a long wide path, black and smooth. They followed it to a large cabin. A wasicu came outside with a weapon. Long Tracks tried to talk to him. No one could understand each other, not even by using trade sign. Yellow Cloud put his weapons down, picked up a bundle of furs to show they only wanted to trade, and moved closer. The man yelled, but no one understood, so Yellow Cloud kept coming closer until the man shot and killed him. Then Long Tracks put an arrow in the white man, went inside the cabin and killed the woman.

Long Tracks was enraged and spent time with the wasicu to teach him a lesson, but the man cried and carried on like a child, so he let the man die. He took scalps and went through the cabin, amazed at all the rich goods. He made one bundle and gathered more for another. Spotted Calf was tying the bundle and the white man's rifle to a horse. When they heard a strange noise, they saw an iron wagon drive up the black path very fast. Long Tracks moved toward the wagon, and had notched his arrow when a white man hopped out of the wagon and shot him.

Spotted Calf remembered Two Elks teaching him a good warrior never rushes, but looks, listens, and knows when it's time to fight or wait until the conditions are on his side. Seeing the weapon used on Yellow Cloud, being shot at by a similar weapon, he knew it wasn't time to fight. Spotted Calf helped Long Tracks onto his horse and they returned as quickly as they could.

Two Elks thought the two men who killed his scouting party may have come for revenge after Long Tracks had killed the wasicu man and woman.

He wasn't sure it mattered. Death was coming. His warriors would have to use patience, guile, and their knowledge of the land. He had twenty-five winters of experience. He didn't win every battle, just most of them.

Two Elks kept the tribe moving slowly toward where the intruders lived. His scouts explored far and wide, while some skirted closer in. Returning reports confirmed it was obvious where the landscape had changed. Everyone was told not to be seen, to hide, not to fight. They'd pick the time and the ground. First, they must learn as much as possible about these new rich enemies with strong medicine, perhaps with thunder spirits on their side. No reason to rush. They stayed within that circle of ground which clearly differed than the surrounding land.

Sometimes they'd see machines flying over their heads, more often in the last few days. Two Elks remembered the story about people flying inside them and now believed. It worried him, although he didn't show it to his people. If people could fly like eagles, had canoes that went upstream with no paddles, travel in iron wagons that didn't need horses, they could have powerful medicine, but he knew they could die just like other men.

Long Tracks still lived, although not for much longer. The ball from the rifle had entered his side. He had a fever, and the wound had soured. People said his strength must be the reason he'd lived this long.

For the last three days, the enemy had been approaching, with each side scouting the other. When reports reached Two Elks, he knew he'd made a mistake. He couldn't win. Instead of his forces surrounding the enemy, they'd surrounded him. He'd been the strongest leader around because he had over fifty warriors, but they had hundreds. The enemy had not only one iron wagon, but many, some so large that ten men could fit inside—wagons with enormous weapons bigger than he'd ever seen. He'd heard stories about wars in the east and knew of cannons. He knew about the wasicu victory in a recent war in Ohio, where they killed or displaced all the Indigenous people.

It was too late to find a safe camp for the women and children, but he sent some off with a few of his best warriors to find other bands. Even if the thunder people wiped his tribe out, they'd continue to fight. He wanted to send his own family away, but as a leader, he couldn't.

Last night he shared his concerns with Black Rabbit, one of his best advisors. She'd said, "Don't fight, we'd die for no reason. Talk, smoke, parley. Let them think you believe their lies. Trade, but watch, wait, learn. After they invite you into their homes, learn their weakness, and when their guard is down, you strike. It may take a long time. They are a powerful enemy. We need to learn their medicine, so our tribe is strong."

Two Elks felt much love for Black Rabbit and opened his robes for her. It'd been a long time between the two of them as it made Many Horses mad.

The enemy camp was close. His scouts watched as they set it up. It was huge, filled with many square tents like the white men used, but bigger and shinier. There were many iron wagons he later learned were called cars or trucks, and many other strange items, many soldiers. Many of the soldiers wore matching clothes, with color patterns to resemble the land outside, making them harder to spot. Many wore black vests.

Two Elks told his scouts, "No matter what happens, don't kill or even fire at them."

They left their bows behind, taking only knives. He didn't want to anger them so they wouldn't talk. Two Elks situated the camp between two big streams for protection. The enemy couldn't cross the water easily. In front, he placed his best warriors' tipis in a protective line. Two Elks considered how to meet the enemy as he rode toward their camp. He knew about the white flag's meaning, but he had no desire to surrender. He was thinking of riding alone into their camp when two of his scouts ran towards him, shouting.

Two scouts, Makes Smoke and Black Stone, who had been watching the enemy camp, had crept in closer for a better look when one of them tripped on a wire. It made a loud shriek, which alerted the entire camp. Within seconds, three men and one woman surrounded them, all holding weapons and yelling at them in a language they didn't understand. By gestures, they were told to kneel on the ground. They blindfolded them and tied their hands behind their backs. They were raised up and walked into a camp tent and tied to chairs. Then, someone removed their blindfolds. They knew they were about to be tortured for information and each wondered how long he would last.

After a long wait, a Lakota man came in dressed like the others and asked their names. He said his name was Lou White Mountain, and that he was a sergeant in the Changleska Guard, but he really was a marine. They didn't know what that meant. He gave them water from strange clear bottles and asked whether they wanted food. They declined. He asked whether they needed to urinate; they did. More soldiers took them to the back of the camp. From the smell, they knew where to go—a board covered a slit trench with seats cut into it. Next to it lay a pile of rags and bottles of water, whose purpose they guessed at. There was even a separate area for women. Afterwards, the soldier who accompanied them insisted they wash their hands. He showed them how. After the soap, there was a large jug of water on a frame of sticks. They pushed a board at the bottom with their foot, pulling a string, tipping the jug so the water flowed out to rinse off their soapy hands.

Hearing this worried Two Elks. If they'd achieved that level of organization just for their elimination in a camp for only a few days, what would their war capabilities be like?

After the scouts were returned to the tent, Lou White Mountain asked the scouts what they did for Two Elks, surprising them with their knowledge of their leader's name.

"What was his plan? Why sneak into their camp? Did Two Elks wish to be friends or enemies? How many warriors? How many women and children?"

Questions they didn't answer, wondering when the knives would come out. Another man came in and asked more questions that Lou White Mountain interpreted. He inquired again whether they wanted food. They were insulted; they were warriors. To stay clearheaded, they'd accept water, but wouldn't eat the enemies' food. How weak did they think they were? They were given a message for Two Elks and sent back. Upon returning to their own camp, now free, they expressed to each other their offense at not being tortured to prove their strength. They were prepared to bite their own tongues out before answering questions. Happy to still have their tongues, they hurried to find Two Elks.

The message for Two Elks was simple, the people who called themselves Changleskans wished to talk, to listen; they hoped to trade. When the sun reached its peak, which they called noon, they would visit. They stated they would bring many soldiers and trucks, so there'd be no need to be alarmed. Their desire was for peaceful trade, not war. They only brought these things because they knew how fearsome the Lakota were. It would be their way of showing respect.

Two Elks knew all wasicu were liars, even with the many Lakota with them. He didn't trust their words. He remembered his promise to Black Rabbit and prepared to meet them peacefully. They set up the meeting lodge right in front of camp, including a fire pit, since the weather was chilly. He had heard wasicu were soft, not liking even a little cold. He had women prepare food while he waited and worried, trying not to show it, telling everyone about the lovely gifts and trades they'd be getting.

Two Elks heard their trucks long before he saw them. Shocking him to his core, two huge trucks pulled up on the other side of the stream he thought protected his camp, pulled out long pieces of metal, and before he even understood what was happening fit the pieces together, built a bridge, drove over the stream, and surrounded the camp.

Others drove to the front where Two Elks and his advisors waited in front of the large lodge, as that was the obvious spot to meet. Two Elks had been standing watching them build the bridge. Seeing the big weapons on top of the trucks, he realized something. They didn't need to build that bridge. Those weapons would have reached the camp easily. This was for show. He smiled. This he understood. Always show the enemy how strong you are.

Many men and a few women came out of the trucks. Behind them rode others on fine horses. Most stayed back. A handful from the trucks and a couple on horseback approached the fire. Two Lakota men approached with a tall Black man. Two Elks had heard of Black white men, but he'd never seen one. He'd heard they were slaves, except those who escaped to live with tribes south and east. The Lakota men were dressed in blue tight trousers and red shirts. One had a tall hat with a beautifully beaded band. The Black man was dressed in all black with a black vest. Two other soldiers, dressed in the patterned cloth and wearing hard hats, surrounded the Black man like he was being protected.

A soldier pointed angrily to someone wearing clothing he recognized as belonging to a friend that'd been killed. Someone else noticed a rifle worn by a warrior who killed the men in the truck. The Black man admonished them, obviously telling them to keep the peace. Their purpose for being here was not revenge. Two Elks felt relieved.

Two Elks decided to meet outside instead of the tipi, since he wanted to keep all of them in sight. He motioned towards the fire pit. Before they sat, the Black man said something on a button on his shirt. A voice answered back. *This must be a radio*, thought Two Elks. A young woman came running, bringing, then unfolding a chair, setting it up for the older Lakota man. Two Elks knew some elders had a difficult time getting off the ground. The enemy woman set up another chair and offered it to one of his older advisors who glanced at Two Elks who nodded, and he sat down with a sigh. Two Elks was impressed with the chairs. He'd seen nothing like them before. He was used to only stools and had never seen ones that folded up.

Everyone else sat on the ground, the older man translating: "My name is Joseph Chasing Hawk. This is my son, Gray Chasing Hawk. The Black man is Oliver Jackson. He's the Executive Councilor for the Changleska Coalition and Minister of Defense." He didn't introduce the others.

Jackson asked Joseph how to pronounce Two Elks' name in Lakota and tried to say it. It sounded terrible. Better not to bother. He asked for permission to use his English name instead. Two Elks learned the sound of his name in English and repeated it. Joseph translated, using the radio so everyone could hear.

Jackson began, "We're happy to meet with you. There's a lot we can learn from one another. We want to trade."

Two Elks stared at him for long seconds; he knew this game. "Why trade? You're on our land. Everything in it belongs to us."

A nearby soldier exclaimed something loudly and there was no need to translate. Two Elks knew it was the equivalent of "come and get it if you think you can." One of Two Elks' young warriors behind him bristled at the tone.

Jackson looked between the two men, then at Two Elks and said, "Young men are all the same, always want to fight, us older ones need to teach them you can often get what you want with no one dying."

Good start, thought Two Elks.

Jackson told him about Changleska and all he had heard from Big Stink. Two Elks realized he didn't know his people had heard this before. Best hold that close. The less an enemy knows what you know, the better. Two Elks said he'd be happy to trade. He wanted weapons. They told them they hadn't yet made the weapons, but they would only trade them to their most trusted allies. They had a few they'd gotten from Big Stink they could trade, but that was it for a while. Jackson promised if they joined Changleska, they'd share defenses. Lakota would share their knowledge of the land and their skill with horses, and Changleska would operate their weapons on their behalf. He explained they couldn't replicate all their weapons, which had originated from their old world, and thus had to use them sparingly.

A weakness, thought Two Elks in triumph, knowing the wonderful gun that Long Tracks had brought back was useless without the shot that fit. Jackson caught his expression, although Two Elks was usually careful in hiding his thoughts.

Jackson told him, "Our weapons may be limited in the future, but they work fine now. Would you like a demonstration?"

Two Elks agreed, curious. Jackson pointed to a big rock on the top of a small hill above the camp, a long way away. *Not even a cannon can reach that far*, thought Two Elks. Jackson told Two Elks to be sure none of his people were below that rock. Two Elks quickly sent a message. On that rock, he had stationed a scout for overwatch.

Two Elks asked, "Give us a little time, we need to check. Perhaps women were gathering plants underneath."

They both knew it was a lie. Jackson looked at him with new respect. When Two Elks assured Jackson it was safe, he spoke on the radio. Following an incredibly loud boom, the entire rock bigger than three tipis came sliding down the hill. While that demonstration impressed Two Elks, he knew he was right. They didn't need that bridge; their guns went very far. He also knew if he depended on their weapons to defend his people, his tribe would become their subjects. He didn't want to have his people subjugated by anyone.

Two Elks knew his pride sometimes interfered with his judgment. Better to remain silent. But today, he couldn't help himself.

He told Jackson, "Your weapons may be powerful. You may kill all of us today, men, women, and children. Not all my people are here, all the Lakota respect the Two Elks tribe. You will think you have won, sleeping easy in your beds, and you will wake up to your women and children dead. We will leave you alive so you will know how you failed to protect them. When you try to find us, we will be like ghosts in the wind. Little by little, you will find your horses gone, your trucks destroyed, your food supplies ruined, and all your powerful weapons spent. It will take a long time, and some of us will die, but in the end, we will win, because this is our land, our home, and we will never give up."

Jackson didn't look surprised or intimidated. Two Elks didn't know what to make of that.

Two Elks said, "Perhaps you don't believe, would you like a demonstration?"

Jackson agreed. A request was made by Two Elks for Jackson to speak on the radio and warn people not to stand in front of the juniper tree in the middle of their camp. Two Elks communicated a message to his warriors, who swiftly passed it to others through hand signs. A few minutes later, they heard someone on the radio exclaiming loudly. Two Elks didn't need a translation, but thought swearing might be involved. He was relieved. It was a shot from his best hunter, who'd been up a tree for a long time. He might have missed. Jackson talked on the radio and the people around stirred, everyone getting uncomfortable.

Jackson said, "We can kill you, you can kill us, but why should we? We want to keep Lakota lands from the white man. Big Thunder brought us here for a reason. Let us help."

Two Elks' pride was still up. Jackson made sense. Remembering Black Rabbit's words, he tried to think of a way to get back to talking about trade without losing face.

Suddenly Jackson said, "Two Elks, let's stop measuring dicks, make peace and trade." Two Elks just heard English.

Joseph said, "Jackson, I can't say that! I don't even know the word for dicks in Lakota."

"You know the word for penis, right?"

"Yes, there may be cultural issues. We don't know anything about the Lakota this far back."

"Joseph, since men first came out of caves, they have been measuring dicks."

"Translate it, exactly how I said it, except use the right word."

Two Elks didn't know what was being said, but figured it was a disagreement about translation. Then Joseph told him what Jackson had said, exactly. Two Elks looked at Jackson for a second or two and laughed. And passed it on to people around who didn't hear. Pretty soon everyone was laughing, especially the women.

Two Elks got up off the ground still laughing, said to Jackson, through Joseph, "I have to make water, let's go measure our *ché*."

They both walked a bit away, and stood a respectful distance apart, peeing on a bush. When they returned, Two Elks said quite seriously to everyone, "His is bigger, we would lose. We must make peace and trade instead." Everyone cracked up.

Hotah said, "I'm glad I wasn't the one to go over there. We'd all be living in tipis and shitting in the woods for the rest of our lives."

Which invited more laughter, especially after being translated. They started to talk trade.

Before they got into details, Jackson felt it had to be said. "We think we know what happened when you came to trade. Carl Ryobi shot Yellow Cloud. We know Yellow Cloud didn't have a weapon. This was a tragedy for everyone. Yellow Cloud's body was treated respectfully in the way our historians believed was proper. We will return him to you if you wish."

Two Elks found it surprising they knew Yellow Cloud's name and stated returning the body was unnecessary. He felt curious about the methods used, but decided that it wasn't the right time to inquire.

Jackson asked, "Did your wounded man survive?"

"My brother still lives, but barely."

"Your brother? We have powerful medicine. We can help."

"I doubt it. The wound soured, he is feverish, and he barely wakes now."

"Hold on."

Jackson walked away, talking on the radio, the two soldiers following him like shadows. Two Elks thought, *too bad they would not help Long Tracks.* He loved his brother, but he was their enemy. Two Elks knew when a man killed another holding a weapon, that was one thing; killing a woman without one, something else. Soon a truck pulled up, and a woman jumped out, not young or old, not white, from a tribe Two Elks was unfamiliar with.

She came up to Jackson, bent her head at him for a moment, a respectful gesture, and said, "Councilor."

Two Elks watched intently. Their conversation wasn't being translated. He was trying to pick it up from context. This woman *chan* was a healer. That part was obvious, but why the arguing? The woman folded her arms in front of her chest in the universal sign of "no, I won't." Then she talked on the radio. Everyone was looking uncomfortable. He figured it out. The woman healer, who may have been related to the people who were killed, refused to treat Long Tracks. However, he heard that both the people who were killed were wasicu, and it was obvious that she wasn't. He didn't understand.

Jackson said something to her. One word he heard was "Oath" which he had heard several times in the earlier argument. This time the woman straightened her back, put her hand on her heart, carefully and slowly repeated words. Jackson repeated back the last words she said, then said them again. The woman grinned joyfully. She pushed on her radio and started barking what appeared to be orders. People began running, bringing things from the truck. Soon came more orders, and more things.

Jackson, through Joseph, said, "Our doctor will look at your brother. We don't know whether it's too late, but our medicine is excellent for 'infections.' We can't promise he'll live, but without our medicine, he'll die. I promise you we'll do everything we can, as if he were my own brother."

Two Elks looked at Jackson. He knew how to read people and saw Jackson was telling the truth. He'd do everything in his power to save Long Tracks' life, like his own brother. While they waited for the doctor, Jackson asked where the tribe was heading. Two Elks tried to explain where the valley they would winter in was. Jackson spoke on the radio. Someone else ran out with a case in his hands. Two Elks thought, *did these people ever walk when asked to do something?* More radio talk, and more things brought running. Someone quickly arranged a small table, two chairs, and a laptop. Two Elks felt pleased that he'd remembered that word.

By now, Two Elks had seen many items from these thunder people that were all surprising, cunning, and different, but nothing prepared him for the laptop and Google Earth. They said in their old world you could use it to see any location on the planet. The entire planet wasn't a concept in Two Elks' frame of reference. The picture on the screen could get bigger or smaller, showing where they were now, and the diameter of the Circle of land brought by Big Thunder. Jackson said the center was at a place called the circle, with many cabins built together in the middle, a tipi-like structure taller than four of his tipis stacked on top. Two Elks thought *they were lying again, but why?*

On Google Earth, he saw the valley where he had planned to camp; they said it was about twenty miles from their Circle; it was close. He couldn't tell if they thought that was bad or good. *Bad*, he thought, judging by the lack of translation and the number of radio calls.

Jackson said, "We've brought gifts, not trades. We expect nothing in return. We'll trade later."

After a radio message, trucks started bringing boxes and bags. Jackson reached into one and pulled out a paper folder. Inside the folders were maps from Google Earth showing all along the river, all his territory. How did they know? Jackson apologized the maps weren't accurate for today. The maps showed buildings from their world they'd not brought back with them. Even the rivers had changed. He looked through the other gifts, feel pleased that he'd remembered that word.

By now, Two Elks had seen many items from these thunder people that were all surprising, cunning, and different, but nothing prepared him for the laptop and Google Earth. They said in their old world you could use it to see any location on the planet. The entire planet wasn't a concept in Two Elks' frame of reference. The picture on the screen could get bigger or smaller, showing where they were now, and the diameter of the Circle of land brought by Big Thunder. Jackson said the center was at a place called the circle, with many cabins built together in the middle, a tipi-like structure taller than four of his tipis stacked on top. Two Elks thought they were lying again, but why?

On Google Earth, he saw the valley where he had planned to camp; they said it was about twenty miles from their Circle; it was close. He couldn't tell if they thought that was bad or good. Bad, he thought, judging by the lack of translation and the number of radio calls.

Jackson said, "We've brought gifts, not trades. We expect nothing in return. We'll trade later."

After a radio message, trucks started bringing boxes and bags. Jackson reached into one and pulled out a paper folder. Inside the folders were maps from Google Earth showing all along the river, all his territory. How did they know? Jackson apologized the maps weren't accurate for today. The maps showed buildings from their world they'd not brought back with them. Even the rivers had changed. He looked through the other gifts, all wonderful, bright-colored clothes, pots and pans, knives. If these were gifts, he wondered what the trade goods would be like. Another radio call summoned another truck.

"Where would you like the corn?" Jackson inquired. "No reason to carry the bags. They are heavy. Undercover would be best, or perhaps we have an extra tarp."

Corn? thought Two Elks. So much to put under cover, heavy bags? He peered in the back of a truck, and saw bags and bags of corn, enough to feed his entire tribe for the winter. He was so utterly astonished he had no words.

Jackson looked smug. "You should thank Mary, our chief. Some people advised us to give you a few bags and trade the rest, but Mary said well-fed people make better trade partners. I'm sorry we'll need the bags back after they're empty. They're difficult to make."

Two Elks was getting over his shock, surprised about a woman chief. He'd thought Jackson was the chief. Women chiefs were unusual, but not unheard of. The two sides decided to wait a few days for further negotiations. They'd meet up when the tribe moved closer. No one felt the need to rush, and both sides were glad no one was dying today.

The doctor returned. Joseph told Two Elks, "The doctor thinks there's a good chance we can save him, but there's no guarantee. He needs IV therapy and surgery in a hospital—that's a big house of healing. The trip would take many hours to get to the hospital in the truck because of the lack of roads along the way. It would be bumpy, and the bullet might move and make things worse. It'd be best to go by 'helicopter' so he could be there in twenty minutes. The helicopter was close. They'd prepared for casualties and stationed it nearby."

Two Elks was getting overwhelmed with all the new information and words. The doctor came to him and put her hand on his arm. He looked up, surprised. She spoke gently, and Joseph translated again.

"We can fly him in the air like a bird, smooth and fast. He'll be there soon and he'll have a better chance of surviving than if he went in a truck."

Two Elks wondered whether he was doing the right thing to send his brother to die with strangers, but it would be better for him not to die. The thunder people seemed to think he would live.

He asked, "Can I send people with him?"

Two Elks wanted to go himself. He couldn't leave his people, but was curious to see how much they claimed was true. The doctor spoke on the radio.

"The helicopter can take one other person, but not bring them back. They'll have to stay with him for many days, but it'll be very different, possibly frightening. Does he have a wife or mother?"

Their mother was long gone, but Long Tracks' first wife, Good Voice, would be good to send. She was older, sensible, and a keen observer. His two younger wives had small children. They decided where the helicopter should land, and the doctor left to see to the transfer. Two Elks sent for Good Voice, letting her know she might be gone for weeks. He knew his women would throw a fit if they had to be gone for weeks and hadn't packed properly. After the helicopter landed, Long Tracks and Good Voice flew away inside the giant noisy bird. Two Elks thought about his brother, whom he'd already regarded as dead, who now might live. Yes, thunder beings had sent these people, but was it a warning or a great blessing?

Chapter Twenty-One
Elliot

ELLIOT WOKE UP grumpy, unhappy to go to work at the same job he'd held before Big Thunder five weeks ago. He didn't like his job then and hated it now. Being the only lawyer available, he practiced criminal law at the Tribal Law Center because there was no one to take his place. He was stuck. It was a real job that paid the bills, so he was double stuck. He wanted to work full-time on the Law Committee. He was an officer, the Secretary, responsible for documentation. Because of the enormous amount of paperwork, Changleska paid him the highest monthly stipend offered, $500.00 a month. Which wasn't enough to live on, especially with prices on anything from the old world sky-high. A bag of Cheetos was going for a hundred dollars if you could even find one.

He finally convinced his Auntie Mary to allow him to participate in the treaty negotiations with its first Indigenous tribe, the Two Elks band. He didn't get anywhere at first. The Law Committee didn't want to bring it to the Council since they didn't consider his request urgent defined as an immediate threat to health and safety even though he tried to argue it was. He cornered Mary on her way somewhere and told her he needed to be present at all meetings between Two Elks and Jackson. She reminded him that Jackson had already turned him down, as he believed that fewer people should be present.

Elliot told her, "Jackson is clueless. You know he has Joseph Chasing Hawk interpreting, who speaks a different dialect than Two Elks. We may be agreeing to different things."

"Jackson says it is important not to be seen as adversarial. He's spent years studying nonviolent interactions."

"Spending years teaching cops not to kill innocent people is not applicable. An expert in treaty law is."

Mary sighed. "What do you suggest?"

"It is essential for me to attend all meetings, review all written materials, and have the historian examine them. I spent years studying treaty law to prove the United States' violations, to protect our rights and regain land. I've never been on the other side before."

"All right, I agree this is historic. The first one sets a precedent."

"It is like writing a prenup. Nobody starts out thinking there'll be a divorce, but when it happens, someone usually gets screwed."

Elliot could see Mary was coming around.

"For language, we need Gift of Thunder present. Her English is getting better. She is the only one who can speak both."

"You're kidding? You want to send a fourteen-year-old girl to the man who killed her family, enslaved her, then sold her to be raped?"

"She's not as delicate as you think. Have you been around her? She and Kimi sing with my cousin Darla. I see her often."

"No way. We need to protect that child."

"Should be her choice. I've heard her say she wants to visit. It'd been her family since she was nine years old. She practically raised Two Elks' son by herself."

"I heard about that. What is his name again?"

"Bites the Dog."

"I thought we had funny names."

Mary took a moment, obviously thinking. "I agree we need you or an expert in treaty law at all future meetings with Two Elks. Your role is contingent on your work not being neglected at the Law Center. As to Gift, I'll ask Hotah, as her legal guardian. He can ask her. If they both agree, she can go."

"As of Monday, he is her legal father. The adoption papers went through."

Mary smiled happily. "That's wonderful."

"I'm sure you'll get an invitation to the formal ceremony and party. Should be soon."

Elliot was waiting for word from Two Elks about the next meeting. Gift was excited about being allowed to go and was picking out gifts for everyone. Two Elks was in no rush. He had one excuse after another: a buffalo hunt, a ceremony, or settling into winter camp. Elliot knew it was a game in negotiation. He wondered whether Jackson did.

He tried to stay available in case the meeting were to come on short notice. His schedule was flexible except for court dates, which were set in stone. He had court tomorrow, a case he was dreading, involving Rose Chasing Hawk's son, Luke Trenton. Since they were still using the old laws, there were jurisdictional problems. The crime happened on tribal land. Lower Brule was still a sovereign nation, but Luke wasn't a member of any tribe. It was a nightmare. Because Luke was a child present during Big Thunder, he automatically received Changleska Citizenship, although he wasn't eligible to take the oath until age eighteen, or seventeen if he joined the service. So far, Changleska laws hadn't addressed juvenile offenders. Until new laws were written, the old state or federal laws applied.

The drug lord's attempted coup had infuriated everyone; Elliot included. He had relatives who were wounded. The county district attorney threw the book at Luke, then threw the whole library, including conspiracy to commit murder, treason, and other charges. Tried as an adult, Luke could get a life sentence, although unlikely, a death sentence was possible. After Caballo (real name, Anthony Riveria) had been executed and his cohorts had died, there was no place remaining for people's rage; they wanted to blame someone. At tomorrow's hearing, he'd fight to have Luke tried as a juvenile. It worried Elliot if he lost, it might be a fight for Luke's life.

Elliot had always opposed capital punishment—those executed were mainly people of color, poor, or usually both. DNA or other additional evidence exonerated too many death row inmates. The US was one of the few countries in the developed world that still executed people.

Elliot not only witnessed everything in the Big Bear room that horrible afternoon, but he missed getting shot by inches. Elliot realized his stand on capital punishment was an old-world indulgence. Here and now, capital punishment was a given. He'd help write the new law to make it quick, with no endless appeals, and no time on death row, humane, painless as possible, and foolproof. He pointed out capital punishment shouldn't be the first law passed, important for history. After they ratified laws passed by the Acting Council, the first law passed was the legalization of cannabis, including recreational use for anyone over twenty-one. Next were other laws that the committee had ready, waiting for the election. Capital punishment ended up being the eighth law passed that first day, passed seven to zero.

The Law Committee chose hanging as the method of execution, which was prevalent in 1791. The concessions to modern sensibilities included not holding executions in public, including not announcing the dates and times beforehand. They debated whether to allow families of the victims to observe. They ended up polling those whose immediate family members had been killed, and four out of the eleven witnessed the execution through closed-circuit TV, with no recording.

Three doctors randomly picked decided the best method of hanging someone humanely. It turned out to be more complicated than anyone realized. They decided not to build a gallows, as there were plenty of sturdy beams in the jail, used for that purpose by plenty of inmates over the years. They got an engineer to check out the beams, found a likely spot, and thought they had a foolproof system.

Everyone assumed, as in the movies, the accused would calmly walk up the steps, allowing the executioner to place the bag over their head. They would pull the lever, and it'd be done. However, no one expected Caballo to fight wildly and refuse to walk up the steps. Eventually, he was tased, handcuffed, heavily sedated, and dragged up the steps before the deed was done. Witnesses later expressed regret for watching, as it didn't bring them closure. However, one man, who had lost his wife and whose daughter had been wounded, was disappointed that they didn't record the execution. He wanted to watch it again and again.

=..=

Elliot made his breakfast of cornmeal mush with sorghum syrup, distracted enough not to miss Captain Crunch or eggs and bacon. He wondered whether the military would make an exception and lower the recruiting age from seventeen to sixteen so Luke could join. His birthday was only a month away. It would solve several problems and be best for Luke.

The Changleska Guard, or as he teased his cousin, "Guardians of the Galaxy," was trying to figure itself out. After the election, attempted coup, and threat of Two Elks, the National Guard joined Changleska. Jackson liked "Defense Force" while General Gardner favored Changleska Guard. The marines wanted a separate unit. They pointed out that water would be their primary mode of transportation, so they started planning a Navy with a marine unit. The term Air Guard was easy, with only three planes and a helicopter under the command of General Gardner. No aerospace engineers were conveniently staying at the resort during Big Thunder, so Changleska was unlikely to build planes anytime soon, but there was an online forum for balloons or lighter than air.

Everyone in the National Guard unit said their oaths at a big ceremony at the same time. Most people were happy about it, except Clyde Folsom, who had a fit on the radio, along with a few county diehards on his side. After the election, he'd rebranded himself as a religious leader and was quickly gaining a cult-like following.

When the new military was announced, older veterans came out of retirement to help train the new recruits. Before the merge with the National Guard, they thought they were starting from scratch. The old vets couldn't agree on a protocol to follow, especially with rank and salutes. Saluting in the military historically had a lot of rules, and if someone forgot them and saluted an officer in a combat zone, the enemy could target them. People also pointed out that saluting began as menials doffing their caps at superiors, a reminder no one liked. The when and where of the new 'salutes' was still under discussion.

Elliot liked the new protocol developing: a respectful head nod accepted as a salute and placing a hand on the heart when a direct order was given as a reminder of their oath. Oaths were starting to be taken more seriously than in the old world. Accusing someone of being an oath breaker was a serious accusation.

Elliot's cousin, Theo, and his friend, Scott, joined up to serve their new country. It surprised Elliot how the military changed them. Before Big Thunder, he wasn't sure if Theo would ever get a job, or if Scott would ever move off his couch. Now they got up early, stopped drinking and smoking weed, and even cleaned up after themselves. It thrilled Elliot they would move into the barracks as soon as construction wrapped up.

After the election, the second law passed was a hefty military budget. Rose Chasing Hawk insisted on implementing an accounting system with multiple levels of checks and balances to ensure that government funds were well spent and didn't go astray. Omímeya paid all the government bills for now. As soon as the new system was in place, Rose would ensure that the proper accounts were repaid back to the penny.

=..=

Elliot was relieved cell phones were working, at least for those with Tribal TeleComm SIM cards, which were in short supply. Unfortunately, there is no way to create replacements. However, they programmed the Verizon and T-Mobile towers, so now signals reached about twenty-five miles beyond the Circle. Landlines were back in a big way, especially since the only way to get NewNet in your home was to have a landline for DSL or to live close enough to use someone's Wi-Fi.

The old-world internet was gone forever, but NewNet was growing, becoming more useful every day. Currently, NewNet was free, but was under review. The question was how people who ran it would get paid. Ownership was complex. Prior to Big Thunder, Omímeya obtained all the software, like Internet-in-a-Box, multiple databases, and bought extra servers and computer hardware. They hosted the servers, provided space and security, and paid IT staff to develop and maintain NewNet.

Elliot had concerns about a private corporation controlling the Internet, even though it was benign now. There were discussions about nationalizing NewNet, making it part of Infrastructure. Unfortunately, NewNet was still slow and hard to use. They needed more computer engineers and a way to pay them, but the Changleska government faced significant financial challenges.

Their bank loan was about gone, and it would take time before they had other sources of income. Taxes on businesses were in the works, but there was a debate about whether to tax a business on its entire year's income or only on its income after Big Thunder. Elliot thought if the government controlled NewNet, there'd be little incentive to pay to improve services, being a monopoly for the foreseeable future. Would the government put NewNet improvements on the back burner when they had cutbacks?

Elliot also had concerns about any corporation or government controlling the Internet, a government he's now a part of. He knew that information itself could be a weapon, a way to control people, and worried about the specter of online censorship, convinced that a free society hinged on unrestricted access to information.

His work in environmental law frequently relied on the Freedom of Information Act. While he understood the necessity of restricting access to certain defense forums, he found himself puzzled by the abundance of password-protected forums elsewhere. Some cases were straightforward, with working groups seeking to maintain the integrity of their discussions. However, sometimes the rationale behind the restrictions was far from clear.

The community forums were becoming the heart of organization for Changleska. Elliot took part in many besides the law forums. He followed the East Coast Expedition forum closely. Unlike the other members, he did not care about meeting George Washington; instead, he wanted to work on treaties. He'd studied many treaties that were being written now. He knew he had to focus on Changleska, not try to right the wrongs done to all tribes.

As an officer of the Law Committee, he held a level one security clearance. He was present at discussions of how much access to technology Changleska should share with the outside world. Most people didn't realize that Omímeya had the entire Wikipedia on its servers, since it was only slowly releasing vetted pages. The dilemma was how much to tell the world about time travel and possible futures, including the fate of individuals. Others argued it was a distraction from the core mission of the Covenant.

Elliot was in the meeting when they sent the first expedition four days after Big Thunder. At first, there was a theory circulating they were sent to an alternative universe with a different history. To find out, they prioritized sending a French speaker to interview the asshole rapist called appropriately Big Stink. There was much debate about allowing him to carry messages about Changleska to the world, but since no one had a better idea, they agreed.

Rose suggested writing a letter to the Hudson Bay Company (HBC), a powerful corporation during this time. They had history of treating Indigenous people fairly and maintained strong business connections around the world. HBC could become an important trading partner. People argued against rushing into anything, but knew time was running out. They needed to set the agenda to control the conversation. They decided to minimize the usage of the term "time travel". "Big Thunder sent us here from a different world to save the Earth." That's our story, and we are sticking to it.

Elliot congratulated himself on hiring Carrie Sorenson as a part-time assistant. It took his whole stipend from the Law Committee and then some. The law office had a receptionist and a paralegal, both so overworked they couldn't assist him. He knew he couldn't keep up with the Law Committee and this job. Something had to give, that was part of his paycheck. Carrie made his life easier. When Elliot got to the office, the materials he'd requested on juveniles being tried as adults were in his inbox, as well as historical documents on capital punishment for minors. Carrie listed details about other upcoming cases and their status. He didn't know how he'd manage without her. He was trying to get her hired as permanent staff, but it wasn't clear how the law office would stay open with the staff it had.

Elliot met Carrie during the election campaign for Jerome Brown's run for the Executive Council. Elliot had a run-in with Carl Plenty Crow about pesticides. Some people assumed all Natives were back-to-nature types. In South Dakota, Native ranchers often used herbicides, pesticides, and chemical fertilizers. The next day, he used his precious gas to drive out to White River Farm to take Jerome to a meeting. He knew Jerome and his girlfriend, Shelly, well. After convincing Jerome to run against Carl, neither thought he could win, but talking about the risks of agricultural chemicals was important, so he agreed. Elliot doubted Jerome would've agreed if he'd thought he would win. The Council was a full-time job, and Jerome had the farm to operate.

Nine days before the election, Elliot and Shelly decided a campaign event was in order. Elliot got Kathy's Bus to pick people up from White River Farm. Afterwards, they realized theirs had been the only organized campaign. Folsom didn't enter the race until the last minute. Everybody voted for whomever was better known or more popular.

Elliot tried to explain how conservative people were around here. He pushed for access to showers and regular clothes to make a better impression. He persuaded Rose to let the group use the gym and pool showers, though the pool was closed due to staffing shortages. The farm had solar showers, but long, hot showers and clean clothes were more appealing. They crammed sixty people onto the twenty-five-person bus, leaving disappointed people behind. Elliot had no idea that campaigning would be so popular.

Rose refused to donate meeting space for a private campaign function, but would be happy to rent him a meeting room. The campaign met at the community center instead.

After spending a few minutes with the supposed organizer, Carrie took pity on Elliot and took over. She tasked people, made lists of talking points, organized calls, and planned what was needed. At the initial meeting, she gave pointers like "Ignore comments about Jerome the hippy, mention his degree, or don't tell people Carl Plenty Crow is an oath breaker; just because he is talking about looking into something doesn't mean he'll do it."

After hearing boos from the room, she said to the crowd, "When they go low, what do we do?" The crowd obliged, "We go high." Then she had them repeat it louder.

Jerome's victory in the election didn't surprise Carrie, but both Elliot and Jerome were shocked. Elliot was so impressed with Carrie that he'd thought she was a professional campaign manager. Nope, she worked part time at an insurance office but was a dedicated activist. She wasn't unhappy about leaving her life behind; in her mid-forties she was single with her parents gone. She hated living in primitive conditions, so she was glad to move and take the job with Elliot. He was able to find her housing with one of his aunties getting on in years but not ready to live at the Living Wisdom Centers. She'd moved stuff out of her craft room, traded rent for minor chores and companionship. Carrie didn't even have to cook as Auntie was over sixty-five and ate at the community center.

=..=

During the election campaign, Elliot met a woman whom he was both attracted to and repelled by. He didn't know what to make of the whole situation, so he focused on work. She kept finding reasons to run into him, like the way she showed up at Luke Trenton's hearing. He suspected Carrie was the fink who'd shared his schedule. It embarrassed him to see her there, dressed inappropriately for court, in a weird combination of clothes from the donation bin. He tried to ignore her, but she kept waving.

Rose inquired, "Who's that woman who keeps waving at you? I thought we're the only case today."

"We are the only case. She's someone who lives out at White River Farm."

"I think she likes you."

"That's what I am afraid of."

The hearing went well. The judge ruled in their favor to try Luke as a juvenile, but he wanted to schedule the final court date sooner than Elliot wanted. He thought the longer it took, the greater the chance the anger towards Luke would fade. He was able to delay it for three weeks, citing the serious nature of the charges.

Everyone wanted to close the jails and detention facilities by the first of the year and use work crews instead. Luke started out as a stupid, privileged kid. The longer he stayed in the juvenile system, the more criminalized he would become, and the worse his chances were of having a normal life. Elliot saw it every day, one reason he hated criminal law. Elliot hoped to use his position on the Law Committee to change the criminal justice system. It didn't offer justice and mostly taught people how to become better criminals.

After the hearing, he escaped his admirer/stalker by walking fast and talking to Rose as they left the building. Her name turned out to be Morning Star, born Debra Cohen. She said she got her name during an ayahuasca ceremony. She was the exact type of person they called a "pretendian."

When he mentioned some people found whites taking Native names offensive, she said, "So you can take a vision name, but no one else can? I never liked Debra Cohen; I love Morning Star."

Elliot assured her he wasn't offended, but others were. She was pretty and thin, which he liked, but he found her long dreadlocks mildly repulsive. He had worn long hair all his life and felt his hair was an extension of his nervous system. Brushing and braiding his hair in the morning woke him up and cleared his mind. If he left his braids in for a day or two, he felt groggy. Why a white person would never want to brush their hair was beyond him. He also thought it was cultural appropriation of African culture, who had good reasons to wear their hair like that.

Morning Star, he thought as he decided to respect her name of choice, was good at adopting aspects of Native culture she liked and scoffing at what she didn't. She reminded him of people who came to Standing Rock, not respecting the Native culture, or understanding when people were offended.

Elliot and Morning Star shared a passion for protecting the Earth. She hadn't been to the Standing Rock protests but was active in environmental political. She studied herbs and was a doula, a professional labor coach. When he told her about the new midwifery school that wouldn't require nursing as a prerequisite, she was thrilled. She said she would need to move into town to attend, but housing was hard to find. Then she said she heard his cousin Theo was moving into the barracks soon. Elliot ignored her subtle and not-so-subtle attempts at getting him in the sack, but he felt sexually attracted to her. It bothered him. He tried to keep busy and not to be alone with her. He never invited her to his house. But they started spending more time together, and he found himself liking her more and more. She was smart and funny.

She talked about the plans people were making out at White River Farm. Although Jerome and Shelly were Rosebud tribal members, almost all the displaced people there were white, except for a couple of Blacks and people of other ethnicities. Although Elliot knew nothing about permaculture, he appreciated what Jerome did out there. They'd scheduled him to speak at their event the Sunday after Big Thunder on Indigenous environmental issues, which, of course, he missed. Since Elliot couldn't call, Jerome had assumed something serious came up. Later they laughed about it, Jerome saying the only valid excuse for missing a speaking engagement was being transported to 1791.

One day Elliot and Morning Star got into an argument, but not as they often did, debating in the way intelligent people do that can be fun. On this occasion, it got heated. Elliot didn't feel he was wrong, but he expressed himself badly, in a hurtful way. She was a vegan, like many of the displaced at White River Farm still were. Good thing they had literal tons of soybeans. No one else wanted to eat beans with game and buffalo so plentiful. She trotted out the theory of how eating meat was killing the planet. He acknowledged her point about factory-farmed meat in the old world. Elliot patiently explained that buffalo and cattle hooves dug up and aerated grasslands and their manure spread seeds far and wide. Both were a necessary part of keeping down greenhouse gas and creating a healthy ecosystem. She kept going on about veganism like a Christian trying to convert him.

He tried, "Name one vegan Indigenous tribe anywhere in the world." Of course, she couldn't. That made her angry, retorting there must be a tribe somewhere.

He should have let it go and walked away, because next he said, "You are vegan because of your white privilege, money for all the fake meat, eggs, and cheese, which takes way more processing than any animal. You are so worried about animal rights. Around here, humans are bought and sold. One of them is a friend of mine. Try doing something for someone who does not support your point of view for a change."

Now they didn't talk, he found he missed her. A long time later, Elliot ran into Morning Star at the community center for one of his relative's fiftieth wedding anniversary party. It surprised him she knew both people, and her appearance shocked him. She'd cut off her dreads and sported a very short, cute haircut. Her figure had filled out, still slender but curvier. She looked clean and well put together. She had gotten a job as an aide at the Living Wisdom Center close to where he lived.

While the midwifery program didn't require nursing or education beyond a high school diploma, it had very limited openings. The births she attended as a doula counted towards the fifty births required for graduation but didn't qualify her for admission. One year of caregiving experience was required. A home health aide, nursing home, or even caring for a relative might count. Morning Star didn't qualify, as she had done nothing along those lines. She moved out of White River Farm and found a shared apartment with five others who worked at the care center, all Hispanic women. She was taking Lakota classes and volunteered at the food pantry. Elliot invited her to his house for dinner. He said he'd make something vegan. She said, "No need, left my privilege in the old world." She never moved back to her shared apartment.

Chapter Twenty-Two

Jamal

JAMAL ALSTON MISSED his cat. In the five weeks since Big Thunder, he should've missed his family more, but it was his cat, Sprinkles, he thought of most often. Not that he didn't miss his family terribly. Last year, he'd had all his wisdom teeth removed at once. The procedure itself didn't hurt. When the anesthesia wore off, he had a low level of pain, but if he probed an empty socket with his tongue, then it really hurt. This was similar. If he thought about losing his family, he could barely stand it, especially the loss of his mother. At twenty years old, he was still a mama's boy. He called his mother every Sunday at 3:00 pm, and they rarely missed it. Both texted each other almost every day.

Both of Jamal's parents were prominent Black attorneys who worked in a big Chicago law firm specializing in civil rights and wrongful death claims. He grew up attending elite private schools and lived in an upscale neighborhood. His parents paid for his college education, a nice apartment, a new Lexus hybrid car, and a generous allowance.

Jamal met Nels when he'd just turned nineteen, in his freshman year at the University of Colorado, Boulder, where he was studying mechanical engineering. He'd heard that opposites attract, and certainly he and Nels were opposites. He was short, five-foot-seven-inch, stocky, and average-looking. Nels was tall, six-foot-three-inch, thin, with blond shoulder-length hair and blue eyes, and gorgeous. Jamal thought he looked like Thor in the superhero movies. They met at an LGBTQ event during Pride Week. Jamal was utterly surprised when Nels came up and talked to him. They hooked up that night, and the next, and every chance they had until Big Thunder threw them back to 1791 and they were living with a bunch of people where they had no privacy.

Nels and Jamal hadn't been together long when they got themselves a rescue kitten, Sprinkles. No one had wanted her because she had a bladder problem that needed expensive veterinary care. Getting that kitten was like having a child, or so they both felt. Nels, a junior in environmental science, loved the outdoors, hiking, and camping. Although he had no experience doing it, he loved the idea of permaculture. Nels convinced Jamal to attend a permaculture gathering in rural South Dakota. Jamal didn't find the subject interesting enough to justify the long drive and being away from home and Sprinkles for ten days. But they went, because when you love someone, you make compromises. Nels attended rap concerts even though Jamal knew he didn't like the music. At this event, the workshops would only take place on Friday, Saturday, and Sunday. Participants could arrive a week early and extend their stay for an extra week. Many people did, particularly those who had traveled a long way. Nels wanted to stay for the full two weeks, but Jamal's classes started the Tuesday after the event. Nels' started too, but he was willing to miss his first few days of classes. Jamal put his foot down, which he rarely did.

When Jamal came out to his parents in high school, his mother said she already knew. Jamal believed his dad might have felt disappointed, but both his parents had always shown their love and support. Nels' family was religious. When he told them he was gay after his first year in college, they cut him out of their lives completely. Because Nels was under twenty-six and his family was middle income, he didn't qualify for grants, and didn't have good enough grades for scholarships. He relied on student loans and worked as many jobs as he could to stay in school.

When they'd only been dating for a few weeks, Nels mentioned his rent was due, and he'd have to take extra shifts working at his gig delivery job. It was obvious Nels would move in. They were both surprised he was still there over a year later.

It was Jamal's first relationship. Nothing compares to the intensity of first love. After Nels moved in, they discussed monogamy. Both agreed they were too young and weren't ready to settle down, but as it worked out, they were monogamous, which made Jamal happy. It surprised him as Nels was such a free spirit, and so good-looking he could be with anyone he wanted. Nels had a hard time settling for anything. This interest in permaculture was new. He had a passion for forests and chose an environmental degree, but he didn't want to work for the Forest Service. Then there was the animal rights phase. New causes he was excited about came and went. He was attending the Buddhist temple, popular in Boulder, when he met

Jamal, who had no interest in going. Nels dropped Buddhism with no apparent regrets.

Jamal hated camping. He was a clean freak. Being away from hot showers or being dirty was hell for him. He went on a couple of camping and hiking trips with Nels when they first got together; it wasn't for him. Nels went without him after that. Nels assured him this event wouldn't be the same as a camping trip. There were showers and bathrooms. Only a few of the workshops interested Jamal, but he decided if he could work on his project, he'd go. Jamal wasn't happy about the lack of cell phone coverage. He'd never been out of touch with his mother for so long, but she encouraged him to go. She thought it would be good for him to do things out of his comfort zone.

Jamal always loved taking things apart and seeing how they worked. No small appliance was safe in his house growing up. His parents bought him every fancy Lego kit, erector set, and building toy they could while he was growing up. It surprised no one that Jamal chose mechanical engineering as a career.

Jamal started his project at the end of the spring term, worked on it all summer, and intended to present it as a final project for his sophomore year. He conferred with his professor, who told him he should patent it. He downloaded all the forms, mindful of the legal process as he worked on building it.

Jamal knew, in the larger scheme of things, that his project wouldn't make a big impact. In a course on the history of engineering, he learned how some projects changed the world. He wanted to build something like that. Nels' idealism was contagious. The only people whom his invention would really impact were cat owners, particularly those with cats who had long hair. Sprinkles shed long hair over everything. Jamal's high-end vacuum cleaner worked fine on floors, but on furniture, the vacuum's handheld attachment didn't work well. They had a separate handheld that worked a little better. Once, Nels had forgotten to plug the charger of the handheld in, so Jamal used an old manual carpet sweeper on the couch. It worked okay. He took it apart, and saw that the rollers only went one way, but if they could go both directions, the carpet sweeper might work better. It was more complicated than he had imagined, but he thought he could make a manual cat hair removal tool that worked better than a vacuum.

He brought his project and all his tools to South Dakota. For the trip, Jamal bought a deluxe two-room tent, a double-size air mattress, and enough camping gear to make his stay more comfortable. He included a portable table, chair, and a light to set up space to work on the project. Unfortunately, everything didn't fit in the Lexus, even with the rooftop carrier. Besides paying fees for the event, participants were supposed to contribute specific items of food. They were supposed to bring a fifty-pound bag of brown rice, five gallons of soy sauce, and several other items that used up a lot of space. As they were discussing options such as renting a bigger vehicle, Jamal emailed and asked whether he could donate food money instead. He offered double the amount he'd already spent on food and found the organizers were happy to take cash, Venmo, or PayPal.

After they arrived, the camp they set up was comfortable enough, but Jamal was unhappy with the other facilities. The solar shower was warm for only a couple of minutes. The compost toilets were interesting with a urine diverter, but he missed flush toilets. He helped with a couple of work projects when they first arrived but escaped to their tent to work on his own project as much as possible. He got into a zone when he worked. Everything else faded away; he focused and built.

=..=

Jamal was in a workshop on making rocket stoves when Big Thunder happened. People experienced a weird fog and a giant clap of thunder that was intense for a minute, then the workshop continued like nothing had happened. It took two days after Big Thunder for anyone at White River Farm to realize something was amiss. There was never cell phone coverage that far out, and only the main house had electricity. It frequently went out, and the landline too; no one thought too much about it. All day Saturday and Sunday they kept doing workshops, eighty-five clueless hippies having a great time while everyone else lost their shit.

Sunday afternoon, those with long drives headed home, found the roads gone, turned on their radios, and heard the unbelievable news that Big Thunder had transported them to 1791. Many campers didn't find out until the next day. Jamal didn't want to accept the new situation. He had Nels drive on the return trip because he was so freaked out. Nels wasn't that upset about not ever seeing his parents, and the idea of living in 1791 and being able to change the world excited him.

A week after Big Thunder, a group from the farm was being sent to campaign for Jerome Brown, who was running for Executive Council. They would go to Omímeya to get hot showers first. They encouraged everyone to bring their devices and fill out skills surveys, upload caches, and download message forums. After they got there, Jamal quit after a few minutes because the data was crawling because of the high number of people using their devices.

People were calling everyone staying out at White River Farm "the hippies." It bothered Jamal a great deal to be called a hippy. He didn't even smoke weed, although Nels did. The Omímeya resort was impressive, but he was still so depressed about the whole situation he didn't appreciate it.

After they returned, Nels spent a lot of time in meetings trying to save the planet, while Jamal sat in the tent. He had gotten a portable solar panel to charge lights and phones. All day he sat looking at his phone, reading and rereading his mother's texts. He didn't know how he would get through life without her. He finally resumed working on his project as a distraction. Finally, Nels told him he had to get out and work; they needed engineering help with the hempcrete projects.

The process of making hempcrete involved fermenting hemp into a paste called "hurd," adding lime and water, and then pouring it into molds, resulting in the formation of concrete-like blocks. It was lightweight and provided excellent insulation, although its production was labor-intensive, which kept the price high. Constructing with hempcrete was more sustainable than using conventional building materials, and as a bonus it removed carbon dioxide from the air. Unfortunately, it lacked strength, which made it unsuitable for load-bearing walls. Even though Jamal had never studied structural engineering, he had textbooks on his iPad, which had useful tables, enough to be helpful. Jamal knew Nels was right; he had to get out of the tent.

He didn't know he would get out of the tent permanently. About three weeks after Big Thunder, there was a windstorm. Jamal and Nels were in bed listening to the intense winds, Jamal hoping another storm might send them back to their old world. Suddenly a tremendous gust of wind came, and the tent collapsed on them. They later discovered that the poles had snapped and were unrepairable. They took out their sleeping bags, left everything in the tent, and made their way to the main kitchen area. Their tents weren't the only ones that had collapsed. Jamal and Nels ended up sharing an eighteen-foot tipi with another couple and a single guy. Nels thought sleeping in the tipi was cool. It was secure from the winds, but there was little room and no privacy. Jamal hated it, even though it was temporary. They were making hempcrete blocks to build tiny houses as fast as they could. The hope was that they would finish enough tiny houses by winter to allow at least some people warm sleeping spaces. They'd be simple small block houses, nothing like the beautiful demonstration model.

=..=

Everyone at White River Farm, including Nels, spent much of their time in endless meetings, which appeared to accomplish little. Jamal got out of meetings by working. There were many projects on a working farm. Machines break often, especially when being used by inexperienced workers. There was one other person who was a mechanic. Between the two of them, they could fix most things.

Typically, the first thing people asked was which work group or committee meeting you attended. It reminded Jamal of how you would ask people where they were from in the old world. People refrained from asking that, as it might prompt the question of who got left behind. The future was everyone's focus, saving the planet, and enacting social justice reforms centuries early. Everyone was so sincere. Jamal felt guilty. He didn't want to change the world; he wanted to see his family and make money inventing a new cat hair removal tool.

When Nels commented on how down Jamal was, he responded, "I miss my family so much. Living here, away from everything we knew, it's just ... it's hard, more difficult than anything I ever imagined."

Because he was gay, everyone, including Nels, expected him to get behind the new referendum being proposed to include the word transgender in the constitution. According to Jerome, when Changleska's founders wrote the constitution over a long night, it was a simple oversight; no one thought to include it. Jerome said he wasn't sure anyone in the eighteenth century even knew what transgender was, and thought the sexual orientation part would be protection enough. Jamal agreed with Jerome but felt pressure from Nels to attend the meetings. He felt bad for Micha, the one transgender person transported by Big Thunder. They were young, having a hard time coping like he was. Jamal felt bad for them. Being the only trans person had to feel lonely. At least he wasn't the only Black or gay person. The rule for a referendum to change the constitution was that it could only take place after one year and needed two-thirds of citizens to vote to pass. The same rule applied to changing laws, but the law had to be in effect for three years. Jamal thought the trans meetings were a prime example of futile debating, since they couldn't change anything for a year. Even after a year, it'd be unlikely that two-thirds of South Dakotans would want to change the constitution over this issue. When he finally spoke up and said the Council wouldn't change the referendum rule for one person, everyone glared at him. Addressing discrimination for one meant addressing it for all. He had to stop attending and found other meetings to attend.

One of the many work groups, teams, and committees Nels was active in was the Antislavery Committee. It was a sizeable group of mostly white people, which was no surprise, as they were in South Dakota. There were only about fifty Black people living in the entire area before Big Thunder, and a few more caught passing through. Jamal was one of three on White River Farm. There was one person of South Asian descent active in the antislavery group. Jamal didn't know that in the eighteenth century, slavery was big in Asia.

Growing up with parents active in civil rights, he'd learned the history of slavery and civil rights in the United States from a young age. His family often went on trips to museums dedicated to this history, and they even visited the National Museum of Slavery in Angola during a trip to Africa. Jamal felt a deep obligation to his parents to work towards ending slavery seventy-four years early. However, he worried that his enthusiasm for the cause didn't match that of others.

Nels would send his phone into town to download messages from the forums and briefed him on the meetings' discussions. Despite Nels' enthusiasm for the group, Jamal often felt that participating was mostly a waste of time. People seriously discussed all kinds of crazy ideas, from fighting the Civil War early with modern weapons, staging commando raids on plantations to free slaves, to raising money to buy them all. Usually, each proposal ended with the realization it wasn't workable, for one practical reason or another. Realistic suggestions would all take time, and some would require decades. Supporting the growing abolitionist movements, which weren't as active in the United States as they were in Britain in 1791, was one good long-term idea. Most wanted something more immediate. Jamal liked the idea of reprinting *Uncle Tom's Cabin* by Harriet Beecher Stowe, a seminal book on the evils of slavery that helped change minds when published in 1852. But someone pointed out that it propagated harmful stereotypes, so they sought another novel. The best plans involved undermining the economics of slavery. Finally, Jamal realized he could help. There was something he could do that he was uniquely qualified for. He started feeling better for the first time since Big Thunder.

Jamal discussed his plan with the Chair of the Antislavery Committee, who said, "I love the idea. But we're running out of time. Have you considered talking to the expedition leaders directly?"

He knew an expedition was leaving for New Orleans soon. Several members of the antislavery group were going. When Jerome Brown became Councilor, they allowed him to use one of the fifteen-person electric shuttles if he agreed to make a few stops along the way. White River Farm could fill the entire van with people every day, so Omímeya limited their group to five passengers. There was a rota for spaces. Even with the shuttle running five days a week, there were limited spots, which were highly coveted. Jamal considered using the last of his gasoline, but he offered to trade for someone's spot in the van by taking over their composting toilet cleaning duty. The job was as disgusting as one might expect. Believing that his mom would be proud, he persevered.

Upon arriving at Omímeya, he requested a meeting with Jenny Abrams, Rose Chasing Hawk's assistant. The staff directed him to wait in the lobby, and soon a young, pretty woman approached him. It surprised Jenny to find out that he hadn't completed a skills survey, but she was excited to find a mechanical engineer, even if he was only a student. She immediately offered him a job and asked how committed he was to living at White River Farm. When he admitted hating it, she told him he could now afford housing with flush toilets, and he was thrilled.

When he explained what he wanted to do, Jenny became serious. "Rose needs to hear this." She stepped away from him and talked on the radio. "We have a meeting with Rose in two hours. Why don't you use the time to fill out the job application and look for housing on Craigslist?"

Jenny put him on a Level Three pay scale. She explained that at first, they'd tried to hire people at the rate they were paid in the old world, but that didn't work. Some lawyers and doctors made a fortune, while other highly experienced people didn't get paid fairly.

Level One was entry level or any position requiring less than a year of training, defined as either academic or on-the-job instruction. Level Two corresponded to two to four years of training. Level Three, four to ten years, and Level Four was over ten years. Most doctors and experienced engineers fit Level Four. There was flexibility in assigning a pay rate after reviewing someone's life and work history.

Jamal had enough cash to buy a cup of coffee. It surprised Jamal to see prices listed in both current prices and those from 1791. His seven-dollar cup of coffee would cost twenty-seven cents in 1791 currency. He heard Changleska was only intending to use electronic transactions and coins instead of printed bills. You could still pay with them but wouldn't get bills back in change. Checks were making a comeback. Within months, they planned to switch to 1791 prices.

Jamal met Rose Chasing Hawk and Jenny in a rather corporate-looking office on the fourth floor.

He began, "There's a way to change the economics of slavery, which may end it years early. Eli Whitney invented the cotton gin in 1793. It's a machine that separates seeds from cotton fibers. A single device could produce up to fifty pounds of cleaned cotton in a day. The cotton gin helped make cotton a profitable export crop, which further promoted the use of slavery. Prior to the invention of the cotton gin, slavery had been on the downturn. The cost of slave labor made growing cotton unprofitable."

Rose asked with a concerned look, "Do you propose we do something to Eli Whitney?"

Jamal answered with a grin, "Yes, offer him a job. Whitney never saw much profit from the cotton gin because of legal and patent issues. Later, he developed the mass production of interchangeable parts. At first used in the manufacturing of muskets, such parts became the foundation of modern manufacturing."

Rose said, "Changleska wants to start a firearms factory, using modern methods with materials from the eighteenth century. Let's talk to that Committee about offering him a job; a good salary and access to modern tools may tempt him."

Jamal had done a report in middle school about the cotton gin, its role in slavery, and Eli Whitney's life. He knew he hadn't yet married and had just graduated from Yale. Jamal had drafted a letter to Whitney. He wanted to include that letter in an information packet. He pondered different engineering designs from their time they could include.

Rose said that the message was too important to trust to eighteenth-century mail. They'd also need to send someone in person, and she'd speak to the leaders of the New Orleans expedition, including Oliver Jackson, the Minister for Defense who oversaw expeditions. The East Coast Expedition would leave from New Orleans. It will be necessary to find someone to deliver the packet in person.

Jamal felt happier than he'd been since that awful day he found out he'd never see his family again. Jenny gave him an advance on his salary directly on his citizen card. He ate a great burger at Buffalo Burger, glad vegan Nels wasn't there, but didn't feel guilty. On Craigslist he found a rental in Oacoma, a nineteen-foot travel trailer next to someone's house, with full hookups, and access to Wi-Fi for an extra fee inside the house. Jamal emailed the owners, letting them know that a gay male couple, one of whom was Black, was interested. He thought it was better to inform the owners first instead of just showing up.

Jamal was so excited about getting a job and finding a place outside of White River Farm that he was surprised that Nels didn't want to move.

Nels said, "I'll stop going to so many meetings, and work full time on the tiny house. If you would work with me, we could get it done in two months."

"When would it have inside running water and a flush toilet?"

"Not soon, but we could use a bucket for emergencies."

After more futile arguments, Jamal said he was moving into town; Nels could come visit anytime he liked. They both hurt, knowing what that probably meant.

Jamal and Nels had talked extensively about Eli Whitney and the cotton gin. Nels was proud of Jamal's idea. Nels mentioned that without spending hours and hours at all the antislavery meetings, Jamal had accomplished something substantial, more effective than many of the grandiose plans being discussed.

After a while, Nels said, "Didn't you say Rose wanted to send someone to convince Whitney in person? What if I go? I heard there were a couple of openings on the expedition due to last-minute changes of mind."

"That is because it is dangerous."

"No more dangerous than people living in slavery."

"They hang people for being gay in the eighteenth century."

"So, I won't get caught."

Jamal thought he could talk Nels out of going. He had to drive into Oacoma to check email about the trailer and check in with Rose. He hoped she'd find someone else, and he could tell Nels there was no need for him to go. The trailer owners said they could rent it, but because there would be two people, the price doubled. Jamal was pissed because he believed they wouldn't treat a straight white couple the same way. He thought about reporting them. If the owners were citizens, they could be fined for discrimination. Jamal felt too stressed out to bother. He looked on Craigslist for another place, but nothing private was available, and he was tired of shared housing.

Jamal thought about being away from Nels for six months to a year and knew their relationship wouldn't survive. He thought about his mother and the values his parents had raised him with. He knew he had to do more. Writing letters while living comfortably wasn't enough. He emailed Rose and asked if there was room for both him and Nels on the expedition.

He didn't hear back by the time he needed to leave, and he waited until they were alone to tell Nels. Jamal thought Nels would be happy he wanted to go with him, but Nels felt frightened for him.

"It's too dangerous. What if you get captured and sold as a slave?"

"I'll have freedom papers, like other Black members of the expedition."

"Papers could get lost or destroyed."

They argued for hours. The more Jamal argued about the reasons he should go, the more he started believing it himself. Then the question arose about who'd take the spot if there was only one available. The compromise they made was Jamal wouldn't go alone.

After the White River group heard what they were doing, they were given priority spots in the morning shuttle. Both planned on going to Omímeya the next day.

It was good they came to Omímeya; Rose wanted to talk to them both. They met in the afternoon with Rose, the Executive Council Chair, Oliver Jackson, and some of the expedition leaders. It was a long interview. They faced tough questions about how they'd cope with the harshness of the eighteenth century. They emphasized the importance of keeping their relationship a secret, which may mean they couldn't have sex for some time. The interviewers asked them about their response to witnessing someone beating a slave or child. If chosen, they'd have to remember that the mission must come first, which may involve ignoring individual wrongs to make a right for a greater good.

Jamal and Nels left the interview, sobered and determined. Neither of them spoke about it, but the idea of going without sex was daunting. Both were young, healthy men in their twenties. Because of the short time frame, they were told they could go right away, if they were both cleared by Medical. When told about needing an HIV test, Jamal wondered whether they were treating them differently because they were gay. He understood HIV would spread like crazy in the eighteenth century, with no testing, and no drugs. While Jamal was getting examined, he asked the doctor, who said everyone got tested for everything. Hepatitis B, a contagious blood-borne disease that many people didn't know they had, was a bigger issue.

His relief at both of their negative results was short-lived, as the doctor brought up another issue. Nels was too underweight for his height. With Nels' permission, the doctor spoke to them both. He said if Nels was determined to go, he'd have to change his diet. Nels said he wouldn't eat meat, so they compromised on him adding eggs and dairy. He handed Nels a case of Ensure, assuring them there was plenty. Jamal realized the older patients no longer needed it. The doctor stressed they didn't know the conditions they'd go into. Having cooking facilities to make vegetarian meals was unlikely. Nels had no reserves, so little body fat that he could have heart issues if he didn't gain weight before he had to go without meals for any period.

They received information about the volume and weight allowance of their belongings, as well as the time and location of where to meet. They received lists of things to bring. Many they had, a few they didn't. Because they missed the orientation, they'd need to do a lot of catching up. They returned to the farm in time to pack. Jamal was thankful for the high-end camping equipment he'd purchased, most of which was compact and lightweight. There was a small stove that ran on alcohol or small pieces of wood, nesting pots and pans made from silicon. Top-of-the-line portable solar panels and charging stations for their electronics.

It surprised them when they saw someone had posted their expedition packing list on the bulletin board. During their farewell party, everyone signed a beautiful handmade card. People graciously offered them items they couldn't spare and found hard to refuse because of the genuine generosity behind the gestures. They received necessities like socks, soap, rubber bands, safety pins, lighters, and pens.

Terra from the kitchen crew said, "I heard Nels needed to gain weight. Here is a jar of peanut butter and a quart of olive oil. Take two teaspoons of each a day."

Jamal was incredibly moved, as both were irreplaceable for the foreseeable future.

Jamal said, "I never realized how much these people cared about us, Nels. It's beautiful. I didn't get why you loved them so much; now I do."

Chapter Twenty-Three
Rose

IT HAD BEEN six weeks since Big Thunder. Every time Rose thought she'd adjusted, something happened that made her miss the old world. It was the little things, like not having her preferred brand of shampoo. She knew she was lucky to have any at all, but damn, the cheap hotel stuff wasn't the same. Other times, her concerns were more substantial, like wondering what might happen to her son, Luke. Juveniles were being sentenced like adults to hard labor until they turned eighteen, sometimes twenty-one.

The Law Committee reviewed eighteenth-century punishments for crimes. Branding was a typical punishment. A thief, sometimes as young as fourteen, might have a "T" branded on their cheek. Fortunately, the committee decided not to recommend branding people, but judges routinely required those convicted to wear a bright yellow safety vest with words clearly written on the front and back: "Thief." The Law Committee labeled anyone convicted of any level of assault, including a drunken bar fight, as a "Violent Offender." There was someone who'd been labeled "Rapist." He disappeared from the work crew. No one looked for him. Same as the man labeled "Sexual Predator." There was talk of castration for sex offenders, but so far just talk. Elliot told her, one charge the District Attorney had proof of was Luke stealing and selling porn from IT. Rose was terrified they'd make him wear a vest that said "Pornography Dealer." There were a few others around wearing that vest. A new law stated it was not illegal to own it, but illegal to post it online or sell it. It was enforced.

If an offender was caught in public without wearing a vest, their sentence would be doubled. The work crews often comprised both paid workers and convicts, working on roads or recycling. Those wearing vests were visible. Jails were being closed. Luke was one of the last in the juvenile center. Elliot Gray Owl made a persuasive argument for a new system of justice. After spirited debate in the law forums, the Law Committee proposed new laws and changes were being made. Juveniles were now allowed weekend passes at home, contingent on good behavior.

Rose tried to stay home whenever Luke had a pass, but she couldn't always engage with him successfully. He played fewer video games and started paying attention to his horse, stabled now at Omímeya. Gift had been riding him, but her uncle Chaske gave her a horse as an adoption gift. For his twelfth birthday, Hotah gave Luke a beautiful colt he named Socks. He loved and cared for that horse until suddenly he lost interest, stayed in his room, and played video games. Rose didn't realize for a long time that it coincided with her and Hotah's breakup.

=..=

Horse talk became like car talk, especially with young men—breeds, ages, bragging about speed. As much as she could, Rose encouraged Luke to ride during the weekends. Even though horses came with them during Big Thunder, there weren't enough. A big quarter horse farm had several prize-winning lines from rodeos. There were no racehorses, but there were excellent breeds, and an extensive selection of horse semen, protected by a generator. They were breeding as fast as they could, crossbreeding with a horse called the *Nakoda* the Indigenous rode, which had become nearly wiped out. Nakoda horses were smaller, sturdier, and more acclimated to the tough prairie grasses. The Lakota here even fed their horses buffalo meat during the deep winters.

A similar ranch focusing on prize cattle breeds also had freezers full of the "good stuff." Unfortunately, few dairy cows or pigs other than a few 4H (youth agriculture club) projects were brought with them. There was one small commercial chicken farm that was working on hatching chicks, as people wanted backyard chickens. Changleska was working on constructing barges for animals, and now the grain barge was ready to go. They planned to sell special breeds of cattle and horses and to bring back dairy cows, pigs, and other farm animals.

It surprised Rose how fast the culture changed, mostly for the better. If a Councilor entered a room where everyone was seated, everyone stood up respectfully. Councilors were called by titles Mr. or Mrs. with a respectful head nod. Jerome Brown was no longer called Jerome the hippie, but Mr. Brown. After the tragedies of the coup attempt, former rez/county division lines started to fade. People often stopped and hugged anyone who looked Native when they went to Chamberlain or the neighboring towns.

It was resort guests and locals from the rez who'd attended that night. Almost everyone had a relative or knew someone who'd been shot.

Clyde Folsom continued to stir up divisiveness. There was a minority of people advocating an election for county independence, including a surprising number of Natives. An election was unlikely, as no one put out an effort to organize it. Lyman, Buffalo, and Brule counties merged to conserve resources. The county was heavily in debt, and talks were underway about merging with Changleska. The county was struggling; the banks loaned them money with property as collateral, but they had little income. They cut staff to bare bones. There was talk about charging people for county services like the police. The county could keep funds from the state sales tax, but Changleska was talking about abolishing all sales tax, as tribal borders were getting so blurred.

The culture underwent other transformations as well. Young people were signing up in droves for the Changleska Guard. The name finally decided, soldiers now called guardians. Unless you had specialized skills, the only way to get on an expedition was as a guardian. They planned many trips, with the first one leaving in days. Young people were excited to meet other tribes, see the 1791 world, have adventures, and prove their courage. Older people didn't want to leave flush toilets.

Because of the impending birth control shortage, including condoms, the midwives and doctors did rounds of sex education talks everywhere young people gathered, in both gender-separated and coed classes. What was taught was simple: "Fool around all you want but save intercourse for someone you wish a child with." Fooling around was described in embarrassing and sometimes interesting detail, depending on the audience. They were told that exploring and finding out what pleased your partner would make things better once they went "all the way." Sexual intercourse outside of a committed relationship was now considered old-world. The line, "Don't stick it in, if you won't stick it out," was repeated often, especially to a couple leaving a party together. People were reminded they'd have to adapt to eighteenth-century mores.

Prior to Big Thunder, South Dakota reservations had some of the highest rates of suicide in the US, particularly among young people. After Big Thunder, almost no young people killed themselves. There was hope, pride, and a shared mission to save the Earth. Initially there were quite a few suicides, mostly people who'd lost their whole families, and a few others, but the incidents were tapering off. Substance abuse dropped like a rock, probably due in part to the Caballo Raid as it famously became known.

After Caballo was executed, someone informed Phil Gallo of the secret location of the drug lab complex, which was isolated on the Crow Creek reservation at the edge of the Circle. Sophisticated technology jammed overhead surveillance, and other high-end security systems were in use. During the coup attempt, all Caballo's crew had died, making the raid the next day anticlimactic. No shots were fired. Only five women and one young man were left behind, all badly strung out, as they'd been used to sexually service everyone except one woman, Rivera's "special," who wasn't a drug addict. The others said she'd helped with the planning. They tried and convicted her of conspiracy and related charges. She became the second person executed, ten days after Rivera. Evidently, the execution went better. No one wanted to observe. The court considered the addicts as victims and imposed mandatory treatment on all of them. After two years of staying clean, they could be released.

The Crow Creek reservation claimed everything under forfeiture laws. It was a rich haul. They donated the tech to the military, including the three drones. The tribe kept the huge weapons cache but was considering selling it to the military. They sold the alcohol to Omímeya for its bar. They donated food to the tribal pantry and sold everything related to drugs, including two double-wide mobile homes housing sophisticated drug labs and shipping containers full of precursor chemicals, to IHS and the hospital, which had merged.

The tribe kept the three newer mobile homes, trailers, cars and trucks, greenhouses growing weed, cash, gold, jewelry, and so many high-value items that inventorying the haul would take a long time. It didn't come as a surprise to anyone that cigarettes and toilet paper weren't on the submitted inventory list. The Crow Creek tribe became financially solvent overnight, drawing envious mutterings from Lower Brule and even the county. It was obvious the thefts had come from all over.

Rose could catch her breath and take a day off now and then, often on the weekends. Most of the guests were gradually finding jobs and housing. Many doctors moved to Chamberlain; the medical committees met in the hospital. A few doctors rented houses or apartments together, joking it was like having college roommates again. They had more doctors than a population their size needed, so they recruited many for curriculum development for the medical school.

The 6,000-square-foot, two-story building that was supposed to be the fancy golf clubhouse would be repurposed for the medical school. It would be headed up by Dr. Begay. The building structure had been finished, with power, water, and geothermal already in. Two big commercial kitchens were ready to have all the stainless-steel tables installed after flooring. The construction crews had been scheduled to complete the inside work during the winter months. They had materials stored in the triangle. Other than a few specialized workers who lived in Pierre, they had everything they needed. The building would be done by spring as planned originally, just not for golf. An architect among the guests had been promptly hired to make the change from golf clubhouse to medical school, prompting lots of jokes about how much doctors love golf.

Other doctors developed protocols for the outreach teams to use to teach disease prevention in a variety of settings. In the early days, Rose enjoyed listening to various meetings whenever she had the opportunity and was surprised to see one group dedicating a significant amount of work to writing different health papers for distribution. She interrupted and uploaded files to show documents on the overhead screen. Kyle had downloaded all the US-AID documents, including all the health information packets. Everything had already been written. Most of it was written for developing nations fifty to seventy years prior, which was better because much of it was low tech. The materials covered everything from how to prevent disease through hygiene to how to sterilize instruments. There were thousands of PDFs, not only about health but also about how to build a country from the ground up, from digging wells to building a small hydroelectric plant. All free and downloadable on public sites. There were also a series of books from the Hesperian Foundation,

Where There Is No Doctor, which was designed for giving care in low-resource areas, as well as ones for no midwife or no dentist.

Rose said, "There's no need to redo all that work, although editing may be required."

She reminded everyone that all documents released publicly had to have the dates removed, anything that could infer a specific timeline. Everyone knew they couldn't keep time travel a secret forever, but wanted to keep the world in the dark or guessing for as long as possible. 1791 was still a deeply religious time. They were leaning into that. Atheists were not amused.

Omímeya usually took the tipi village down the first week in October. It consisted of twenty-one beautiful tipis made by the Nomadic Tipi Company, which ranged from fourteen to twenty-two feet, including a twelve-foot empty play tipi for the kids. The tipis had raised wood floors covered in Native-patterned rugs, probably made in China. They used safe indoor propane heaters instead of fire pits. They provided rubberized foam pads for sleeping. Guests provided their own bedding, or they could rent bedding. During the busy months, reservations for the tipis would often fill up. There were seven empty on the day of Big Thunder. The campers, mostly families with children, were stuck. Rose didn't want anyone to winter in canvas tipis, although she knew the Indigenous tribes did. It took almost a month, but she finally found homes for everyone and could shut the tipi village down for the winter.

Tom's old Riverside Cabin, now hers, seemed too big with Luke gone so much. Kimi and Gift had fixed up their room but were rarely there. She felt guilty having so much space for herself, especially since she still worked so many hours at the main building two miles away.

The Begay family came up with a great solution for their three-bedroom cabin. They put their two teenage boys in one room and invited the doctors, Shawn and Roger Caris, to have the other bedroom. Since both Shawn Caris and Theresa Martinez had seats on the Council, they had housing allowances and good salaries. Even the exorbitant Riverside Cabin rates were manageable. They all got along great. They were close by for Council meetings. The Councilors who lived further out were going to have a problem getting to meetings as winter set in. NewNet didn't have the bandwidth for Zoom.

The wedding party rented one cabin. The bride and groom got the prize for the worst wedding story: "At our wedding, we were all transported to 1791." As was common at big weddings, the bride and groom had rented the bridal suite in the main building, and family members rented a cabin, squeezing in as many as possible. The cabins were designed with that in mind, so the bedrooms had Murphy beds in the walls and trundles underneath the beds, and the couches all folded out. The three-bedroom cabins slept ten to fifteen people, depending on how cozy they wanted to be. Since only eight family members of the bridal party had arrived before Big Thunder, they were staying for now. Most of them were younger and able to work, with a few having working credit cards.

The two-bedroom cabin was rented by an older retired couple, wealthy from inherited money and investments. Neither had marketable job skills. Their credit cards weren't with the local banks, who turned them down for new cards because of their age. They were both in their early seventies, active, and healthy enough. Shawn Caris came to the rescue and housed them in a Living Wisdom Center as Companion Helpers, the new work-trade jobs.

Rose was going to need to rent that cabin. Omímeya no longer hosted conferences and weddings every weekend. Even with the reserves, they wouldn't stay solvent for long at the current spending rate. In the spring, Rose hoped the first of the visitors would be coming. They might rent the cabins as embassy buildings. Rose kept it empty for now, for use as a temporary emergency shelter if a family had a fire. House fires were becoming all too common with people using home-built wood stoves and old space heaters.

As rooms in the main resort emptied, people were shuffled around. Rose's goal was to empty as many floors as possible, one wing at a time. Geothermal energy was limitless, but not the parts for the plant.

Wayne Becker said, "Even though there were spares for all critical systems and the best 3D printers available, something would break. Without a spare, they'd be up a creek without a paddle. I don't think electric conversion was even possible with the technology they have now. They built Omímeya from the ground up for geothermal."

Many people saw Omímeya as a cash cow with resources and rooms with free heat, while people were crowding into small, cold apartments.

This was without knowing about the basement resources. Rose had to harden her heart and look at the big picture. She knew it'd get worse before it got better. Rose was now corporate, the thing she'd hated about her job before. Now she was the one that people would blame.

Because of the labor shortage, Rose hired a few guests as staff. They received staff discounts and rented the lesser-tier rooms; she looked the other way at how many people slept in each. They tried letting people clean their own rooms. That was a disaster, but people could pay for fewer housekeeping visits a week. Staff became eligible for profit sharing after six months. Most moved out if they could find cheaper housing that offered more room. Almost all the ranches offered work-trades for housing. All Changleska citizens had full medical/dental/vision coverage, an immense relief to Rose, as it had been such a major expense before.

=..=

As Luke's court date neared, Rose felt an overwhelming sense of anxiety. Elliot was moderately optimistic. The court proceedings started with the judge reminding Luke that Mr. Rivera had shot his mother in the head, only less than a centimeter from taking her head off. He showed a video of what a similar caliber weapon did to a watermelon; it turned it into a smoothie. Rose wondered if it was as instructive as the judge hoped. The judge went into detail about what would've happened if the coup had succeeded, suggesting Luke's role in a Rivera administration would have been as a sex slave, like the seventeen-year-old young man they'd found. That seemed to sink in.

The judge admitted that the crime of Luke selling pornography had occurred prior to the law taking effect. He admonished Luke that his actions might lead to a decrease in information on NewNet because people might choose not to upload their data, feeling that their privacy had been invaded, despite being assured it was secure. The judge decided to let the charges of underage drinking and marijuana smoking stand.

He said, "I saw the videos. Don't argue it was tea or tobacco. I'm not stupid."

The judge dropped all the treason charges. "I could see no evidence that Luke was trying to take down the government."

The judge said he didn't believe Luke knew the two men planned a coup and killing spree, including killing his own mother. However, he didn't buy Luke's protestations of innocence on what they discussed. There were too many inconsistencies in the police interviews. Luke knew something, no one knew what, other than he lied during police interviews. Luke could have told Security about people asking suspicious questions. He didn't. For those reasons, he found Luke guilty of underage drinking and smoking marijuana and charged him with eleven counts of conspiracy to commit murder and thirty-nine additional conspiracy counts involving attempted killings. Stunned silence followed by sobbing from family members in the back. Tears were running down Rose's face.

After a moment, the judge said, before sentencing, "I understand you have a statement. I'll tell you your sentencing will be determined by what you say next, young man."

Luke read from a sheet of paper, prepared with Elliot's help. Luke apologized and admitted the men had asked him questions about casino security. He'd thought they wanted to rob the casino; he'd told them it was impossible, because of how good the security was. It would've been better if he'd said nothing. He would regret until the day he died that he didn't inform security about their questions. Seeing his mother shot in the head had been the worst moment of his life.

The judge gave everyone an hour's break before they returned for sentencing. During the break, people crowded around Elliot, who said in the worst case the judge could sentence Luke to hard labor until age twenty-one without weekend passes. If Luke were anything less than an ideal prisoner, the district attorney could file additional charges extending his sentence as an adult, but Elliot doubted they'd give Luke the death penalty. Elliot said he'd proposed an alternative which the judge might accept if he felt Luke showed enough remorse.

After the break, the judge said, "There are many people in court today, not sure how many are Mr. Trenton's family or friends." The entire Chasing Hawk family was there. "Would everyone please stand if, despite what Luke did, you still love him?"

Fourteen people stood, including Elliot. Luke turned around, seeing his family, tears running down his face.

"There are two paths from which you may choose, which will determine the course of your life. One is the path in which you remember people love you despite the horrible mistake you made. On the other path, you continue to think only of yourself, of how you were wronged, and you do not learn. I hope you choose well." Luke looked stunned.

"I am sentencing you to hard labor until age twenty-one without weekend passes. However, I will suspend that sentence if you meet the following conditions:

You will apologize to all the wounded persons from that night, if they are willing to see you. If not, you will write a letter on paper, which they may or may not choose to read. You will ask each of them if there is anything you can do to help. I understand one woman coming home from the hospital needs a wheelchair ramp built. If any of the victims say they need someone to come over twice a day and wipe their butt, you will do it with humility and grace.

You will complete high school or its equivalent through Khan Academy. An apprenticeship in an employable field would also be considered. If you choose an online program, it must require the same hours as high school: six hours a day, five days a week. IT will monitor all your online activity.

Your home and devices will be cleared of all video games and related tech. You are not allowed to enter the resort arcade. Frankly, I do not know why that was not done earlier."

The judge glared at Rose.

You will work after school five days a week, three hours a day, at the horse stables—mucking or whatever needs doing. You may substitute another job at Omímeya, except for IT.

On the weekends, you will work at the 11:11 memorial. I understand there is still construction underway on the arbors and landscaping.

You may not leave the secure Omímeya grounds unless accompanied by two family members. I will accept weddings, funerals, powwows, or rodeos if the family escort condition is met.

You are personally responsible for paying Mr. Gray Owl's legal fees. If your mother has already paid him, you will reimburse her and submit records of your payments to the court until the debt is paid in full.

If you meet all these conditions, the conspiracy charges will be dropped, allowing you to be eligible to serve in the Changleska Guard. You must complete your diploma or equivalent before serving. The underage drinking and smoking charges will remain, but they will be the only offenses on your permanent record.

Mr. Gray Owl proposed reconciliation rather than retribution for juveniles and first offenders in our new justice system. You're our first test case. I hope you take advantage of what we have offered."

Afterwards, the family crowded around Luke and Elliot, clapping their backs and hugging. They teased Luke about how many butts he'd need to wipe.

A cousin said, "I was there that night and I'm traumatized. Would Luke come wipe my butt?"

Relief alone didn't describe how Rose was feeling. She had fears of Luke becoming a lifelong criminal due to how much time he spent in juvie. She knew plenty of good kids who'd turned bad that way. Rose knew Elliot Gray Owl had saved Luke's life, literally. He was worth every penny, and she was looking forward to presenting Luke with the bill.

=..=

The day after the coup attempt, while everyone else was busy with the election and grieving, the Chasing Hawk family started to construct the 11:11 memorial. Kimi asked Kyle to find the exact center of the thirty-mile-radius that Big Thunder brought. He determined that the exact center was located away from all the buildings, inside about 1,500 acres of former hay fields, currently being used for horse grazing and the proposed golf course. Kimi walked unerringly to a spot Kyle had been trying to pinpoint with the GPS and there she placed a rock from the river.

Rose felt overwhelmed in dealing with the aftermath of the attempted coup. Many parts of the building had been closed off, as it was still a crime scene. Rose was traumatized, like everyone else who was there. No one could take time off. Working was the only coping mechanism Rose had. She and Jackson bonded over trauma, him sharing with her the difficulties he'd had coping after Iraq and sharing a few violent incidents from his childhood. They both needed counseling, but neither could prioritize it, but somehow talking to each other helped.

In the center of the memorial was a circular altar made from rocks, which wasn't completed that first week. Every time people came to the memorial, they brought a rock, and eventually, the perimeter was made using so many rocks. The altar ended up being a flat-topped four-foot-diameter circle, four feet high, which could hold tobacco, sage, sweetgrass, and other medicine objects during ceremonies. Twenty feet beyond the altar stood a circular arbor, like what they used at powwows, with openings in four directions to allow people to come and go. A large thin cabinet lined with bulletin board cork backed each section of the arbor, using recycled windows for weather protection.

People brought photos of those left behind the Circle in the first section of the arbor, devoted to day one of Big Thunder. Some people posted pictures of the old world. There was a magazine photo of the Statue of Liberty. The next section commemorated people who'd died since, from shootings, suicide, or lack of access to medical care. They included photos of loved ones with names and dates of birth and death. These dates seemed odd, for example: "Born July 26, 1982, Died September 28, 1791." Sometimes people added brief notes about the person, some funny, most sad. Another section began with those who had died in the attempted coup, the newspaper article about it posted as well. No one objected when tragic mothers posted pictures of their sons who'd been the shooters. There was room for more photos in the remaining sections still being built.

The news spread on the first Friday after the attack. Instead of observing a minute of silence on Saturday in the main building, there'd be a service at the new 11:11 memorial beginning at ten am. Kimi and Nicole organized everything. There were tribal drummers and singers, as well as the choir from St. Agnes. The four biggest churches had their pastors or priests each talk for about ten minutes. At exactly 11:11 am, there was a minute of silence, followed by most people joining in the Circle song.

Every Saturday after that, people would meet at the memorial. Services were shorter, starting at about ten forty-five, but at 11:11 it was always the same, a minute of silence followed by the Circle song. With the weather getting colder, it wasn't clear whether services would continue through the winter; fewer people attended every week, although a couple of people came every day.

Once Rose realized what was happening after the service that first Saturday, she authorized funds for the memorial's construction. She accessed building materials from the warehouses and funded logging crews to get wood. Omímeya construction crews fit the donated stones together for the altar. They used the recently discovered secret of self-healing cement using quicklime, which enabled Roman buildings to last for millennia. The altar would last thousands of years. Work on the memorial would also last for a long time. Luke would be there every weekend, as both penance and healing.

=..=

One of many reasons Rose was so happy Jackson won the election as Councilor was he no longer worked for her. Clyde Folsom would've been a disaster. She wasn't sure her new country could've survived. Jackson was wonderful at his job, her respect for him increasing every time she heard him speak. She found herself deeply drawn to Jackson, especially now there was no longer an employer/employee relationship. With that barrier now removed, she felt a shift within herself. Slowly, she opened the door to her heart she had tightly closed, allowing herself to explore the depths of her feelings for him.

Rose thought Jackson was completely out of her league. An attractive single man in one of their new country's most powerful positions, he was in many women's sights. She felt that at thirty-six years old, she wasn't physically attractive, being overweight. Her husband had left her for a skinny nineteen-year-old. That they broke up long before he met Nicole she forgot in bouts of self-pity. She had a demanding, time-consuming job, two teenagers, three if you counted Gift, and Luke with all his trouble. She felt she had no chance with Jackson and was determined to keep him in the friend zone, even though her heart felt different. Rose assumed Jackson was still deeply mourning his fiancée, which was why he'd shown no interest in dating.

Rose didn't realize Jackson had feelings for her. Since she never gave him any hint of her interest, he didn't reciprocate. Jackson had women making the first moves on him his whole life. He did not know how to woo a woman; it had never come up. Jackson even wondered, in an egotistical male way, if she was a lesbian. He'd met women who'd been married who came out later in life.

Soon after she moved into the cabin, she realized she was alone for the first time in sixteen years. Luke hadn't started having weekend passes yet. Kimi and Gift were rarely there. She never liked to cook. Cooking for herself wasn't an option. She ate at the Red Oak restaurant every night. As she was arriving one evening, she saw Jackson sitting at a table eating alone. She spotted Jenny, who was leaving.

Rose grabbed Jenny and said, "Come join me for dinner."

"But I already ate."

"I don't care, have dessert, I'll pay, I want to sit with Jackson but not alone. I don't want him to think I am coming on to him."

"He gets that a lot. Okay."

They joined Jackson for dinner. Rose and Jackson connected, their conversation flowing effortlessly as they shared stories and laughed together. They were oblivious to Jenny's presence as they engaged deeply with each other.

Rose decided a regular group dinner was in order. She missed her family dinners. She invited Jackson, Jenny, Kyle, Mary, even Phil, and a few others. Rose would pay, but only if they were prompt. It would be from 6:00 -7:00 pm Monday through Friday. Meals at the Red Oak were the best around thanks to basement food storage, often serving food found nowhere else. They had raised the prices; it wasn't cheap. People offered to pay for their own dinners, but Rose said since her housing was included, the kids were mostly gone, and there were few places to shop, she had virtually no expenses. Treating her friends to dinner was a pleasure; she enjoyed their company. She didn't mention how much she helped Hotah's family and others in the community through anonymous donations.

About ten people usually attended Rose's dinners. People coveted the invitations, and some would bring a plus-one after texting Rose first. It surprised her to meet Kelly Rosenburg, Kyle's girlfriend. She didn't know he had a girlfriend. She was a nurse at Chamberlain Hospital. They'd been dating for six months prior to Big Thunder. The restaurant reserved a spot in the private room used for rehearsal dinners and similar events. When people arrived, they told the hostess Rose's Dinner, and Rose swiped when she left.

Red Oak still served cafeteria-style; people got their food, sat, waited until it looked like everyone was there, and said a prayer. Rose asked different people each time to say the prayer; even the atheists said something. The only work talk allowed had to be funny, inspiring, or something that made them happy. When serious work-related topics came up, which was often, Plus, Rose reminded everyone this was dinner and the only talk allowed had to aid digestion. Soon Rose wasn't the only one who reminded people.

Jackson almost always attended. He and Rose constantly sat together. People would move a place at the table to make room for them when they arrived at different times. All her friends would glance at her and Jackson, engaging in interesting conversations with knowing looks. However, there was never a touch, never a suggestive hint from Rose, or a move from Jackson. It was obvious to everyone around them they had a thing. They just didn't realize it themselves.

PART V
Months Two to Three

It is not the strongest of the species that survives, nor the most intelligent. It is the one that is most adaptable to change.
— Robert Charles Darwin (1809–1882), Naturalist, Author.

Steam Barge *Endeavor's* maiden voyage

Chapter Twenty-Four
Gift of Thunder

GIFT HAD NEVER imagined her life could be so happy or so interesting. Two months ago before Big Thunder, she could only see misery in front of her. Now the endless possibilities in her future astonished her. She loved her new family, and she admired and was in awe of her sister Kimímela. Her new big house on Crow Road, with her father, his second wife, Nicole, his sister Zitkala, even the cousins, felt like home already. Her little cousin Emma was so sweet, and the two boys, Ethan and Evan, exasperated her to no end, but she loved all of them. The boys reminded her of the young boys of her tribe, making messes, fighting, and causing trouble. Emma wanted to do whatever she and Kimi were doing.

School was challenging. At first, she was afraid of all the new people. There was so much English. She was learning quickly, but not fast enough. Initially, Kimi stayed with her to translate, but the school decided it was beneficial for both girls to spend time apart during the day. They had a class for English as a second language students, for Spanish speakers. Gift wanted to learn Spanish but decided to wait until her English improved. The middle school and grade school were adjacent; Gift spent part of the day in the grade school with the younger children. Learning to read was difficult for her. She helped the younger children with Lakota; they helped her with learning her letters and sounds. Numbers were easier. At least she had the concepts beforehand. Gift hadn't known anyone who could read or write.

Gift had so much stuff, everyone had so much stuff, and wanted more stuff. They complained they could no longer buy new stuff, only old stuff. When Gift first arrived and later with her adoption ceremony, people brought her so many clothes, shoes, books, pictures, and beads, cloth, and more stuff. She couldn't even fit it all in her room at Crow Road.

Having lived most of her life in a twenty-four-foot tipi with five people, Gift had no idea that people used so much space to live their lives. Two Elks' tipi was large and rich compared to others. Gift felt more comfortable at Crow Road, the closeness of being with others. Even though the house was bigger, the rooms were smaller. The Riverside cabin had big open spaces, while beautiful with all the polished wood and stones, felt empty to her. She and Kimi spent little time there. They rode the school bus on Friday, spent Friday night, were there for Saturday 11:11 Ceremony and usually caught a ride back with someone. They rarely spent the entire weekend, but they could ride the bus to school on Monday morning. Kimi knew it made her mother happy, but she preferred Crow Road as well.

At first, Gift was uncomfortable around Luke. She didn't think of him as her brother. Lately, he'd been changing. He was interested in what she showed him about caring for his horse's hooves, using sage and buffalo fat. Not long after his court hearing when he moved full time to the Riverside Cabin, Luke asked her what her tribe did to punish criminals. The Two Elks tribe had little crime; she informed Luke, but if it occurred, if minor, the person may be beaten, but if serious, they may be banished. Other tribes would receive information about the exiled member and the reasons behind their banishment. No tribe wanted a criminal. Living alone, the person often died.

When Luke questioned that, Gift said to him seriously, "No one can live alone, no one."

Luke's attitude changed; he started working harder around the memorial. When it started getting colder, the attendance at the memorial dropped. They were discussing closing down for the winter. Luke suggested a solution. There were four circular sections of the covered arbor, separated in four directions by walkways. The back of each arbor held the photo cabinet, and the sides and front were open. They had just finished the last section, the one facing north. Luke suggested enclosing the sides and front of the covered arbor, installing two big doors and a heating system, and replacing the photo cabinet with a small table that could be used as an altar. They could store the folding chairs used by the elders there. There'd be room for about fifty people, but if they built the doors to open, in warmer weather, people could stand outside.

The Saturday 11:11 Ceremony gradually became more than a memorial, although it still drew the bereaved. It became a way to connect with others, to discuss what Big Thunder meant for them, and to share the vision of how they could change the world. It wasn't formal, like a church service. Although clergy often came, people shared songs, stories, or prayers if moved to do so. Only the minute of silence at 11:11 remained the same.

=..=

Everyone was interested in her life in the Two Elks tribe. The teachers at school asked her to speak to different classes. She was asked about the Lakota Seven Values: "Courage, Generosity, Kinship, Prayer, Respect, Wisdom, and Compassion," Buffalo Calf Woman had passed down. She learned them not as a specific list, but as integrated into many teachings. Buffalo Calf Woman came as a beautiful woman dressed in white buffalo robes. As she approached the Lakota camp, she carried a sacred pipe, the čhaŋnúŋpa, and imparted to them the rituals and prayers associated with it. This gift of the pipe symbolized the unity of all living beings and the importance of harmony with the natural world. Buffalo Calf Woman taught her people the importance of honoring the Earth as a sacred being, understanding that every plant, animal, and element has its place and purpose in the web of life. She taught the values needed for people to live in a good way.

So many people asked to speak to her that her father put his foot down and told Gift she wasn't an anthropology specimen. When translated, it surprised her that people got paid to learn about how other people lived. Gift was learning about professions and often heard from those her age what they planned to do when older. This was new to her. She had only expected to gather and prepare food her whole life. She'd been learning herbs and songs, but no more than other women. Gift knew of women who had a calling to become healers of the body or spirit. Women warriors were rare, but not unheard of. Occasionally, a woman had an affinity with horses, sewing, or art. No one discouraged women from following a different path. It was the burdens of motherhood and food production that left little room for anything else.

Gift didn't know what she wanted to do. There were so many choices. Many young people wanted to join the Guard, even the girls. Another popular option was medicine, but Gift became discouraged when she discovered how much schooling was involved. Kimímela was interested in

275

midwifery, especially with her new sibling being born this winter. She also liked the fact that there was less schooling involved.

Rose liked to tell the story about how she had Kimi at home because of her terrible experience when giving birth to Luke in the hospital. The midwife almost didn't arrive in time because it happened so fast. She joked she almost named him Justin Thyme.

Rose told the girls about the big fuss between the doctors and the midwives. They were captivated by the story. The doctors who were planning a new medical school added a nursing school at the Chamberlain hospital. The doctors all wanted the midwives to become nurses first, which would take years more schooling and would require learning a lot of patient care not needed by midwives. There were already a lot of nurses and a few nurse-midwives, many nurse practitioners, which took even more years of training. They were strongly against direct-entry or non-nurse midwives, arguing that the extra years of training were necessary.

One direct-entry midwife, Evelyn Tillerman, was an older woman married to one of the newly arrived doctors. When she started her training in 1978, there were almost no midwives in the United States. Midwives taught themselves and started their own professional organization, over decades changing the laws to license midwives, allowing them to work in out-of-hospital settings. Because of the fear of malpractice lawsuits, obstetrics became a very technological specialization. Almost no doctors delivered babies at home. If there was a bad birth outcome outside of a hospital setting, which happened sometimes, doctors blamed the midwife's lack of training, although they wouldn't train midwives or have them be part of their team, like in Europe. Evelyn, now retired from active practice, taught occasionally. She had on her laptop an entire midwifery school curriculum, as well as all the professional guidelines. The midwifery school could start training immediately. The doctors and nurses were months away, as they had to create a curriculum from scratch or piece together parts from different sources.

Evelyn pointed out it took fourteen or fifteen years to train an OB/GYN, or ten years for a family practice doctor, but only three years to train a midwife. Direct-entry midwives could save many more mothers and babies by working as a team with doctors. Most births were normal. Midwives received training to spot complications and to determine when to refer to a doctor. Evelyn asserted, "Thousands of mothers will give birth during the extra four years it would take to train a nurse midwife. Every one of those mothers deserves a midwife." The doctors finally agreed, but some weren't happy about it.

=..=

There was still so much Gift didn't understand. Translation missed so much. Gift asked Kimímela why she wasn't close to her mother.

Kimi said, "Rose spends too much time with her spreadsheets."

Luke overheard the girls and laughed with Kimi. Gift was shocked. She knew what sheets were; she loved them, and she knew what spread meant. She assumed Kimi said Rose spent too much time spreading sheets for her bed, meaning another euphemism for sex. Gift was learning there were many words and euphemisms for sex. She wished people would talk straight. In her tribe, it was bad, a taboo, to discuss sexual matters across different generations. Frank discussion was common among those of similar ages, but not across generations. She couldn't believe Kimi and Luke would say such a thing. Luckily, she refrained from speaking up, as it would later embarrass her upon learning what a spreadsheet was.

Gift and Kimi spoke an interesting mix of languages all the time. Gift wanted to learn English quicker. The young and the very old spoke Lakota, but only a few of the middle years did. She remembered Janet telling her how the white man stole their language. That made her sad because she still remembered Arikara. She knew losing language meant losing part of your heart and soul.

Kimi promised that someday they'd find the Arikara. Changleska had plans to send expeditions to all the tribes west of the Mississippi. Gift loved Kimi for offering, but felt she was Lakota now, especially since she was adopted and part of the Changleska tribe.

Mary, whom Gift and Kimi called Auntie Mary, asked whether Gift had been told about Christianity. Mary said that everyone had a different spiritual path. The Lakota followed what some called the Red Road, while others followed Jesus or even Buddha or Allah. She said there were only Christian churches around here, but Gift should visit each to see if any spoke to her heart. Mary emphasized that which church wasn't important, but the faith and belief it represented. You should only put your faith into

277

beliefs that resonate with your soul. It was faith that brought you close to the spirit. Sharing with others strengthens faith. It was good to look at all the options before settling on a belief system. She said some Christians believed you should only have one religion, and their church was the only right one. Others acknowledged there could be different paths to the same goals. She said her Catholic church accepted Lakota values and symbols, but it wasn't always the case. In the past, her church and many others did terrible things to Indigenous people.

Hotah and Kimi agreed Gift should learn about religions, even though neither was Christian. Each Sunday, Kimi and Gift would visit different churches, surprising the pastors or priests who'd ask them if they were there to sing. She would explain in her halting English that she was there to learn about being a Christian. Gift said she was just learning, not sure what path she would take, but her Auntie Mary said she would know it in her heart. When word got out, all the clergy were thrilled. Churches as far away as Oacoma and Presho offered the girls rides to visit their churches. Hotah didn't allow the follow-up home visits and didn't accept the many invitations to Bible studies and potluck dinners, saying they wanted to visit as many churches as possible. Gift and Kimi always visited the Sunday school classrooms and asked the children to teach them new songs, even if they already knew them. They sang, *"Jesus Loves Me," "This Little Light of Mine," "'Tis a Gift to Be Simple,"* and others. This was how they spent Sunday mornings. Gift loved it; Kimi, not so much.

=..=

Gift, Kimi, and a few other girls around their age were singing together regularly, both Lakota and English songs. One girl, Darla, who was sixteen, took it upon herself to teach Gift how to be an American teenager because all Kimi was interested in was herbs and horses. They talked about clothes, makeup, boys, and played a lot of different music. Darla shared her precious nail polish and painted her toenails. Darla had brought face makeup she'd gotten from her mother and did a "makeover" with Gift. The makeup didn't cover up the smallpox scars, only diminished them slightly. Since the makeup was a lighter shade than her skin, it made her look like a clown. Darla presented Gift wearing the makeup, complete with lipstick, eyeshadow, mascara, and a new outfit to the group with a ta-da!

278

The other girls applauded, but Kimi said, "You look terrible. Wash it all off."

Gift was mortified and started crying. Darla was upset. Everyone was mad at Kimi.

When Gift returned with it washed off, Kimi told her, "Your smallpox scars are a badge of resilience, of who you are, a survivor. They show your strength."

Kimi told the other girls, "Makeup is old-world, what we are getting away from. Beauty is within. Singing creates beauty."

Kimi then started a new song she'd recently learned and wanted to share.

Even though Kimi was two years younger, Gift found her wise and insightful. Occasionally, Gift would find herself out of sorts, and Kimi would say Gift had been staying inside too much. Kimi explained that, being raised in nature, Gift would get depressed if she spent too much time indoors. The two girls would go walking or riding in all kinds of weather. Gift found that as much as she loved the warm house and all the things that made life easy, she needed to feel the earth under her feet to feel like herself.

When it came time for the adoption ceremony, it surprised Gift what a big event it turned out to be. Gift had only expected immediate family to attend, with a prayer and one or two gifts. Legally, only Hotah's name was on the adoption papers. However, Rose and Nicole took part in the ceremony as her father's first and second wives. Rose insisted on a big party at Omímeya and said the staff missed hosting parties. Gift felt overwhelmed by the elaborate and beautiful party, with its enormous crowd and abundant food. So many people gave her gifts, she wasn't sure where she would put them all. She was most excited about the beautiful horse given to her by her Atéla (uncle) Chaske. Gift was introduced to so many relatives, she couldn't remember all of them.

=..=

Gift knew Kimímela had a strong connection with the wakíŋyaŋ or thunder beings. She'd heard them hours before Big Thunder. Kimi sometimes knew things before they happened. On the night of the attempted coup, Kimi told her as they were going into the Big Bear room that something was wrong, but she didn't know what. Right before the shooting started, she yelled, "Get down!" A warning that may have saved her entire family. Guilt overwhelmed Kimi; she thought she should've warned everyone earlier.

Kimi was eager to hear the stories that Two Elks' father, Sings in the Morning, had taught Gift, knowing that many Lakota stories had been lost. Gift shared tales of the *Heyókȟa*, or thunder dreamers, the people who could communicate with the wakíŋyaŋ. These stories described the Great Thunderbird, a majestic bird-like being with sharp claws and enormous wings, revered as a guardian of truth and a protector of the Lakota people.

According to the stories, wakíŋyaŋ granted the *Heyókȟa* powerful abilities. They could bring joy to others in times of sadness, summon rain during droughts, and even control the direction of storms. The Two Elks tribe wasn't blessed with one, but when they visited other tribes, Gift shared funny stories about *Heyókȟa* walking backwards, telling jokes, and playing pranks. Despite the lighthearted nature of these stories, Kimi felt a sense of unease. She admired *Heyókȟa*'s ability to bring joy, but didn't want to be seen as a clown because of her connection to thunder.

Kimi wanted to learn how Gift's previous tribe communicated with spirits. She paid close attention to anything involving holy people. She wanted to learn all the healing songs. Gift only knew the songs for fever and sleep because she used them with Bites the Dog. The other women in the tribe could teach Kimi, but without contact with Two Elks' tribe, that wasn't possible. The breach in the relationship with Two Elks' tribe was blamed on Kimi, causing Gift to feel terrible about the whole thing.

A couple of weeks earlier, Gift had been excited to go back to Two Elks' tribe to see everyone. She spent a lot of time picking out gifts. Rose had given both girls allowances on their citizens' cards. Gift now had money, an unfamiliar concept which differed from trading. Gift didn't think she'd earned it, but Rose assured Gift that since her job paid her a lot of money, it was only right she shared it.

Kimi warned her that if she weren't careful, she'd buy more than she needed, a cause of many problems in the old world. Her aunt Zitkala borrowed Rose's electric car and took them shopping, another new experience for Gift. They spent the entire day going to Chamberlain and other places. The stores had turned into trading posts, both buying and selling various items. Anything new had an exorbitant price.

Kimi was growing fast and needed new clothes, but she was most excited when she found a new pair of boots. She gave her old pair to Gift, who loved them, in part because they had belonged to Kimi. They were cowboy boots, but the toes were square. Gift bought nothing for herself but bought clothes and toys for Bites the Dog, clothes and a new pot for Black Rabbit, and, after hesitating, bought cloth for Many Horses. Since Many Horses hated to sew, it was a backhanded gift.

When they got to Two Elks' camp, the men went into the big lodge to smoke and talk. Gift and Kimi went to Two Elks' tipi to find his family. Black Rabbit was happy with the gifts, as was Bites the Dog. Many Horses politely accepted her gift, but she knew all the cruelty she'd inflicted on Gift hadn't been forgotten.

When they returned to the big tipi, the men had just stepped outside. First, Two Elks noticed Gift, who immediately lowered her eyes and shrunk herself smaller. That angered Kimi. Then Two Elks noticed Kimi and stared at her, particularly at her breasts, with a clearly lustful look on his face. This angered Kimi even more. Then Two Elks turned to Hotah, asking whether this was his daughter. His intention of asking for a bride price was clear.

Hotah said, "My daughter Kimi speaks to the thunder beings. It's not for me to give her to any man. When she's ready, she'll choose her own." That angered Two Elks.

Kimi said angrily to Two Elks, "You're the man who killed Gift of Thunder's family and took her as a slave." Two Elks nodded, amused at her fury. "She took care of your father like her own kaká (grandfather) and cared for your son as if he were her own. Instead of letting her marry into the tribe, so she'd no longer be a slave, you sold her to someone who raped her."

Two Elks, surprised by her anger, said, "She couldn't have been raped because Big Stink owned her. No one can rape their own slave."

Kimi took a deep breath to calm down. Power emanated from her as she spoke. Standing straight, close to his face, looking him in the eye, Kimi told Two Elks that her people considered those who bought or sold slaves the worst criminals, the lowest of the low. The very worst were those who sold young girls for sex. She said in her world they had jails to lock up criminals, where they'd never again see the sun or feel the grass. Criminals would spend their lives never touching a woman again and would live in a cage with other cruel men. These men would rape any man who couldn't protect himself. Even those criminals believed men who sold young girls into slavery were so horrible they often killed them themselves.

Two Elks looked uncomfortable, but Kimi didn't let up. Waving at the negotiating team, she stated, "My father and these men believe it's for the greater good to make you an ally when they could wipe out your entire tribe in hours."

Jackson looked like he wanted to interrupt, but Hotah held him back.

She continued, "You won't be a good ally, not because of what you did to Gift, but because you will not change. When given a chance of knowledge to help all your people, to save mothers and babies from death, and to learn important knowledge, you want to stay with your old ways. You won't be a good ally because you're not a good leader. A leader puts his people first. You put your pride and your old ways first."

Two Elks looked angry at her rant and was about to say something, but Kimi put up her hand. "I'm a young girl. My elders will decide who to ally with, but if it was up to me, I'd ask them to find a tribe whose leader cares about the welfare of their people. The thunder beings sent us from another world to protect the Earth. You think you know more than the thunder beings. You should listen, learn, grow, and be prepared to change, otherwise your people will suffer."

Hotah gently led Kimi away. Joseph said to Two Elks in a conciliatory tone, "Young girls have tongues not fully grown, often saying things they wouldn't say when older and wiser."

Gift was shocked at the way Kimi had stood up to Two Elks. She heard someone say as they were walking away, "Not sure what she said, but she sure told him off. Please tell me someone taped that."

Two Elks didn't want to go back to the lodge to continue discussions and cut off contact afterwards. Jackson was upset with Kimi, but other people thought what she'd told him was right. Someone filmed the encounter with their phone, had it translated, and posted it on NewNet. It was the source of controversy. Kimi felt bad because she'd lost her temper, Gift felt guilty that Kimi had been defending her, and many people were mad at Kimi because now there was no communication with Two Elks. People said there might be war.

Gift didn't know what would happen with Two Elks' tribe, but she was asked to go to a meeting with General Gardner, with Kimi translating, to share what she knew about the other tribes in the area. Two or three tribes would often gather in the spring and the fall to trade and exchange news and stories. It was a time for young people to find mates not of their own tribes, as everyone knew those who mated within their own tribe too often had sick and weak children. Gift answered specific questions like: Who was the leader? How many in the tribe? Were they considered good warriors? She hoped her information might be helpful. Gift loved her new country, her new tribe, and wanted to do anything she could to help.

Often people said or did things that confused Gift. She struggled to learn English. Occasionally, she missed the simplicity of her old life. She was slowly adjusting to the many differences. Even when things were difficult, much more was so wonderful. Gift had never felt so loved, protected, and cherished.

Chapter Twenty-Five
Mary

MARY FELT LIKE the day embodied the saying, "When it rains, it pours." Two months ago, when Big Thunder changed everything, it had been a torrential downpour of challenges. She pulled her first all-nighter since college. It took weeks before things settled down. Setting the agenda was her responsibility as Chair of the Executive Committee. Mary quickly set a forty-hour workweek with weekends off, although some worked longer hours or overtime for urgent matters. Finally, things were settling into a routine.

It was Saturday, and she was looking forward to spending the day alone at home with Daniel. Bridget had taken the girls to a friend's place to ride horses. Mary felt annoyed when the phone rang, but seeing it was her new work phone, she knew it must be important. She'd left her old phone to go to voicemail for friends and relatives, redirecting them to leave a text message.

The news was grim, starting her day on a terrible note. There had been no ethanol production in the area prior to Big Thunder. With no experience and incomplete knowledge, using jury-rigged equipment, people trying to make ethanol had accidentally started a fire outside of Reliant, causing nearby propane tanks to explode. Several people had died or suffered severe burns so far. The firefighters hadn't yet contained the fire, which posed a risk to nearby buildings. Despite many inexperienced people experimenting with dangerous materials, there had been surprisingly few accidents before this. Changleska had sent fire trucks to assist, but most were fifteen to twenty miles away.

Mary had a lifetime of experience in dealing with this sort of crisis. She immediately started organizing support for the affected families, such as meals or rides to the hospital. She requested the use of Omímeya electric vehicles from Rose, as the bus didn't go to Reliant on weekends. Mary arranged pastoral home visits to notify the bereaved, wondering whether the radio had released the names. She turned on the radio and was pleased the station adhered to the old-world convention of not announcing the names of the deceased before notifying their next of kin.

Mary was still in the middle of texts and calls about the fire when she got another call, which added more to the rainfall of her day. A Guard patrol riverboat about forty miles north of Omímeya had spotted a voyageur canoe, the type of canoe used by the HBC to transport furs across the continent. After stopping and talking, the guardians found out there was a passenger who was the HBC representative they'd asked for.

The canoe, paddled by six muscular men, carried trade goods. Mary knew from her study of history that voyageurs could paddle 100 miles a day, faster than some modern boats, carrying over 5,000 pounds of cargo. Voyageurs had a distinct culture and dress, usually colorful sashes. They were often illiterate, and HBC wouldn't allow them to trade on their own. They spent most of their lives paddling canoes, delivering cargo and furs.

Mary knew Rose had hoped the packet they had sent reached the HBC. It conveyed an invitation to send a representative to verify Changleska's claims of being from another world and to open trade negotiations. Along with various small modern items, postcards, and calendar prints, the packet included a list of goods they desired and what they offered in exchange. They'd sent the sealed letter with Big Stink, and it contained the information the bearer of the letter wasn't welcome back. Mary and Rose were not sure when or whether the HBC representative would arrive. Long voyages posed many dangers. Whoever received the letter might think it was a hoax and throw it away. Mary was relieved they had arrived, but she was annoyed at the timing since she was focused on the fire.

Fortunately, the patrol boat had given them advance notice. It would be three to four hours before the canoe arrived. Mary was debating whether she needed to go to work. She'd need to meet with the HBC representative. If she got it out of the way today, perhaps she could have Sunday off.

=..=

The rain of her day kept pouring. Mary got a call from Jackson in his role both as Law and Defense Minister. A rancher had shot and killed a man, presumably one of Two Elks's warriors, outside of Presho. Those warriors had been entering the Circle and stealing horses, cattle, laundry off the line, and whatever wasn't nailed down since they'd settled in their winter camp a month ago. The Council instituted a policy of not responding with violence. People were asked on the radio not to shoot intruders but to use fencing, alarms, and scare tactics instead. Changleska reimbursed those who'd had property or livestock stolen, but it was getting expensive. Two Elks still refused to come to the negotiating table, using one excuse or another. The situation was becoming untenable, and now with one of his warriors dead, they had to do something. That meant she had to go into the office. Mary received a gasoline allowance for this reason, so she could drive. Her usual electric van shuttle didn't run on weekends.

Mary called her assistant, Travis Hazelhurst, to come in and planned to pick him up on the way to the office. She was lucky to have Travis; it had only been a few weeks, but she couldn't imagine how she had managed without him.

Travis and his girlfriend, Melody, had been graduate students driving on I-90 during Big Thunder. Rose insisted all the Councilors needed administrative assistants and sent a list of potential candidates from the job application pool. When Mary got around to interviewing candidates, she found the other Councilors already hired the best. She started searching in the skills survey database but wasn't having luck under the terms secretary, administrative assistant, or office worker. Finally, she tried "researcher" and found Travis. He was a graduate student majoring in English literature, specifically the work of William Blake, one of Mary's favorite poets. He'd no office experience and had never been an assistant, but Mary knew as a college educator how much organization and research skills were involved in graduate studies. Travis was thrilled to get the job since he and Melody were still living in a displaced person shelter. He organized, anticipated Mary's needs, and acted as a gatekeeper for all the people who thought they needed to see her now. They also discussed William Blake occasionally.

=..=

Since she rarely came to work on Saturdays, she was happy to find no line at the gate as she drove in. Although the guard knew her, he still asked for Travis's ID. She wondered whether blind obedience to rules was a good

286

thing. Construction workers were finishing work on an expanded gatehouse on one side and a large barracks on the other.

After Mary got to her office on the fourth floor, in the west wing above the casino, she looked out at the river for a moment. The flowing water helped center her. The spacious, elegant corner office featured a spectacular view of the river, a beautifully crafted wooden desk, a cozy leather couch, and exquisite Native art adorning the walls. That office used to be Tom Durrell's. It should have gone to Rose, especially as she was CEO besides the General Manager. Rose said she'd rather stay in her old office, in the thick of things, with her staff. She also said it was important for the Chair of the Executive Council to have the best office. It would be their Oval Office. Sooner or later, they'd need to impress people.

Rose was right. Today was the day. Mary knew how important the HBC was to all their plans. She looked around the office. It was all in order. She'd kept all the art Tom had left; she had nothing of the same quality to replace it, but she placed many of the little animals Daniel had carved in various places. It gave a whimsical touch she liked.

Mary tasked Travis with the fire aftermath. She handed him her personal phone and let him respond to the incoming texts from various community members, offering help or asking questions. She sent him to Communications to get more updated information. Mary understood now why Rose wanted her office to be where the main administration was. Communications had been located there since Big Thunder in a converted hotel room next to Administration. Communications had staff that monitored radios 24/7 and wrote reports. Phone communication had improved, but there were still gaps. They still used GMRS and ham radios to communicate in various locations. In an emergency like this, there'd be a lot of radio traffic. Travis had to go downstairs, cross the lobby, go to the north wing, and up again to the fourth floor to get to Communications. The layout of Omímeya was artistic, not efficient.

Mary texted Jackson, asking to be informed when everyone arrived at the meeting about the Two Elks situation. The meeting of what they now called the Security Council comprised Jackson, Kyle, Rose, General Gardner, Billy Fast Dog, Phil Gallo, and her.

As she awaited the Security Council's arrival, she reviewed the updates about the fire. Travis had coerced an early report from Communications.

The death toll had risen because people with severe burns over fifty percent of their bodies didn't qualify for extended care under the Ethics Board's guidelines. The firefighters contained the fire, which was still burning but no longer threatening nearby buildings.

Mary got another call, her rainfall of a day turning into a deluge. Bridget called to say Cecilia, her eldest daughter about to turn twelve, had fallen off a horse onto a pile of scrap building materials, broken her arm, and hit her head. Cecilia had lost consciousness briefly; she was being taken by ambulance to the Chamberlain Hospital because of concerns about a head injury. One thing about no longer worrying about lawsuits, Bridget could ride in the ambulance with Cecilia.

Mary immediately wanted to leave and meet Bridget and Cecilia at the hospital, but realized how much she was needed where she was. She knew she could do little at the hospital except offer Bridget moral support. If it was just a broken arm and a bump on the head, Bridget could handle it. Mary needed to be at the Security Council meeting, not to mention meeting the HBC representative. Then she thought of Cecilia having a brain injury and the possibility of horrible consequences. If she were to live and become disabled, she might not meet the criteria for continued medical care under the Ethics Board guidelines. She knew some people, perhaps the family members of the burn victims today, chose euthanasia over a painful and lingering end. Euthanasia was considered a private matter between doctors and families. Mary knew it often happened when there was little chance of recovery or when long-term medical intervention would be necessary. Mary and Bridget were Catholic. Euthanasia was out of the question.

Mary criticized herself for jumping to negative conclusions and attempted to find a proactive solution. She realized the best brain doctor in the world, Dr. Begay, lived at the resort and was probably home. No reason she shouldn't get his opinion. She texted, asking him to call her for an urgent medical consultation. He called back quickly, assuring her he was at home and available. His calm, clinical questions reassured her even if she didn't know the answers, like how long had Cecilia lost consciousness? Were her pupils reactive and equal in size? Dr. Begay said he would call the hospital. Would she please contact Bridget and have her let the hospital know he'd be consulting? He requested her to arrange a vehicle for him to drive to the hospital if needed. Mary assured him that'd be no problem. If he went, would he please go by her house and pick up Daniel?

Mary felt better. Even if she couldn't be there, Bridget would have her daddy for emotional support. Bridget said they were working on Cecilia's arm. The hospital staff recommended admitting Cecilia to the hospital overnight because of concerns about a potential head injury. Relaying this information caused Bridget to cry and left Mary feeling terrible. Mary told Bridget that she'd leave work and come if needed. Bridget declined and mentioned that she knew about the fire. News was all over the hospital. She'd also heard about the shooting. Bridget asserted Mary needed to stay. When Mary told Bridget her dad was on the way, she could hear relief in her voice. Mary called Dr. Begay back with the news they were admitting Cecilia overnight. He said he would leave right away and pick up Daniel, and Mary arranged for him to use an electric work truck.

After hearing from Jackson, Mary headed downstairs to where the Security Council was meeting. Elliot was there, as she expected, since he had been involved with the Two Elks negotiations, but it surprised her to see Bruce Milsham, an attorney who'd been staying in one of the high-end suites during Big Thunder. According to Phil Gallo, Bruce was a skilled gambler, known for his success in sports betting and blackjack. A high roller but not a partier, he spent time with his wife when not in the casino. They left two grown children behind the Circle. He worked in a big prestigious law firm, specializing in hostile takeovers of corporations. Normally, Phil knew the net worth of all the high-end gamblers. Phil said he couldn't find out what Bruce earned, which meant he had good Internet security. He likely earned millions a year.

Mary remembered uncomfortably when she first met Bruce. After she agreed to let Elliot accompany Jackson when he met Two Elks, Elliot said they needed an experienced negotiator. Elliot was clear that neither he nor Jackson had ever negotiated a contract, which is what a treaty was. She agreed and added Bruce to the team. At a meeting to discuss strategies of approaching Two Elks, Bruce criticized Mary's decision to give Two Elks all that corn. Now his band had enough food for the winter and a healthy cushion for the future. Trade goods from Changleska were all luxury items. If Two Elks was smart, he'd be careful his people didn't become dependent on manufactured goods.

Mary told Bruce she knew from Gift many starved each winter, including the old, and babies whose mothers' milk had dried up.

Mary asked Bruce, "Have you met Gift and Kimi, Rose's daughters?"

"No, but I've seen them singing at various events."

"How old do you think they are?"

Bruce looked uncomfortable. "The one with the pockmarks, eleven or twelve, the older one fifteen or sixteen?"

When Mary told him that Gift was fourteen, soon to be fifteen, and Kimi had just turned thirteen, Bruce looked surprised.

"That's the difference between a healthy diet and long-term undernourishment. I asked Gift, she said they fed slaves the same as everyone else."

Mary reminded Bruce that Changleska had more grain in the silos than could feed twenty times its population. Even with turning some into fuel, unless they could sell it, most of the grain would spoil. Did he think that letting babies die and children go malnourished while they had excess was a good negotiating tactic? He never conceded he was wrong, said he understood Mary had her reasons, and let it go.

They met with Two Elks not long afterwards, but that was the last time. There was an incident with Kimi at that meeting. She spoke up and berated him, much to either the delight or dismay of listeners, depending on their point of view. Mary was in the delight camp, but realized she had to take the long view. You had to make deals with the devil sometimes. Following the thwarted attempt at negotiation with Two Elks, all communication ceased, and the incursions stopped. Last week, reports from the Guard crossed her desk saying they had restarted. Two Elks was stirring up trouble again. Now with one of his warriors dead, the Guard feared war may be coming.

When she arrived, Bruce was already speaking: "What we've been doing isn't working; Two Elks isn't coming to the table. He thinks he has a chance of either winning or causing so much damage and disruption that when he resumes negotiations, we'll be desperate to settle. Two Elks counts on our desire for peace and considers us weak."

General Gardner agreed, using examples from Afghanistan to illustrate his point.

At this point Phil excused himself, saying to Kyle, "Text me if you need me."

Jackson started to lecture about the six principles of conflict resolution: affiliate, empathize, engage, own, self-restrain, and build trust.

Bruce said to him harshly, "Take your cop hat off. You're the Minister for Defense. Think like a soldier."

Jackson looked abashed; Gardner looked relieved.

Gardner said, "They believe we're on their land. That they can come in anytime and take what they want."

Billy interrupted, "They have a point. This was their land."

"After they stole it from the Arikara," answered Bruce.

"That doesn't change their point of view."

Mary intervened before the discussion could escalate.

"General Gardner, what's your recommendation?"

"Treat them like enemy combatants. They're probing our defenses for a reason, not just to steal horses."

"You won't like this," he said, looking at Mary. "Lift the proscription on shooting, including the Guard. Not offensively, just to defend our territory."

Billy asked, "What about the warrior that was killed? I understand the body is still there untouched other than photos taken."

"Leave it there, send a message to Two Elks: 'Come get it before the coyotes do,'" replied Gardner.

Jackson asked, "What about the rancher who shot him? That couldn't be called self-defense because he shot him far out of bow range and the warrior didn't carry a rifle."

Elliot responded, saying, "Prosecuting a home invasion is difficult, even if one's life isn't directly threatened. The Constitution allows for the carrying of arms to protect one's property."

Kyle stepped in, "Don't forget we are in a survival situation. Maybe in this case, what he attempted to steal wouldn't have threatened the family's survival, but there may be a situation when stealing or damaging something critical could endanger a family or affect an entire community."

Bruce asked General Gardner, "If we lifted the shooting proscription, how many warriors would likely be shot?"

"Depends on how many he sends, of course, but if we are looking at the last week, five or six."

Jackson interjected, "That is unacceptable."

"Why?" asked Bruce.

"Because we can resolve this without violence."

Bruce replied, "Can we? You must get someone to the table before you can negotiate. This will cause Two Elks to take notice; nothing else will."

Gardner said, "He is right. Here is what I propose..."

Mary stopped listening while she looked at her texts. She needed to call Bridget.

Before she said her goodbyes, she said, "I hate to admit it, but General Gardner is right. He is a professional. Unlike any of us, he'd been paid to do this job before Big Thunder, so let's trust him to do his job. He has my vote. Sorry, I must go."

Bridget said Dr. Begay had arrived with her dad. They'd just taken Cecilia in for a CT scan. The hospital initially refused to scan her, since they had severe restrictions on all tests using modern machinery. Bridget said Dr. Begay used Mary's name in vain, as well as his expertise as neurosurgeon, to get the test run.

Bridget said it initially worried her as the other doctor didn't think it was necessary, but when the other doctor left the room, Dr. Begay winked at her and said, "It's probably unnecessary, but even if the chances of brain damage are extremely remote, let's not take a chance."

Mary felt relieved but also guilty for using her position to provide Cecilia with care others might not receive. Most parents would go to any lengths to protect a child or grandchild. She felt guilty because she'd always detested the medical system's practice of ordering unnecessary tests, "just in case." Mary sighed. She didn't have to be logical, she only wanted Cecilia to be healthy and safe.

Mary let Bridget know she'd tell Rose not to expect her at work on Monday. Bridget had been hired as the new Human Resources Manager. Rose had been complaining about the lack of an HR person, and Mary mentioned Bridget. Rose immediately hired her without an interview. They had manuals and textbooks on file, and Bridget could learn on the job. It worked out well.

She went back to her office; they were still waiting for the HBC representative, who should arrive anytime. She was wearing a long skirt and a nice top, nothing special, but better than what she otherwise would've worn. In addition, she wanted to touch base with Travis regarding the fire.

While waiting for the HBC representative and news about the fire, Mary thought she might as well get work done and turned on her computer to review budgets. The initial startup loan the bank had given was almost gone. They'd got a loan from Omímeya, but Mary wondered how long Omímeya could keep underwriting their new government, without conferences and few paying guests, and little casino revenue.

Instead of reducing the amount they gave to the Lower Brule Tribe, Rose increased it. They also gave funds to the Crow Creek Tribe. Mary supposed they would have to print more money. Actually, it was electrons since they didn't print money. Governments did this all the time, fiat money not based on gold, but according to Rose, it was a dangerous precedent.

Mary was no longer the Chair of the Lower Brule Tribal Council. She'd heard from Lou White Mountain, the current Chair, Rose had asked that both tribes send her a list of all current unfunded projects in order of priority. Both tribes' income was minimal without federal funding. They still had rental and utility payments, and a few minor projects, but that was it. Changleska paid for medical care, including substance abuse treatment, feeding of children and elders, fire and rescue, which lifted the burden from the tribes, but they still had unmet needs.

Rose said if things went well with the HBC negotiations, Omímeya might help with the housing shortage or the heating problems. Many houses were heated with natural gas, which they no longer had. With winter coming on, wood stoves and wood became priorities. Housing being in such short supply with so many people living with relatives, it was becoming a crisis; they needed solutions before the weather got too much colder.

Travis came into her office and told her he had bad news. Communications had received the names of those who died in the fire, and her nephew William was one of them. Mary felt a mix of grief and disbelief when she learned about William's death, which devastated her. She didn't know he'd been working in Reliant. He was a welder, probably working on the tanks.

William was Daniel's sister's son, around the same age as her two boys, in his late thirties. When younger, the cousins spent a lot of time together. Because Mary had a house right in town and William's family lived rurally, he'd often spent the night at her house. Mary wondered when she should tell Daniel. He couldn't go to see his sister while at the hospital with Bridget. She wanted to tell him in person, not on the phone, but realized that was a luxury she may not be able to afford.

Rose texted, "HBC rep arrived." Mary called and found out they were getting the voyageurs settled. They'd set up their tents on the platforms in the tipi village, next to their cargo. Only the representative would get a room in the hotel. Rose would bring the representative to meet her in her office within the next two hours. Mary wondered what the delay was. They could take a golf cart from the tipi village and be here in ten minutes. Then it occurred to her that Rose probably wanted to take the representative on a tour first, to pump up the wow factor. A lot was riding on this meeting.

The Hudson's Bay Company was one of the most powerful corporations in the world during this time, the equivalent of Amazon or Microsoft. The East India Companies, both English and Dutch, were the largest, but HBC wasn't too far behind. They not only had vast wealth but exerted powerful influence politically. Rose emphasized the importance of securing HBC as a trading partner for Changleska's economic survival.

More important than a trading partner were their political and business connections. Rose had told Mary, if they could get the HBC invested in Changleska, they'd have a much better chance of survival. Rose always harped on the importance of the economy for survival. Mary believed people would flock here to witness the biblical miracle, as well as to see all the modern wonders. No one was sure how big tourism was in eighteenth-century America, and Phil said visitors would be more likely to show up wanting plunder.

When the HBC rep arrived, it surprised Mary how young the man was, early twenties. He spoke English well with a slight accent. Not surprising, as Rose specified to only send English speakers. He looked around, obviously awed. Rose and Mary exchanged a satisfied glance. The first thing he did was offer condolences to Mary. Rose said since the HBC party had several weeks before they were due to return, they wouldn't start meetings until Monday or Tuesday, and Mary was not strictly needed until things were further along.

Mary asked Henry whether he was a Catholic. He said he was. Mary asked Rose to please arrange a ride for him to St. Agnes for the 9:00 am Mass. She'd meet him there. Sensing an obvious dismissal, they departed for the rest of the tour. She noticed Jenny had arrived to take over. *Nice touch, Rose*, thought Mary, as the two good-looking young people might end the tour with dinner. Pleasant and pretty company always greased the wheels of negotiations.

Bridget called back with the results of the CT scan. Since Cecilia was fine, they could release her early, so Mary felt less guilty about having it done. They would all squeeze into the truck to catch a ride back with Dr. Begay. Mary asked to speak to Daniel on the phone, not sure if she should tell him on the phone, but realized she couldn't put it off. After relaying the sad news to Daniel, she asked him to have Dr. Begay drop him off at Omímeya, and they could both drive over to his sister's place together.

While on her way outside to meet Daniel, she swung by Red Oaks to grab food to bring. John Murphy already prepared a large quantity of food for her. He refused payment and informed her it was paid for. It had been part of an order for grieving families, and he was happy she could deliver it. There were several catering platters like she hadn't seen in ages. She wondered how Omímeya kept serving food that no one else had. After Daniel and Mary got to his sister's house, after the tears, hugs, and eating, the two stood on the back porch in the cold, escaping the crowded house, holding each other. Mary thought, *even on a day like today when it pours, I have Daniel; he protects me from even the worst storms.*

Chapter Twenty-Six
Elliot

TWO MONTHS AFTER Big Thunder, Elliot didn't think he should be this happy. Many people were stressed and struggling to adjust to life in 1791. He knew he had it good compared to others. He still lived in his two-bedroom rental. It had been heated with natural gas, but he had been lucky enough to get a couple of electric space heaters before the trading posts ran out. People had moved around, living with relatives, many packed into a small space. After his cousin Theo and his friend Scott moved out, he had new roommates with whom he got along well: Travis and his girlfriend, Melody. Elliot's new girlfriend, Morning Star, had moved in recently. It was going surprisingly well. She even paid a small amount of rent.

Most of all, Elliot was happy with his new job. He finally got hired as a full-time lawyer for Changleska. Because Omímeya no longer had to repay the loans to the casino consortium, it could direct more funds to the tribes, which could now afford the Law Center. It had been difficult, but Elliot found someone to take over his old job, which freed him up to work full time for Changleska. After talking to every lawyer who came through Big Thunder, he finally found someone—a divorce lawyer who'd been staying at the casino with her family. Because she needed a job, she was open to learning criminal law and now found she enjoyed it. She was also working alongside Elliot on the subcommittee to reform the criminal justice system. The Law Center could now afford to pay his former assistant Carrie, who was becoming a paralegal. Elliot no longer had to pay her salary. With his new salary and roommates, he was doing better financially than he had been before Big Thunder.

Morning Star worked from 3-11:00 pm. He usually worked from 9:00am-5:00 pm, so they had little time together. They usually shared breakfast while they spent a little time catching up. He was beginning to miss coffee less. She made prairie tea and a pot of cornmeal mush for the household. This morning, she was doing homework; she was trying to get all her prerequisites for her midwifery program done. Elliot looked at what she was doing, surprised because it was on paper. Because of paper and ink shortages, almost everything was read electronically. Using a set of colored pencils, she was coloring an anatomical drawing of the female reproductive system, taken from a book called *Birthsong Midwifery Workbook*. She would color the part, then color the hollow letters that were the name of the part. He thought it was a great way to learn.

Seeing the name of the author, Daphne Singingtree, he said, "I know that woman!"

Morning Star wanted to know the entire story. Elliot said he didn't really know her but had met her twice, once during the Standing Rock protests. While he was there, Elliot had caught a cough that was going around. He went to the Rosebud camp where Daphne had organized doctors and herbalists to work together in a big tipi set up with herbal medicines. They gave him fire cider, a blend of garlic, horseradish, cayenne, and other herbs in vinegar; elderberry syrup; and tea with elecampane, osha root, mullein, and coltsfoot.

"Daphne is an older, big woman," Elliot said, demonstrating with his hands a big circle, "the size of my aunty Carline. She'd been in a car accident years before and could barely walk, used a walker. But she drove from Oregon, raised funds, organized medical supplies and doctors. Arranged for donated tipis from the Nomadic Tipi Company."

Elliot continued, "I wouldn't have remembered her, but she lived in Eugene, where I went to law school. The woman I was dating at the time wanted to attend a workshop she was teaching, 'Herbs for the Zombie Apocalypse.' I didn't realize it was the same woman until we arrived at her house, where she held the workshop. She had converted her yard into herb gardens, trained interns who helped her, and ran a small business selling products she grew and made."

"What herbs did she recommend for zombie bites?"

Elliot said, "The class was about preparedness. I don't remember specific herbs, but they were for smoke from wildfires or issues that may come from being in a shelter. She also talked about pandemics; this was a few years before COVID. What I remember most is what happened during the break. Someone asked Daphne what tribe she was, and she answered, 'Standing Rock.'"

His date mentioned Elliot was one of the protesters, had been at the camp the entire time. She didn't remember him, but they talked about the camp for a couple of minutes. When everyone returned, she said she wanted to acknowledge Elliot.

"Water Protectors are warriors. Warriors go toward danger to protect others. Some warriors are soldiers, or firefighters, even police. They put their lives on the line to protect others. Water Protectors did the same."

She asked Elliot, "How many times did you get teargassed, shot with rubber bullets, or sprayed with water in freezing temperatures?" He didn't know, but more than he could count.

"Water Protectors went toward danger to protect the water, to keep DAPL from putting in a pipeline. We may have lost that battle, but our warriors showed their commitment to protect their communities."

Daphne presented him with a gift she had made for all the Water Protectors. Then she shared a song she wrote during the protests; it was short, and everyone sang with her.

Mni Wiconi, Water Is Life,
Clean Water, Clean Water Is Everyone's Right,
Protecting the Water with All Our Might.

Morning Star told Elliot he should teach that song to his cousin, Darla. He hadn't remembered it until he related the story. She asked about the gift. He went to his room and came back with a leather-wrapped turkey feather and a necklace that looked like water with small turquoise beads at the bottom, years before he burned the sweetgrass and sage.

=..=

Elliot had to rush out the door to meet the shuttle, with Travis not far behind. Another nice thing about his new job was that he qualified for the door-to-door shuttle and didn't have to walk in the cold to the bus stop at the school at six am He could leave at a reasonable eight-thirty with Mary, Travis, and nine others. Mary wasn't on the shuttle today, probably on bereavement leave after her nephew's death on Saturday from the fire.

Elliot's first meeting of the day was with the Hudson Bay Company representative. They met in the boardroom on the fourth floor, with its spectacular river view, exquisite art, plush chairs, and the conference table made from one beautiful slab of highly polished wood with inlaid stones.

That table probably cost more than some houses his relatives lived in. He had never attended a meeting there before. Elliot, Rose, and Bruce Milsham met forty minutes before the representative to review what they wanted to present and to discuss strategy.

Henry LaChamp arrived on Saturday but waited until Monday to discuss business. Everyone took not working on the Sabbath seriously in the eighteenth century. Bruce had been working on this for weeks beforehand. When Elliot opened the document, the extent of the work Bruce had already completed surprised him.

Jenny ushered LaChamp in. He looked around the room, obviously impressed. He noted one chair at the head of the table was empty. Rose told him she didn't expect Mary to be present for the first meeting, as she needed time with her family. Jenny excused herself, and Travis joined them to take notes for Mary, but he didn't sit in her chair. Henry began by saying how impressed he was with everything he'd seen so far. Jenny was going to take him to the hospital later this afternoon. He was looking forward to seeing the rest of Changleska. He gushed about the various wonders he saw, saying how shocked he was at the showers, the unlimited hot water from the tap, and how clean and beautiful everything was, and nothing smelled of smoke.

LaChamp expressed his surprise and awe at everything he saw. He expressed his admiration for the cars. He had visited a farm and had seen modern farm equipment and grain silos. It was obvious the young man was full to bursting with excitement over all the new ideas.

Rose surprised Elliot when she told LaChamp that Bruce and Elliot were there for the negotiations because she had been the former general manager's assistant and she had to take over when he was left behind the Circle.

With a vacuous expression, Rose said, "There's so much to learn."

According to what Elliot had heard, Rose had done much more than Tom ever did and was more than his assistant, essentially running the place. Rose smiled at LaChamp, looking like this was too much for her. Elliot knew she was the one who'd thought of writing to the Hudson Bay Company in the first week after Big Thunder and had worked closely with Bruce to outline the negotiation strategy.

He didn't understand the helpless female routine she was performing, but LaChamp fell for it. "Of course, it would overwhelm anyone with this much responsibility, and I understand you have three children," he said.

"Teenagers, that helps."

LaChamp turned to Bruce, the older white man, and started addressing him. He ignored Elliot completely, and only occasionally included Rose. Elliot wasn't sure if he'd ever seen a man so patronizing and was certain LaChamp ignored him because he was Lakota. Elliot was angry.

They spent several hours reviewing the material Bruce had prepared, discussing various aspects of the proposed business. They negotiated a deal for the rifles, gunpowder, and coffee that had been sent, and agreed on a price for more.

The HBC wanted to buy plans to build steam engines and other modern technologies. Bruce was clear selling plans outright was off the table, but they could partner for manufacturing of some. They hadn't discussed it beforehand, which is why Rose interjected. She said she realized the Dakotas were remote and difficult for shipping, but they would consider a joint venture in St. Louis for manufacturing. LaChamp looked at her, surprised she'd made a good suggestion.

After the meeting was over, Elliot asked Rose why she'd acted like an airhead. He knew she wasn't. Rose explained even in their day, men underestimated women, especially in business. He was a typical eighteenth-century man, even more chauvinistic, if that was possible. If she hid beneath the silly female smile, he'd think he had the upper hand. She had no problem working through Bruce. She also said it annoyed her when she found out LaChamp's job title. The HBC sent a very junior clerk, not even a secretary to someone important. She said she downgraded his room from a suite to a regular room when she found out. He had no authority to make decisions, make agreements, or sign contracts. These meetings were for show, but they were a first step. Hopefully, the company would send someone else with more power next time. The pace of communication was difficult, with messages arriving months apart. Soon, winter would shut down everything, causing further delays.

Elliot returned to his office two doors down. The casino comptroller was left behind the Circle, and Elliot had lucked out by getting his office. It was nicer than the other administrators' offices. Like the West Wing of the White House, having an office close to Mary was being close to power.

Elliot got a message the Black Hills expedition had returned, and there was a meeting at 2:00 pm to discuss the findings. He had time for his semi-regular lunch with Jerome at Buffalo Burger, which now served buffalo stew and cornbread at a reasonable price. All cattle were now free range. Buffalo was becoming more of a staple than beef.

Jerome told him he was having a lot of luck convincing farmers to switch from hay and feed grain to hemp. Growing hemp was easy, farmers could easily adapt their machinery for it. Hemp grew fast and cleaned the air. It didn't need pesticides or chemical fertilizers. There were many uses for hemp, such as cloth, paper, rope, soap, a plastic substitute, and hempcrete. People or animals could use hemp seed for food. For biofuel, hemp proved superior to corn. In 1941, Henry Ford built a car largely out of hemp, that ran on hemp fuel. The challenge would be developing all the manufacturing needed. For example, they would need to create looms for cloth. Hemp was a big crop in the eighteenth century. Elliot suggested to Jerome perhaps the expeditions could find people already using it and recruit them to move.

=..=

At the meeting, Elliot was excited to hear from the Black Hills/Paha Sapa expedition. They heard little from the expedition after it left. He was on that committee and was anxiously awaiting their return. *Očhéti Šakówiŋ*, also referred to as the seven council fires, is the collective name for the seven bands of Lakota, Dakota, and Nakota speakers. The original names were Brulé, Oglala, Itazipco, Hunkpapa, Mnikoju, Blackfoot, and Two Kettle. Later, the government agencies that forcibly resettled the tribes gave them reservation names. Some kept their own tribal names and others were reclaiming theirs. For example, the Rosebud Sioux Tribe was more properly known as Sičangu Lakota Oyate or Burnt Thigh People. Throughout the years, the tribes had formed their own unique identities. Each functioned as a distinct sovereign nation. All Ocheti Sakowin held

Paha Sapa sacred. Many felt strongly that no mining of any kind should take place in Paha Sapa. Others argued mining could be accomplished in environmentally sound ways, with safeguards in place to avoid desecrating sacred sites.

A few brought up the only way to protect the Paha Sapa was to raise the money for the purchase and Changleska Guard forces to defend it. They argued gold seekers were probably already heading there now. They couldn't stop the hordes with gold fever, but they could contain and manage the situation. Discussions got passionate. Paha Sapa was deep in people's hearts.

Some argued about how strong Changleska would be in 50 or 100 years, but everyone agreed the charter should include a provision stating that the Black Hills would always be held in trust for the Lakota people. They finally came up with two proposals: one was no mining at all, the other allowed it with claims that avoided sacred sites and had environmental protections. As a compromise, it required all claim holders to have one Lakota person on their permit who was free to inspect the site at any point.

It was too big a decision for a committee to bring to the council for a vote, so they held a meeting and conducted an online poll of every member of the Ocheti Sakowin. There were a lot of enrolled Lakota from different tribes between the conference and those who lived locally. Almost everyone either came to the meeting or voted online. The proposal to allow limited mining went through. A smaller committee would work out the details of how to accomplish it.

Concerned a gold rush was already on the way, the committee sent the first Paha Sapa expedition within days. They selected the two Lakota families because they regularly participated in powwow and rodeo circuits. With their camping gear setups, four-wheel-drive vehicles, horses and trailers, and two tipis, they were packed and ready to go. Each time they returned from an event, their gear was all cleaned, restocked, and ready to go for the next trip. Both families spoke Lakota, although the younger members were more fluent.

The only thing they needed to stock was grain for the horses and more food, which they planned to supplement from hunting. They added a few trade goods, but had little room, as they also had to bring chainsaws, road clearing tools, and additional fuel.

The families were ready before the committee finished writing all their guidelines, but still received samples of permits. They weren't planning on doing much mining, but were there to contact the Indigenous tribes and to patrol the area for unpermitted miners. In case Indigenous tribes encountered gold seekers, they sent examples of permits. In order to make the permits difficult to forge, they printed them in color and notarized them to create a raised surface.

Jack Tilson and his two grown sons, Ed and Larry, comprised one of the families sent. Jack and Larry left their wives at home, since they knew the trip would be hard and dangerous. The other family was Darren and June Iron Cloud, their sixteen-year-old son, Ely, and their twelve-year-old daughter, Collette. They all had experience as riders, hunters, and campers. Between them, there were three vehicles and eight horses. All the vehicles had four-wheel drive, except for the trailers, which weren't designed for off-road use. Whenever the road was bad, they had to let the horses out and sometimes winch the trailers over a rough patch. The 250-mile trip would have taken five hours on an existing road. It took five days.

They chose I-90, assuming it had been surveyed to avoid major obstacles during construction. Alongside old paper maps, they had excellent Google maps. They acknowledged they were constructing the beginning of a road which would facilitate the path for others. After they left what was left of I-90, they noticed tracks in the dirt, showing that someone had already passed through. The first 100 miles, the path showed evidence of someone felling trees, but then the tracks took a different direction. They wondered if a broken chainsaw had caused someone to stray off the I-90. However, they never saw tracks again.

The families brought radios that could communicate with aircraft if they could hear it flying overhead. Regularly, the Air Guard performed reconnaissance to look for tribes and locate buffalo herds. The expedition had only caught the plane twice since they left, with not much to report except they'd arrived safely and had encountered no one, despite seeing tracks earlier. The second time the plane made its radio check-in, the families heard there was a large tribe about 100 miles north moving slowly south, and a few smaller tribes closer by.

The expedition located a suitable campsite with a nearby stream close to the Deadwood Gulch, where gold had been found. It had rich mining sites and wouldn't need major excavation. NewNet contained historical data that gave exact locations for every mining location in a password-protected site they could access.

After setting up their tipis and the camp kitchen, the men built an inípi or sweat lodge and held a ceremony. The women chose not to do so this time. Kyle Ward had given them perimeter alarms and other military surveillance gear. The fact a casino owned such equipment surprised them. Although they had hunting rifles, Omímeya supplied them with a few automatic weapons, but instructed them to avoid hostilities with the Indigenous tribes. By bringing two women, including a young girl, they hoped to avoid appearing like a war party. They were more concerned about white men who may have better weapons than the local tribes and so tried to stay alert.

A few weeks after they settled into their camp, one morning before dawn, they heard the piercing shriek of the perimeter alarm they had set up in the horse corral they had built. The men came rushing out of their tipis, weapons in hand, all still in their long johns. A couple had got feet into boots. By the time they got outside, there was no trace of anyone. They were debating whether it was an animal when suddenly an arrow struck Ed Tilson, the younger of the two sons. They turned over the table in the kitchen area and took cover.

Before anyone shot back, Darren started shouting in Lakota. "We are here to trade. Let's smoke and talk. My woman will make you good food."

Ed's shoulder was bleeding from the arrow. His dad was trying to apply pressure, grabbing a towel from the kitchen behind them. Fortunately, the wound wasn't deep. Later, June sewed it up, even though she had never sewn up a person before, and said it couldn't be harder than a coat. They had been provided with a good medical kit, including suture materials and antibiotics.

Two Lakota warriors approached slowly, weapons still in hands, but not raised. Darren asked Jack to cover him and came out from behind the table unarmed with his hands raised.

Darren in Lakota asked, "Have you ever eaten pancakes? My woman makes the best. Come join us for breakfast. The sun will be up soon."

Everyone relaxed. They turned the table back over and turned on the overhead LED camp lights. The warriors all came in for a closer look.

Darren showed them the solar panels on top of the canopy the kitchen was under, and how it hooked to a battery that charged the lights. The scouts wanted to trade for the lights. Darren said they needed those, but had some smaller ones he could trade for, and more where those came from.

They weren't a war party, they were scouting for the bigger tribe that had been spotted north, the Red Eagle band of Oglala. It was currently seven or eight days away. June had come out and was working on Ed's shoulder. The scouts observed closely. It was getting light, and when done, June started breakfast. Collette came out of the tipi, fully dressed, holding a rifle. Darren gave her a look.

"I know you told me to stay inside, but I had to pee," she said in Lakota. Everyone laughed.

As everyone was about to sit down to eat, one scout gave a sharp whistle and two more scouts appeared from the shadows. June said, "Guess I will make more pancakes."

She really made great pancakes. One scout mentioned he'd tasted maple syrup before, explaining it'd been traded with tribes from the northeast.

After breakfast, they brought out their limited trade goods, which included a wind-up flashlight. The scouts had little to trade. It was more gifting than trading, but everyone understood. The tobacco they gave them was appreciated. Darren showed them their vehicles and gave rides, which they loved. The scouts said their tribe had wondered about the airplanes, which had flown low over the camps.

Before they left, when discussing how to approach the Indigenous tribes, they'd decided not to emphasize Big Thunder and why they had come yet, rather to focus on protecting Paha Sapa from unscrupulous gold miners. The rest could wait. They all talked about Paha Sapa gold. The scouts knew what it was, traders valued it. It surprised them it could be found in streams that came from the hills. Darren requested to see the sacred sites they should avoid. This confused the scouts, as all of Paha Sapa was sacred, but there were places for different ceremonies and numerous burial sites. Figuring out which sites to avoid was going to be more complicated than they thought.

When asked, they confirmed they hadn't seen any white men. A sturdy envelope and copies of the permit example were given to the scouts. The scouts liked the colorful permit with its gold foil seal and were directed to feel it.

Darren taught the scouts the English phrase, "Show us your permit."

They explained that if the white men didn't have the paper with the raised seal, they shouldn't be allowed to mine on Lakota lands. In the future, only white men who had a Lakota with them could mine gold. The hope was that the local tribes would offer their services to miners for trade or a portion of the gold. Changleska would teach any Lakota who wished to learn how to mine. It was now Changleska law the gold must remain in trust for the entire Ocheti Sakowin benefit. That gold would help the Lakota prosper with trade goods, enable them to buy weapons. The scouts appreciated the explanation that many wasicu would come, and they'd have to protect their lands.

Darren explained their chief would want to meet Red Eagle, and would offer many trade items. When the scouts asked about weapons, Darren explained they had to be made, could take as long as two or more winters. They informed them they considered taking slaves bad medicine, they'd only give the best goods and weapons to tribes that didn't take slaves and agreed to become an ally and join Changleska.

Everyone was pleased with that first meeting. Instead of going to meet Red Eagle yet, they stayed put, drilled test holes, and panned for gold. Panning didn't result in any big finds, but some color and a couple of tiny nuggets. They had all caught gold fever and would have been happy to stay longer, but the weather was getting cold, and they didn't have the needed gear. Before they broke their camp down, they decided a couple of guys would patrol to look for vehicle tracks. They'd seen no one yet, and they weren't sure if they should be relieved or worried. After discovering downed trees and tracks, they followed the trail to an abandoned campsite. What was left was mostly trash, and four dead, naked, mutilated bodies of white men.

Jack said, "I guess they didn't have a permit." Ed threw up.

After taking pictures with their phones, they buried the men and looked for any identification. There were no wallets or personal effects, or much of anything else from the campsite. After locating two trucks, they discovered that the upholstery had been trashed, but no one had opened the hoods, suggesting they probably still ran. They couldn't find any keys, and none of them knew how to hot-wire a car. They noted the location on their maps and returned to their camp, packed up, and returned home.

After hearing the story, Elliot and the others were unsure what to make of the whole situation. The idea of killing and mutilating trespassers was difficult to swallow, even if the men had been in the wrong. Early on through media statements, they informed people about the need for permits, even offering assistance to miners with maps. No permits had been issued yet, as they were waiting for the first group to return with information about sacred sites to avoid. No one was sure if the miners who had been killed had attempted to apply for a permit or not. They released a statement about the deaths, saying the men didn't have identification, gave make and model of the trucks, and family members could check photos. Their hope was none would, since photos of even the face were horrible.

After much discussion, they decided not to take any action. When they met with Red Eagle, they'd ask them nicely not to kill or mutilate any trespassers, please. It was good to meet another Lakota band. Two Elks was still not being cooperative; there had been incursions but no more deaths. They recalled the outreach team who'd been staying at the winter camp at Two Elks' invitation to have his people learn English. Jackson thought, *Two Elks could use the outreach team as hostages.*

=..=

Elliot's last meeting of the day was with members of the Medical Committee. They wanted legal advice about the vaccination policy. The issue had come up because COVID was going around again. Most people at risk had already died from underlying health conditions because of a lack of medications. Those vaccinated only experienced a mild flu. The medical committee was concerned that COVID could devastate the Indigenous population. Two Elks' band had frequent contact through the trading posts.

There were thousands of doses of COVID booster vaccine available. The problem was no one was getting vaccinated, despite their pleas on the media. The committee wanted to determine if it was possible to pass a law to make vaccines mandatory, as they believed it was the government's duty to protect people. They admitted they weren't as concerned about COVID, but what would happen when the new smallpox vaccine became available? This was a controversial topic, with passionate arguments on both sides.

Elliot felt it represented an interesting legal question, but passing a law requiring vaccines, even to protect community health, was going to pose social problems. He understood they were trying to prevent the genocide that white man's diseases brought to the Indigenous people. As Elliot pointed out, Clyde Folsom would use his opposition to vaccines as a flash point to further his political aims, making the situation complicated. They tossed around alternatives, such as a mandatory quarantine for those who refused vaccination. They discussed making people wear yellow vests saying, "Stand Back. I believe my health is more important than yours."

Elliot asked, "For COVID, instead of requiring our people to vaccinate, why not vaccinate the Two Elks tribe and other Indigenous we meet?"

The doctors all looked at each other, surprised to have a lawyer propose such a simple medical solution. Although it was a good idea, it didn't address smallpox or other vaccines. Elliot promised to look at the entire issue and put it on the agenda of the law committee.

Elliot had to rush to catch the 5:00 pm shuttle, grateful to Mary for insisting on the nine-to-five schedule. He could have easily stayed later, especially considering the day's fast-paced nature and the commitment of his colleagues. It was Morning Star's day off, with their opposing work schedules, spending time with her had become increasingly important to him.

As he reflected on his day, Elliot realized how much he loved his job. The environment was dynamic, with everyone dedicated to making real change that could impact the future. Each day brought new challenges and opportunities, reinforcing his passion for the work he did.

Chapter Twenty-Seven
Two Elks

UNCERTAINTY FILLED TWO ELKS. It'd been over two moons since Big Thunder brought the thunder people to his territory and disturbed his peace. Two Elks faced many difficulties in his role as leader of his tribe, but none had challenged him as much. He didn't know the right thing to do. Being a leader meant being decisive. Knowing where to go and what to do was as much of a part of him as breathing. Sometimes he made wrong decisions, especially when he didn't have enough information. But he always had clarity about the path that should be taken.

It was hard to believe that the Thunder Beings had brought an entire people, complete with all their marvels, in a perfect circle, on his lands. Although they'd shot his brother, Long Tracks, they'd healed him with their medicine and machines. Choosing to send Good Voice had been a good choice, as she was an excellent observer. When Long Tracks was returned a week later, the intelligence Two Elks received from her was both enlightening and terrifying. These people were weak in so many ways. He couldn't believe how a people could survive, being so soft. When his scouts returned and told how they were captured then questioned, nobody beat or tortured them; instead, they were offered food and water. They healed his brother, an enemy who'd killed one of their own, including an unarmed woman. Killing unarmed women was shameful for a true warrior. It happened occasionally, particularly if the warrior was in a rage like Long Tracks had been.

Good Voice had an interpreter, a young girl named Jenelle. She'd asked the girl lots of questions and had gathered a good picture of life in what they called Changleska. Good Voice had chosen to stay in the hospital with Long Tracks, despite being offered a place to sleep in someone's home. The nurses had brought her blankets so she could sleep next to Long Tracks' bed in a chair that folded out.

Everyone in Changleska missed their old world and didn't know how to live in this one. The hospital was full of people who were sick and dying from the lack of medicines they no longer had. There was such a shortage of medicine doctors had to choose to let some people die. Good Voice talked about several families she'd seen in the hall, arguing with doctors, crying, trying to save loved ones.

Changleska was filled with large people, taller and more robust than their people. Many people were fat, some were so fat they could barely walk. Good Voice had seen nothing like it before. Jenelle said that people whose ancestors ate mostly meat and little grain had what she called a different metabolism. When the white man came, they killed all the buffalo and gave the people flour and lard, which they made into fry bread, which helped make them fat. She said in her old world lots of poor people were fat from eating lots of starches, and the rich people were thin. That made no sense to Good Voice, but she was told rich people could afford healthy food, had the time to exercise. Once people gained weight, it became more difficult for them to exercise. Some ended up sick because they couldn't afford to eat right. Good Voice ate fry bread when she was there. It was good, but she would get fat too if she ate lots of it every day.

Men came and wanted to talk to Good Voice about Jesus, which was confusing. Afterwards, Jenelle told her that to feel the Creator, they went once a week to special buildings to sing and pray about Jesus. They didn't believe the Creator lived in the earth, water, trees, and animals, it was something outside and separate; you had to believe in Jesus to feel the Great Spirit.

Good Voice said lots of people wanted to talk to her. She ended up sitting outside of Long Tracks' room to avoid disturbing him. She couldn't understand why they were asking her those questions. For example, people asked her how well she got along with Long Tracks' other two wives or how they divided up the work. Or what kind of food they gathered, or who attended women when they gave birth. Few people spoke Lakota. She had to rely on Jenelle, but everyone was respectful. No one treated Long Tracks like an enemy, even though everyone knew what he had done.

All of this was confusing to Two Elks—enemies that didn't act like enemies. When they got to winter camp, they asked if they could send "medical and outreach teams." He agreed, curious about what they would do. They examined people, listening, prodding, poking with needles, and even drawing blood. He had heard white men believed taking away bad blood could heal people, but he'd seen no one do it. The outreach people asked lots of questions, but also taught English. They told people sickness came from dirt, so they had to cover their feces and wash their hands.

They offered to build outhouses with composting toilets for the entire camp. Two Elks had heard about outhouses from the scouts and allowed it. They tried to get the men of the tribe to help build the structures, but the men would rather watch them and joke. They ended up bringing in a bunch of soldiers to finish the job. The few who spoke Lakota shamed the men, saying they had to stop doing their own work to come do theirs.

Two Elks didn't understand what kind of war leader would have his warriors stop training to build outhouses for a potential enemy. It made no sense. The thunder people could wipe out his tribe, and his inability to understand why they didn't made him uneasy. A key to success in warfare was understanding why an enemy did what they did.

They had built a road to the camp to bring their trucks. After the outhouses were done, Two Elks told them they must park two miles away and walk or ride into the village. Two Elks wanted to maintain some level of distance. His people would ride into town to go to the trading posts. They returned with goods, many of which were less useful than the warm buffalo robes they'd traded for. People didn't need thin bright clothes, or the many other items that were made from "plastic," that had little practical use.

Before they arrived, it'd been rare for anyone to steal. Everyone knew everyone else. It was easy for people to identify a stolen item. There was severe punishment for thievery. Since people started going to the trading posts, it became common for items they got to be stolen. A popular item was "blue jeans." All the young men wanted a pair, sometimes even trading medicine bags, or quill-decorated shirts their mothers made for them. Unlike clothing made specifically for individuals, blue jeans looked alike. This meant if a pair got stolen, the thief could wear them without getting caught.

Two Elks heard from Good Voice thievery was common among Changleskans. He also heard many were "alcoholics," the disease of drinking too much whisky. Since whisky was hard to get, few drank enough to catch this disease, but it was easy to find at the trading posts. He worried for his people. Two Elks considered forbidding people from going to the trading posts, but he knew they'd find a way. He didn't want to issue an order that wouldn't be obeyed. Unsure how to proceed, he would start by talking to them. He did not have to agree to anything, but talk did not hurt.

When he'd agreed to negotiate, Two Elks met Joseph Chasing Hawk's granddaughter, Butterfly Chasing Hawk. She'd berated and shamed him before everyone. He had never seen a young girl so stunning, even more striking than Many Horses. She had a power about her. Her name fit her, beautiful like a butterfly, but chasing a hawk, something many times more powerful. He wasn't used to young girls speaking up to him. There were plenty of strong women in his tribe, but only the older ones spoke to leaders, and none spoke like she did. Butterfly Chasing Hawk told him he was a bad leader, and why. The thing that troubled him the most was wondering if she was right.

Two Elks knew what it was like to lose a child. He and Many Horses had lost a little girl. Two Elks felt surprised by how much tenderness he'd had for the baby girl. He'd hoped she would grow up to be as pretty as Many Horses. The baby would sleep on his chest, small and sweet. When she was three moons old, she died after getting sick. Many Horses was inconsolable; Two Elks felt her pain and his own. Before this, Many Horses had been vivacious and happy, but she never returned to her old self. It was a dark time in his life; he felt he'd lost not only a child, but a vital part of his woman. He also remembered when Big Star, who hadn't been named yet, was three winters old, got so sick he didn't wake from a fever. Two Elks remembered that fear, as Big Star was his firstborn and only child at the time. *The thunder people's medicine could have saved his little girl.* Could he deny any parent the same, the possibility of saving their children?

Black Rabbit heard what Butterfly Chasing Hawk said. Everyone had. According to her, she was angry because she thought his action had harmed Broken Pot, now named Gift of Thunder. Black Rabbit said she didn't doubt that Gift of Thunder had been hurt; she was small and Big Stink was a large man. It was obvious that Butterfly Chasing Hawk loved her new sister; she was defending her. Black Rabbit told Two Elks that he was lucky she didn't curse him. Anyone who met her could feel how much power she had. She'd heard the Thunder Beings hours before Big Thunder. To right the wrongs she believed Two Elks had done to her sister, she could have cursed his manhood until it withered and fell off. She had that much power. He was fortunate she only told him he was a bad leader if he didn't put the welfare of his people first.

Now Two Elks had something else to worry about. After that incident he stopped talking to the thunder people altogether. He withdrew and thought, trying to find the right path. He knew Butterfly Chasing Hawk was right about some things. Her people's medicines would allow children to live, and his people would hunger less. But would they also steal more, drink more whisky, get fat and lazy, not be able to feel the Great Spirit without going into a building and reading a book about a dead leader?

Because he didn't know what to do, he did nothing. This angered the young men, especially his oldest son, Big Star, who'd become a leader of the younger men, always wanting to fight. As Two Elks remained silent, Big Star's faction became stronger. Two Elks wondered whether the time had come for him to step aside, as all old men did. Two Elks loved his son but knew he didn't have the needed experience as a war leader, or the wisdom to resolve conflicts within the tribe, as all good leaders did.

Big Star had been leading raids to steal horses, clothes, anything they could easily grab from outlying farms without either permission from Two Elks or an order not to do it. Then he got a message from a young man, dressed as what they called Guardians, not Joseph Chasing Hawk, who had always been the messenger before. He was told to come get a dead warrior's body before the coyotes did. Two Elks was surprised to learn they didn't show any respect for the dead, unlike his previous experience. He didn't like what this new attitude had foretold.

Two Elks remained unsure of his next move. Scouts reported the voyageurs had reached Omímeya, carrying a substantial cargo of rifles, gunpowder, and other goods. Two Elks also heard the Red Eagle tribe had met with the thunder people. Red Eagle was not an enemy, more of a rival. Their tribes traded sometimes or sent war parties to the Crow together, but he didn't want Red Eagle to get more rifles and to align with the thunder people. Two Elks decided doing something was better than doing nothing, and if he showed strength, he'd be in a better negotiating position.

The man who had been killed was Big Star's friend and he wanted revenge. He was planning an attack and assumed Two Elks would say nothing, as he had been quiet for weeks. But Two Elks came into the young men's lodge and asked what they were planning.

Changleska had two military bases on the river, north and south of their Circle. They had planned to send most of their force, forty-two warriors, against the southern base. Two Elks knew an attack there would fail. He recommended a bold strategy: cross the river. Changleska forces didn't think the Two Elks tribe ever crossed the river. They rarely used canoes, and crossed the river with horses, but it wasn't easy. The river was wide, horses didn't like to swim in the cold, and this time of year it was dangerously cold. But they had "lighters" and "space blankets" from the trading posts. With organization and planning, they could warm up quickly. Surprise was the advantage they needed against those powerful weapons. They could do it if they came from an unexpected direction.

Two Elks stayed behind, leaving Big Star to lead the attack. Black Rabbit wanted his younger son, Six Feathers, to stay behind, but Big Star said he was a man now, and Two Elks allowed him to go. He wondered if he would lose two sons in a day. He knew Changleska possessed more weapons than what they had revealed, but they seemed soft and unwilling to kill.

They heard nothing for days after the attack on the southern base. Two Elks tried to show others he had confidence in his son. He hid his worry, but worry he did. When they finally learned the outcome, it was worse than they'd suspected. The strategy for most raids was: Go in fast, arrows or shots fired, a few people injured, one or two to die, and a few to be captured for hostages or slaves, then retreat. This was the nature of warfare as Two Elks understood it.

Like a good leader, Big Star stayed a little behind to send messages and to coordinate the attack. That didn't save him, nor most of the warriors. When they attempted to retrieve the wounded they were fired on. Of the forty-two warriors sent, none returned; only two of the three horse boys sent returned, as one drowned trying to cross the river. Two Elks had rarely even heard of such a massive defeat. Only in the big wars with the wasicu did so many get killed.

They'd selected what they believed to be a perfect target—an isolated ranch with two houses located so far from any populated area the sound of gunshots wouldn't easily carry. The plan was to take the two houses and use them as a base for further raids. The returning boys hadn't seen or heard enough to learn exactly what happened. They didn't know who'd lived and who'd died until the next day.

At Two Elks' camp, the forward scouts heard the trucks. They saw the two war vehicles and two trucks come to the spot where they had parked before. They stopped and unceremoniously dumped thirty-one bodies and returned without firing a shot. Big Star was among the dead.

Knowing he should've stopped Big Star's foolish raid, Two Elks was devastated. It was his pride, and not wanting Red Eagle to gain the rifles, clouding his judgment. He realized he couldn't beat these people the first time they met, yet he'd let both of his sons fight a losing battle. The fate of Six Feathers, whether he lived or died, tormented Two Elks. He wasn't among the dead, but it was possible they didn't return every body. If Six Feathers lived and was wounded, would they treat his wounds, or let him die a lingering death with a sour wound? These questions haunted Two Elks.

The terrible grief that consumed Black Rabbit was heart-wrenching. Sorrow consumed her as her heart shattered. She cut her hair, her arms, sat and keened for hours. Black Rabbit was so furious with Two Elks that she refused to speak to him or cook his food. It was clear she blamed him.

Two Elks was desolate. A sense of emptiness settled upon his heart. He cut his hair, and despite the snow, he went off by himself to camp, fast, and pray. For four days, he asked the spirits for guidance, but the spirits remained silent, offering no answers.

Two Elks returned to his people, consumed by sorrow for his son. He knew he couldn't change his son's fate, but he refused to accept defeat. There had to be a way to save his people, and he was determined to find it.

Chapter Twenty-Eight
Jamal

AFTER TWO MONTHS of feeling disconcerted and out of place, Jamal finally sensed a glimmer of being on the right track. Jamal and Nels were about to embark on a journey through the late eighteenth century.

"I can't believe we're actually going to experience what it's like going back in time," Jamal said, his voice tinged with excitement and a hint of nervousness. "It's like something out of a movie."

Nels replied, "Other than a few Indigenous, we have encountered no one from this time period. Everything is the same here as it always was. We will enter a looking glass, Alice."

The meeting site of the expedition was south of Oacoma, close to White River Farm. They got a ride on the farm truck. They rented a nearby barn to store Jamal's car, which they filled with the belongings they were leaving. Jamal debated bringing his tools, but since so many were irreplaceable, he left most of them. Changleska paid both Nels and Jamal as expedition members. The pay wasn't as much as Jamal would earn as an engineer, but it was helpful. They laughed about being government employees.

Jamal would work for the engineering subcommittee under Infrastructure. They gave Jamal a list of projects he could work on while he was gone. Since he'd listed his experience in patents in the skills survey, many design patents were downloaded onto his laptop. His job was to review them for viability from a mechanical engineering standpoint, suggest improvements, and figure out how to build them using currently available materials. He couldn't help but wonder how these inventions would change the course of history in the eighteenth century. It wouldn't be easy. They needed to build the tools to build the tools. He loved the project and would've happily spent hours at the computer doing it.

When Jamal and Nels arrived at the expedition departure site, they were surprised to find it resembled the beginning of a military base. They were stopped by a guardian who asked for their citizens' cards, which were checked against a list. After entering a fenced area, they heard construction all around. They saw shipping containers, a few mobile homes, rows of neatly arranged tents, and several large tents. They asked for the expedition's leader, Lieutenant Mateo Rodriguez, and were directed to an office in a repurposed bedroom of one of the mobile homes. Rodriguez, a smaller Hispanic man, wasn't much older than they were, late twenties, but had a commanding presence.

The first thing he asked them was why they hadn't joined the Guardians. They were both under twenty-five, citizens, and each had a two-year service requirement. They looked at each other. Honestly, Jamal had completely forgotten about that requirement. Nels and he had never discussed it. *Maybe*, he thought, *it didn't apply to them.*

Nels said, "I'm not sure if there is a religious exemption. I'm a Buddhist. I won't carry a weapon or take a life."

"Sorry, no religious exemption, but we can assign you to support or, since you're on an expedition, you can be a medic."

Nels looked uncomfortable. "Okay."

"You're the engineer?" Rodriguez said, looking at Jamal.

"Yes, sir."

"We need one. You can be useful."

He looked at them critically and explained there wasn't time for them to go through basic training before they left. Since this was a military operation, they could credit their time on the expedition toward their two-year requirements. They'd take the Guardian Oath and be subject to the same rules and regulations as the rest of the guardians. Jamal and Nels looked at each other, realizing this was the best they were going to get, and agreed. Rodriguez said they'd take the oath in the morning and directed them to IT, which was conveniently in the living room of the same mobile home. The information provided to new recruits was transferred as PDF files to their phones, which were filling up fast.

All their gear had been dropped off near the entrance; they had to haul it all to their assigned tents. They knew they were intentionally assigned to separate tents. A cot was assigned to Jamal, and he was told to fit all his personal gear into the footlocker. If he'd brought more than could fit, he could speak to the loadmaster.

Jamal and Nels spent the afternoon repacking their gear, reading the materials provided, and meeting their teammates. No women were going on the initial expedition, and except for one or two older men, they were all young. There was a sense of camaraderie he didn't expect. They all teased each other and horsed around. Most were helpful, explaining how to pack more efficiently, what they might need during the voyage downriver. They all called him Alston; no one used first names. Sergeant Dunning, not much older than he was, led his squad, which was composed of the eight men in his tent.

Dunning took him aside and said, "I realized you didn't get basic, but all of us will help you get up to speed as quickly as possible. Don't hesitate to ask for help. Your mission is important. We're all here to protect and help you."

"I don't know anything about the military, all the rules. I didn't even play Call of Duty. No idea how I'll do."

"You'll be fine. Remember, even if the rules make little sense, there is a reason for them."

He also told him he knew he and Nels were a couple. As long as they kept their private time discreet, no one had a problem. Dunning reminded Jamal of the severe consequences of being gay in the eighteenth century, and if discovered by outsiders, it could impact the entire mission. There was already a rule about no PDA or public displays of affection for all guardians on duty. It was being extended to them for anytime they were around others on or off duty. They extended this rule for their safety, as they had to be aware of how outsiders would perceive them. Even a casual touch could expose them.

At a ridiculously early hour in the morning, dark and cold, someone roused him for physical training or PT. They expected him to run the two-mile track around the base. The last time he'd run was in PE class in high school, and he still hated it. A plumpish young Native woman joined him as he dropped behind, struggling beside him. His pride was up, so he somehow finished. The woman said her name was Kearsley. Jamal was not sure if that was a first or last name. Kearsley said she was a cook and pointed to her name patch, which was yellow for support. Jamal wondered if the yellow color for support was an intentional slight and was glad they'd assigned him to engineering.

Jamal and Nels took their oaths right after PT. At the morning assembly, there were four others, no one else going on the expedition, but locals joining. Nels' name patch was white with a red cross. They gave Nels coursework on his laptop. He'd shadow the doctors and medics during the expedition. Jamal's engineering patch was brown. Once they checked in at a large tent marked "Supply," they received their patches and other gear. They received a list with numbered items, like seven pairs of socks, four t-shirts, and a few new items not on the earlier provided list. The young woman at the supply tent gave them everything they were missing. She said she was happy when they handed the list back, as most of those displaced had far fewer belongings. She also gave them a heavy needle and thread to sew their own patches on. Jamal had never sewn anything in his life; fortunately, Nels showed him.

Jamal had a lot of orientation material to learn, and no time for the engineering projects. Learning ranks, acronyms, and military terms was overwhelming, but he'd always been an excellent student. He worried about Nels, though; he'd often helped him with his term papers.

Every evening after dinner, a crew set up a movie projector in one of the big tents, and everyone watched movies, mostly period war films. Despite their unrealistic aspects, the films might show the culture, manners, and expectations of this time. They warned everyone to be very polite, as duels would often resolve perceived insults. Spanish culture dominated where they were heading. It dawned on Jamal why so many guardians were Hispanic on this trip.

Four doctors and three guardians trained as medical support would serve on this first expedition. They'd add more medical staff in the future to establish an outreach clinic in New Orleans. All the doctors were Native: two Cherokee tribal members, one Choctaw, and one Seminole. The doctors had copies of treaties on their devices, showing the history of how they were broken.

Although the Council aimed to give priority to tribes located west of the Mississippi, they recognized the significance of assisting individual tribal members in reconnecting with their ancestral tribes. The Choctaw and Seminole doctors would leave the expedition, taking with them one guardian each. Given the enormous risks involved, the chances of everyone returning were slim.

There were lectures from the medical team, emphasizing the use of mosquito nets and repellent. Malaria, cholera, yellow fever, and smallpox were prevalent, and there were no vaccines. In their time, many existed, including a new malaria vaccine, but none had come through the Circle. Two doctors who'd traveled in the developing world had been vaccinated, but no one had a smallpox vaccine. Fortunately, they had a good supply of PPE available.

=..=

The flotilla comprised two big bass boats, a couple of canoes, and the barge they named *Endeavor*. Canoes and the boats with depth finders would go ahead, marking the path. They would mostly float downriver. To power upriver for the return, the barge had converted a diesel truck engine to steam. Modern boats didn't have room for bulky steam engines. They were hoping for an alternative fuel source for the boats soon. The boats could tow the barge, but they were hoping the steam engines would reduce or even eliminate that need. The expedition planners were expecting failures and were creating backups because there were too many unknown factors.

They'd built the barge using salvaged materials. It carried six shipping containers. Four on the bottom held cargo. They'd converted one shipping container to house members of the expedition, another for kitchen facilities and food storage. The other container held the navigation center, and the top had a deck where people could hang out during the day. The back had a paddle wheel operated by steam engines run by diesel with a wood burner as a backup. They included an alternator and pulley drive system so they would have twelve-volt electricity to have power to run saws and charge a battery bank for lights and electronics.

It was roughly 800 miles to New Orleans. The bass boats averaged around four miles per gallon, which meant they needed to carry over 5,000 gallons of fuel for the round trip, more if they had to tow upriver. Fortunately, several fuel trucks had been caught inside the Circle during Big Thunder. They simply backed one of the full trucks onto the top of a shipping container, dropped the tank in place, and drove it back down. Not having to custom-build a fueling system saved considerable time.

This was intended to be the only trip of its kind, and it would consume a significant portion of their fuel reserves. Around fifty people collaborated on the project, each playing their part under tight deadlines. The Guardian Engineering Brigade provided critical support.

Most of the expedition members would set up a base in New Orleans. The East Coast contingent would go to Philadelphia to meet George Washington, and Jamal and another guardian would go to Boston to meet Eli Whitney and accomplish various tasks. They had a long list of things they wanted to bring back, like coffee, foodstuffs, and seeds, as well as various chemicals and minerals. They sent grain, modern clothing, toys, taxidermy animals, and junk they thought would sell, items like someone could find at any yard sale. There were four of the "Big Mouth Billy Bass" singing fish on wooden plaques with extra batteries, a popular gift in fishing country that no one really liked. This was one item they hoped would bring a good price. No one knew the value of twenty-first-century items, but they thought that rich collectors of rare items were universal. Since taxidermy hadn't yet been developed, the stuffed animals might be valuable. If they could trade for things they could use, that much the better. They did not want to bring too much grain on this first trip; no one knew if they could sell it.

After debate, they sent a four-wheel-drive truck. They thought driving around would help convince the locals. They sent printed materials and were instructed to find or buy a printing press to print more. Almost all the printed materials were health-related, although one was *The Big Thunder Story*. The Omímeya marketing department had written its first propaganda piece in an eighteenth-century style, describing their arrival and the forming of the Changleska Coalition. It contained copies of their Declaration of Independence and the new Constitution.

=..=

According to the historical briefing, a Spanish census of the time reported about 5,800 people lived in New Orleans. Limited information existed about this time period in the libraries, and on NewNet, there was a lot of guesswork involved. Expedition members had multiple missions to complete. Setting up trade relationships was foremost. Jamal and his group would head to Boston to meet with the leading shipbuilder of the time. They hoped to trade plans for ships that were more advanced in exchange for constructing ships for Changleska. They had access to gold or trade goods but were hoping the plans would be enough. Threatening to go to the competition might help secure a deal. They were looking to build both ocean-going and river ships, like barges and paddleboats. South Dakota, even in 1791, had little timber, nor did it have the equipment or expertise necessary for shipbuilding.

They had letters for George Washington and the Spanish governors of St. Louis and New Orleans, containing what was becoming a standard packet. They included pictures from old-world calendars—beautiful, large, photo-quality prints of landscapes, animals, and modern scenes—which hopefully would have an impact. Photography didn't exist yet; the color printing of the time was very basic. The prints took up little space.

Approaching George Washington required a delicate balance of caution and confidence. The Changleskans needed him on their side but didn't want him to covet their military assets or technology and decide conquest was better than becoming an ally. Information about their military was deliberately vague. The guardians sent on the initial expedition were primarily messengers. The plan was to pave the road to send diplomats and more doctors in the spring, hopefully to open an embassy. They needed to be recognized as a country before they could approach Spain or France in order to complete the Louisiana Purchase twelve years early. Since Napoleon hadn't yet come to power, it was possible to bypass him. However, Spain gave up the territory to get land in France they wanted, so they may have to deal with France.

Besides the packet, they brought a laptop and an LED projector to show films to Washington and whatever staff he wished. Changleska had made a special forty-eight-minute film for him. They started with the Big Thunder scenes from the first video they'd made. A narrator introduced him to the Chair, Mary Landrau, and Oliver Jackson; each gave a short spiel mentioning Washington and something from his past. They hoped the written biographies were right. There was a glimpse into a Council meeting showing a vote on a proposal. Then a narrated video tour used aerial footage to show the hospital, cars, airplanes, and helicopter. They produced a similar video both in Spanish and French, to be shown where applicable, with nothing about George Washington.

The narrator said they wouldn't show their military capabilities, as he was sure Washington understood. Instead, they would show them a demonstration of peaceful contact with a potentially hostile tribe that was becoming an ally. They'd filmed the visit to Two Elks camp and included that footage. It showed the building of the bridge, guardians surrounding the tipis, and the smallish-looking weapon producing the tremendous bang destroying the rock. If the expedition leader felt there was a threat, a selection of war movies had been sent; he could show them at his discretion.

It was approaching December; they hoped to get to New Orleans without running into ice on the river. They didn't know how late in the year ships ran. Individuals were prepared to winter in New Orleans if necessary. The barge would return home as soon as possible. Jamal and Nels would be part of the group that would winter in New Orleans if needed.

The night before they were scheduled to leave, a screeching noise and flashing lights startled them awake. They all got out of bed, armed up, except Jamal, who hadn't passed the exam to carry a weapon. He didn't mind. Before he came, he'd never touched a gun in his life and wasn't looking forward to carrying one. His teammates assured him he would get qualified soon; they'd all help him. He wished he'd said carrying weapons was against his religion like Nels had done.

When they got outside, they were told it was Indigenous scouts testing the perimeter; they did that periodically. They liked to slip in and steal whatever they could carry off, mostly to show they could sneak in whenever they wanted. Fencing and perimeter alerts were always getting better, so they may have been surprised this time. They had orders not to fire and to let them go, but it was creating resentment.

Everyone returned to bed, unable to go back to sleep. Jamal listened to conversations between his teammates, a few sympathetic to the Indigenous Lakota, saying this was their land, they were the intruders, others pointing out they would offer them a good price if they'd negotiate. They had hundreds of miles of territory in all directions; they had no need of this thirty-mile circle. After a few rounds of this, Dunning told them all to shut it and go to sleep.

Jamal was friends with two guardians, Lucas and James, two Black guys from Chamberlain who were active in the Antislavery Committee. They'd joined the expedition to proceed to the Caribbean, hoping to meet a man named Toussaint Louverture, who had risen to prominence as a general in the Haitian Revolution.

The Haiti revolt—only just begun in 1791—ended in 1804 with the former colony's independence. When the Black population had become citizens of France, Louverture joined the French army. He helped France combat and eventually defeat Spanish and British forces. The French promoted Louverture until he became a prominent general. In 1802, Napoleon had gained power and wanted to reinstate slavery. France invited Louverture to parley but arrested him upon his arrival. He died of starvation in prison a year later. He missed the last battles of the revolution, but his influence helped the Haitian army achieve final victory. It was the only slave uprising that led to the founding of a state which was both free from slavery and ruled by non-whites and former captives.

Lucas and James, who both had authorization to sign trade agreements, hoped to join the revolution and convince Louverture to distance himself from France. Once Haiti was secure, they hoped to spread rebellion across other slaveholding colonies. Besides getting the plantations to use paid labor, Louverture had amassed a large, well-trained army and had negotiated trade agreements between the United States and Britain. They wanted to send back sugar and willing workers to Changleska.

Jamal believed their plan was one of the better ones for combating slavery. With all the letters sent East, a plan for the Caribbean, and knowledge that could stop the cotton gin, they could change the economy of slavery. Back in Changleska, members of the Antislavery Committee were divided on buying slaves to free them. With limited funds, the debate arose about the acceptability of buying another human, with many people arguing against it under any circumstances. The compromise involved purchasing skilled slaves, such as blacksmiths, who were offered the choice to repay the funds used to buy them by working for Changleska at a fair wage or to opt out of repayment, remain free, and seek employment elsewhere. The hope was that the newly freed slaves would work and contribute to Changleska while earning enough money to support a family, maybe even purchase their family members if possible. If enough freedmen signed on, Changleska could afford to "buy" more.

Even this stirred up controversy, with a few individuals strongly believing people should be freed without any expectations. Afterяться2.

After completing the Louisiana Purchase, they could enforce their law, which would ban all slavery west of the Mississippi. They considered the potential trouble from angry plantation owners but ultimately determined the benefits outweighed the risks. Freeing as many people as possible was the goal.

Jamal felt good about being part of the expedition and was even getting accustomed to military discipline. The morning of their departure greeted them with a crisp, cold breeze and a clear, blue sky. A thin layer of snow that had fallen overnight dusted the ground. It was a beautiful morning. They were all cleaning up in their best for the departure ceremony. The Council and family members were coming to see them off.

The guardians didn't have uniforms yet. Those designated combatants wore camouflage, Mossy Oak or Realtree patterns mostly, since it was hunting country. The original National Guard stood out in their former uniforms. He noticed most of them were officers. Fortunately for Jamal, the other teams wore black for formal occasions, as they normally wore jeans. He had brought plenty of clothes on the initial trip because he knew there was no laundry, and he usually wore a lot of black.

He got a spot next to Nels for the ceremony; they were both excited. Jamal and Nels looked at each other, wanting to clasp hands but restraining themselves.

Jamal quietly said, "Thank you for pushing me. I never would've done this without you. I love you."

"Just don't get yourself stolen and sold. Love you back."

VIPs from all over the Circle came. They had a ceremony involving various churches, with Lakota prayers and songs. There were speeches by various Council members, thankfully not all of them. Then the expedition flotilla pushed off. Jamal couldn't believe he was looking forward to seeing what the eighteenth century was like. The mission to meet with Eli Whitney, while important, paled with the upcoming adventure of the journey.

Jamal read a quote from Roald Amundsen, the first person to reach the South Pole: "Adventure was just bad planning." He hoped that wasn't true. A lot of planning had gone into this expedition. They'd sent a lot of irreplaceable equipment, including goTenna phones and portable ham radios. Jamal hoped for an adventure, but a safe one. From what he had been hearing, it was unlikely to be safe. He thought about Lucas and James fighting and maybe dying in a war for freedom and thought he had the better of the tasks. Throughout his life, Jamal was aware of the privilege he had—the best of everything, nice clothes, the latest Nike sneakers, new cars, his choice of college. He'd never known hardship or hunger. He had never personally experienced violence or even encountered overt racism or homophobia. Not that those things didn't exist, but he was isolated from any ugliness in the world by having money. The path he was on would be dangerous, but how could he not do everything in his power to fight against the cruel and inhumane institution of slavery? His parents had given him everything, including an innate sense of justice. This journey might cost him his life, but if he could make a difference, it was a price he knew he had to pay.

Chapter Twenty-Nine
Karl

KARL HAD NEVER been so fit. After two months in 1791, he'd adapted and adjusted to his diet of mostly meat. When they first left on the expedition to New Orleans, he wasn't sure how he'd cope, but somehow, he managed. Paddling a canoe was harder than he imagined. The first week, he thought there was no way he could continue. Every muscle in his body hurt. Of his two companions, he hated Raul, the leader who never failed to rub it in he was in charge, and Anthony, whom he liked.

Anthony was twenty-one, amiable and easygoing, the opposite of Raul. He'd been working at a farm prior to Big Thunder. Raul was thirty-two, a father of a baby girl. He was Mexican and Apache. His wife was Pueblo, and they'd moved from Arizona to take jobs at Omímeya a few years ago. Raul and his wife lived in a small one-bedroom apartment. He hoped to use the money he would earn from this trip to put a down payment on a house.

It surprised Karl he liked Anthony. He rarely liked anyone, but Anthony was one of those people who brought light wherever he went. After the first few days of paddling, Anthony said during the historical briefing, he'd heard that the voyageurs would sing to help keep the rhythm and pace. They didn't know any voyageur songs, so they sang whatever songs they remembered the lyrics to, mostly old rock songs. Karl had the lyrics to a bunch of Beatles songs on his phone. He'd wanted to impress Hannah, who'd said she liked them, so they sang a lot of Beatles while paddling.

Something started happening to Karl between the exercise and the singing. The black fog that had been present most of his life started to recede. For the first time since Hannah had dumped him, he didn't feel miserable. Anthony said he had read somewhere that singing was good for depression. Karl had never considered himself depressed. He didn't take medication and was fully functional, but had to admit he had a better attitude than usual. The harsh conditions were still difficult, but manageable. He still didn't get along with Raul, but he and Anthony got along fine. Anthony asked him questions about life in Germany and was genuinely interested. He found he was looking forward to what life would be like in the eighteenth century, instead of bemoaning the fact he was here.

Anthony and Raul talked about Changleska like it was their dream come true. Especially Raul, who had harsh things to say about what the white man had done to the Indigenous, as well as what it was like to live in the US as a Mexican American. Their idealism and enthusiasm did nothing for Karl. He may have let his cynicism show. Karl talked about how he believed monarchy was an excellent form of government, which they all argued about.

When they arrived at St. Louis, it surprised them as a small city of contrasts. It was dirty, especially the people. The few Indigenous they saw looked like they'd been drinking. Everyone smelled bad, even the women they saw. Evidently, the better class of women didn't venture outside often. But when they did, they were richly dressed, followed by servants or slaves, and normally holding packages. Houses were small log cabins, or the larger ones built with quarried limestone and brick. There were signs of prosperity, areas of bustling activity. They visited the Auguste Chouteau Mansion, both a trading post and a residence. Curious, they walked by the governor's mansion, but not to go in, as that was the job of the second expedition.

They'd received instructions to fit in, to look and act like fur traders. Their clothing was supposed to resemble the style of the time, it didn't. Many things made them stand out as outsiders. For one thing, even after nine days paddling a canoe, they were cleaner than almost anyone. Their teeth were white, and they had all of them. Their speech marked them as outsiders, regardless of language. Not only were accents different, but word choices and the names of things were different. Nobody had expected the extent of language drift in 233 years. They had a hard time understanding others, even those who spoke English.

It was Karl's turn to stay with the canoe and guard their belongings, so he wasn't at the meeting with the priest, but Anthony told him about it. Even after seeing the video on the laptop, the priest was having a hard time believing they weren't from the devil. Raul asked if he could give confession as he was Catholic, and that mollified the priest. He said it was clear they weren't French fur traders; they should claim to be adventurers instead. When the priest discovered their other companion was German, he suggested they should claim Karl was a wealthy nobleman and they were his hired guides. Raul wasn't happy about that but saw it made sense. It was clear their story wouldn't hold up otherwise.

They stayed in St. Louis for a week. They found a grain buyer; it was easy, there was only one. He didn't know or didn't want to tell them about buyers in New Orleans. They had a hard time wrapping themselves around 1791 prices. They received silver coins that vaguely resembled the Mexican coins of the time. Apprehensive during their first attempt to spend them, they discovered that many types of coins were in circulation. An ounce of silver was worth about a dollar twenty-five, which was a small fortune. They could buy enough flour, bacon, cheese, apples, even coffee for the three of them for the rest of the trip, for less than two ounces of silver. One reason Anthony was chosen for this trip was because he was an excellent hunter. He kept them in fresh meat.

Raul didn't allow alcohol in the canoe but didn't stop Anthony and Karl from frequenting the public houses and drinking. They'd planned to leave a few days earlier, but in one of Anthony's and Karl's drinking forays, they were hungry and ate stew at the public house. They both came down with a case of diarrhea. Raul showed no sympathy. They'd been warned never to drink water or eat food you hadn't observed boiled for at least five minutes.

Karl and Anthony were worried they had cholera, but Raul asked the priest and no one else in town had it. After they recovered, they continued their journey. Raul was pushing them. They'd planned to arrive in New Orleans six weeks before the next expedition. Now, it looked like closer to three weeks. The nice thing was the further south they went, the warmer it became, although the mosquitoes were getting worse. They hadn't brought enough mosquito repellent. As they approached New Orleans, the risk of malaria and yellow fever increased because of mosquitoes transmitting it from one person to another. They saved their repellent and coated themselves with mud. Now they were as dirty as everyone else.

They saw few other people. Occasionally, they saw abandoned villages close to the river as they paddled by. Once they saw four Indigenous men dressed differently than Lakota paddling a big canoe which came up swiftly behind them. They slowed and exchanged a few words in French, as they didn't understand Spanish, English, or even the few words of Lakota that Raul knew. Unfortunately, they didn't understand the hand sign trade language the Indigenous men used. They traded a bag of corn for a bag of dried venison. The expedition party did not need it, wanted to trade something. Neither party left their canoes, pulled to the side and stopping. After completing the trade, the Indigenous men pulled away and swiftly disappeared from sight. They paddled faster afterwards, but it was obvious they'd been outclassed. Anthony made jokes about it, which made everyone feel better.

About a week before they were due to arrive in New Orleans, they were getting ready to break down camp for the day. Anthony had gone down to the river to wash. They heard him yelling and swearing. A snake had bitten him, then swam away quickly. Anthony didn't see it closely, but they assumed it was venomous, probably a water moccasin. They had a snakebite kit and quickly used it on Anthony. At first, he seemed okay. They had him rest while they packed up the rest of the camp. By the time they were done, his leg was swelling, and he was having trouble breathing.

Pressing on, their only hope was to find a settlement where someone might have an herb or remedy for Anthony's worsening condition. They knew not all water moccasin bites were fatal, and they had used the snakebite kit right away. Anthony's leg continued to swell. He was in so much pain he started thrashing about, so they found a place to stop. Karl and Raul were distraught they couldn't do anything for Anthony. Their medical kit had a small amount of painkillers, and they wondered whether they should use them now. They also discussed amputating his leg. Neither had medical knowledge or even a saw, so they gave him the pain medicine. Karl and Raul held him as he struggled to breathe. Anthony died a few hours later.

It was horrible. Karl had never had anyone close to him die before. Anthony had been the first friend he'd had since college. Raul and Karl buried him under a tree. They only had their little shit shovels, so it took a long time, but neither minded. Raul pointed out they didn't need go six feet down, or be full length. The body could be curled up. As Karl stood by Anthony's grave, he grappled with a new sensation, one he'd never experienced before. Grief. Anthony had been more than a friend; he'd been a lifeline in this unfamiliar world, a beacon of warmth amidst the cold reality of their situation.

=..=

The journey continued. They no longer sang. It was like singing would be disrespectful to Anthony somehow, although they knew it made little sense. Frequent arguments characterized their interactions, with Raul pushing for progress while Karl insisted on taking breaks.

One morning, as they were packing their gear in the canoe, Karl was in a foul mood and not paying attention. Shifting slightly, he had to readjust his foot to regain his balance and heard a crunch. After running the solar charger, he had failed to put his laptop back in its protected case. Karl knew without looking he'd broken it. The screen was dead. He was furious, mostly because he had no one else to blame but himself. All his historical data was gone. He only had a few printed encyclopedia pages on Napoleon and Prussian royalty. Because of the paper and ink shortage, he couldn't print as much he'd researched. Everything was digital. He also had details on various inventions that might bring a fortune to the right person on his laptop. His grand plans, now reduced to ashes, were all dependent on the laptop.

Not only for the information they contained, but to dazzle and entertain the nobility he hoped to meet. In hindsight, he should've had backups on his phone with extra memory cards.

It didn't seem possible for his mood to get worse, but it did. He and Raul continued to argue. Raul told him he had left word in St. Louis that Karl wouldn't make a good agent, as Karl didn't believe in Changleska, was only out for himself, and Karl shouldn't expect any additional money for a ship's passage. Karl was outraged because he'd counted on those funds.

When they got close to New Orleans, Karl was told to stay back with the canoe so Raul could rent a place in a dockside warehouse to store their gear. As soon as Raul left, Karl searched the canoe, finding Raul's laptop. It needed a thumbprint to open. Karl knew what he had to do. When Raul returned, he looked in the canoe. Karl had tried to be careful, but he had aroused Raul's suspicions. Karl woke up early the next morning, grabbed the pistol he'd been given, and while Raul was beginning to stir, he shot him in the head. He had expected he would feel sick from killing someone, but he didn't.

He got the laptop out, took it to Raul's body, opened it, and placed Raul's thumb on the sensor. After accepting the thumbprint, it asked for a password. Karl couldn't believe it. He was sure he'd seen Raul use the laptop with only a thumbprint and wondered if he'd added the password last night.

Karl searched the canoe, found the letters to the priests and others, which he burned after reading. He felt he owed nothing to Changleska and didn't want to do anything that might help them or impede his plans. In Raul's clothing, folded next to where he was sleeping, he found a pouch of coins containing a few ounces of silver. Karl figured Changleska wouldn't sent the expedition with so little money. They were supposed to be spies, which usually involved payoffs. It didn't matter what year it was; payoffs were the way business was done. He carefully examined every bit of gear and discovered five gold coins. That was worth about a hundred dollars in 1791. He wasn't sure that was enough for a ship's passage, but gathering from the prices he'd seen in St. Louis, he was hopeful.

Karl wanted to be gone from New Orleans before the next expedition arrived. He considered telling them a story about how Raul died so he could get his pay and his ship's passage paid, but every story he imagined might fall apart under questioning. Leaving Raul's body at the campsite, he took everything else. He considered disposing of the sleeping bag that had gotten bloody, but it was a modern down bag. He knew it would fetch a good price. Dragging the bloody end behind the canoe to wash, Karl paddled alone the rest of the way to New Orleans.

As he approached New Orleans, Karl saw an increasing number of various types of watercraft. He shouted in French and English, asking everyone for advice about where he should stay, safely store his belongings, or sell his stuff. After a while, he got better at asking the questions, learning the right words.

People were happy to give recommendations, usually with the words, "Tell him Pierre sent you," or whoever.

Karl figured if a place got recommendations from three or more people, that's where he'd go. Without asking, nearly everyone suggested their favorite whorehouse. He found a well-regarded warehouse at the dock where he could rent space to store his gear. He still had small change from St. Louis and probably overpaid dock workers to move his stuff from the canoe to the warehouse.

New Orleans was bigger than St. Louis and filled with a vibrant population of people of all colors and walks of life. The number of Mexicans surprised Karl. Mexico and Cuba were New Orleans' primary trading partners. A lot of trade from the Caribbean came through as well. Many languages, including French, were in frequent use. There were slaves and freemen, hard to tell apart sometimes, many of obvious mixed ancestry. Since strangers often arrived by ship from far away, Karl found it easier to fit in than in St. Louis, where the differences were less noticeable.

Karl carefully observed the way people dressed, especially those of the upper classes. Karl's plan was to pose as the priest had recommended, as a German nobleman on an adventure to the wilds of America. He asked for the best hotel and had no problem getting a room. He wanted better clothes, but during this time, clothes were all custom-made. Requesting recommendations for a tailor, he made it his first stop. The tailor wanted to sell him the latest fashions, but he ordered something simple. He had two outfits made, one suitable for formal occasions, and one for everyday wear. Even with a rush order, getting them would take a week.

Next, he visited the whorehouse. He'd heard about the high prevalence of syphilis among prostitutes in the eighteenth century. Because of the possibility of condom breakage, he'd no intention of engaging in risky activities. When he got there, he didn't choose the youngest or prettiest, but someone older. When he requested only oral sex, she wasn't surprised, but she provided him with a washbasin and asked him to wash first. After they were done, he gave her an extra coin and asked for information.

Karl had never used prostitutes before. He was surprised by how cheap and easy it was. He knew he'd be back. His real purpose was information, which was why he'd chosen someone older. Karl needed a fence, someone who would buy his modern goods yet be discreet about where they'd come from.

He'd hoped their expedition would be considered lost. If items came with the story of an odd German who sold them, that may present problems. Discretion and a high return for his goods didn't go together, but he thought he shouldn't take a chance. He wasn't worried Changleska would do anything to him, but if he was trying to build a narrative about himself, he couldn't have a reputation as a thief and a murderer follow him. He told the woman he'd give her a bonus if his sales were successful.

Losing both laptops drove him crazy. Once he got into his hotel room, which was small and dirty but had a small table, he took both laptops out. He was trying to see whether he could connect the unbroken monitor on Raul's machine, which he couldn't access, to his laptop. His efforts didn't work. After a while, it occurred to him even if he could get them connected, the graphics card and software might be incompatible. Raul's computer was now useless. Unsure if he should bother carrying both around with him, he knew they had valuable components. Karl considered leaving the laptops for the Changleska expedition, possibly with the priest, but decided the risk was too great. He kept them with him, at the bottom of his luggage.

Over the next week, he sold everything, including the canoe. The modern items brought a good price. Karl was glad he'd washed the sleeping bag. He kept his and a few other modern items, consolidated everything into a large trunk and a smaller travel bag common to the era. Karl found a ship leaving in a week for Cuba, which wasn't expensive. He figured he'd have a better chance of finding a ship to Europe from the Caribbean at this time of year. He'd asked around for prices. Between the gold and the sales of everything, he had enough money to not have any trouble posing as someone wealthy.

The story he had fashioned for himself was he was German nobility, born on the wrong side of the blanket, sent to live with relatives in Canada as a child, which could explain his funny accent and word choices. He'd set off on an adventure and now wanted to return to Germany to see home for the first time since childhood. The story wouldn't hold up to much scrutiny. Without the laptop, Karl didn't know the genealogy of his supposed dead father. At this time, everyone, including illegitimate children, knew their genealogy. He'd thought the story would get him to Europe until he could figure out his next plan.

Karl's original plan was to make money with modern inventions from the laptop, marry a nobleman's daughter, and support Prussia and the Holy Roman Empire. He intended to keep Napoleon from conquering Austria and Prussia to save Germany. Without historical data and design plans for machines, that would no longer be possible. The encyclopedia pages he still had covered Napoleon's rise and fall. He could use that.

Previously, Karl had considered assassinating Napoleon before he conquered Austria. But he knew now he wouldn't have the money or influence to take power for himself. He'd need to go to Plan B, advise and help Napoleon, warn him of things that might go wrong. He could tell Napoleon not to go to Russia, or how he might lose at Waterloo. If Karl proved to be useful enough, Napoleon would reward him. After all, he made his brother the king of Spain. Perhaps he could make Karl the King of Germany.

Chapter Thirty

Martin

AS MARTIN APPROACHED his sixty-third birthday, thoughts of mortality crept into his mind with increasing frequency. Each passing day seemed to bring mortality closer, a weight he couldn't shake off. Almost three months on the 1791 diet had worked wonders on his waistline. He felt great. Martin suspected his blood pressure and cholesterol were down. He was even friskier than usual. In the old world, people were active and healthy into their eighties and nineties, but that was with modern medicine. Without it, he wasn't sure how long he could last. It wasn't the thought of dying that bothered him as much as leaving Anna May alone that scared him.

Things were better between Anna May and him than they ever had been. Their relationship had always been transactional. He provided the money; she got the lifestyle she enjoyed. It was a comfortable arrangement; he even went along with her ambitions for his career. Now that all the money was gone, everything had changed. Martin had started relying on Anna May. She had the plans and the strategy to better their situation. Something changed in how he felt about her. They shared the grief of the loss of their sons. He loved her as much as ever, but now he admired and respected her. It was the first time in twenty-three years that they were truly partners.

They were living on the bank credit line, with the patents as collateral. Soon, payments had to be made on it, but they lacked income. Initially, they thought it would be easy to find someone interested in manufacturing and selling medical devices, but they were unaware of the issues that would come up. The first problem was finding someone willing and able to make them. People with skills or a willingness to learn were busy creating different things. The problem with the medical devices is hospitals and clinics had everything they needed. The market was the outside world, but only if they could find people interested. Which meant training outside doctors in their use. Getting a return on investment was many years away.

Another problem was the shortage of stainless steel. They needed an electric arc furnace to make it, but there was only one in the circle. In addition, stainless steel needed iron ore, nickel, chromium, silicon, and molybdenum. It was unlikely that they would have those things soon. The only option was recycling stainless steel. Someone, probably Kyle Ward, foresaw the need, and the trading posts were all buying stainless steel by the pound. It was available to the first people to buy it. Without money to buy stainless steel, they could not make their devices.

Usually, Martin never discussed finances with Anna May. He had inherited millions from his parents, and Anna May did not know the details. In his will, he left most to his children, some to charity, enough for Anna May to live her same lifestyle until she remarried. All irrelevant now.

Martin told Anna May, "We can't keep renting this big house, paying Ella and Soren's rent, and pay the credit line. We need income soon."

"We could sell stock in the medical device company, but I don't know that much about the new stock market."

"I only heard a few things, but it is complicated to start one and I have no idea when it will happen."

"I have faith in you, learn as much as you can, and I will work things from my end." Oddly enough, he was reassured.

=..=

Right after Big Thunder, Omímeya closed the spa and moved the employees to other departments. The massage therapists were unhappy, some had occasional private clients. They ended up finding jobs in other places. Survival was on people's minds, not facials and mani/pedis.

When Anna May told Martin she was going to see about opening the spa, as she might turn her expertise into a little income, he was thrilled. Martin looked over the proposal, helped her with the financial portions, and appreciated working together. Since he was not present, he enjoyed hearing about the meeting she had with Rose Chasing Hawk after she got back.

Anna May dressed conservatively after waiting a week to get the appointment. Rose knew the topic of the meeting in advance and was ready to dismiss her arguments about opening the spa. Anna May first asked her about how the trauma counseling was going. After the coup attempt, many people who were in the room suffered from posttraumatic stress disorder. There'd been several mental health professionals who'd come with them, as well as those that lived locally. Some worked out of two hotel rooms that were converted into counseling rooms. Changleska paid them. They were fully booked. Rose said they wanted to expand, as the need was greater than expected.

Anna May presented her professionally printed proposal, complete with graph charts, a budget, a projection of profit and losses, and a list of services. The proposal was to create a Self-Care Center using the spa facilities and expanding it. Anna May had done her homework. Next to the spa on the ground floor, there were eight wheelchair-accessible hotel rooms. As people in wheelchairs rarely traveled at this time, they only needed one or two. They could use them to expand the number of counseling rooms, decorate them to be more inviting. Since the counselors were all paid through Changleska, that program would be self-sufficient.

In addition, Anna May wanted to add back all the usual spa services, with the same rates as before. She argued that some people, especially physicians, had discretionary income and were used to these types of services and would pay for them again. More importantly, the new tourists whom she knew Rose was trying to attract would experience these services for the first time. Even in the eighteenth century, women influenced their men on travel. Travel to health spas was common in Europe. With the pool right across from the spa, they could heat it a few more degrees, people could "take the waters". They expected people would come for treatments of various conditions, contributing to medical tourism. In her proposal, Anna May illustrated how to target the eighteenth-century consumer for marketing.

Anna May made a compelling argument to reinstate massage therapy. Her proposal outlined the health benefits, including statements from Dr. Martiniz, who cited studies. The doctors all recommended the opening of a self-care center and emphasized how the reduction of stress was necessary for good health.

Anna May also suggested converting one room into a hair salon. She pointed out most in town had closed, there was equipment and out of work stylists. While chemical hair dyes would be gone soon, there were natural alternatives. Feeling good about yourself was an important part of self-care. Women who tended to take care of everyone but themselves needed places they could go for self-care. Everyone was working very hard, under stressful conditions. A day to spend getting your hair and nails done, going for a swim, getting a massage, would both relax and energize those who needed it the most. She pointed out it was an activity that women often did together, bringing friends and family.

Anna May said she did not want to forget the men. The proposal suggested two days a week would be men's days. One Sunday afternoon and one mid-week. The hair salon would have a barber come in. She expected men would use it less. It could be a low-key day for staff.

Anna May impressed Rose by sharing her experience of visiting spas around the world. There were suggestions for improvements, new treatments, all things easily done. The presentation impressed Rose. She rescheduled her next meeting to spend more time going over the finances with Anna May. Afterwards she approved it, stating it was nice to be the boss, she could decide quickly.

Rose said, "You would be great as a manager. Would you like the job?"

"Sorry, I have other projects, but I could be a consultant."

They discussed fees, and Anna May got what she thought was fair, and Rose probably thought was too much. For a small monthly retainer, she would submit a regular report on services, review profit-and-loss statements, and make suggestions as needed. In addition, she would consult on the remodel. The contract included profit sharing, with the condition that her monthly fee would decrease if they incurred losses. They both left satisfied.

When Anna May told Martin what she would be paid, he was thrilled. The initial consulting fee was generous, the monthly fee was just enough to cover the payment to the credit line. Martin wondered how he ever doubted her.

=..=

The new stock exchange had not yet opened, but it was getting closer. Before Big Thunder Martin followed the stock market to keep track of his investments, but his financial manager did all the trades. They were risk averse and stayed with blue chip stocks. It took a bit of study for him to learn enough to be useful.

There was a stockbroker staying at the casino during Big Thunder. He dealt mostly in commodities, in farm futures. He was knowledgeable enough to start up the new stock market working closely with the Banking Committee. The banks were closing branches because of the labor shortage. A branch of the Interstate Bank in Lower Brule closed, becoming the site of the stock market.

It took a long time for the committee to decide the rules. Early on, Rose insisted on all banking rules being no longer than five pages and easily understandable by any sixth grader. They condensed them to ten pages, requiring at least a high school graduate to understand. A similar approach was being taken with securities laws, aiming to simplify and reduce unnecessary regulations. However, this process was time-consuming.

Another delay occurred because the bank had been heated by natural gas. They were on the waiting list for a wood stove. Until the stock market opened, no one could sell stock in their new companies. Many people were anxiously waiting.

After Big Thunder, if a business was owned by a corporation left behind, ownership could fall to the employees if they wished to continue. Most did, a few did not, mostly places like fast-food restaurants. If employees did not register within thirty days, the property reverted either to the tribe, if tribal land, or the county.

Businesses, especially larger ones, had plans to manufacture everything from the Sunshine Header Harvester and the McCormick Reaper, farming devices that doubled crop production, to the Pelton Water Wheel used for generating electricity. They all needed investment to pay for retooling, patents, materials, and workers. Many had investors lined up, but if their companies were to be publicly owned, they needed a stock market. Most were private corporations for now, like the hospital and Omímeya. Publicly traded companies could raise funds quickly. Many people wanted the stock market to open as soon as possible.

Anna May suggested they start a corporation to make not only their medical devices, but all durable medical products. As a public corporation, they could sell stock and keep a large share. By selling stocks, they would have the funds to hire a CEO, as well as buy stainless steel before it was gone. She suggested doctors were more open to long-term investments, not needing quick returns. Medical professionals also knew the value of what a company like this could offer in the long term.

While they waited anxiously for the stock market to open, Martin and Anna May worked together on the prospectus. Normally, Anna May would host dinner parties to get people to sign on to one of her projects. Because of the gas shortage and the bus schedules, they couldn't host at their home. She looked over the Omímeya schedule and found a meeting that most doctors would attend. It was on a Saturday, from 9:00 am to 5:00 pm, the topic was eighteenth-century diseases. Fun.

Their brand-new company "Durable Medical Corporation" would host a reception with finger food and a cash bar, from 5:30-7:00 pm on that day. All the physicians in the area received invitations. Anna May figured most would attend. Free food was a draw, but people would be curious. The invitation noted the shuttles would run late.

Martin and Anna May hoped the stock market would be open by the time of their reception so people could buy stocks right away, but if not, they would proceed anyway. To get a head start, they started a search for a CEO. Martin did not have the skills or the desire to run a manufacturing company. They had a very hard time finding anyone either through their ad on Craigslist or the skills database. Other companies had already hired anyone with industrial experience. They finally gave up finding anyone who knew anything specific, and thought if they could find a good manager, it would be their job to find the expertise needed. They ended up hiring a displaced man who had previously run a small company which made protein supplements for gyms. In his late forties, he'd left an ex-wife and two boys behind. Currently employed at the meat plant, he was eager to do something different and offered his help in setting up the company for stock, with a salary once the stocks were sold. He had an MBA and fifteen years' experience, so his pay rate should have been a level four, but he was willing to start at a level three for the first year. He was currently working at a level one, so he was happy.

They worked as a team for the presentation, keeping it short but concise to hold everyone's attention after just having sat in lectures all day. It was a resounding success. Anna May was in her element. She wore one of her new dresses she'd had commissioned to resemble eighteenth-century fashion. One thing they failed to consider was how much people missed the trappings of the old world. Free finger food to hear a sales pitch on buying stock in a new company would normally not be much of a draw, but almost all the physicians attended.

When the stock market opened the next week, they sold almost all the shares. Martin took some of that money and invested in a few companies that promised early returns, like farm equipment and steam engines. Fuel would be a good investment, but there were so many choices and problems with development, he waited. He had been following the forums and knew what companies were close to having salable products.

Dakota Grain and Mill was a large company that came with them. It bought and sold most of the grain in the area. Despite its name, it did not operate a mill. They milled the grain in a faraway location. There were tons of wheat and other grain in silos all over the circle and no way to turn it into flour. Some small grinders, but nothing on the commercial scale. Because it had been previously owned by an out-of-state corporation, the new owners were struggling, as no one was buying or selling grain. The company would go public as soon as the stock market opened to raise money to build a commercial milling operation. Martin thought that would be good to get in on the ground floor.

They finally had some room to breathe financially. Anna May was becoming quite popular online. More people were learning who she was, an online presence was important now as it used to be, but with fewer people, it made a bigger impact. She advertised the Self-Care Center and started forums to promote the arts and eighteenth-century clothing.

Martin spent most of his time online on the expedition and steamship forums. Oacoma was becoming the manufacturing center for steam engines. Most of the shops that delt with auto repair, body shops, and machinists were located there or in Chamberlain. They were working on converting existing car and truck motors to steam, rather than starting from scratch. They had made some progress, but there was a long way to go.

On the forums he took part in, there were a lot of online arguments. Sometimes honest disagreements about the best way to do something, but more often, it was someone's ego trying to push their viewpoint. He used his years of management experience to soothe ruffled feathers and to direct people to find workable solutions. Anna May took notice of what he was doing and encouraged him. She would often direct him to other forums where there was a conflict that needed mediating. Martin found it satisfying to use his management skills, as he did not have knowledge or skills in any of the areas under discussion. He started doing it in so many forums; he was getting emails asking him to look at different groups to see if he could help.

Martin was enjoying living in the farmhouse. They were lucky it had a wood stove and some firewood. They found a young Native couple with a small trailer to live on the property for security. The man, David Ocha, had useful skills none of them had. Besides hunting and fishing, he helped them get more firewood, and was handy at repairs. Martin had never lived with a group of people before and found he enjoyed it. He wished Anna May would not treat everyone like staff, but people still liked her, surprisingly enough.

Anna May surprised him by transferring all the money she made to their joint account. She said, "You had always handled the family finances before. Why change now?"

One change was that she informed him rather than asked if there was a big expenditure. It did not happen often; there was little to spend money on.

One morning at breakfast, Anna May said, "Today, I will go to the trading posts to buy fabric and clothes that I can reuse the fabric from. I am also looking for seamstresses and it will not be cheap."

Martin was miffed. "Why do you need more clothes?"

"For New York, of course. Paris will have to wait. The clothes are for both of us."

"New York!?"

Anna May told him, in the same way she told him to apply for a company promotion, he was going to be the new Changleska Ambassador in New York. He could not believe she would consider leaving the comforts of home, flush toilets, and the spa. She admitted trepidation about the journey, but said once they got settled, it would be easier. She pointed out that money made everything simpler. As an ambassador, he needed to show the wealth of Changleska. They would have ample resources provided to them to achieve that. Anna May discussed parties and political maneuvering. It wasn't just the luxury trappings of her old life that Anna May missed, but the calculating machinations of it. Martin had to admit she was good at it.

Martin asked, "Why would they select me as an ambassador if I have no training?"

"No one else has training around here."

Anna May suggested he become more active in the New York Expedition forum, particularly in the discussions of the approaches to Washington, the Spanish and French. Anna May spoke a little French. She downloaded a French language program that she planned on using when they no longer had NewNet access. Her forums were taking up a lot of her time. Martin realized she was developing correspondence with several influential people, besides her online presence.

Martin knew with Anna May so determined, he would be the new Changleska ambassador. He started following the New York forums more closely, adding his own opinions instead of just mediating arguments. By staying busy with thinking about new challenges, he worried less about his age, and stopped worrying about Anna May. He knew now she could take care of herself.

Chapter Thirty-One

Jackson

JACKSON COULD NOT believe it was almost Christmas. He'd arrived on the Fall Equinox, September 21, and now it was the Winter Solstice, December 21. The thought of Christmas without his family was painful. He couldn't get away from work in recent years, but when he did, Christmas was a big deal in his family. Housefuls of relatives cooking up a storm, attending church, always a niece or nephew in a school play or singing somewhere he had to attend. Jackson and Rose had a conversation about this last night at her dinner. Rose said, a lot of displaced people weren't coping well. Even the locals were having a hard time. Not being able to find the traditional foods and other items found during this season put a damper on celebrations.

Omímeya planned a big Christmas Eve party and hoped that would cheer people up. Jackson knew there was a Lakota Winter Solstice Ceremony tonight at the 11:11 site, but has no desire to be out in the cold and has no plans to attend.

The Council was on winter break from today until the first of the year. Jackson was relieved. Being on the Council was much harder than he had ever imagined. They'd worked out a manageable system finally. The Council required all proposals to be submitted seven business days in advance. Prior to the vote, the Council members discussed the proposals on their private forum. If anyone had questions or needed clarifications, they could email the Committee Chair. The rule was that all correspondence to and from Committees about proposals had to be cc'd to everyone in order to keep everything as transparent as possible. Private lobbying to Council members wasn't allowed. Not that everyone read every email, but it was a start.

By having the proposals in advance, the Council could limit the time all seven members needed to be present. Now down to twice a week and hoped to go to weekly. In addition, votes were a formality mostly decided beforehand. Rarely, someone changed their mind at the last minute. Votes had become ceremonial. The entire Committee came, sometimes with family or supporters. The Chair read the proposal carefully on the record. Occasionally the Council would ask a question, but most often it was a comment, often praising the Committee's work or articulating their objections. After the vote, if passed, all the audience members would cheer and hug. If it failed, the Council had to explain why. The Committee members would stay and listen. They could try again in a year.

The last thing Jackson ever expected was to be a government official. Although challenging, he didn't mind deciding which proposals to vote for. Where he was having trouble was as the Minister for Defense. The law part was fine. He enjoyed the innovative ways the criminal justice system was being reorganized.

Jackson in the old world would have been the Secretary of Defense, but unlike the old world, he was also the Commander-in-Chief. They decided that was a better fit than the Chair, unless in the future the Chair was also the Minister for Defense. It made sense; he was better apprised than Mary about what was going on in the military. General Gardner was in charge. He made all the decisions normally, but in major decisions of policy, go or no go, it was all him. The situation with the Two Elks tribe still haunted him.

When he first started taking nonviolence training, he realized he had a real deficit in his education in this area. He never went to college, was not a good student, read little. He started reading Martin Luther King, Jr., Gandhi, Nelson Mandela, and the Dalai Lama. Jackson felt committed to nonviolence not only as an ideal, but truly believed violence was a terrible way to resolve conflicts. He loved the Asimov quote, "Violence is the last refuge of the incompetent." As a cop, he learned that pragmatism won over idealism many times, but he wasn't willing to give up on his ideals.

Although hesitant, he approved the proposal in the Security Council meeting to lift the no shooting order for incursions of Two Elks' warriors. He wouldn't have approved it if he'd known it would turn into a massacre. At least it wasn't the military; it was the Neighborhood Watch that did it. Although it wasn't his direct responsibility, he still felt bothered by his inability to find a nonviolent solution.

Soon after Big Thunder, Kyle started the Neighborhood Watch. Combined aspects of the FEMA Citizens Emergency Response Team (CERT), the old Neighborhood Watch and a citizen militia. CERT trained volunteers to work in cases of natural disasters in first aid, communication, and ways to assist professional emergency workers. Things like how to remove someone safely from earthquake rubble or how to coordinate with authorities.

The Watch divided everywhere within the Circle into neighborhoods comprising twenty to one hundred people. Rural areas had fewer people and bigger areas, urban areas about five blocks. At first, they assigned a leader to each neighborhood and encouraged them to vote for a new leader if needed.

Initial leaders were military, medical, or professionals with good organizational skills. Participation was mandatory for all citizens, and noncitizens were encouraged to join. Individuals who were older or had mobility issues were assigned to roles in communications, medical, or other logistics. All able-bodied individuals were expected to do weapons training alongside the Guard at least once a week to start. The requirement would go down to once a month once they had enough people trained.

Most people in the area had guns. All Changleska citizens were required to have at least one person in each household receive training and to own a weapon. Citizens who didn't own a weapon could get a zero-interest, low payment loan to purchase one. The controversial measure received one of the closest votes they'd had, despite the frequent mention of Switzerland. Jackson voted against it. He'd seen too much gun violence to think more access to weapons would make anyone safer.

Jackson had to admit the Watch had benefits no one expected. One responsibility of the Watch was to survey all residents to find out if anyone had medical or special needs, or what resources were available in their neighborhoods. Those resources might have been physical, such as buildings, or people who had useful knowledge or skills. Weekly meetings took place in whatever neighborhood venue was easy for people to access or in individual homes. Online forums specific to each neighborhood were limited to residents only. Between the meetings, online communication and the shared activities, a real sense of community was developing. Neighborhoods saw elders or isolated individuals making connections with others. Things like babysitting, barter, rides, loans of tools, help with minor projects all started occurring.

Rural areas already experienced that connection between neighbors, but in town there were people who had lived next door to each other for twenty years that barely spoke two words to each other.

The day of Two Elks' raid was the weekly meeting of the Watch. Everyone had brought their weapons. There were two members of the Guard present to train them. General Gardner believed the best way to learn something was to teach it. He had experienced and new recruits take part in each Watch training, the recruit training others, and the experienced guardian supervising. The supervisor that day was Lou White Mountain, a former marine, with combat experience.

They received a perimeter alert only moments before they spotted the first warriors. They were all minutes away in a barn, but they all grabbed their weapons and White Mountain directed them to roofs and under cover. When the warriors approached and started shooting, they responded and shot back quickly. Since they didn't have radios and couldn't hear the cease-fire order over the shooting, they kept firing until only eleven wounded were left. On their side, the only casualty was someone who fell off a roof and broke his leg.

Jackson felt sickened by what happened. He brought up at the next Security Council meeting that Two Elks lost most of his effective force. While that may bring him to the negotiating table, it wouldn't be as a capable ally, but as a client serving as a subservient role. They needed powerful tribes to show others they were good allies and trading partners. Wiping out tribes with superior weapons wouldn't serve them in the long run. Two Elks wasn't a threat. What would they do when the ammunition ran out? Guns, mostly automatics against bows and arrows and a few flintlocks, was not showing military superiority, it was showing cruelty.

Even Gardner looked thoughtful at Jackson's rant. He pointed out that they didn't come for a quick raid; they had many pack horses with supplies. Gardner suspected they had chosen that place to hit because of its isolation. Planned it being a base for further operations. He insisted on staying with the program he outlined previously, saying the deaths shouldn't go in vain. The bodies were dumped near Two Elks' winter camp. They didn't pass any requests for communication or messages of any kind.

Gardner and Jackson both agreed that the enemy's wounded should be treated, despite the medical resource restrictions. Jackson's reminder emphasized the importance of treating the enemy's wounded fairly, as it reflected who they were as a people. They couldn't agree on what to do with the prisoners, so they postponed the decision until the wounded were healed enough.

=..=

Jackson wondered what he'd do with himself over the break. Mary sternly warned all the assistants not to post any proposals online. Jackson couldn't review them, which took up a lot of his time. Because they required no action on his part, he'd read little in the expedition forums. Expeditions fell under defense, but it encompassed a broad area, logistics, diplomacy, as well as defining goals. He rarely had time to look at any plans. During the break, he was unsure if his assistant would be completely off. He realized how much help she was in prioritizing projects.

Without his input, they assigned an older woman named Charlotte Evans as his assistant, who'd been in the Air Force and worked as an aide to a colonel. She was efficient but humorless. The other Councilors got to choose their assistants, but Gardner insisted on someone who had held a previous security clearance, someone who knew how to maintain military secrets.

He moved into a suite; the cost covered with his housing allowance. All the Councilors received rooms to use as offices or suites if they wanted sleeping spaces. For Councilors who lived far away, it was helpful. Although the front of the suite was public, where the assistant worked, the bedroom was private. There wasn't a lot of traffic in the offices. Since the front gate opened, it was rare that random people stopped by. Occasionally, someone wanted to see if he was available to talk about an upcoming proposal, but Charlotte kept a lid on that. He was the only Councilor who lived in his suite full-time. It was a huge cost savings, not to mention a twenty step walk to work.

=..=

The Security Council meeting was the last of the day. He hated these meetings. Being Commander-in-Chief and having the powers of war didn't sit well with him. He knew the ugliness of war firsthand. They'd upgraded his security clearance to a three and given him a tour of the weapons in the basement and the triangle bunkers. All the shipping containers filled with weapons, military surplus purchased at a steep discount, disturbed him. War plans for an invasion by Washington or Napoleon were underway. Gardner pointed out that armies of fifty to one hundred thousand were normal at this time. They moved across the country in mass. Washington's armies were still intact, fighting tribes in smaller numbers. A big campaign wouldn't be difficult for him.

For someone who believed in peace, seeing war may be necessary was a hard pill to swallow. On his computer was a copy of Barack Obama's speech when he won the Nobel Peace Prize. He reread it, finding comfort in the words of a man he admired who said, "To say that force may sometimes be necessary is not a call to cynicism — it is a recognition of history; the imperfections of man and the limits of reason."

Obama spoke about how lasting peace came from freedom from want, from inherent rights, and from the dignity of every individual. Jackson knew Changleska could offer that to the world, but it might take war to achieve it. He thought of Obama's words, "Clear-eyed, we can understand that there will be war, and still strive for peace."

Jackson was upset about the situation with the Two Elks tribe and was trying to think of a solution. If you conquer someone, they're not allies. An ally is independent and has a choice. They not only removed Two Elks' ability to wage war on Changleska, but took away his ability to defend himself, weakening his tribe to be prey to others.

At the meeting, Jackson couldn't help pointing out the problems created by decimating the tribe's warriors. That wasn't helpful, nothing anyone could do. They all questioned why Two Elks sent so many warriors. What was the point? He knew about their military capabilities; the repeated incursions verified it.

Billy informed them he'd heard from the voyageurs they'd met Lakota scouts just north of the Circle. The scouts knew they carried a load of rifles and gunpowder for Changleska. Billy said it wouldn't surprise him if Two Elks knew that the Red Eagle tribe had been in contact with the Paha Sapa expedition.

"I don't understand why they'd attack, even if worried we may ally with the Red Eagle tribe."

Billy responded, "Even though over half of us are Lakota, they consider us all wasicu or white men."

"We have told them we're trying to protect them from the white men who'll steal their land, that we'll protect them."

Billy explained patiently, "They don't want us to protect them. They want to protect themselves."

He let them know the nearby trading posts were selling alcohol to the winter camp. He learned from the trading posts that theft had risen in their camp, whereas before, it had been almost non-existent.

"If I was Two Elks wanting to protect my people, my way of life, I'd have nothing to do with us."

Jackson was upset hearing that, "We need to do a better job of showing them and other tribes how much good we can do."

"Not all people believe change is good."

Unable to reach any kind of decision regarding Two Elks, they moved on to the other item on the agenda, Clyde Folsom. Phil directed everyone's attention to the transcribed speeches Folsom had given on the radio and at his church, highlighting certain parts. Phil told everyone Folsom kept the radio addresses lower key. The sermons from the church were clearly treasonous in promoting taking over Omímeya and Changleska for the new nation, Christian America. Folsom had taken the oath. Trying to overthrow the government was treason.

Jackson asked how they got copies of Folsom's church sermons. Everyone looked at him like he was a simpleton.

Phil answered, "We have spies, of course, don't all governments?"

Jackson knew Phil oversaw the new intelligence service they were calling First Shield Command, or FSC. It was a combination of CIA, FBI, NSA, and Homeland Security. Knowing they were just getting started and didn't know what they were up to. No need to know, he supposed.

Folsom had taken over the church he attended, although not ordained. The pastor gave opening and closing prayers, Folsom gave the main sermons. They were exploring larger churches or venues because it had grown so much. They broadcasted the services live over the radio every week.

Folsom gave speeches, not heard on the radio, for his closest followers. The county was finally getting ready for an election to become an independent nation, spurred on by Clyde Folsom.

Kyle stated, "Folsom represents an existential threat. This divisiveness will undermine our survival. Most of his followers are county, where the manufacturing base is, and the equipment we need to survive. If he gains power and this becomes Christian America, think *The Handmaid's Tale*, or *1984*. We must stop him any way we can."

Gardner said, "If he contacts Washington, we can assume he'll come in force to take our military resources."

Phil answered with, "Folsom could've an accident, perhaps a fire at the radio station."

Mary, who had been quietly listening the whole time, quoted, "Will no one rid me of this meddlesome priest?"

Everyone stared at her. "It's a quote by King Henry II. Are you not familiar?" All shook their heads no.

"Our education system is terrible. Henry II said that to a group of knights who assumed he meant they should kill the Archbishop of Canterbury, Thomas Becket. When they killed him, they turned Becket into a martyr and a saint. The controversy almost took down the crown. Henry was trying to reduce the power of the church and just made it worse."

Jackson said, "I'm not sure how this is relevant."

Mary sighed, exasperated.—we may hate Clyde Folsom and everything he believes, but he has a right by our constitution to believe it. He has freedom of religion, speech and dissent. If we shut him down, or the radio, we harm ourselves more in the long run. We must stand by our beliefs, even if they're not comfortable."

She looked around the room sternly. "I don't even want to hear a joke or even a whisper like what I just heard. That's not an option."

Kyle asked, "Can we arrest him for treason?"

Phil replied, "I forwarded a copy of the transcripts to Elliot Gray Owl. He said treason is hard to prove in a court of law. It'd be more likely to galvanize his followers."

Jackson added, "Looking over these transcripts, he talks a lot about how oppressed he's by the government, how we're trying to silence him, a classic 'us versus them' strategy."

Billy asked, "What can we do?"

Jackson thought about it for a minute, trying to put on his peacekeeper hat. He remembered the county was finally getting ready for an election to become an independent nation, spurred on by Clyde Folsom.

"We need to reconsider our stance on the county's independence," Jackson suggested, his expression grave. "I understand the arguments about not having to pay medical and infrastructure costs, but stopping county independence may be the only way to stop Folsom's rise to power."

Phil said, "Polling suggests most residents are in favor by a large majority."

"We have polls?" asked Jackson. Phil just gave him a look.

Mary suggested, "We should put the hippies on it. Look what they did for Jerome Brown."

Everyone called them the hippies, the displaced people who were attending the permaculture conference. Most had moved away from White River Farm for jobs and better housing, but they were becoming the most powerful political group. They remained on numerous committees together, had a private forum, met regularly at the Oacoma community center and the White River Farm. They've been instrumental in the passing of dozens of laws so far. Now the majority are on the Environmental Committee, which they renamed the Gaia Committee. They proposed and passed laws banning the production of new pesticides and herbicides and severely limiting the use of stockpiles. Created strict laws on recycling, and other environmental laws.

One unpopular law had been passed, which restricted the number of trees that people could cut for firewood in certain areas to minor thinning. In modern times, dams destroyed all the woodlands next to the rivers. They had evidence to show how this loss adversely affected these vital bio-systems, which supported many species. In addition, the Indigenous tribe's horses ate the bark from cottonwood trees when the snow was too deep to find grass.

This meant firewood crews had to go further, using more fuel. People were working on solutions, but there weren't simple ones.

The hippies were active on other committees as well. Whenever they proposed a law, the accompanying documentation was clear, concise, cogent, with supporting evidence. They earned a lot of respect, which was kind of funny considering hippies were previously thought of as flakes and druggies.

The election for county independence was scheduled for mid-January. There was little time. They raised a question about running this plan by Rose and the other economists because of the potential financial impact.

Kyle said, "If we don't stop Folsom, none of this will matter. We don't have time."

They unanimously passed a motion to use whatever resources needed to oppose the county's independence. Jackson offered to talk to Rose.

Jackson appreciated an excuse to talk to Rose. Although it may be a hard conversation, he knew how conservative she was about finances. Having dinner with her on weeknights was the highlight of his day. He tried to get out of meetings on time so he wouldn't miss it. The rule against talking shop meant they could talk about lots of other things. They talked about family and told funny stories. They laughed a lot together. After everyone else had left, they'd often linger over tea and talk. Jackson shared his concerns about being an aspiring peacekeeper and the nominal head of the military. Rose listened and offered good advice. He listened to her talk about her children and troubles with the resort staff. They both shared fears and hopes for the future.

His attraction to her was unique, unlike any he had felt towards other women. He'd been with a lot of beautiful women, since so many came on to him, he had his pick. While being pretty and self-confident was a factor, a big bust or booty a plus, he'd never rated intelligence high on his list before. Although he still mourned Denise, he knew he had to move on. Women were still coming on to him, more so since he became Councilor. He knew women were attracted to alpha males because of their wealth, power, or preferably both. It was getting annoying.

His libido was returning, this was the longest he'd ever been without sex. Jackson always tried to not allow women to become emotionally attached or hurt. He had observed that while men seemed to be happy to spread their wild oats about, women wanted to settle, wanted a provider. It was an instinctual survival mechanism to propagate the species. Birth control changed human sexuality, separating it from procreation. He realized at this time in his life he no longer was interested in recreational sex. Nothing was wrong with fucking for the pure pleasure of it. But after Denise, he wanted the deeper emotional connection of making love.

Jackson felt the temptation. There was a woman, Maria, who worked in the laundry. She was beautiful, Afro-Caribbean from the Dominican Republic. As one of the few young Black women around, he expected many people, including her, thought they'd get together. When the usual flirtation didn't work, she'd contrived with the seamstress to come to his room to check the measurements for another suit he was having altered. She kneeled right in front of him to measure the inseam of his pants. He turned her down, even though it was hard.

Jackson felt sure Rose liked him in that way. He thought he knew why she didn't act on it, but he was still unclear. Recently, he'd had a conversation with Luke that made him reevaluate his feelings. Usually, Luke came with his mother to the dinners she hosted, but he rarely sat with the adults, eating alone or with others his age. One evening, Rose had to leave early to deal with some minor crisis or another. As Jackson was finishing eating, Luke sat down next to him.

"Hey, Jackson, can I ask you something?" Luke's voice was casual, but there was a curious glint in his eyes. "What's going on between you and my mom?"

"We're friends," Jackson replied, but his eyes flickered with uncertainty.

"It's obvious you're more than friends; I see the way you look at each other."

"I'm not sure your mom feels that way about me," Jackson confessed, a hint of vulnerability in his voice.

"Of course she feels like that about you. I hear her talk to her friends. She doesn't want to be one of your admiring hordes of women."

"If she did, would it bother you?"

"Only if you hurt her. She's been through enough. Don't bother unless you're serious."

Now Jackson had to decide how serious he was. He'd put off proposing to Denise because he didn't want to commit to being with only one woman for the rest of his life. The more he thought about it, the more he realized a life with Rose was more than sex or companionship. It'd be a partnership of shared goals and values. He thought about how he felt when he saw

Caballo pull a gun on her, how despite all his training, he threw himself at someone holding a loaded gun.

As he examined his heart, he couldn't ignore the undeniable reality. Rose was the center of his world, and he couldn't imagine a life without her. The question persisted, weighing heavily on him: was his love for her sufficient? Like the young people all said now, if he stuck it in, was he willing to stick it out?

=..=

Rose was too busy with the remodel for lunch, but agreed to meet him later that afternoon. He was working in his office when he got a call from General Gardner for an emergency meeting about a military matter. When he got downstairs, there were several officers and Elliot Gray Owl in the meeting room. Gardner informed him they may have their first court martial. A guardian assigned to guard the prisoners was caught making out with a prisoner.

"What?" exclaimed Jackson, confused.

Gardner expanded, saying that Courtney Bravebird, a young woman guardian, had been assigned to guard the prisoners because she was fluent in Lakota. Evidently, she and Six Feathers, one of the wounded, who'd recovered, been spending a lot of time together. She even came in on her time off to bring him food and talk.

"We'll review the procedures that allowed that to occur, believe me," Gardner stated.

Jackson said, "We should take this as serious as if it was a female prisoner and a male guard. There's a power differential involved."

The military people all agreed, discussing if there should be additional charges besides dishonorable discharge.

Elliot said, "Hold on a minute there. Is there an issue of consent? Have we talked to them separately?"

Gardner reviewed the file. "They say they want to marry. Six Feathers has asked for the return of his three horses, so he can give them to her father."

Jackson rolled his eyes.

Gardner added, "Courtney said she'd move to Two Elks' camp if necessary."

Elliot responded, "Before we can court martial her, were the prisoners officially charged? I thought they were hostages as much as prisoners. As far as I heard, we're not planning on doing anything to them."

"That's a point," replied Jackson.

"Did you say Six Feathers? You realize that's Two Elks' son."

"This gets better and better," said Gardner.

"Where's the girl now?" asked Elliot.

"We sent her home; she lives on the rez close to here," answered Gardner. Elliot proposed to bring the girl in. He'd review all the statutes, but there were bigger political implications here with Two Elks' son involved.

Because it was the last day before the meeting rooms would be shut down for the break, they scheduled to meet again at 4:00 pm

When it was time to meet with Rose, he went to the temporary office set up with the architect and the contractor. He watched her for a few minutes before she noticed him. She was directing people, answering questions, multitasking efficiently. He realized that was another thing he loved about her; she was competent, utterly competent.

Chapter Thirty-Two

Rose

THE DAY OF the Winter Solstice dawned cold and clear. Rose was happy because the planned ceremony Kimi and Gift had created involved looking at the stars. Rose knew those who wanted an alternative to the Christian holiday looked at the Solstice for celebration, ritual, or ceremony.

The Lakota, while recognizing the shortest day of the year, traditionally didn't have a solstice ceremony. The girls created their own, something unique, incorporating Lakota traditions with others from around the world. She was looking forward to it but had a long day ahead of her.

A pang of sadness washed over Rose at the thought of Christmas morning without Hotah. Even after they split up, they'd have Christmas with the kids. She remembered the excitement of the kids as they rushed down the stairs to open presents and how both parents shared their joy in their gifts. Later in the day, she and Luke would go to a big family dinner at the Crow Road house, but it wouldn't be the same.

"Luke, have you thought about what you want to do on Christmas morning?" Rose asked as they set the table for dinner the night before.

"Not really," Luke replied, shrugging. "I guess we could make breakfast together or something."

Rose was happy with that answer, getting another response besides "I dunno," Their communication had improved, as well as their overall relationship.

When Luke was struggling, Rose complained to Theresa Martinez, who was becoming a friend. She asked for advice, as her two teenage boys seemed so well adjusted. Theresa asked her if Luke had spent a lot of time in front of screens before the age of two. Rose admitted he did. She knew as a baby his babysitter would put him in a playpen in front of the TV, where he spent all day. When they were at home, she often used screens as a babysitter while she did homework, as she was still in school. It was different after Kimi was born; Hotah was making good money, and she could focus on being a mother.

Theresa explained as an epidemiologist, she saw a lot of studies about how detrimental any screens were to a child's developing brain, especially before the age of two. Learning difficulties, behavioral issues, autism spectrum disorders, and delayed developmental milestones were all clearly linked. Rose said she didn't know about it. Theresa mentioned many of these studies were recent, but studies challenging established paradigms were often unknown outside of professional Circles. Screens were too easy for parents. Theresa said she understood. She had kept her two boys away until they got older but gave in and now her boys played limited video games. She said video games were an addictive drug, giving the brain dopamine and other pleasure hormones. Luke just turned sixteen. His brain was still developing. The more Rose could keep Luke away from video games, the better. Rose sighed. She knew she gave in to Luke too easily.

These last few months had been a wake-up call. She'd prioritized spending more time with her kids, realizing the world didn't fall apart if she was away from work. Rose knew no one ever said on their deathbed, "I wish I'd spent more time in the office."

Luke became friends with the Begay boys, all close in age. Rose made a point of inviting them to spend the night. She raided the basement reserves for junk food, kept the fridge stocked, and encouraged them to spend time at the house. They were there a lot, playing board games, watching movies. Rose loved hearing them laugh; she knew how valuable the bonds of friendship were at this age. They were a good influence on Luke, helped him with his homework, and he taught them to ride before the weather got bad.

=..=

Most people would enjoy a winter break, except Rose, who'd have extra projects. Everyone who could be let off work was using vacation days or half pay. Guests were offered the choice to clean their own rooms or to pay an additional fee, which meant extra cleaning when the staff returned, but everyone needed time off. The exception was construction and maintenance, who'd work overtime. Additionally, they hired people from the outside. The goal was to complete the projects before New Year's Eve.

Rose had worked a lot with construction over the years and thought it was doable. She also knew how easy it was for one problem to throw an entire schedule out the window. The structural remodel would be finished over the break, but the entire project wouldn't be complete until spring.

They were going to remodel several conference rooms to a Changleska Council Chamber and more offices. With the planned medical school, there was less need for conference rooms. They were still working to separate the finances between Omímeya and Changleska. Changleska would have a long-term lease on rooms. Eventually, rents would match those in other capital cities of similar square footage. They also had the option of expanding as needed. No one knew what the future would hold; they all hoped it would become a thriving capital and wanted to look ahead.

Rose had a firm commitment to keeping Omímeya a resort instead of government offices. She hoped she wasn't being short-sighted; her identity being so intertwined working in hospitality. Rose had worked there a year before it opened. She was part of the design process. It was her baby, a growing child now. It was her vision, slowly coming to life before her eyes, and she couldn't help but feel a sense of accomplishment. Her dream was that Omímeya would be a center for which people would come from all over to learn to create a better future.

They hoped by spring to be getting outside visitors. Henry LaChamp, the HBC representative, told them there were rich nobility arriving in Quebec with the French revolution coming and would flock here as soon as they saw luxury accommodations. She sent him back with plenty of brochures and postcards.

Rose felt a surge of pride as she surveyed the work. Besides the Council Chamber and offices, they'd work on the spa expansion, modifications to the pool, build the new hair salon, expand the day care center, paint and do a deep clean of carpets and common spaces after the construction was over. The space planned for the Council Chamber had limitations. Originally, the north wing was chosen for conference rooms because the back had a view of the triangle. No one wanted to look at the industrial mess. The largest room was boring with no natural light, seating about 100. The smaller meeting rooms had windows with river views along the sides. The back of all the rooms held risers for speakers and HD screen projectors.

They consulted the architect who worked on the medical school remodel, designing something simple and beautiful. Anna May's eyes sparkled with excitement as Rose described her ideas for the Council Chamber remodel. They opened the walls of the smaller meeting rooms to integrate the hall and the larger back room, creating one big room that allowed light and river views in. When finished, it would seat about 400, more than needed now. The most to come to a Council vote was 200, and recently about thirty to forty. It may seem cavernous for now, but in the long term less so. The size gave it an open and airy feeling, important since they couldn't raise the ceilings.

Anna May suggested keeping the largest projector in the rear to showcase art, show videos, or digitally display the new Changleska Flag.

"We could use local artists for the murals and a large sculpture," she suggested. "It'd not only support the community but add a wow factor."

She bubbled with ideas and pulled out her phone to show Rose examples of various local artists' work. Impressed, Rose did not know the extent of Anna May's connections within the Circle's artists.

The current Council setup consisted of three standard, six-foot conference tables arranged in a semicircle. At the center, a small circular table, covered with a buffalo hide, held tobacco, sage, and feathers. Positioned towards the front, but not entirely enclosing the circle, was another standard-sized table where the Committee Chair, Secretary, and Treasurer presented proposals for a vote. Spectators sat in back rows on standard conference chairs.

The new Council Chamber would maintain the same table arrangement, but with a significant upgrade. Instead of artificial wood, the tables would be crafted from gorgeous walnut slabs from Oregon, originally intended for the remaining Riverside cabins. These slabs would be joined to create the appearance of one large, slightly curved piece of wood. Finished with marine-grade tung oil for a high gloss sheen, and supported by small tree trunk legs, the table would be truly spectacular. The Committee table would feature the same style. A local artist was crafting the small round center table. The elevated stage would support the entire setup to be above the audience. Local artists would paint a beautiful mural on the walls on both sides of the screen. Hidden behind the murals, storage rooms held video equipment, extra chairs, first aid kits, a weapons locker, and other security features.

The best craft workers in the area were working on the project. The chair for the Council Chair would be slightly bigger and more ornate, somewhat thronelike. It'd take too long to get one woodworker to complete seven chairs. Anna May pointed out they didn't have to look alike. Other than the "Chair" the rest would be the same size, worked on by different wood workers. Each chair would be unique, a beautiful work of art that would last hundreds of years.

=..=

After Rose checked in with the construction crews, she headed to the board meeting. All the people who held level four clearance were on Omímeya's Board of Directors. Besides herself as CEO, there was Phil, Kyle, Billy, and although he complained, Wayne. Rose thought he secretly enjoyed it. Five people were a small number for a board of directors for a corporation that was growing as fast as they were. They discussed ways of bringing more people in, but it kept falling on the priority list.

On the agenda was the threat of nationalization of NewNet. Before Big Thunder, Omímeya bought the hardware and software needed to restart the Internet in case of a disaster. Afterwards, they hired many new programmers and had their own IT working nonstop to recreate as much as possible. During the first days after Big Thunder, Kyle and some others went around buying as many electronic devices as they could find, in addition to guns and ammo. This gave cash to the stores and people they bought from, but also gave Omímeya a near monopoly on computer parts and other modern items.

Besides Omímeya, there were computer servers at cable and phone companies, the hospital, and the community colleges. The computer stores had a fair amount of hardware they were hanging on to. While NewNet was not all housed at Omímeya, most had the impression it was. The information was synched, ensuring everyone had the same amount of information, except for secure private data. That didn't seem to make a difference to public perception.

There was a lot of discussion questioning whether a private company should control the Internet. Google started with the goal of not being evil, but most now thought it was evil to control so much information. Omímeya did not release all the data they had preserved, even to Changleska. Data such as current historical information, weapons manufacturing, and even some patents that may prove valuable. The board decided there was no rush, they may release the data later.

Omímeya bought many Raspberry Pi computers as part of their backup plans. Raspberry Pi are small, low-cost single-board computers about the size of a credit card which worked with any input and output device, such as a keyboard, mouse, or monitor. They could replace or extend computers in low resource areas. They hadn't needed them yet, but they could expand their computer capabilities in the future easily. Omímeya had more computer power and resources than anyone knew, and the Board had no particular desire to share that knowledge.

A forum about freedom of information stressed how dangerous it was to have only a few control what gets published, especially a big corporation. The forum highlighted the use of the internet as a tool of repression in China. Some hippies were vocal opponents of Omímeya, saying many of the old-world problems were because of the one percent holding the world's wealth. They argued for laws to control Omímeya and other large corporations. Proponents argued NewNet should be part of infrastructure, government funded and controlled, with low or no costs to consumers.

The Omímeya board was concerned about the proposal to nationalize NewNet, which would include their servers. Their systems were designed with robust security systems to keep hidden resources such as military materials, making this unacceptable. They couldn't allow people not vetted anywhere near their systems. Board members pointed out that Omímeya had invested a considerable amount into NewNet. It was fair to want a return on the investment.

There was the question of who should pay whom and how much. The biggest provider, Interstate Communications, no longer a cable TV company, provided the landlines that carried NewNet to the area's homes and businesses. Since they were an out-of-state corporation, after Big Thunder, the employees took over. They planned to keep charging the same fees and to reinvest in services. Their concerns were nationalization would redirect funds to other government projects. The Lower Brule tribe badly needed the income that Tribal Telecomm brought in, which nationalization would jeopardize.

Omímeya's media subscription service was still free for anyone who uploaded original content. Most people had a year or two paid in advance, but when that expired, those small monthly payments would add up. The hippies wanted that service nationalized as well, even though Omímeya paid for the IT staff and hosted it on their computers.

Phil said he could assign intelligence staff to follow the forums more closely. He reminded everyone not to underestimate the hippies. They'd passed laws before the industries concerned knew what happened.

Rose suggested they meet with other stakeholders and create a NewNet Cooperative. Hippies loved co-ops. The new co-op could share payments and resources according to what each company brought to the table. That way, it wouldn't be one company controlling NewNet. The hippies could even nominate board members. Omímeya and other companies would still control their own data and resources and share what they want. This way, Omímeya could keep the subscription service, their software, and hardware. Everyone considered this a brilliant solution and moved on to other agenda items.

Rose thought Jackson had influenced Rose. He talked often about compromise and cooperation instead of conflict.

In order to separate the finances with Omímeya, Changleska finally hired a comptroller and an accounting team. Now Omímeya could stop paying the bills. Changleska still owed a large loan to Omímeya. They could chip away at it as early tax payments. Taxes were yet another thing to work on. Without taxes, Changleska would need to create more fiat money. Governments often ran on deficits, but at some point, there'd be a reckoning.

During the rest of the meeting, they focused on deciding how much of each resource to release and when to do so. Billy emphasized the secrecy of the reserves was essential for the long term, short-term hardships were necessary to protect it.

=..=

After they adjourned, Rose felt less alone. Burdens shared were burdens lightened. She texted Jackson to say she was free and where to meet. She was looking forward to seeing him, even if it was just for business. Rose was getting the idea he liked her. She knew he wasn't dating anyone else, despite the many who tried. Everyone assumed they were a couple, except them.

Rose thought about Jackson a lot. He took rent space in her head, which was a precious commodity, considering everything else she needed to think about. She'd only gone out a few times since Hotah and her separated, and those were a waste of time. Rose wasn't looking for a man in her life. She told herself her kids and work were enough until she met Jackson. Jackson was unlike anyone Rose had ever met before. His warm smile and genuine demeanor made her feel at ease, and the hours they spent talking flew by effortlessly. Jackson's presence in her life made her realize that maybe, just maybe, she'd finally found someone whom she could share her life with.

At the meeting, Jackson explained about the new proposal to oppose county independence and why. Rose agreed with the rationale, saying it would create economic issues in the short term but be better in the longer term. All the bigger businesses would be in county areas and would provide a larger tax base. When they were done, Jackson told her all about the problem with Courtney Bravebird and Two Elks' son, Six Feathers.

Rose laughed and said, "Don't you guys realize this solves our whole Two Elks problem?"

"I don't understand."

"Any women in the room when this came up?"

"No, but I pointed out there was a power differential. We should treat it the same way as if it were a female prisoner and a male guard."

"Good for you." Rose beamed at him, thinking, *wow, what man considers power dynamics? He is so different from any man I have ever met.*

Then Rose told him why they were wrong. Here were two young people who had fallen in love and wanted to marry, one the son of a tribal leader, the other a Changleska guardian. When two kingdoms were at odds with each other, they often solved the problem through marriage. They should not court-martial Courtney but keep her on active duty. Sure, give her a suitable 'you broke the rules' punishment, something minor.

Rose asked, "Does Six Feathers want to stay in Changleska?"

"Word is he loves it here, especially cars. He's been hanging out with the mechanics at the base garage."

"Two Elks had been badly defeated and his oldest son killed. He would likely go far away in the spring. Who knows how much trouble he could cause later if he wanted revenge? Possibly even rallying other tribes against us."

Rose pointed out, "This marriage could solve that problem. They should tell Two Elks through marriage their two tribes were now related. His son would live in Changleska, his grandchildren would grow up here. Two Elks would be welcome anytime."

Jackson admitted, "This could be a face-saving measure. Two Elks is a very proud man."

"No mother, if it could be helped, would allow her son to get married without her or agree to never see her grandchildren."

Rose offered to have Omímeya host a big wedding for the young couple. She had heard Two Elks refused to come inside the Circle, even to see Omímeya. Jackson admitted she'd heard correctly. Rose said she would offer the smaller Riverside cabin for the Two Elks family and his advisors. They could all come to the wedding and stay for a few days after to negotiate a treaty. The staff would love a big wedding.

Rose said, "It should be as soon as possible, perhaps late January."

"That'll be challenging. We need gas for the snowplows to keep the road accessible for emergency vehicles."

"This wedding can bring peace. It needs to be a priority."

"I agree with you. Let's go to the meeting and you can share your proposal and get the others on board."

At the meeting, everyone was open to the idea, even Gardner, relieved a simple solution had fallen in their laps. Rose suggested if Six Feathers became a citizen, they could make the ceremony a big deal before the wedding and invite Two Elks.

Rose stayed to meet the girl; she'd met her mother once or twice. When Rose saw her, she was surprised by how young she was, eighteen years old, the same age as Six Feathers. Courtney was ecstatic she could have a big Omímeya wedding. In this area, it was every girl's dream. Courtney admitted she didn't want to live in a tipi and never see her family again, but she loved Six Feathers and would follow him anywhere. At that moment, all the older people looked at each other and smiled. They couldn't help it; she was as cute as a puppy.

=..=

Rose left to help her girls get ready for their ceremony. She told Jackson she understood he didn't want to go to the outside ceremony, but they were having a small party at her house afterwards and he'd be welcome. A special shuttle would be running.

"Okay, I'll see you at the party." They smiled at each other, and she left.

The Winter Solstice ceremony took place at the 11:11 memorial under the canopy of stars. As each participant approached, an elder smudged them with an eagle feather, filling the air with the scent of burning sage and sweetgrass. Drummers were under the arbor, closer to the warmth, but the sounds of the drumming carried across the night, like the heartbeat of the earth.

The ceremony began with a call to the four directions. Kimi, Gift, and two friends, Darla and Caitlin, walked around the stone altar. After speaking, they each lit a candle next to items representing the direction they chose.

Facing East, Kimi opened with, "The shortest day of the year brings the promise of spring renewal to let go of the past and to face the upcoming year with a grateful heart."

Darla asked the spirit of the South, "During the dark months to remind us of the warmth of the summer and the abundance of the Earth would return."

Gift faced West, "The spirit of setting sun invokes change and death that is part of the cycle of life, that brings new growth."

Caitlin faced North, "The cold winds of winter help us face inevitable challenges that give us strength."

They sang a short song so everyone could learn it and sing with them.

Light is returning even though this is the darkest hour

No one can hold back the dawn

Let's keep it burning, let's keep the flame of hope alive

Make safe our journey through the storm

One planet is turning, a circle on her path around the sun

Earth mother is calling her children home

After singing, everyone stood in the shared energy in the silence for a moment. Then the girls blew out the candles, so it was very dark. Everyone looked up at the stars. An elder began telling a story in Lakota, one girl translating a part to English, until all four took part. The story was about the star people. How they came to the Lakota and the gifts they brought.

When it was over, they directed people to the arbor enclosure which had a wood stove burning. There were cups of tea and hot cider, and gingerbread cookies.

As the ceremony started, and everyone was gathered around, Rose felt someone standing close to her. She looked up, surprised to see Jackson. He'd brought a big warm blanket; they snuggled in it until the ceremony ended. Rose told him she needed to head to her house to be there before the guests. They walked to River Road and started towards the house. The first shuttle drove by, but they were talking while they walked, holding mittened hands. Jackson waved the shuttle past. They continued walking, covering over a mile, their happiness mingling with the chill in the air.

They arrived after the guests. No one minded, or probably noticed. The caterers were there serving. Rose had raided Tom's safe room stash and offered many gourmet goodies. They served top-shelf liquor, hot cider, and even difficult to find soft drinks. She and Jackson orbited around each other, speaking to people in the room, but not each other. Still keenly aware of the other's presence.

She chatted to Elliot about County politics and to Morning Star about midwifery. Anna May looked gorgeous in an eighteenth-century styled gown and Rose spoke to her and Martin for some time. They talked about the approaches to Spain and France about the Louisiana purchase. Rose found it surprising how knowledgeable they were on the subject and was even more surprised when Anna May expressed her desire to visit Paris in the eighteenth century, as it was one of her favorite cities.

She saw Mary and Daniel engaged in a lively conversation with the Begays. She approached and became captivated by their discussion about the inspiring transformation taking place among the youth in the community.

Rose looked at Kimi, surrounded by teenagers laughing. But she seemed distant and sad, so she went to put her arm around her and told her how lovely the ceremony was.

Kimi replied, "Everything seems good now. We have food, warmth, and family, but it won't last. We'll have hunger, be in pain, and lose those we love. There's such a hard journey ahead, and I only get glimpses of the path we should take. How can I help if I don't understand the direction the Creator wants us to take?"

Rose held her closer. "Oh sweetheart, the Creator doesn't make mistakes. You were chosen to share these insights, but this burden isn't yours to bear alone. Have fun, be a teenager, hang out with your friends. The world and its problems will be here tomorrow, and together we will face each problem as they come."

Kimi replied, "Okay Mom, thank you. I think you know this already, but Jackson is the one for you."

When the caterers began to pack up, everyone took it as their cue to leave. Jackson started picking up glasses and plates, bringing them to the kitchen. Luke looked at Jackson, looking at Rose.

Luke said to Chaton and Theresa, as they were putting on coats to go home with their boys, "Can I spend the night at your house?"

They looked surprised. The boys usually slept at Luke's, then Luke glanced at Rose and Jackson. They smiled, saying, "Sure, get your stuff."

Once the caterers were gone, Jackson and Rose exchanged a long, meaningful look, their hands intertwined. They sat for a moment, their eyes locked, feeling the weight of their connection. The room faded away, leaving only the two of them in their own little universe. Without uttering a word, they understood. They sat in silence, their hearts racing, aching with longing. The desire between them surged like a powerful river, overwhelming and undeniable. In that moment, they surrendered to the current, knowing that this rare and precious moment would not slip away easily.

Jackson was unsure what he should say. He knew Rose was waiting for him to break whatever barrier existed between them, preventing them from taking that next step of intimacy, to share their love.

Instead of anything profound or romantic, he blurted, "I want to stick it out."

"Good, because I want you to stick it in." They laughed, breaking the intensity of the moment.

Rose took his hand, leading him into the bedroom, letting go of her insecurities and fears, only wanting him. Rarely, the first time two people had sex was it the best. It could be awkward or embarrassing. Understanding each other's preferences and what truly pleasured your partner was a gradual journey, one that required patience and open communication. For Rose and Jackson, it was different. When they fell into each other's arms that first night, it felt as though it was the most natural and fitting thing in the world. Making love became an effortless fusion of their bodies, minds, hearts, and spirits. This magical connection transpired between them not only during that first time, but every time after that.

This concludes the story of those first three months. What follows are the records left behind, a reality check, and the author's notes. The journey continues in **Book Two: Expeditions: A Time Travel Journey,** *and in* **Book Three: Thunder Calls,** *due Summer 2026.*

PART VI
Echoes & Foundations

*The advancement and diffusion of knowledge
is the guardian of true liberty.*
— James Madison (1751–1836), Fourth President of the United States

Changleska Coalition Flag

Selected Newspaper Articles,
Fall - Winter 1791

Collected by the Changleska Historical Society

Chamberlain Free Press

First Issue—September 23, 1791

"Big Thunder" Strikes—Entire Town Displaced in Time

Eyewitnesses describe deafening roar, no lightning, and sudden isolation

By June Danner, Staff Reporter

Chamberlain. At precisely 11:11 am CST on September 21, 2024, a thunderclap of extraordinary force rocked the region, echoing for miles without lightning, rain, or storm activity. The phenomenon, now widely referred to as "Big Thunder," marked the beginning of an unprecedented event: the complete temporal displacement of a thirty-mile radius surrounding Chamberlain and the Omímeya Casino and Resort.

Since that moment, all contact with the outside world has ceased. Roads, pipelines, and communication lines end abruptly at what surveyors confirm is a perfect circle, encompassing much of Brule, Buffalo, and Lyman counties. The land beyond the border no longer resembles 2024. Aerial observations revealed herds of buffalo, smoke from traditional encampments, and an absence of modern development. Sioux Falls and Rapid City are gone. In a confirmed encounter, local fishermen Jake Hostler and Brent Cagle reported speaking with a French fur trader who identified the current date as September 21, 1791.

No scientists were immediately available for comment, but Chamberlain High School science teacher and amateur astronomer Allan Bramster confirmed the timeframe based on star positioning and lunar phase, stating: "Since we have no idea how we got here, there may be no way to return to our own time."

Mayor of Chamberlain, David Burrer, expressed concerns of maintaining city services for the health and safety of city residents without access to outside resources like antibiotics and other modern technology.

An emergency meeting was held Thursday at the Omímeya Resort, attended by elected members of the Lower Brule and Crow Creek Tribal Councils, along with officials from Brule, Buffalo, and Lyman counties. With tribal members forming the legal majority of the displaced population, the assembled leaders began outlining a joint governance structure and discussing the formation of a new, sovereign entity.

Brule County Commissioner Ed Robinson offered a steadying message: "This is a serious situation, and it's going to take all of us to get through it. Stay calm, stay informed, and stick together."

In contrast, State Senator Clyde Folsom insisted on maintaining ties to the US Constitution: "According to South Dakota law, I'm the highest-ranking elected official and should be governor. We should join with the United States, not create a new country with the tribes."

Despite political disagreements, the assembly reached a foundational milestone: the creation of the Changleska Coalition, named for the Lakota word changleska, meaning hoop or Circle—a symbol of unity and mutual responsibility.

Among its first acts was the drafting of a Declaration of Independence, printed in full in this issue. Early proposals include the possibility of negotiating with New Spain to purchase lands historically known as the Louisiana Territory.

The *Chamberlain Free Press* will continue to provide updates, advisories, and meeting notices as information becomes available. In the meantime, residents are encouraged to remain calm, cooperate with local leadership, and do their part to support neighbors and maintain order.

Columbian Centinel, Boston

Monday, October 31st, 1791

A Most Remarkable Occurrence Upon the Western Frontier

A town hitherto unknown is said to have appeared suddenly upon the banks of the Missouri River, accompanied by uncommon thunder and lights

A letter received from our correspondent in Philadelphia, dated October 15th. Several gentlemen lately returned from the territories west of the Mississippi bring news of a phenomenon most extraordinary. It is related that, upon the 21st day of September, a great and unnatural thunderclap was heard for many miles, though no storm nor clouds did accompany it. Thereafter, persons traveling the upper river did observe, with amazement, a settlement of considerable size and novel aspect, situated upon the western shore.

This place, which some now call Omímcya or Changleska, is reported to contain buildings unlike any known to our age, constructed with vast panes of glass and strange substances. Horses are said to be absent, though carts and wagons are seen to move swiftly, guided by persons dressed in unfamiliar garb. A few claim that machines of steam or fire are employed within, though no clear understanding of their origin is yet offered.

The Spanish authorities, it is believed, have been apprised of these reports and may issue a formal declaration in due time. In the meanwhile, these tidings are received with caution, some attributing them to fable, others to divine providence.

We await further dispatches.

Pennsylvania Gazette, Philadelphia

Saturday, November 12th, 1791

Strange Reports from the Mississippi

A foreign town said to have appeared without warning; new peoples, unknown instruments, and rumours of unnatural knowledge. From various traders and voyageurs returning from the southern territories, we receive accounts most curious and scarcely credible. It is stated that, upon the river's western bank, a town now stands where none had before been known. This town, occupied by a company of Natives and others calling themselves "Changleska," is said to contain strange devices and contrivances never before seen by civilized men. Lanterns that burn without flame, voices heard through wires, and carts propelled without beast nor wind are among the wonders reported. The inhabitants are said to speak English and the Native tongue with equal fluency, and to possess garments and instruments unknown in our time.

Are they Indians from the far interior? Others say they are the agents of Spain or France, though no flags or sovereign symbols are seen. There are even whispers of these folk claiming to come not from another land, but from a future age, a notion rightly received with disbelief and alarm. Whether these tales be truth or trickery, we advise prudence in judgment and await confirmation from our appointed ministers and officials. Some persons of learning propose that these individuals are descended from ancient Phoenicians or some lost tribe of Israel, returned to our continent by means unknown. Others call them illusions or signs of divine judgment. What is certain is that no ordinary explanation suffices.

We await further testimony from churchmen, officers, and the Crown's representatives, that the truth of these strange occurrences may be made plain. Until such time, let no man act in haste nor spread idle speculation.

═•═•═•═•═•═•═•═•═•═•═•═•═•═•═•══

Letter from Padre Tomás Rivera to His Grace, Bishop de la Torre
San Luis de los Illinueses, Upper Louisiana
10th December, 1791

Your Grace,

I write to inform you of a most singular and disquieting encounter. Not many days past, I received two men who claimed to have come down the Missouri by canoe. Their clothing was of fine quality yet foreign to all fashions known here. Though they made themselves understood in Spanish and French, their speech was marked by a peculiar cadence and unfamiliar expressions. Even their English was oddly formed.

One of them, darker of complexion and perhaps of Indio blood, asked me to hear his confession, which I did. Afterward, they revealed an object unlike anything I have ever beheld. It was smooth and dark like volcanic glass, and when they pressed it with their fingers, an image appeared within it as if by sorcery.

The image moved. There were people speaking in Spanish, walking beside carriages that moved without horses. Great towers of glass and steel reached into the sky, and winged machines passed through the clouds with the speed of musket fire. I could scarce believe my eyes. The men explained little, save to say they came from far away and sought not only my discretion but my assistance.

They asked that I bear witness to what I had seen, and requested that I post several sealed letters to the Holy Father in Rome. I agreed, though with some apprehension. Before they departed, they placed several pieces of fine silver upon my desk and thanked me for my time and silence.

Since their visit, I have slept poorly. I know not whether these men are harbingers of something divine or diabolical. I only know that they were real, that I saw what I saw, and that the world has shifted in some unseen way.

I remain your most faithful servant in Christ,
Padre Tomás Rivera, S.J.

NAVAL REPORT: ROYAL NAVY | HMS WINDWARD | NEW ORLEANS STATION

Filed by Lieutenant Thomas Ainsley, R.N.
20th December, 1791

To the attention of His Majesty's Admiralty:
Sir,
At first light on this date, an unknown vessel was observed ascending the river toward New Orleans. The craft bore no sails or oars and emitted neither smoke nor sound, yet proceeded upriver at a measured and unwavering pace. Its form and fittings are unlike any presently known to naval architecture.

The vessel was broad of beam and low to the water, with a long, rotating wheel affixed astern. The structure above deck consisted of metal frameworks and multiple containers or enclosures of uniform construction. A wheeled carriage resembling a wagon, though without trace of harness or animal, was secured to the foredeck.

At its mast flew a banner unfamiliar to any man aboard. The flag was red, with a white circle at its centre, within which was braided greenery encircling a disc quartered in black, white, red, and yellow. Its meaning and origin remain unknown.

The crew, though not in uniform, displayed coordinated appearance and bearing. Their garments, though modest, were manufactured from fabric of a type unfamiliar to this station. Many wore belts bearing tools or objects not immediately recognisable. The party made landfall near the Spanish port quarter and was observed speaking with local officials. From this distance, no words could be discerned, but their conduct appeared deliberate and composed.

Mounted upon the sides of the vessel were several long-barrelled implements, possibly of martial design, though differing markedly from any ordnance known to this service. No overt display of aggression was made, but the bearing of the vessel and crew was indicative of preparedness and organisation.

Reports from upriver suggest prior sightings of similar parties near the Missouri. Clergy and merchants have relayed accounts of advanced implements, unfamiliar speech, and disciplined behaviour. The matter may be of strategic interest and warrants prompt attention.

Respectfully submitted for consideration by His Majesty's Government.

I remain, your most obedient servant,
Lieutenant Thomas Ainsley, Royal Navy
HMS Windward, New Orleans Station

Founding Documents of the Changleska Coalition

Declaration of Independence

On September 21, 1791, representatives of the people brought by Big Thunder from another world gathered at the Omímeya Resort in the Nation of Lower Brule in order to declare independence from Spain, and we claim the lands from the Mississippi River to the Pacific Ocean and bordered by what was in our world, Mexico and Canada. We assert that all these lands belong to the Indigenous people who live there. We recognize those tribes as sovereign nations with inherent rights and responsibilities to their own people and to the Earth. From this day forward, we declare these lands to be held in trust for the good of all. On this day, we create a new sovereign nation, the Changleska Coalition. Its purpose is to protect the lands west of the Mississippi River and the people who dwell upon them. Our covenant as a nation is to protect the Earth and interconnected bio-systems such as waters, plants, and animals from pollution, contamination, and exploitation, to be preserved healthy and whole for future generations.

The Constitution of the Changleska Coalition

Preamble We, the citizens of the Changleska Coalition, united by purpose, memory, and vision, establish this Constitution to protect our people, restore balance to the Earth, and govern ourselves with justice, transparency, and care for future generations.

Article I – Structure of Government the Changleska Coalition follows a form of government rooted in Indigenous traditions of shared responsibility, consensus, and stewardship. The national government shall consist of a seven-member Executive Council, elected for seven-year terms, reasonably but not extravagantly compensated for full-time service. The Chair shall facilitate meetings and send agendas, with no additional powers unless emergency action is required and all other members are unavailable. The Council has the authority to remove any member for cause, using standards adapted from Lower Brule and Crow Creek Tribal guidelines.

Article II – Powers and Responsibilities of the Council the Executive Council shall not originate laws. Its role is to vote to approve or deny proposals from citizen committees. All decisions are made by majority vote. If a proposal is denied, the Council must provide transparent reasoning unless it endangers national security. Rejected proposals may be resubmitted after one year.

Article III – Committees Committees may be formed to address specific areas of national concern. At least two thousand people are needed to create a committee who can propose laws. Each committee may have up to eighteen members and must include:

Chair, responsible for guiding discussion and presenting proposals.

Secretary, to document proceedings.

Treasurer, to budget resources including funds, materials, and labor.

Article IV – Citizen Rights and Referendums Any issue may be brought before the Council through a public referendum, bypassing committees, if approved by two-thirds of eligible voters. Referendums to change this Constitution must wait at least one year and require two-thirds approval to pass. After the first year, changes to the constitution may occur every ten years. Referendums to change laws must wait three years after a law is enacted and also require a two-thirds majority.

Article V – Citizenship To become a citizen, be eligible to vote, serve as a Council, Committee, or Court member, and receive all the protection and collaborators of citizenship, a person must:

1. Be 18 years of age or older and either brought by Big Thunder within the thirty-mile circle or be born to someone who was, regardless of their original tribe, country, or county of birth. Dual citizenship is allowed. If not brought by Big Thunder, the person must have lived within the Changleska Coalition borders or a related community for two years.

2. Have sworn a sacred oath of the Covenant of the Earth before witnesses, of which one must be a citizen, and be duly recorded in the legal record.

3. Have agreed to support and defend the four freedoms and accept the four responsibilities freely, without reservations or purposes of evasion.

Oath of the Covenant of the Earth

"I solemnly vow, by all that I hold sacred, to safeguard the Earth and its interconnected bio-systems, including its waters, plants, and animals, from pollution, contamination, and exploitation. I pledge to preserve them in a state of health and wholeness for the benefit of future generations."

Four Freedoms *Every citizen has the freedom and right:*

To be free from slavery, torture, or rape. This includes the right to be free of discrimination based on race or ethnicity, religion, gender, sexual orientation, or political affiliation. Citizens have the right to justice, not to be subject to incarceration, cruel or unusual punishment, or death without the judgment of a court of law. Every citizen has the right to basic health care.

To worship or not worship as they choose. Everyone has freedom of religion or spiritual practice if they do not coerce or compel others to follow their beliefs.

To express dissent: This includes freedom of speech, via written or other forms of communication, freedom to gather, to engage in peaceful protest, and freedom to exit or travel. This freedom does not include the right to foment violence, insurrection, or treason.

To bear arms to protect themselves, their family, and their property. This right does not apply to those convicted of a violent crime, or who pose a danger to themselves or others as determined by a court of law.

Four Responsibilities *Every citizen has the responsibility:*

To protect the Earth for future generations, to use resources sustainably, and to stop those who would damage the ecosystem.

To protect their nation. All able-bodied adults from the age of eighteen to twenty-five shall be required to serve two years of military service either in an active or a support role. Those enrolled in either an educational or apprenticeship program may defer service for up to four years.

To aid in the care of those who are vulnerable, such as children and elders.

To support the financial stability of the nation by tithing ten percent of all gross personal income. Business income is taxed at a higher rate, determined by annual income and number of employees.

PART VII
Author's Notes
& Reality Check

*I am not afraid of truth. I am only afraid of people
who are afraid of truth.*
— N. Scott Momaday, (1934–) Kiowa author and Pulitzer Prize winner.

Pine Ridge Agency 1891

About the Author

Daphne Singingtree is an educator in plant medicine, midwifery, and emergency preparedness. Her journey started as a street kid at age twelve. At a young age, Daphne became an herbalist, then later a midwife, an educator, and an author. She started midwifery in 1974, leading to an active practice in home and birth center settings until her retirement in 2002. Her influence extends beyond her practice, as she played a pivotal role in shaping midwifery education and accreditation. She is the founder of Zaníyan Center, a nonprofit organization that promotes plants for health and a connection to the earth. Daphne is also an urban homesteader, promoting permaculture, and food resilience. She emphasizes the importance of emergency preparedness, not just for personal survival but also for the ability to aid others. Her heritage includes Lakota from the Standing Rock Tribe, Spanish, and Scottish. She is the mother of four grown children and the grandmother of eight. She calls Eugene, Oregon, home, and is where she grows herbs, makes medicine, and is an activist for protecting the earth and water.

Other books by Daphne Singingtree

Circle for the Earth, Book Two: *Expeditions: A Time Travel Journey*.

Coming Summer 2026: *Circle for the Earth*, Book Three: *Thunder Calls*.

Nonfiction

Birthsong Midwifery Workbook; The Emergency Guide to Obstetric Complications; Training Midwives: A Guide for Preceptors; Eagletree Herbs: Guide to Medicine Making.

Daphne's Great-grandmother Helen Brown (Fisher Woman)0

Acknowledgments

Writing a book takes a village. I'm incredibly grateful for my village, who provided me with encouragement, advice, constructive criticism, and practical assistance to bring this book to life. To my family and friends to whom I eagerly showed my unedited book while it was more a book-shaped blob than a book. I apologize and hope you'll give it a chance now it has undergone proper editing. Special thanks to my friend, Janet Russell, who volunteered for the first edit, long and full of far too many errors—that I thought the software would catch but it didn't. Thanks to her and her husband, Jerry, who are supporting the publication of the book through the nonprofit Zaníyan Center. A heartfelt thank you to my beta readers, Ken Smith, Sophia Maki, James Davies, Clair Strawn, and Dawson Lewis. My publishing assistant, Mary Glo Cuda, has helped so much in marketing and graphic design. My developmental editor, Nakiska Papenfuss from Reflection Harbor, who gave fantastic feedback to turn it into something more readable. Also, to my editing and formatting team, Michael Pilgrim, Amanda Shellnut, Lili Marlene Booth, and Calvary Diggs. As AI is increasingly involved in art, I'm especially thankful for my human graphic designers Savanna Stamp, Carlos Proveda, Robert Gillespie, Van Halen Cunanan, D.A. Suraj, and Yosama Sun. I want to extend a special thank you to my home helpers. Since my car accident, everyday tasks have become difficult and time-consuming. Their assistance allows me to write. They are my friends and support system, always there when needed. Thank you, Shari Arthur, Sharon Cohen, and Cindy Herzog. To my children and grandchildren, who continue to support me no matter what crazy thing I'm doing, and writing a novel was just the latest, you're all my pride and joy.

Would you do me a favor?

As a self-published author, I rely heavily on reviews. They make a huge difference. Every review counts. Please visit www.circlefortheearth.com for more content, feedback, and suggestions. Your feedback will help make the next books even better. You can email: daphnesingingtree@gmail.com

What is Real?

Fact or Fiction?

Location

Circle for the Earth takes place in an actual location in South Dakota, on the Lower Brule Reservation. The area transported back in time starts in the center of a loop of the Missouri River and extends in a thirty-mile circle. This includes the towns of Chamberlain, Presho, and other small towns. The towns and businesses included exist, with some names changed. The loop of the river is the size and shape described. Currently inside the loop is farmland. The entire casino and resort inside are fictional. There is a Lower Brule Casino in a different location. There is a hospital in Chamberlain owned by an out-of-state corporation.

The Lakota in History

- The Oceti Sakowin, or Seven Council Fires, is a confederation of seven allied bands: Brulé (Sičangu), Oglala, Itazipčo, Hunkpapa, Mnikoȟu, Blackfoot (Sihasapa), and Two Kettle (Oohenonpa). They speak one of three related dialects: Dakota, Lakota, or Nakota.
- The word "Sioux" comes from a term meaning "snake" given by their enemies, but they prefer "Lakota," "Dakota," or "Nakota," which means "friend" or "ally".
- Originally from the Great Lakes region, the Oceti Sakowin migrated westward and settled in the Great Plains, establishing the Great Sioux Nation, which spanned North Dakota, South Dakota, Montana, Wyoming, Colorado, and Nebraska. The Oceti Sakowin emerged as a powerful military force in the region, resisting encroachment from neighboring tribes and later from European settlers and the US government. They established a formidable reputation for their equestrian skills, strategic warfare, and fierce defense of their lands and way of life.

Lower Brule and Crow Creek Reservations

- The Lower Brule Tribe has its own buffalo herd, and an electric school bus. The community college has a teacher training program.
- They cultivate over 3000 acres mostly in popcorn, which they sell to Jiffypop and Orville Redenbacher.
- Crow Creek Hunkpati Oyate Tribe is in Fort Townsend and in the surrounding area. They operate a boarding school.
- While most Lakota Reservations are food deserts with few large, lower-cost grocery stores for many miles. The Crow Creek reservation has one store, and one is being built on Lower Brule.
- While some tribes own their own utility and cell phone companies, Lower Brule and Crow Creek do not.

Lakota/Nakota/Dakota Reservations

- While substance abuse, crime, suicide rates, unemployment, and poverty are very real for Lakota Reservations in the Dakotas, none are specific to Lower Brule or Crow Creek alone. Significant disparities exist between life in the United States and on the reservations. Crime is between six and twenty times the national average, depending on the reservation. Poverty is the highest on Lakota reservations than any other place in the US. Drop-out rates for high school, teenage pregnancy, substance abuse, diabetes, obesity, and other health problems are higher. Every metric that measures the health and well-being of society is significantly worse on these reservations.
- All the Lakota reservations have suffered from a loss of language. Lower Brule has about 14% native speakers. The local schools are teaching Lakota, as there is a growing interest in language restoration.
- Everything about the protests at the NoDapl protests at Standing Rock was real, including the author's participation.
- While some drug cartels have been found nationally on reservations, cartels have been found operating in all 50 states.

Lakota/Nakota/Dakota Tribes

Cheyenne River Reservation
BANDS: Mnicoujou (Planters by the Water), Oohenumpa (Two Kettle), Itazipco (Sans Arc or Without Bows) and Siha Sapa (Blackfoot)

Crow Creek Reservation
BANDS: Mdewakanton (People of Spirit Lake) and Ihanktonwan (Dwellers at the End of the Village) and Hunkpathi (Lower Yanktonais)

Flandreau Santee Sioux Reservation
BANDS: Mdewakantonwan (People of Spirit Lake) and Wahpekute (Leaf Shooters)

Lower Brule Reservation
BANDS: Sicangu (Burnt Thigh or Brule) Kul Wicasa Oyate (Lower Brule Tribe) and the Heyata Wicasa (Upper Brule Tribe)

Pine Ridge Reservation
BANDS: Oglala (Scatter Their Own)

Rosebud Reservation
BANDS: Sicangu (Burnt Thigh or Brule)

Lake Traverse Reservation
BANDS: Sisseton (Fish Dwellers), Wahpeton (Forest Dwellers)

Standing Rock Reservation
BANDS: Hunkpapa (Campers at the Horn) Siha Sapa (Blackfoot), Ihantonwanna (Little Dwellers at the End of the Village) Ihanktonwan (Dwellers at the End of the Village)

Yankton Reservation
BANDS: Ihanktonwan (Dwellers at the End of the Village)

Lakota Language and Culture

For cultural accuracy, go directly to the tribal websites linked above. For language, there is controversy around the Lakota Language Consortium, the largest organization, because of concerns about ownership and how outsiders are profiting. Additional resources:

- Othokahe: An online hub for Dakota/Lakota language courses taught across Standing Rock and beyond.
- Lakota Language Learning Dakota Texts and White Hat Orthography
- Facebook has a number of active Lakota Language groups.

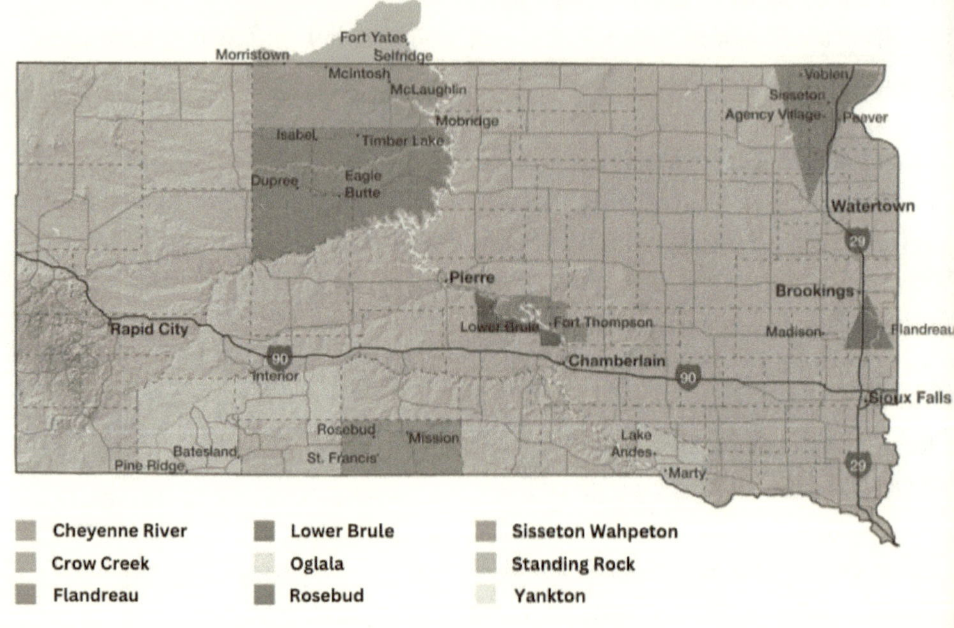

Alternative Energy

- There are no geothermal plants in the area, however, the benefits of geothermal energy are not fictional.
- The two wind farms in the area both sell power outside the area, including to Walmart and Boston University.
- Triple H Wind project is in Hyde County, South Dakota.
- NextEra Energy Resources is located outside of Stephens, South Dakota.
- Solar energy is a renewable and clean energy source that doesn't produce harmful emissions or greenhouse gases. Solar energy systems are low maintenance, requiring only occasional cleaning.
- Lithium extraction and disposal of lithium batteries can have a significant negative environmental impact. Lithium mining is destructive and is being fought by many Indigenous tribes.

Boarding Schools

- Indian Boarding Schools historically were designed to convert natives to Christianity and take away children's culture and identity. The legacy of Indian Boarding Schools is one of deep trauma and loss, as countless Indigenous children were forcibly removed from their families and communities. Many children endured physical, emotional, and cultural abuse, and the impacts are still felt today, as generations struggle to reclaim languages and traditions that were systematically suppressed. National Native American Boarding School Healing Coalition is working to address some of these issues.
- St Joseph Indian School is real. They have had a boarding school since 1927, now they operate a museum, and a group home style of boarding school. Unlike historical Catholic boarding schools, St. Joseph's has embraced Lakota culture and teaches the language in its schools.

Books

- The *1632* series by Eric Flint is real, and you can download a free copy at Baen Books.
- Starhawk writes both fiction and nonfiction, the quote is from the *Fifth Sacred Thing*.
- Hesperian Foundation is a nonprofit which provides books, apps, and other health and medical materials like *Where There is No Doctor* and *Where There is No Dentist*.
- Daphne Singingtree is the author of the *Birthsong Midwifery Workbook* and other midwifery publications. You can get her work at www.eagletreepress.com

Communication and Emergency Preparedness

- goTenna is a real mesh phone that works off grid without cell towers.
- There are apps to create mesh phone systems that work without cell towers.
- Baofeng radios is one brand of handheld ham radios anyone can buy, but you need a license to transmit.
- There are two radio stations in the area, one Christian, and one NPR affiliate.
- Internet in a Box is real, a mini-server with a wireless access point, allowing nearby devices like smartphones or laptops to connect and access pre-loaded content like Wikipedia articles, educational videos, and digital books without needing an active internet connection
- Raspberry Pi computers are real, credit card size open source computers capable of running the basics of most computers.
- Khan Academy is a real preK-12, online school.
- The Community Emergency Response Team (CERT) is an FEMA program that educates volunteers to help in natural disasters and other emergencies.
- AT Microfiche Reference Library by Volunteers in Asia, has 1050 PDFs of books and resources on all areas of self-reliance and do-it-yourself technology. It is available to purchase from Village Earth.

Hemp

- Hemp is environmentally beneficial (for the soil, air, and water) It can regenerate and replenish the environment it grows in, is incredibly resilient and can flourish no matter the soil or air quality, or with limited rainfall. It takes less water to grow compared to cotton and trees.
- Hemp cleans the air, producing oxygen during their growth cycle.
- Hemp grows in just about any condition without chemical fertilizers or pesticides. It is resistant to disease and pests.
- Hemp improves soil quality and purifies water. It can soak up to three times its own weight in water, improving dry climates and farms with moderate or low rainfall. It only uses about 37% of the amount that cotton does per acre cultivated.
- Hemp actually cleanses the soil it's growing in, preventing erosion and acidity issues, and leaves the soil rich in nitrogen.
- Hemp production preserves wild animal habitats
- Hemp is stronger than cotton and other natural fibers; it's literally stronger than steel! Since hemp fiber is stronger than cotton and naturally UV resistant, it makes the ideal material to manufacture durable fabrics for clothing, shoes, and backpacks.
- Hemp is stronger than wood fiber and create almost anything— from hempcrete for construction materials, furniture and as a wood substitute.
- Hemp has the potential to be transformed into plastic materials that are 100% biodegradable and recyclable, yet they have many of the same uses as petroleum-based plastics.
- Hemp can be used in the production of biofuels.
- Hemp is bee-friendly. Many beekeepers use hemp plants as an alternative when other flower sources are not as abundant.
- Hemp can produce paper and packaging products that surpass the eco-friendliness of wood-based papers and can be recycled multiple times.

Doulas and Midwives

- Doulas provide physical, and emotional support before, during and shortly after childbirth. They do not provide obstetric care.
- One study found that doula care reduced the odds of cesarean delivery by 52.9%. Doula care reduced risk of postpartum depression and anxiety, reduced risk of low birthweight, increased likelihood of breastfeeding and improved maternal health outcomes.
- Certified Professional Midwives are direct-entry midwives who train without becoming an RN first. They can get their training through apprenticeship and/or attending an educational program. They primarily deliver babies in out-of-hospital settings.
- Licensed direct entry midwife is a midwife who is legally permitted to practice midwifery without first obtaining a nursing degree. Licensed by the state to provide prenatal, intrapartum, and postpartum care, typically working in home or birthing center settings.
- Certified Nurse-Midwives (CNM), must be registered nurses who graduate from a master's or higher-level nurse-midwifery accredited education program. They are required to work with physicians.
- Information from the Network for Public Health Law about Direct Entry Midwives www.networkforphl.org/resources/direct-entry-midwives-across-the-nation
- According to research, midwifery care is considered safe for low-risk pregnancies, with studies showing that women attended by midwives often have lower rates of interventions like cesarean deliveries, while experiencing similar or even improved birth outcomes compared to physician-led care, particularly for first-time mothers.

Permaculture and Farming

- Permaculture or permanent agriculture, is a philosophy of working with, rather than against nature, looking at plants and animals in all their functions, rather than treating any area as a single-product system.
- White River Farm is fictional, loosely based on a similar place, OLCERI on the Pine Ridge Reservation that hosts permaculture gatherings.
- The Dakota Lakes Farm is an actual place who teaches sustainable farming practices.
- Dakota Grain and Mill buys and sells the many tons of grain grown in the area, and yes, they really don't have a mill in the area.
- This area of South Dakota has a great number of conventional farms producing corn, soybeans, hay and wheat.
- It is true that runoff from pesticides from farms in the area a major cause of pollution in the Missouri River.

Police and Military

- The South Dakota Highway Patrol has an office at the location in the book, near the I-90 rest stop. However, it does not have a police armory full of riot and military gear (as far we know).
- Tribal Police in Lower Brule and Crow Creek reservations are both under-funded, with very few officers. Having three on duty at a time is overstated and fictional.
- South Dakota police have a plane, just not a new Cessna 206, although that is a plane used by police forces.
- Martial law can suspend civil liberties, such as the right to free speech, free movement, and protection from unreasonable searches. Martial law can also suspend habeas corpus laws.
- The Chamberlain Armory exists and is home to the 200th Engineering Brigade of the National Guard, who served in Iraq in 2017.

About Zaníyan Center

100% of all proceeds from this book go to support Zaníyan Center, a 501(c)(3) nonprofit organization dedicated to promoting health through plants and connection with the earth.

We offer workshops and publish educational materials that reflect our vision and values:

- The healing power of plants nurtures body, mind, heart, and spirit.
- Sustainable, resilient food systems are key to food sovereignty and long-term community well-being.
- How we birth, breastfeed, and care for the young shapes lifelong health and the future of the planet.
- Elders hold knowledge and wisdom that are essential for cultural survival, continuity, and care.
- End-of-life care be loving and dignified, and we honor the sacredness of the body after death.
- In a time of increasing disruption, we promote self-reliance, resilience, and preparedness rooted in community and connection to the earth.

At Zaníyan Center, we believe that connection to the land, reverence for life, and practical skills are essential for building a just and sustainable future.

Visit zaniyan.org for more information.

Tax deductible donations are always appreciated.

A Prophecy Remembered

Upon suffering beyond suffering, the Red Nation shall rise again,
and it shall be a blessing for a sick world. A world filled with broken
promises, selfishness and separations. A world longing for light
again. I see a time of Seven Generations when all the colors of
mankind will gather under the Sacred Tree of Life and the whole
Earth will become one circle again. In that day, there will be those
among the Lakota who will carry knowledge and understanding of
unity among all living things and the young white ones will come to
those of my people and ask for this wisdom. I salute the light within
your eyes where the whole universe dwells.
For when you are at that center within you and I am that place
within me, we shall be one.

– Crazy Horse, Oglala Lakota Sioux 1840-1877

9 780967 443126